G000138529

The Signature
From Tibet

The Signature From Tibet

A NOVEL

⁓

Alison Demarco

Based on a True Story
Editor and Technical Advisor, James R. Coffey

First Edition 2015

Copyright © 2015 Alison Demarco
All rights reserved.

ISBN: 099321651X
ISBN 13: 9780993216510

Book cover design by: www.kontemptcreations.com
MAIL: KONTEMPT@INBOX.COM

Alison would like to thank her family and friends for their continued support during the writing of this novel.

And to David Mackenzie
for his additional research and guidance.

Disclaimer

Though based on a true story, this is a work of fiction and therefore not intended to reflect or suggest any actual historical events.
While interaction with real-life, living individuals is a feature of this work, these interactions are purely literary invention designed to illustrate the sentiment of the story and not intended to reflect the actual personage.
Any false depiction of said individuals is purely unintentional.

Prologue

EACH MORNING AT THE BREAK of dawn from its rickety wooden roost in the back garden the cockerel would wake her. She would then force herself to get out of bed and walk on unsteady legs to the china basin that sat on her small dressing table. Next to the basin was a jug full of cold, fresh water, some of which she poured into the waiting basin. Bracing herself for the icy-wet sting, she would plunge her porcelain white hands into the clear, chilled liquid and, stooping over, splash her half-awakened face. She repeated this several times. Then with eyes stung closed she would feel for the coarse linen towel she knew lay next to the basin. Then rubbing briskly over her smooth, pale and youthful skin with the small coarse towel, the chill was replaced by an invigorating warmth. Now she was awake.

Before she left her bedroom she dressed. Firstly with the tempered smoothness of her undergarments, then her white blouse with its starched and irritating collar, followed by a pair of black woollen knee-length socks, and finally her pleated black skirt which she fussed over to make certain its length was proper: half-way between her knees and ankles. Her black bolero-style jacket, white cap and black patent-leather shoes she put into the bag she'd carry with her. Her own wool coat and leather brogue shoes would keep her warm and her feet dry when she left the cottage. As she clattered down the bare wood of the narrow stairs that led from the small attic bedroom to the ground floor, she heard a familiar voice mildly chastise her:

"Ye better hurry, lass, ye don't want to be late again!"

"Ah know, Gran," she replied in a mocking tone of exasperation.

"A've left a glass o' milk and slice o' buttered bread out for ye to eat before ye go," replied her grandmother.

As she entered the small scullery, the bag containing the jacket, cap, and patent-leather shoes was placed carefully against the leg of one of the wooden chairs which surrounded the stout, well-worn table. Between gulps of milk and mouthfuls of buttered bread she confided sheepishly to her grandmother, "I think he will be at the house today."

"Och--you and your thoughts of that boy, ye want to get them right out o' your head," was the admonishing response.

"Gran, it's only a wee bit of fun! Must be away, see you tonight." With that she picked up the bag and was off, the front door of the cottage pulled tight behind her.

As she walked briskly past the last few cottages in the row that made up the little hamlet where she lived, she was soon out in the open countryside she knew so well. There was 'Old Man Grant's' farm cottage, set back a wee bit from the main road. She remembered as a child playing with her friends, daring each other to see who could get the closest to the cottage without being seen. They would sneak up the overgrown drive, crouching and hiding amongst the tangle of bushes and unkempt grass, expecting a face to appear in the window. *What mysteries and goings-on happened in that cottage?*--their young imaginations would run wild. The rustle of a lace curtain or unbolting of a door was enough to make them jump and run giggling and screaming all the way back down the long driveway to the safety of the road. She now shivered and quickened her pace at the thought of those childhood adventures. A bit further on she came to Mrs. MacPherson's cottage, which was quite different from old man Grant's. A whitewashed exterior, clean windows, lots of brightly-coloured flowers, herbs and bushes made it a very cheery sight. Billows of smoke emanating from the chimney were a sure sign of warmth and homeliness and safety.

Hedgerows, farm tracks, tall pine trees and fields of lazy and contented animals passed her by. But her mind was elsewhere. Then she arrived at Corbies Glen and the two tall stone pillars that marked its entrance. Atop each pillar was a magnificent carved stone eagle, its beady eyes looking downwards; its wings open and spread wide as if about to swoop down onto anyone who dared stop and take notice. This morning, like every other morning, she looked up at the pillar on her right-- and sure enough there was the black crow in its usual place, just under one of the wings of the eagle. As if mimicking the eagle it spread its wings and looked down on her as if it were identifying her in its memory. She shrugged: *stupid bird!* she thought, and set off down the path that ran alongside the driveway and led up to the main house.

Now, this driveway was one she and her friends never played on in their younger days. This wasn't the rundown chaos of old man Grant's, nor the prim tidiness of Mrs. MacPherson's. No: this was grand, wide enough for two carriages to pass, and spread out on either side were fine lawns, raised beds of mature shrubs, and even a pond with patches of tall reeds at its edge that swayed, attuned to the breezes that swept across them. And to cap it all, water lilies floating serenely and at their leisure, in and out of the reeds. He must have had a great time playing amongst all this as a boy. *Not for him--the sneaking between bushes to avoid being detected*--she thought. He most likely did whatever he wanted to do with his friends; after all, his father owned all this—and beyond.

Feeling a chill, she pulled the collar of her warm coat tightly round her neck as she walked past a line of dark green spruce trees that opened out on either side of the driveway to reveal a semi-circle of flattened, fine stone and gravel. There, at the base of this semi-circle stood the imposing façade of Corbies Glen, the estate house of all the land her eyes had taken in on her walk down the driveway and some distance beyond; all the way down to the river, in fact. She smiled ruefully. *Not for her*--the stately walk up the grand entrance steps and through the polished timber double- entrance doors with leaded Italian glass panels etched with the family crest. *No*--she skirted the curve of the half-circle drive to a small, almost unnoticeable, door set back out of view on the side of this imposing family house: the staff and tradesmen entrance. As she pulled this nondescript door shut behind her she could feel the warmth of a crackling fire spreading through the small hallway that led into the staff area. She could also hear the *tut-tutting* of a man's deep and irritated voice:

"You'll need to do better, my girl," it uttered without emotion, "*much* better!" The eyes that accompanied the voice cast a darting glance at the clock that hung judgmentally on the bare painted wall of the hallway. "No doubt dawdling and daydreaming your way up the driveway!"

"Sorry, sir," she offered. "It won't happen again."

"I'm Mr. *Cassels*, girl, not *sir! Sir* is the master of this house!" continued the irritated voice, "and you'd do well to remember that!"

It's going to be a long day, she thought, as she hung her bag on one of the brass coat hooks fixed to a wooden rail just at her head-height behind the nondescript door.

"Now, don't you go worryin' about Cassels, m'deary, you know what he's like. Typical butler, aye full o' airs and graces, but just the same as the rest ae' us!" It was Violet, the cook, speaking. She was also the household seamstress, laundress, and everything else for that matter. She liked Violet; she was like her grandmother. She looked out for her, kept her right, and had taught her the best way to do things as a maid, a domestic servant: how to pass about the main house unnoticed, speak only when spoken to, and how to behave when she was in the presence of her *betters*.

"Wi' better get on, then. Get yourself ready an' away and set the fires," instructed Violet. So she got her jacket, cap, and shoes from her bag, put them on, straightening her brown shoulder hair and dress as she did. "When you've done that come back down and a'll have breakfast ready for serving." She nodded, and off she went. By 8:00 all three fires were lit and roaring, so, she headed back to the kitchen in readiness to take breakfast to the dining room. "Here, lass, the breakfast trays are ready. Cassels has lit the food warmers so get going and fill 'em with this food before it gets cold. Here, deary, take the eggs and haddock then come back for the bread and porridge."

As she closed the door of the dining room after completing her second trip of delivering bread and porridge, she heard hurried footsteps coming up behind her. She recognised the footfalls as she had heard them many times before, and waited with anxious excitement: they were *his*. She could feel her body begin to tingle and her face began to flush, his closeness always made her feel that way. This never happened with the other boys from the village; only *him*. Maybe this was what love felt like?

As she turned to face the oncoming footsteps with her face aglow and her nerves jangling, the boy's face was ashen--white as if he'd encountered a ghost. Rather than the twinkling and cheeky, secretive smile that usually greeted her, his lips were stretched and shut tight as if barely able to hold back his rage. His turquoise eyes were steely cold as he passed her enquiring look, brushed by her and into the dining room. *Something must have happened*, she said to herself. Her mind raced: *Has it to do with me? Something I did? Oh no, he doesn't love me anymore!* What-ifs and dire thoughts tumbled round her head. What would she do if he didn't speak to her anymore? Quickly she scampered back to the scullery.

"I just saw the young master!" she blurted out to Violet. "And--he just brushed past me like I wasn't there! What's happened?"

Just as the cook was about to share what she knew, Cassels boomed out in a pompous and demeaning tone, "It's none of our business what happens between those we serve!" he said, his eyes darting between the two domestics. "And especially not *yours* girly!" She looked pleadingly at Violet who recognised the familiar uncertainty and concern in the girl's eyes.

"M'deary, pay him no mind," she said, motioning for her to come sit beside her. "It's not you, lass, it'll be just another row between the young master and his father." The girl slumped into the chair next to the cook, who could see she wasn't convinced of her explanation. "Have, some hot breakfast. A've kept some eggs and haddock aside for ye." As the plate of food was pushed in front of the girl she baulked at the sight of it--and in a panic knocked her chair over as she raced for the maids' washroom. Violet shook her head: young girls these days, what are they like? After a few minutes the girl returned to the scullery and sat down on the chair Cassels had since righted and returned to its regimented position. "Now, don't get yerself intae such a state over the master's business, an ma cookin's surely no' that bad!" joked Violet.

Holding her stomach, the girl explained, "It's not your cooking, it's just some mornings I don't feel too well."

"Maybe just growin' pains, m'deary. Aye, growin' pains," was the cook's reply, a sly grin on her face and a wink in her eye.

For the remainder of the morning the girl went about her duties, but her mind was not really there; she was thinking about the boy and her. He was a fine looking lad, with a mop of thick blond hair and well known round the area, and someday a fine catch for a rich farmer's daughter--all the grown-ups kept saying.

His mother had passed away when he was still a young boy and he'd spent a lot of time with the servants as his father was always too busy with estate business. Violet had told her this: that she and Cassels had been in service at Corbies Glen for over a decade and had watched him grow through the good and the bad years. Yet the girl felt she was *special* to him, and had been working at the house for just over a year now.

They were about the same age; he, just short of a year older. At first they would just joke round with each other; after all, they were the only young people round the house and the grown-ups lived in their own stuffy and boring world of work and duty. And she had things in common with him: she too had lost her mother when she was young, to the fever that had spread into the countryside from the cities. At first it was just harmless horseplay; keeping secrets between them, a sly glance and fleeting touch that went just beyond childhood games. She'd come to feel different when she was with him; not at all the same as when she was with her girlfriends. Being with him was exciting--almost danger-ous--but yet, not *in* danger. Her mind couldn't really explain it.

As she grew that little bit older, her body changed. And their inti-macy changed. Her skin tingled when he touched her; when he'd lead her by the hand round the house or out onto the grounds--when he should have been at his studies and she at her duties. Their touches became more frequent and more passionate as if they had a special pur-pose. As if they were meant to take them on a journey to a wonderful destination and the journey itself was so exciting that she wanted it to go on forever . . . At times she couldn't wait to see him; to have him near her. Just being round him was enough sometimes. But at others, she ached for him--his beguiling smile, a soft look from his twinkling, mischievous turquoise eyes. She dreamed of his touch, his arms wrapped round her holding her tight; shielding her from the cold.

One such time the summer before when Violet had given her some time to herself, and Cassels and the master away on estate business, the two had been chasing each other round the grounds when they found themselves in the stables. Both full of nonsense, goading and teasing each other with cheeky remarks, they dared each other to climb up to the hay loft. Both rushing to the top by separate ladders, they jokingly argued who'd arrived first. As they lie on the bed of soft cushiony straw that covered the floor of the loft, she could feel his deep and rapid breathing next to her. She too was softly panting, recovering from the spirited climb. As she turned to face him she could feel his hand gently stroking her hair. Without hesitation she put out her hand and lovingly touched the side of his face. From then on her emotions took over . . .

She loved being so close to him. She wanted to get closer, closer, closer still. She felt the tingling sensation in her body overpower her; she couldn't stop, didn't want to stop. Their oneness was all that mattered. She was lost—lost in the moment, lost in her emotions--her body pursuing its own desires. In all this cacophony of emotion her senses became sharper. The rustling of the straw beneath her became the sound of dry leaves blowing round wildly on their branches by autumn winds. The sharpness of the dried and crisp blades, as she clenched them in her fists, were like knives that might cut her youthful skin . . .

For her, it all ended too soon. It had been so wonderful that afternoon in the stable loft--but it had become just another secret to keep. They still teased and joked with each other when they could, but they were no longer just childhood *friends*. Somehow they had both grown up a little that day--

"C'mon, deary! Stop daydreamin'--there's work to be done!" (It was Violet, breaking the spell of her reverie.)

By that afternoon she'd got back into her routine, carrying on with her duties. She hadn't seen him again that morning so it must have been as the cook said: just another row between him and his father. But her fear returned as she walked past the master's study as she could hear raised, angry voices. She didn't want to stop and listen as Cassels might happen by and catch her, but it sounded like the master and his son. She went on about her work. An hour later as she again passed the study the voices where still emanating--now louder and angrier--fighting each other to be heard. This time she did stop to listen, hoping to make out at least a little of what was being said. It was difficult, the voices were raging, garbled and emotional, but she knew it was the master and his son and she could pick out some words: words like "grow up," "duty," "family," "me," "own life," and "happy." But no mention of *her*. She still felt uneasy but knew she'd better get on as she only had a couple more chores to do before she could set off for home. Then the voices stopped. There was silence. She heard heavy footsteps just behind the study door. And before she had time to hide or get out of the way, the door flung open--and out *he* strode, the master's son.

Her presence caught him by surprise and she was about to speak, to ask him what was going on--but he raised his hand as if to warn her off. She could see that his eyes were, at first, fiery and defiant, but softened slightly as he looked at her. "That *man* in there!" he forced out through gritted teeth, making his way towards the staircase, bounding up the steps two-at-a-time--clearly in a great hurry to get away.

Her mind was beyond confused: *What's going on?* She hurried back to the scullery to explain all that had gone on to Violet. "Don't fash yerself, m'deary, families have arguments aw' the time. It'll aw have blown o'er by morning. Forget about yer last few chores and get yerself home, dear. I'll see to 'em." Nodding an appreciative thanks she put her jacket, cap, and patent-leather work shoes into her bag and set off to retrace her steps across and down the grand driveway: past the eagle sentinels that guarded Corbies Glen entrance, past the hedgerows and fields. But no thoughts of mysteries and childhood pranks this time. Her mind was flooded with raised voices and memories of summer past.

When she reached home, she couldn't help but blurt it all out: all except the summer memories, they were still her guarded secrets. "Aye, these rich folk, for all their finery and money, it doesn't bring 'em happiness," was all her granny offered. That night the girl barely slept. She couldn't help but think that the argument had something to do with her. She and he were so close, so intimate; what troubled him troubled her. But, what could she do?

The following morning she was up early as today was not a day to be late. She had to find out what the big argument between the master and his son was all about. It seemed to her that it had been quite serious. Hurriedly she washed and dressed. Today the sting of the water and coarseness of her clothes meant nothing to her--she had to get back to Corbies Glen. Familiar fields and farms passed by unnoticed as she nearly stumbled down the road. The ever-vigilant morning crow at the eagle pillars was paid no heed, neither were the formal lawns, pond, and spruce trees. When she reached the side door of the estate house, Cassels was waiting for her: "Ah, good timekeeping for a change, girl. In you go," was all he said. Once in the scullery she searched out Violet, keen to find out any more news of yesterday's row. "Don't concern yerself, m'deary, just get on about yer work," was all she got as the cook looked away, unwilling to meet her eye.

Something is not right! the girl thought. She felt an emptiness. As if his presence no longer filled the house. She looked pleadingly at the cook: "Tell me! I know something's happened—so, please tell me!" she begged.

"It's no ma place to tell, m'deary. Let's all just get on wi' our work," was the reply as Violet again turned away.

"Oh, no! --So something *has* happened! *Tell* me! I've got to know!" she begged, tears welling-up in her eyes. Cassels then appeared at the scullery door.

"What's all this commotion, then? Haven't got enough work to do? I can find you more, easy enough!"

"Oh, please, sir--I mean, Mr. Cassels--what's going on? What's happened?" she implored. "Cook won't tell me—and I have to know!"

"Well, it's really none of our business, least of all *yours*, my girl, but he's left. Gone and good riddance!" Cassels said coldly.

"You're a heartless *lout*, Cassels--so ye are!" spat Violet. "He's just a boy, sent away like that! Aye men, ye can be heartless *bastards*!"

The girl couldn't take in what she was hearing. "*Who's* gone? Gone *where*?" she asked, but not wanting to hear the answer.

"Why, the master's son!" Cassels said coldly. "He's left! Disowned his whole family! Set himself against his own father! A carriage came for him late last night and took him to--*who-knows-where*--and that's the end of it! Now, get on with your work, my girl, or you won't have work to get on with!" With that an exasperated Cassels abruptly turned and left the scullery. Violet shook her fist at his back and scowled, then put her arm round the girl.

"C'mon, now, ah know he was yer special friend, and he'll be back, a'm sure of it."

But this was all too much to fathom. He *couldn't* have--*wouldn't* have--left without saying goodbye! In that moment, her world turned upside down; her life in ruins. Part of her had been ripped out and taken away. His image, her memories of their moments shared, were now replaced with an emptiness, a heaviness that gave way to a painful, hollow feeling growing within her. What would she do now? The rest of the day didn't matter.

Sick again that morning, the cook offered her some breakfast. She then went about her duties as if in a trance, just nodding her head at everything said to her. Cassels became a fleeting phantom who just appeared before her eyes now and then. That night when she got back home she blurted out to her grandmother that the young master had gone; there had been a big argument with his father and he'd gone off on his own!

"Surely not!" comforted her granny. "He won't have gone for good! His father's a good man, he wouldn't have let him just run off!"

"Well, Cassels and Violet think he's really gone! It was a *big* argument!" she sobbed.

"It'll blow over, lass! He'll have gone away to his cousins' in the city for a wee while for things to calm down. You'll see, I'll be right!"

"I hope so, Gran. He's my friend; my *special* friend!"

Sleep would not come to her that night. She hoped her grandmother was right. That it would all blow over and he would be back. Next morning she went through her usual routine and reached Corbies Glen just in time to see a carriage pull out from between the stone pillars and head off down the road toward the village. *It's him,* she thought, *he's back*--and hurried down the drive, past the gardens and spruce trees, round the side of the house and into the servants' quarters. "Was that *him?*" she asked of Violet.

"Was who *what?*" The cook looked bemused.

"The carriage that just left--was *he* in it?" she demanded. "Has he come back?"

"Och, no, m'deary," the cook shook her head, "it wis'nae him. Din'nae concern yersel wi' their business. Let's just get on wi' oor work."

The girl spent the remainder of the day in the sinking hope that when she turned a corner in the house, he'd be there (and she'd get that tingling feeling all over again). But not that day nor the next nor the next was it so. Her hope faded as more and more days passed without him, or even any news. As she went about the house trying to focus on her duties, little memories would force their way into her head: of secret rendezvous . . . fleeting glances . . . stolen moments at places they'd agreed to meet--or chance meetings. That's all she had now. Little memories. She would hold onto them until he came back, she resigned. They were her link to him and she hoped that he, wherever he was, was doing the same. Reliving memories of her in his mind, trying to keep her with him.

The days rolled into weeks. Carriages came and went--but none brought him back to her.

Visitors came and went--but none brought news of him. Her anticipation of seeing him again faded, leaving only the aching loss. At times she would force herself to remember the little things they had done together; insignificant to others, but to her, they were *everything. Everything.*

Violet commented on her being sick every morning, and suggested she speak to her grandmother about it; which she did. And she continued to work as long as she could. But with Cassels' condescending *tut-tutting* every time he passed and the cook's well-meaning but relentless advice, it became increasingly difficult. So it was just a matter of time before she had to leave and get on with her life. That day finally came, when neither she nor the other staff members could hide her condition from the master, so she left Corbies Glen . . .

Left behind the big old house: its nooks and crannies. The stable loft . . . the laughter . . . the fun . . . the touching and the tingling. Left behind the pond, the gardens, the cold and stony stare of the unnerving eagles; the shimmering bluish silver-black of the crow's wings each time she passed. Yet she took with her memories. Memories rich with love and innocent trust.

What would become of him? Would he ever come back to Corbies Glen?

Part I: The Soldier's Story

Chapter 1

CONSIDER IF YOU WILL: THE year is 1939 and an old man is sitting in his ancestral home, a secluded, rambling Scottish mansion set on its own sizable working estate. It is a cold and frosty morning and from a large and panoramic first floor window in his study he can look out over large frost-tinged formal lawns and gardens, with ornamental fish ponds leading down to the banks of the fast-flowing (and at this time of year) icy waters of the River Spey. If he looks to his left he can see, over the tops of the trees, the rolling slopes of the Cromdale Hills, and to his right the more rugged and snow-topped outline of the Cairngorm Mountains. He now spends much of his time in solitude, locked away in his study, surrounded by his past: photographs, paintings, ornaments, and books clutter the room. He feels safe and comfortable here in the company of these old *friends*. Such is his desire for privacy that his bedroom is close by, linked to the study by a door set in a shared wall.

His tall, slim build has changed little over the years. His shaven head and olive skin have taken on a weathered look but his large round eyes are still a piercing turquoise in colour. Interestingly, many people talk of his eyes; they unnerve them. They believe he has the ability to see into their souls. He was once also well known for his sharp tongue and off-handed manner which, to some people who knew him, was a remnant of his army days.

As he sits in his favourite brown leather armchair in his study, the flames of the roaring fire dance and flicker. Beside him on a small table to his left the light offered by the fire sparkles into the amber glow of whiskey sitting pond-still in a crystal glass, untouched from the night before. The light appears to diffuse into a myriad of colours before reforming into one as it leaves the glass and drifts upwards to settle on a sepia-tinged photograph sitting on the mantel shelf above the fire. It is a photograph from times long gone, from another age, of military men looking haughty and proud; some seated whilst others stand behind them statuesque. *What fools*, he thinks to himself. *Where is their lofty pride now?* As he stares into the colours of the crystal glass he sees faint images from his past form and then fade . . . seemingly attuned to the flickering of the fire's light. A dull *thud* breaks the soldier's deep reverie.

"What the . . . was *that*!?" exclaimed the old man aloud. As he begins to rise from his chair he catches a flutter of black feathers on the outside of the window, just before they drop below sill-level. As his eyes adjust from the sombre light of the room to the sparse winter sunlight, an imprint begins to form on one of the window panes. At first it looks like a pressing of flower petals, like those things children collect in books, but slowly its form becomes more distinct. It is of a bird's wings spread out in perfect symmetry on the clear, smooth surface of the glass. *The detail of the impression is amazing!* he thinks to himself. In such a short space of time, and out of such agony for the bird, how could something so beautiful be created? Then just as quickly as it had appeared, another bird comes into view. "Damn birds!" the soldier says aloud. "Get one and more keep coming back—like they *live* here!"

As the soldier drops back down into his chair, thoughts of crows fill his mind. *What is it with these damn birds and me?* he thinks to himself. From as far back as he can remember, crows had been there, making their presence known, on his journey through life. Then before he can ponder further the mystery, a sharp knock on the heavy wooden door sets him off again. "What *now*?!" he exclaims with great irritation. "Come in, then!" A muted 'So sorry, sir' comes from behind the slowly opening door. He knows the voice, of course. It's Agnes his housemaid. "Sorry, Aggie," he says almost sheepishly, "come on in."

Agnes is a cheery girl; a young *woman* really. She doesn't *live-in*, so to speak, but lives nearby in Dulnain Bridge where her family has lived for many decades and close enough for her to be able to walk to and from the estate. The soldier can no longer remember why or when he'd started calling her "Aggie" instead of Agnes, but he's sure it was around the time nine years past when she'd entered his study looking a bit apprehensive and uncomfortable. She was a pretty slip of a girl then, petite with high cheek bones and swept-back brown hair, who normally had a girlish smile set off by rosy cheeks and green-blue eyes. But on that particular day she looked somehow different. "Yes, Agnes, what can I do for you?" the old man had enquired of her then. The maid had seemed to him most uncomfortable in his presence; her eyes rigidly fixed on her black patent-leather shoes. "Come on, out with it lass."

Fumbling with her apron strings her gaze shifted from her shoes . . . to the fire . . . to the old man . . . and then back to her shoes--before taking a deep breath and blurting out: "I'm afraid I must ask to leave your service, sir."

The old man gave a rueful smile and a knowing nod and said, "Oh, Agnes, I see," fully suspecting what she was about to say next.

"You see, sir, I'm pregnant. I'm expecting a wee baby," Agnes mumbled.

"Hummm . . . that's a bit of a surprise, Agnes. And you're not married yet, are you, lass?"

"Aye, sir, not married yet," she continued with a hint of a sob in her voice.

The old soldier, feeling tender towards the girl, got out of his chair and inched near her. Putting an arm around her shoulder he said, "Oh, Aggie, you'll be fine. These things happen! You can carry on with your work here for as long as you feel able, and if there's anything you need, you let me know," he said softly. That was nine years ago. And it was then, in that moment, that he remembered that as being the first time he'd called her "Aggie." And he also remembered that she'd only taken a few months off back then and here she was now--nine years on--a mature woman whom he'd warmed to over the years. *Funny how these things happen in life*, he now thinks to himself.

"Sorry, Aggie. Not snapping at you. That damned crow flew into the window pane just before you knocked," explained the old man.

"There's always been crows round here, sir," Aggie replied by way of a reminder. "My gran used to talk about them sometimes."

"Yes, I remember them when I was a young lad here, interesting birds you know," said the old man. Aggie smiled. "You know, Aggie, I was thinking that it's about time the ground-floor library got a good clean. Haven't been in there for a while, and I bet the dust's gathering."

"Oh, yes, sir. I'll get on to that this morning!" confirmed the house maid. But the old soldier wasn't fooled; he could hear the apprehension in her voice. Agnes was never fond of the ground-floor library. Well, to her it isn't really a *library*. Sure, there are some books on shelves there but it mostly stored glass bottles filled with different coloured liquids, strange-shaped crystals, long tube-like telescope things, and other scientific-type stuff. And from her first venture into that room, when she'd first started working at the house, she thought it was more like a laboratory than a library. And she imagined the master carrying out weird experiments in there.

"Come now, Aggie," reassured the old man. "I don't know why you're still funny about that room, but there's nothing to concern yourself about! Look, I'll explain it to you again!" Aggie's eyes widened. "See this glass here with the whiskey in it? See what happens when I move it just a bit?" As the old soldier rotated the glass round between his fingers, Agnes saw an array of colours appear on the far wall of the study--like a dancing rainbow. "It's all to do with *light*, Aggie. All those colours you see there are just *light*! They're what let us see things, and make sense of our world," explained the old soldier. "Each colour is different, and means different things to us. They have energy and can give us energy--good and bad, mind you! And all that stuff kept in the library has to do with studying and understanding light and co-lours, their frequency and energy."

"Aye, well, that may be," shrugged Agnes, "but that room doesn't feel homely right now, and besides, some of the things in there look aw-fully delicate. I'm afraid I may break them!"

"Well, you're right, Aggie, I've not been in that room for a long, long time. So, could you give it a once-over? I've a mind to spend some time in there soon." With that, Agnes nodded, turned and left the study.

Even with a library full of coloured bottles, crystals and test tubes, and a study full of old faded photographs, tapestries and exotic figurines (which to her were of strange and mystical beings), Agnes had a soft spot for the old man. He seemed to understand people. And he was very good to her when she had to leave to have her baby those many years ago. Always asking if she was okay, and telling her not to do too much lifting and carrying, and to get the cook or his butler to do the heavy work. And if they had any problems with that, they could come and see him!

According to some of the staff, the soldier had acted a bit awkward when he first returned to the mansion after his father had died. They felt that he was a bit out of place; not really the "country laird" type. But he quickly adjusted to the way of life—and the responsibilities that came with it. Rumour had it that the family solicitors had a devil of a job finding him when they knew the old master, his father, was dying. Also, Agnes remembered her grandmother taking a great interest in all the gossip going round the village about the new master. Even now she asks after him when Agnes comes home from work.

As the study door closed behind his housemaid, the old man looked again at the window. But all signs of the crow had disappeared so he turned his attention to the whiskey glass; not to partake of its contents, but to marvel at the colours that danced through it as the meager daylight forced its way through the prismatic glass. From the depths of the liquid in the glass he can just make out a reflection of one of the figures in a photograph on the fireplace mantel shelf. As he strains his eyes to make the image clearer, his mind drifts back: back to a young soldier in a strange land, and to a chance meeting with a holy man.

Chapter 2

IT WAS IN KATHMANDU, NEPAL. The young soldier was a newly-promoted sergeant, a Gordon Highlander, and proud of it. He was in Kathmandu with a military detachment to recruit some local, fit young men into the Army of the British Empire. Well, not the *formal* British Army but the British *Indian* Army, the *Gurkhas* to be precise, as the regiment of Nepal was known. To be selected as a *Gurkha* was an honour amongst the Nepalese, and it took these young men out of what some viewed as grinding poverty, into a worthwhile occupation.

One day when the young soldier was off duty and out of uniform, he'd gone to one of the many small markets that lined the narrow streets of Kathmandu. He'd been rummaging round one stall where the trader had been trying to press a turquoise beaded necklace into his hand when he heard raised voices coming from a stall further down the street. The voices grew louder and louder, with more voices joining in. *A job for the Army*, he chuckled to himself, sorting out the locals. The commotion seemed to be spreading as more and more people got involved, with a lot of pushing and shoving going on. *What could be so valuable at one of these market stalls that warranted such a furore?* He was intrigued. He edged closer to the scene of all the action, where amongst all the flailing brown-hide, skin-covered arms and dull woollen-hatted heads bobbing up and down, a shaven-headed young man in flowing maroon-coloured robes stood out as he pressed his way, politely and smilingly, to the centre of the commotion. Within just a few minutes the arms had stopped flailing and the woollen hats had stopped bobbing, and peace was restored. *Impressive*, thought the young soldier. All that achieved without a single musket, rifle, or sword in sight; not a shot fired, drop of blood spilled. Then as the crowd thinned and the buyers and sellers returned to their business, the red-robed figure walked towards him-- and smiled as he passed. The sergeant couldn't help but blurt out, "Well done, that, man! A fine piece of diplomacy!"

With a slight turn of his bald head the man replied (in near perfect English), "Diplomacy . . . *mmmmm*, diplomacy . . . " as he scratched his head, obviously thinking about the soldier's choice of words. This took the young soldier momentarily aback.

"Courage, nevertheless, to venture into that den," he prompted.

At that the young man turned to the soldier, clasped his hands and bowed before him. "Human nature . . . simply human nature," he said, smiling at the sergeant.

"So sorry . . . where are my manners?" the soldier offered by way of apology. "My name is Donald, Donald Cameron, and may I say again, how impressed I am at your handling of that potentially volatile situation."

"I think you too must have to deal with difficult people and situations in your work?" said the hooded figure knowingly.

"Yes, at times I do. But how did you suspect that?"

"You are a soldier, are you not? That is part of what you do."

The new sergeant gave a startled look, pondered a moment and said, "Is it that obvious? Yes, I'm a soldier, a sergeant with the Gordon Highlanders."

"You can tell a lot by a man's face and his actions," replied the robed man with a cheeky grin. "I am Lama Kunchen, Buddhist monk. Come walk with me a while," proposed the monk. With a nod both men set off in stride, out of the hustle and bustle of the marketplace.

"What was so valuable back there to cause such a commotion?" enquired the soldier.

"Well, it is part of our culture to barter, which involves shouting, pushing, and in general, doing anything that will give someone an advantage over someone else. All of this can be for something as simple and worthless as a small trinket, or for essential everyday things like food, medicinal herbs, and general needs." Donald nodded. "But for some, desire and greed born out of ignorance can take over," sighed the monk. "It is *samsara*. Life and how we live it," he continued. "The way things are in this world. Some are never satisfied, they crave and desire, then crave more; and this to my way of thinking always brings suffering. So part of my job is to remind these buyers and sellers that there is more to their lives than what they can see and want, to show them that we are all interconnected and through the *dharma* guide them on their journey to accept and understand their suffering."

The soldier stopped and looked blankly at the young monk. "*Samsara*; suffering; this world. I don't understand. What other world is there?"

Coming to a stop as well the monk said, "I see you are questioning and curious! Our ways and our lives are simple to you, no doubt. Yet within them there are many hardships, which you too have and will suffer in your lifetime. So, we are not so different! Not obtaining what we desire—as with the arguments you saw back in the market--are small hardships, but to some, very real hardships. So it is set in our minds how we should approach our hardships. It has to do with the nature of the mind; it is perception mixed with solid beliefs and understanding things as they truly are, and it is this that makes the difference in how we view the passage and outcome of our lives," the lama explained.

The soldier looked directly into the lama's face; not only did it give off an air of wisdom, it was also a handsome and tanned oval face with high cheekbones, large dark brown, deep-set eyes, and almost perfect heart-shaped red lips. As they walked quietly along the narrow streets it was the soldier who spoke next. "So, what is *your* life? What do you do each day?"

"I am a travelling lama from Tibet. Many Tibetans are nomads, so I journey across the vast Tibetan Plateau visiting nomad camps and monasteries which lie beyond the great mountains to the north. Other Tibetans have travelled through the passes in these high peaks to live and trade with our neighbours here and in the lands to the east and west, so I follow them. In fact, I have just returned from a very interesting visit to the monastery Dolma Lhkang in Tibet where I received teachings from the Abbot Koncho Samdrup"

The young soldier still wore a puzzled look on his face: "Yes, but how do you survive? Do you have money? How do you eat, drink . . . sleep? Surely you must worry where your next meal will come from, and where you will find a bed for the night?"

"Worry? Yes, I may worry. But such worry, I think we can agree, will not provide a meal or a bed! If they are not there, then they are not there! I am a simple man. A nice woven mat and woollen blanket is a bed for the night, whether it is in the warmth of a friendly home or underneath the open skies! From hardship comes learning," he said. The lama could see from the soldier's face that he was still unsure of his meaning so he continued. "I am a teacher. I teach the *dharma*--the words of the Buddha. People will always need to learn. Learn about themselves and about the world round them. This helps them to understand why things are the way they are, and how they can be made better. For this teaching, my people are kind enough to offer me food and lodgings. So that is what I do. I too have learned the words and the ways of the Buddha, but like others, am still learning."

As the young soldier took in the lama's words, he shook his head. His first thoughts were of power; a holy man of such intelligence could wield an awful lot of power to determine peoples' lives. Yet with this man came intelligence and humility, and a refreshing honesty that would be perceived in the soldier's own society as weakness. *Yes*, he thought to himself again, *this man has power, but not any type of power I have come across before.*

So it was that out of a visit to a local marketplace, an argument and a chance remark, the soldier's worldview had become more than just the British Army. That whole afternoon was taken up with a fascinating conversation between the soldier and the monk. Life, death, suffering, ignorance, greed, peace, happiness--a whole new world of ideas had been set before the young sergeant. Then as the afternoon shadows began to lengthen, the soldier realised that it was time for him to return to his detachment. Offering his hand, the soldier said apologetically, "My friend, I regret that I must be getting back to my job."

"I understand," replied the monk, "and I to mine. I hope we will meet again. I too still have much to learn, and much to teach."

With the lama's words fading, the faint reflection in the old man's whiskey glass disappeared.

He was alone again with the embers of the fire beginning to likewise fade. He reached for the cast-iron poker next to the fireplace and lifted it off its hook, and with some effort stood up and brought the fire back to life with a rattle of the poker. He then took two hefty logs and a handful of peat and laid them against the flickering flames. Quickly the rising fire took to the raw, unsuspecting wood and he could feel the heat tingle the tips of his fingers. The cast-iron of the poker began to nip the palm of his left hand. Returning the poker to its hook he stood back and admired the rich energy emanating forth. As he tried to ease himself into his armchair, he thought he could hear laughter and stifled moans. Quickly he reached out to grab the arms of the chair, feeling himself falling backwards . . .

Chapter 3

"Watch it, Sarge! You'll kick the fire over!" Suddenly the soldier was being pulled upright into a sitting position by two tanned and powerful hands jutting out from layers of mud-spattered heavy woollen sleeves. "Got to watch it at your age, Sarge!" mumbled a cheeky voice, followed by stifled moans of, "Shouldn't be hoggin' the fire in the first place!" and some hoots of friendly laughter.

As his eyes adjusted to the fire's light he could see that he was sitting round a campfire. He could feel the prickle of coarse wool on his shaven head, and as he tried to move he felt weighed down by layer upon layer of clothing. As he gazed beyond the fire's flames he could make out the worn and dark faces of other men peering out from heavy woollen caps and balaclavas. "Go on, Sarge, tell the new lads how long you been in the army--don't spare any of the gory details!" said a voice immediately to the right of him, with mock sincerity. Before he could make sense of all this another voice, this time to his left, chimed in: "Our Sarge, here, joined up in '78, an original Gordon Highlander he is! Trouble at home, so he ran off and joined up, just a lad he was," continued the voice, "seen and done it all! Now he's a top sergeant--and don't you forget it!"

The fog of his memory began to clear. He remembers back to 1903 and the journey into Tibet. Some sort of trouble with the Tibetans, he had been told, so an expeditionary force had been put together to protect some big-wig political officers who were going in there to sort it out. But it is the cold that he remembers most--the harsh, biting cold--and the wind. Heading north out of India and up into the Himalayas was a shock to most of the men. They'd never experienced anything like that before. Sitting round the campfire he could see it in their faces. A real motley crew he had with him: tall, bearded Sikhs; snub-nosed, tough little Gurkhas with whom he was familiar; tall, thin and dark-skinned Madrassi sappers from the warm lowland plains; and a couple of regular Tommy Atkins who gave him all the cheek. All of them huddled round the campfire layered in their standard and extra-issue clothing which still didn't keep out the insufferable chill of the desolate, "God-forsaken" landscape.

Progress for his little group had been agonisingly slow. Sometimes they found footpaths meandering up the scree slides and sharp boulders--which quite easily gave way under foot; or they had to make camp wherever they could so that the sappers could blow up the side of one hill or another and form a route for the following men, beasts, and supplies. Then the officers announced that the worst was over; that the hardest of the climbing was behind them and the land would now flatten out as they neared the plateau. *Finally!* they all thought. No more camps perched on grey rocky outcrops. No more stumbling and fumbling over all-too-yielding ground where half your energy is spent trying to simply stay upright!

After a few more days of stumbling onwards and upwards, the ground did appear to be leveling off, and the mood of the men began to change. What concerned them now was not the climbing and the cold but who, and where, were the Tibetans? So far they hadn't encountered any; just traders calling themselves "*Tibetans*," bent on selling their trinkets and coloured beads. The only other soldiers they'd seen were a few Chinese officers chatting with other officers, all very polite and cordial. Word came back from the head of the expeditionary force that some fighting had broken out between the advanced British forces and the

Tibetan Army further ahead in Chumbi Valley. So the officers had ordered him to advance his men down into the valley and rendezvous with some other units at a Buddhist monastery; from their current position, just a white speck in the distance. As ordered, he and his men set out, down into the valley.

As the land flattened into arable fields separated by stone dykes, the soldier could make out the remnants of crops of barley and wheat and could see and hear the chirping of finches and the barking of foxes. There were groves of spruce trees and patches of gentian and wild rhubarb. And it all reminded him of *home*; of Scotland. All that was different were the *chortens* (or stone *cairns*), draped in small coloured prayer flags, to show him that he was in fact in Tibet--and not back home. As he marched his men forward, the outward shape of the monastery became clearer. It was an imposing whitewashed structure that looked as if it had been carved out of the same stone that surrounded it, and into which it was set on the side of a hill. A couple of hundred yards from the base of the hill an officer rode up on horseback and directed the sergeant to take his men across two fields to the right where they were to guard some captured Tibetan prisoners. Duly instructed, he wheeled his men to the right and off they marched. When they'd covered the allotted distance they came upon a huddled group of some fifty to seventy-five men. *Surely these are not Tibetan soldiers?!* he thought to himself. *They look like a rag-bag of beggars and tinkers--not soldiers!*

"They're all yours now, Sarge," piped up an approaching corporal. "I'd stay up-wind of 'em if I was you, they don't half stink." With that offhand remark the corporal signaled his squad to follow him back to the monastery.

"Wait a minute, corporal!" barked the sergeant. "If this lot are soldiers, where's their bloody weapons?"

"Over there by the wall," the corporal retorted. "Good luck with the Tibetan *Army*," he said with a sardonic smile on his face.

The sergeant strode over to the wall and looked down over what he would have guessed was a pile of scrap wood and metal. On closer examination he could just make out some old flintlock muskets, a few ceremonial swords, and some hand-held catapults. The rest of the pile was just crude clubs and sticks. He then looked back at the huddled mass of humanity, most of whom looked bewildered and lost, and thought to himself: *Surely they didn't try and defend themselves with this collection of junk! What belief made them think they could possibly succeed?!*

Returning to his prisoners, the soldier tried to find out who was in charge. He tried speaking English and what little Urdu he knew, but was met with blank faces. He then tried signing, gesturing with his hands to indicate "importance." A faint flicker of recognition came over one of the poor souls sitting near the front of the huddle, who started pointing toward an outcrop of rock a few hundred yards away. As the sergeant strained his eyes to bring the rocks into focus he ordered some of his men to stay and guard the prisoners; the rest to accompany him. Once they reached the rock formation his eyes were drawn to a large flock of jet-black crows which were strutting round a body, almost obscuring it from view. On closer inspection he saw a slight movement coming from the body.

The body was clad in dark red robes and the soldier realised that it was that of an old lama, lying propped up against a large, smooth-sided boulder. He assumed he'd been shot during the skirmish which had resulted in the taking of military prisoners. He'd come across lamas before whilst serving in the army; one quite memorable, Lama Kunchen, who he'd met at a market in Kathmandu. Something now drew him to this dying lama, so signalling his men to halt and stand guard, he bent down over the lama, who then slowly opened his eyes and smiled benignly. The sergeant was transfixed by his smile; it truly paralysed him. He could not fathom why the lama would smile at him. *Him*, of all people. (After all, it had likely been someone like him who'd shot him.) As he looked into the lama's large dark brown eyes, the soldier sensed the lama's serenity and resolution of his impending death. And from within him a dark and morbid sense of loss arose. It then dawned on him that the Tibetans were so very different in their view of death; they were silent, they showed no pain, and they accepted their fate with a smile.

The sergeant's eyes were drawn to the blood that had dried on the lama's darkened robe. As he looked, the lama extended his arm toward him. The soldier's eyes became transfixed to the box laying in the lama's open palm. He took in the minute details of the small crimson metal box inlaid with turquoise stones and decorated with a double *dorje* design; on the front of the box was an opening clasp set in the middle at the top with two rings on either side that had a long red coral thread attached, and there was a hinge at the bottom of the box. He recognised this as a Tibetan Buddhist amulet. Many Tibetans wore these amulets round their necks in the belief that it would protect them from harm. The soldier watched as the dying lama, gathering all his remaining strength, smiled and nodded his head, gesturing with his eyes for him to take the box. As the soldier took the amulet the lama smiled and slowly let his head come to rest against the smoothness of his stone pillow. The soldier watched the lama's eyelids slowly give up the ghost: he could see the life-force draining out as a strange, swirling mist from the lama's body.

He tried to speak--but then realised that he didn't know the proper words to say. What *could* he say? He had witnessed soldiers die before, many in extreme pain with severe wounds, and had thought that he was hardened against the sight of death. But now he was so moved by this dying lama that he realised that he was actually *fully awake* in this moment; as if there was no one and nothing else round but himself and the dying holy man. He forced a smile, his mind silently searching for the right words. "May we all find such peace . . . " was all the sergeant could think to say as he squeezed the amulet tightly into his own clenched fist. The lama gave him a wry smile with his last breath and the soldier thought he recognised the exact moment the lama's human existence ceased. And it made him feel so very helpless. So very aware of the finality. Stupid that he could not find the right words to say in the lama's final moments of life, and he now wondered why he felt that it had been so important to do so. He turned his back on the dead lama and looked into the faces of the men who'd been watching the dramatic scene unfold, looking for any glimmer of empathy for him or the lama. But there was none.

Was he the only one who'd felt anything of the grace, acceptance, and completeness of what the lama had just offered in his death? In that moment he felt an understanding and release; but also a sense of betrayal and ignorance from his fellow soldiers. He wanted to rail against them for being so cold and dispassionate; to distance himself from this scene--from the huddle of crushed and bewildered Tibetan soldiers with their wholly-useless weapons--from his own superior officers who'd sent him into this land of strange and too-harsh contrasts--but he was a soldier! And he had a job to do! He had to take care of his men! But, *God*! he thought to himself, *we've made a right mess of this!*

As he ordered his men back to their prisoners, he gave one last heart-felt look at the dead body of the lama, round which crows had now returned to act as sentinels and guardians of their own.

Chapter 4

His mind becomes filled with the prevalence of crows: crows round the dark, red-clad body of the lama; a solitary crow perched on a stone pillar; and crows roosting amongst trees, their features distorted through the glass of the window. With a shake of his head to clear his thoughts the old man realised that he is now standing up, looking out across the estate gardens that lead down to the river, his vision now fixed on three crows sitting resolutely on a branch of the nearest-by alder. "Bet you it was one on them that flew into this window," he said aloud. As he turned round to return to his armchair, he instinctively put his hand to his chest and felt the smoothness of the small metal box that hung round his neck on a coral string. He pressed it tight to his skin. Before he could take his seat, there was a sharp knock on the chamber door.

"Yes, what is it!" he barked reactively.

As the door slowly pushed open he heard Agnes report, "It's me, sir, I'm done cleaning the library."

"My, that was quick, Aggie! You've barely been gone minutes," replied the old man in a questioning tone.

"It's been a good couple of hours, sir. And I gave everything a real good going-over," confirmed the maid.

"Is that all for the day, then?"

"Yes, sir, more or less."

"Good, good," continued the old man. "Oh, before I forget. I've been meaning to ask you how's your boy doing? *Alexander*, isn't it?"

"Alex is fine, sir, he's nine now—and a good boy--*most* of the time!" Agnes replied with a proud mother's smile. "Leads his Great Grannie a merry dance at times, but she wouldn't be without him!"

"Ah, that's right!" the old soldier reminded himself. "You live with your grandmother. How is she?"

"Oh, she's fine. Just gets on with it. She's about your age now, sir--if you don't mind me sayin'-- and a bit nosy about what goes on when I'm up here working."

"You tell her there's nothing to worry about. Just an old man here with his memories!" sighed the old man. "Oh--one last thing! My mind's been set on that damn crow again. Can you give the case a good dusting?"

Agnes nodded a reserved affirmation. "Sir." Backing out she pulled the door shut and mumbled under her breath, "Not that glass case again!" Something she'd never got used to, she'd always thought it morbid: a stuffed crow perched on a small branch mounted in a glass case, set on a round black base. And she remembered vividly the circumstances of this crow's fate:

Generally even-tempered, it was rare that the old soldier took any real exception to anyone or anything. But that day, he really had it in for that crow. Marching heavily down the staircase with his old rifle clenched in his right hand and a determined look in his eyes, he strode to the front door, flung it open, and marched out towards the tree nearest the front wall of the house. (This was so unlike him, so Agnes followed--but at a safe distance so as not to be detected.) Agnes watched as he raised the butt of the rifle to his shoulder and sighted into the upper branches of the tree. Then as cool as you like, with his left hand he squeezed the trigger; a sharp crack reporting round the gardens, sending the birds squawking frenziedly in all directions. All except one. A jet-black crow toppled from the tree and landed at the old soldier's feet--with a near-soundless *thud*. Without a word the master picked up the dead bird and marched back into the house, carrying it as though it were some precious trophy. A week or so later the glass case appeared at the bottom of the staircase with the moribund bird inside; perched on its branch behind a wall of crystal-clear glass. Agnes had never questioned it—*not my place to ask*, she thought--but the incident had frightened her and each time she cleaned the glass case she was certain the crow's eyes were watching her, as if it were still alive . . .

To her favour, the old man had always liked his little conversations with "Aggie." He enjoyed her company and at times it lured him back from the emptiness and solitude of the big old house. Suddenly he had a thought: he'd visit the ground-floor library and reacquaint himself with his *colours*; after all, Agnes had surely left it clean and tidy. Mustering his strength he raised himself out of his armchair and shuffled off, out of the familiarity of the study. Walking the short distance to the hall he descended the short but imposing set of polished-wood steps, turned right at the top, and walked the remaining distance--only then realising that he'd left his walking stick standing by the fireplace in the study. Pressing his weight against the old brass handle he leaned in, the door offering no resistance. Agnes had left the curtains open so that by now the late afternoon sun was streaming in, so much so that he has to squint his eyes to regain his bearings.

What is it about this room that Aggie doesn't like? he wonders as he enters. *Could it be all the bottles—maybe reminds her of medicine and doctors and hospitals?* Admittedly, he too was a bit wary of this "colour-studying business" when he'd first been introduced to it after leaving the army. That was a long time ago and the army was the only thing he'd known up to then, really. He'd joined up as a young man—too young, actually, having lied about his age--and there he was, a middle-aged ex-staff sergeant back in the country of his birth, looking for direction in his life. And it was his *colour studies*, introduced to it by another retired soldier at an ex-serviceman's club down in London that had helped him. Maybe it was his time spent in India and the East, and the cultures he'd encountered there, that let him overcome his skepticism and try to understand the deeper value of light and colour.

Slowly he pushed the library door closed behind him and walked to the centre of the room. The range and depth of colours that sprung from the still liquid, protected within the small pyramid-shaped glass bottles placed in regimented lines on the bookcase shelves round the room, welcomed him. Offered peace and comfort. Crystals that hung from fine silk thread from the tops of the window frames swayed gently, reflecting the sun's rays into rainbows of colour across the room, giving life and movement to the otherwise stillness within. He can still remember the meaning of each and every colour and although it is a cold afternoon and an unheated room, he can feel a certain warmth flowing into him. And as he turned to look round the room the colours seem to flow and follow him, like waves pushed along by the light forcing its way through the window glass: there were waves of clear sky blue, deep and rich crimson, and sharp and invigorating saffron yellow that crested and rolled before crashing against the solid and aged brown of the library door. Blinking his eyes he could then see that these coloured waves had instantly taken form, and although faint, were now approaching and becoming clearer, accompanied by the distant sharp clang of bells and the low bellow of soulful horns:

"What's that coming, Sarge? A parade?" boomed an inquisitive voice as a bony and tanned figure pointed in the distance.

"Not sure, lad. Think it may be some more of those Tibetan leaders heading toward the city," replied the sergeant. "There's a big meeting in the city sometime soon to finish all this nonsense off." The sergeant and some of his men had been allowed to go into the city shortly after they'd marched their way through and out of Chumbi Valley and across the Tibetan Plateau. Resistance to their progress had become less and less the nearer they got to Lhasa, the capital city. Before they'd got anywhere near the city walls, the sergeant was overcome by the sight of the palace. *Potala Palace--what an amazing structure!* he thought. Shimmering white in the morning sunlight, a huge white wall of light set into the hillside that guarded over the tiled roofs of the city's dwellings and its people. He'd never seen anything quite like it before. Now he and his men were camped a few miles to the southwest of the city, ostensibly to act as a perimeter guard in case what was left of the Tibetan Army decided to have another go.

"Shall we stand-to, Sarge?" enquired the voice behind the bony finger. "It's getting nearer."

"What is?" enquired the sergeant.

"The Tibetans. Some sort of parade."

"No, lad. Let them be," sighed the sergeant.

The colours of the parade were now clearer and defined. Reds, yellows, blues, greens, and golds were everywhere. Shaven-headed monks in deep red flowing robes were carrying a large, decorative wooden litter, whilst ahead of them similarly tonsured monks clad in saffron were chanting in a deep monotony interrupted only by others ringing ornate bronze-coloured bells or blowing similarly-coloured horns. Seated prominently in this litter was a most majestic figure dressed in the deepest and richest crimson robe, exquisitely pleated and draped down over the seat and over the individual's left shoulder. The face of the figure was that of a youngish man, high cheekbones and deeply-tanned olive skin. (*This is no soldier*, thought the sergeant.) Crowning this powerful figure was the most opulent gold headdress, akin to a bishop's mitre but so much more, and inlaid with gemstones of red, black, and turquoise.

As the litter passed directly in front of the sergeant, the figure turned his gaze towards him. The look that met the sergeant was not one of power and arrogance or of lofty position or rank, but of quiet confidence, serenity, and humility. The figure, the sergeant recognised, was familiar to him. He'd seen him somewhere before. As he watched the procession, one particular monk stood out and as the soldier looked back into the Tibetan face, it suddenly dawned on him: it was the lama in Kathmandu, from all those years before! "No, surely *not*," he mumbled aloud. Before he could collect his thoughts the litter had passed him by, the procession continuing on its way towards the city; the waves of colour and sound receding into the distance. "No, it couldn't be," the sergeant said to himself.

For the remainder of the day the sergeant couldn't clear the images of the Tibetan procession from his thoughts. The face of the majestic man in the litter and the monk that seemed so familiar to him tormented him. Finally he informed his corporal that he was going out for a walk and headed down to the stream that ran across the track into the city to put his mind to rest.

"You be careful, Sarge. Them uppity Tibetans are camped somewhere out that way," warned his second-in-command.

"They won't harm me. They won't harm anybody," he chided the corporal. "They're as far from being soldiers as you can get."

The sergeant's walk took him across clear green meadows, devoid of heavy boot prints and the churned earth of horses' hooves. Only patches of lilac, blue and pink, of the delicate yet hardy ground-cover variety, broke the steady greenness; such a stark contrast to the harsh and sharp grey of the high mountains way off in the distance. His mind full of thoughts jostling for dominance, his solitude was interrupted by nearby shouting, and as he looked in the distance he could see two red-clad monks approaching him, waving their arms in great agitation, and muttering away in clipped Tibetan. As the disconcerted figures neared him, the sergeant raised both arms in a gesture of surrender. A loud, raucous laugh then reached his ears--coming from a figure walking some distance behind the two irate monks. Dressed in the deepest and richest of red robes the figure spoke to his two acolytes, which seemed to subdue their anxiety, and they duly moved out of the soldier's path. As the soldier approached the red-robed figure to the rear, his features became clearer. Although the gold head-dress was missing, it was the monk from the litter.

This red-robed figure spoke directly to the soldier in Tibetan, while the one of the accompanying monks began to translate his words.

"They worry, worry about my safety, worry that someone may kill me" translated the monk in passable English, "but where does worry really get us?" These few words instantly put the sergeant at ease; uneasily calm. He couldn't explain it but he was alert and aware as any soldier--but with an over-riding sense of calm.

"I'm sorry, I appear to have disturbed you," replied the sergeant with a respectful bow of his head and waited as the monk translated his words to the main monk.

The red-robed monk raised his right hand slightly as if to admonish him.

"My name is Khakyab Dorje the Fifteenth Karmapa" the monk continued to translate "and you are a soldier from the camp, I saw you there.

"The *Karmapa*?" queried the sergeant. "I've heard that name before . . . yes, back in Nepal . . . in Kathmandu . . . a market, a trader trying to sell me a turquoise necklace, an argument and a lama I met. Lama Kunchen, I was sure I saw him today. . . do you know *him*.?"

"Lama Kunchen?!" smiled the Karmapa. "Lama Kunchen is a wise and clever man. A great teacher. I'm sure he would have been very interested and pleased to meet you! A turquoise necklace you say, interesting. Are you going on into Lhasa?"

"No, no," replied the sergeant but we have already been in to visit. Most impressive and unusual, I must say. Potala Palace . . . the temples . . . the flags . . . the colours—they're all quite extraordinary."

The Karmapa smile, bowed and bid his farewells to the soldier.

With that the three Tibetans bowed and took their leave, the soldier left with only his thoughts (clearer thoughts) and a prevailing sense of peace. He felt that he had learned something, but wasn't quite sure what. With a shake of his head he set off back to camp, wondering what had *actually* just happened, his mind teaming with thoughts and ideas: the *Karmapa, Lama Kunchen*, the dying lama . . . were they all linked somehow, beyond the obvious?

What a strange country this Tibet is! he resigned to himself. Its fortress walls of the Himalayas so mighty and foreboding; a challenge and struggle to be undertaken before reaching the calmness and ease of the high plains on which he now walked, as if such serenity of nature was a reward for having endured the toil and hardship to get here. As he turned the corner of one of the ceremonial *cairns* peppered across this land, he knew he was on the outskirts of his encampment. But even after blinking his eyes to adjust to a sharp shaft of sunlight, he could see no camp. No picket guards, no corral of officers' horses, and no array of khaki-coloured tents. Just the flutter of the dull beige-coloured linen curtains of the library windows caught in a slight draught coming through a crack at the bottom of the window frame.

Exhausted, the old soldier realises that he must get some sleep. With some effort he made his way back out into the hall, up the full set of stairs, down the upstairs hall and into the master bedroom. *I'll undress in a bit*, he thought as he lay back on his bed and shut his eyes.

Chapter 5

Caught fully-dressed by the first rays of the rising sun, the old soldier woke feeling rested, the warmth of his feather mattress and cotton sheets having shielded him from the chill that always pervaded the master bedroom. For some reason beyond him, he never liked his bedroom cluttered; he kept it simple and functional, perhaps a remnant of his army life. He changed his wrinkled clothes and headed out into the hall, then slowly made his way down the stairs and into the dining room. The smell of breakfast hung invitingly in the morning air; the sunlight glinting off the domes of the silver serving ashettes.

Seating himself in his usual chair at the head of the table he gazed out onto the grounds to the rear of the house. The bay window that opened out onto these grounds is an impressive one. Almost the full height of the room and made up of large and unusually uninterrupted panes of glass so that the view is almost continual, it provided an unobstructed view as if there was no window at all. From his seat he could make out several birds swooping and diving across the lawns, seemingly engaged in some aerial combat. Added to this he could hear the mumbling of raised voices in the distance. He could just make out Agnes' voice and that of the butler; *an argument no doubt*, he thinks, down in the kitchen.

Just then the main clock that stood out in the hall began striking the hour. This grand, free-standing timepiece didn't so much chime the hour as emit a deep and sharply resonant *boom* like a pommel striking the taut skin of a drum. These sounds filled his ears just as the sight of a tangle of wings and feathers outside the window reaching their inevitable climax filled his field of vision. A crow and a magpie had finally got to the point of the chase. As quickly as the two birds had clashed, they parted--and the old man could make out an object spiralling to the ground. But all these sights and sounds were too much for him at this time of the morning. He shut his eyes and covered his ears to keep his senses blind. As he opened his eyes he found himself standing by the side of a dirt-track road with a voice ringing in his ears:

"Here we go again, Sarge. Another one of them parades!" As the soldier looked towards the direction of the voice, he could see approaching some Tibetan monks leading a procession. "Looks like the one we saw near that Lhasa place a while back," continued the voice.

The sergeant nodded. "Yes, a bit, maybe," he replied. "But different, not as posh." The soldier and his men were now part of a column heading south, away from Lhasa. The officers and politicians had done their stuff; the fighting was over and they were on their way back to India.

"Just a few days more, Sarge, and we'll be over them mountains and back to where we belong," continued the other soldier, pointing to the looming peaks of the Himalayas in the not-too-far distance. As the procession drew nearer the sergeant could see that it was indeed different; not so much pomp and colour. In fact, it seemed a sombre affair. A sadness seemed to hang in the air.

"I think it's what they call a *sky burial*," offered the sergeant.

"A *what*?" said the other soldier, looking confused. "What's a *sky burial*? God--these Tibetans and what they get up to!"

"It's basically a funeral. One of the ways they bury their dead. Nothing wrong with that," the sergeant said, his eyes transfixed by the affair.

For some reason known only to him, the sergeant felt that he had to follow this party (which seemed oblivious to the British soldiers' presence). Leaving his men he followed their trail higher into the foothills, maintaining a discrete distance. Leading the procession was a monk chanting what the soldier imagined to be incantations, presumably for the dead. Trailing behind were numerous family members carrying the decreased on a wooden pallet, others playing *damaru* drums, and others spinning hand-held prayer wheels. These objects, the soldier knew, had powerful religious significance for Tibetans: the drum was a small hand-drum with two pommels attached which when quickly rotated emitted a rhythmic, clicking beat; the prayer wheels are said to contain messages of the Buddha's teachings that when spun were given out from the wheel to be spread through the air to reach whomever could listen. As the group moved on, the soldier became more and more intrigued; absorbed in the solemnity and ritualism.

Maintaining his measured distance, the soldier's attention was suddenly drawn to the head of the procession and one family member who seemed to be struggling and stumbling over the rocky ground leading to the high ridge, and was occasionally assisted by other family members. As he focused his eyes he realised that it was a heavily pregnant woman and instantly felt empathy with her. After the group had walked a considerable distance the monk waved his right hand in a downward motion, pointing to the body. The body was then carefully lowered to the hard, stony ground adjacent to a neatly arranged mound of stones and rocks forming a crude *cairn*—a purposefully-built stone marker. Extending downward from the top of the cairn and from differing angles were brightly coloured squares of fabric with Tibetan writing on them. These "wind-horses," or prayer flags, danced wildly in the chill mountain wind. All members of the burial party bowed ceremoniously before the cairn, then the pall-bearers dutifully lifted the body high into the air and the procession (apart from the woman who by custom were not allowed to attend a sky burial) continued on its way up a well-trodden path, up into the foothills toward a monastery that could be seen in the distance.

As the soldier continued to follow the unfolding events, the funeral party finally halted by the monastery at a large, fenced-off meadow; this was the *durtro*, or *charnel* ground, he was later to discover. At one end was a circle defined by large rough-hewn stones; this was where the group stopped and the final ceremony would take place. Prayer flags hung from numerous cairns and smouldering juniper scented and purified the air. All this activity, along with the smell of incense, attracted the interest of lammergeyers, ravens, and crows; the latter much revered by Tibetans. As the vultures circled overhead, some had the courage to perch themselves on the raised stones like worldly, wise sentinels, casting judgment over the proceedings. A more adventurous group of these carrion-devouring birds gathered on the ground, huddled together like a coven of dark witches, a short distance from the funeral bier. Three crows, showing complete disregard for the more intimidating vultures, positioned themselves on the raised stone nearest the funeral party.

Following a signal from the monk, the chanting stopped and the pall-bearers lowered the body to the ground. Some of the men then put on long white aprons. They then unwrapped the corpse-- which was naked, stiff, and bloated. The men then picked up huge cleavers which, after a few strokes on nearby rocks, were honed to razor sharpness. The bright sun and clear blue of the sky made the soldier's eyes squint but he could still make out the glinting blades in the men's hands as they talked amongst themselves in a business-like manner. He then watched in stunned silence as one of the men ceremoniously slashed down into the flesh of the corpse, followed likewise by the others—a *thwack, thwack* sound resonating.

This macabre behavior appeared to incense and excite the vultures, who brazenly began hopping forward in bloodthirsty anticipation; whereupon three of the men brandished long wooden sticks to warn them off. Within a few minutes the cutting and slashing had been completed and some of the dead man's internal organs were removed and set aside. The vultures again tried to move in but were driven back by the gesticulating and shouting of the stick-wavers. Then the body-cutters gave a signal and all the men simultaneously stood back, away from the dismembered corpse. This was the signal--if any were needed--for the flock of scavenger birds to rush in--

Quickly obscuring the body from sight, their cruel and nimble heads disappeared into the body parts as they ripped away bits of flesh. The soldier watched with gruesome curiosity as the vultures balanced on the severed body parts, arched their backs so as to gain extra purchase, and with their enormous talons ripped lumps of flesh from the carcass which they swallowed whole. The earlier sounds of chanting and incantations were now replaced with the squawking and squabbling of the feasting birds. Once sated, the birds, one by one, took to the air, to be replaced by others; while the soldier could only shudder in disgust. After the last raptor had feasted, he watched as the men took what remained of the corpse (now only a bloody framework of bones) and set to work crushing the bones with huge mallets. (To the soldier's surprise, the men talked jovially as they worked, and even laughed.) The bones were soon reduced to mere splinters which were then mixed with barley flour and thrown to the crows and hawks that had been patiently waiting their turn. Half an hour later the body had completely disappeared. Then the men left, their work finished, the family retracing their steps back down the trail--the stone circle and meadow resuming blissful serenity as if the events he'd seen unfold were part of an unfathomable dream. Then just as he was about to turn away, the soldier saw a most gruesome sight: an eyeball of the dead man had rolled a few feet away from the dismembered body— undetected . . .

Suddenly a fearless crow, that had been imperiously watching the feasting vultures, dived in and snatched the eye. But as it flew off with its prize it was spotted by one of the vultures--who immediately gave chase. The soldier's attention fixed, the birds were mismatched in size but the wily crow ducked and weaved from side-to-side, making sharp and speedy turns in an attempt to shake off its pursuer. For its part, the vulture swooped ominously up and down, harrying the crow at every opportunity, as if biding its time until that one misjudged turn from the smaller bird would prove its demise. The soldier could see that the crow's flapping wings were not beating as frantically as when it first set off with its prize, and that its maneuvering to evade the vulture's grasp was becoming laboured: it was tiring and running out of energy and places to go.

As the crow made one final and desperate turn towards him, the soldier saw the vulture set its wings for the fatal attack. Swooping down to just above the crow's neck, in the blink of an eye its sharp and all-enveloping talons had the hapless black bird in its vice-like grip—the two plummeting, coming within inches of the soldier's head. The shock of the capture forced the crow to loosen its jaws and in a flurry of feathers dropped the coveted blood-covered eye. Unable to avert his gaze in time, the dead man's eye struck the soldier's forehead, trailing drops of blood down his face, then landed at his feet, on the stony ground where he stood. This bloody finale to the pulse-quickening chase sent a cold shiver down the soldier's spine and caused him to let out a stifled cry of revulsion. Even though he considered himself a hardened soldier, this last macabre twist was too much—even for him.

Turning and running in a blind panic towards the dirt-track road the funeral party was now following home, before he knew it he had tripped over a large stone and careered forward at a pace too fast to remain on his feet. And as he stumbled, he unavoidably collided with the pregnant woman of the procession--knocking her off her feet--the two tumbling together to the ground, him landing on top of her. Momentarily stunned, the soldier found himself staring into the most intense and mesmerizing brown eyes he'd ever seen. At first speechless he then said, "Oh my—I'm so sorry!" Jumping to his feet he offered his hand--which she refused. Fearing that he'd injured her he then knelt down beside her as she lay on the rocky ground. "May I--" he said, again extending his hand. This time accepting his help, he gently pulled her to her feet and again looked deeply into the woman's dark brown eyes. His heart pounding he felt his pulse race as he held this beautiful Tibetan woman's hand. But it wasn't just the collision and the fall. Or even her mesmerizing eyes. His mind still reeled with the thuds of mallets on severed bones and the human eye that had fallen from the sky.

(*Everything* he'd seen and heard had now merged together—and he had to get away! As at no time before since he was a small boy, he felt he had to run! Run as fast as he could--away from these people and the madness of their rituals and the men with their disturbing laughter—away from the vultures and crows that feasted on the dead and fought over human eyes!)

The soldier bowed respectfully to the woman, while all the others in the party watched on in near horror. Standing before her, her eyes focuses intently on his, as if looking into his very soul. He shuddered—a dozen emotions flooding his senses. "I—I'm so sorry!" he said again, now feeling inept and rather foolish. Then with only the tiniest of nods, the woman turned and with the help of another woman resumed her walk home. The soldier watched, transfixed, as the distance between them grew. He willed her to turn round and look at him one more time but she just kept walking. Then out the corner of his eye he then saw something lying on the ground where the woman had fallen. As he walked towards it he saw that it was a small leather pouch with turquoise and red draw-strings. He bent down and picked it up, turned it round and round in his weathered hands. He could almost feel warmth coming from the pouch--*her* warmth--and immediately felt *at one* with the universe. Raising his head he called out, "Stop, stop! You dropped this purse!" he said, holding up the purse. But his words were lost in the wind and now she was merely a speck in the distance. "Stop, stop!" he yelled again, louder.

To his surprise and relief the woman stopped; turned round to face him as he waved the purse wildly in the air. He was certain he saw a smile come to her face as she turned away and resumed her walk in the other direction. It was no good, he knew now. He would have to keep this beautiful leather pouch, care for it, until the day he could find her and return it. With one last look at the receding party, the soldier turned and stumbled back down the dirt-track road. Once the Tibetan party was out of sight he slowly began to regain his composure and by the time he reached the encampment his breathing had returned to normal and he thought the worst had passed. But still, he didn't trust himself. There was no denying--he was still quite shaken. His head spinning and feeling faint he made a brief, grunted apology to his men and made straight for his own tent.

Retiring early that evening, as he undressed a black crow's feather fell from his tunic. As it floated to the ground on an errant wind its colour seemed to change to a deep turquoise as the light from his bedside candle played upon it. Suddenly the day's events came rushing back to him. As he lay on his camp bed he tried to relax but his mind kept filling with images of the burial party and the sounds of squawking birds and the wrenching of human flesh. And the longer he lay there reflecting on these sights and sounds the more he wondered how a people like the Tibetans, who claim to live such spiritual lives, could have such disregard and disrespect for the dead. To his Western sensibilities, their behaviour and practices seemed barbaric. Irreligious.

In trying to distance himself from such troubling ideas, a voice stirred in the back of his memory; it was that of Lama Kunchen, whom he'd encountered all those years before. He could hear the slow and purposeful (yet pleasing) tone of the lama's broken English as clearly as if the man were standing right next to him. Lama Kunchen had tried to impress upon him a more peaceful and satisfying view as to the purpose of life through meditation, and the cause and effect of peoples' actions. The lama had explained the indivisible nature of the mind: he had said that it had a fluid quality like currents of energy which they called "winds." The Tibetans believed that these *winds* flowed through channels of various parts of the body and served as bridges between body and mind. These *winds* presided over our physical as well as mental functions and manifested through our nostrils as breathing.

The soldier—now, for the first time--considered the five elements Lama Kunchen had spoken of: space, wind, fire, water, and earth--which fascinated him when he realized that they are an essential part of life, as well as part of every human being. As he lingered on the lama's words he realised that part of what he'd been taught was that bone, flesh, and blood were merely a means of carrying the true human *essence* (*spirit* or *consciousness*—some call it) and that once it departs the body to seek its new life, that which remained is but a husk, an empty shell, and as such could be returned to nature to continue the physical cycle of death and life for other creatures. And the more the soldier considered it the more practical a sky burial seemed. The rocky and unyielding landscape of the high plateau and foothills did not lend itself to digging graves; in fact it nigh on made subterranean burial impossible. So employing such ritualistic means of disposal of the body satisfied both the Tibetans' religious beliefs and their affinity with the land they inhabited.

The next morning the soldier woke from a very shallow, troubled sleep, the incidents of the previous day still lingering in his mind. He roused his men and they broke camp to continue their journey out of this strange land. But the sergeant and his men hadn't travelled far when a solitary moving outline appeared on the horizon. Slowly, as the outline approached, he began to make out the dark red and saffron colours of a lama's robes. The lama was perched on a donkey which ambled dutifully along the dirt-track road. As their paths crossed, a flicker of recognition passed between them, and with that they both stopped and looked at each other more closely. The lama smiled and broke the uneasy silence: "The market in Kathmandu, a young Scottish soldier and a young Tibetan monk, I think," the lama said knowingly.

"Of course!" exclaimed the soldier. "Lama Kunchen! After all this time you remembered!"

"My dear Scottish friend!" exalted Lama Kunchen with genuine affection. "It has been a while since we had our interesting conversation-- much *too* long!"

"Indeed," sighed the soldier. "But life's events have overtaken us, and as you can see I've finally made it into Tibet. Wish it were under happier circumstances."

"Yes, some things are not good. But life is change and we must accept that," the lama continued. "And these times are a great change for us all. But let us not dwell on such things! You are a leader of many men now! Not only older but *wiser*, I think!" The soldier nodded reservedly. Lama Kunchen then pointed to plumes of smoke rising in the distance and said, "See that smoke in the distance? It is from a nomads' camp where my brother and his family are camped. You must join me there to meet them and share some yak-butter tea."

"I don't think that would be such a good idea, my friend," replied the soldier.

"It will be fine, they are good people. Trust me. And anyway, it will be good to catch up on old times," insisted the lama.

The soldier did trust Lama Kunchen. That chance meeting in Kathmandu had been running through his mind ever since he'd witnessed the Karmapa's procession outside Lhasa. He felt he should accompany the lama. Maybe get to know the real Tibetans and find answers to some of his nagging questions.

"What's up now, Sarge?" queried a gruff soldier.

"I'll be gone with the lama, here, for a short while," replied the sergeant. "You know what to do. Just keep the lads quiet, and get them on with their duties."

"Off on your travels again, eh, Sarge?" sighed another soldier. "I'd of thought you'd have enough of this place!" The sergeant thought to respond—but then thought again.

There was little conversation between the two men as the wind and dust of the plateau whipped around them. No doubt they both had much to discuss, thought the soldier, but the lama seemed intent on reaching the encampment first. Slowly the extent of the nomads' settlement filled their vista: the black-haired, yak-hide tents with the coloured flags billowing in the wind looked striking against the paleness of the plateau, the vibrant blue of the sky, and the dazzling whiteness of the snow-covered peaks of the mountains. These tents were spaced a fair distance apart so that each had ample land for grazing their animals. Prayer flags were strung along the guy ropes of each tent, reminding the soldier of bunting at a country *fete* back home. He could hear dogs barking and saw them running to and fro in anticipation. This alerted the camp and a party of six approached from behind a line of tethered horses. Following the customary Tibetan greetings and a short verbal exchange, the lama waved for the sergeant to come forward. The no-mad welcoming party bowed in greeting and gestured for him to follow them. From behind the slightly opened doors of the first few tents the soldier could just make out the glint of inquisitive eyes as they followed his progress into their encampment. He could feel an air of unease round him, but then a reaffirming hand on his shoulder calmed the sergeant's disquietude.

"Do not worry," counselled the lama, "they are merely curious. They do not see many people that look like you on their journey. Nepali traders and Chinese, *yes*, but not someone like *you!* Ah, here we are, this is the tent!" motioned Lama Kunchen as its door was pulled open by one of the welcoming party.

The inner space of the large tent was hexagonal; there was an open flap in the centre of the roof that allowed smoke from the dried yak dung and juniper fire to rise up and out into the clear air of the plateau. The fire also served as a stove for cooking. At the back of the tent was an altar on which were placed numerous artifacts including a statue of the Buddha, some lit yak-butter lamps, a bell, a *dorje* (a small sculpted metal hand-held object shaped like a dumbbell), and a *damaru* drum. All these items appeared to be placed ritualistically before two depictions of co-lourfully-robed religious men: one, he thought, must be the Dalai Lama, the leader of Tibet, whilst the other bore a striking resemblance to the monk he'd met near Lhasa. There was a lot of conversation between the nomads and Lama Kunchen once inside the tent, voices became raised, as the soldier was ignored for a few tense moments.

"I am greatly saddened," confided the lama to the sergeant, " I have just been informed that my brother was killed a few days ago and now his wife is struggling with childbirth in the next tent, and I must go to her now." He then bowed and made his way out of the tent, leaving the soldier on his own. An old woman who'd been sitting near the entrance of the tent gestured for the soldier to come and sit beside her, then gave him a mug of steaming hot butter tea.

The soldier sat in silence as the tent emptied of everyone except the old woman, whom he noticed sat low to the ground on a very small wooden stool which seemed to rise only inches from the ground. Her head bowed, she sat staring at the floor as if in a trance. Meanwhile the soldier sat on large, very colourful cushions made from yak wool, staring into the fire as he sipped his tea. A short time later Lama Kunchen returned to the tent.

"Things are not good," he said as he sat next to the soldier. "She is not a strong woman and with the death of her husband she has lost her will to fight for her and the baby's life, and fight she will have to do if both are to survive. The elders are quite concerned for both mother and child. Prayers can only do so much," he said, "but you, my friend, I think can help. I will speak to the elders." Without waiting for a response from the soldier, Lama Kunchen stood and turned to leave the tent.

"*Me?*" questioned the sergeant. "What can *I* do? I'm not a doctor, I'm just a soldier!"

The lama turned and smiled. "You know more than you *think* you do, my friend! It is about trust and understanding, which you have. You have my trust and *yes*, you can help." With that remark the lama left the tent and in a short while returned and nodded to the soldier: "Come with me," he said politely.

The soldier followed the lama out into the cool air, watching not to trip on all the guy ropes that held the tent securely to the ground, and discovered that attached to the back of the tent was another long and narrow tent which looked to him like an animal shelter. As they entered, he couldn't believe his eyes: There was the pregnant woman he'd knocked down at the sky burial, lying on a mat on the dirt floor, obviously in the final stages of labour! There was also animal fodder, churned-up soil, and the most awful smell he'd ever encountered. (He nearly vomited.) How could he possibly face this woman after what had happened? And what could he possibly do to help her?

He stood looking down at the woman as she lay there writhing in pain—hesitation and uncertainty gripping him. He had no skills to help her and now wondered if it had been the collision that brought on her labour. *Did I cause this?* he asked himself, sweat streaming down his face. He would later remember (as if in a dream) bending down and gingerly wiping the perspiration from her brow with a damp white cloth someone had put in his hand. And as the woman gazed up into his eyes he was again taken by their dark, almost black colour, as they seemed to plead with him to help her. He took her hand; it felt limp and lifeless.

Sitting on the ground beside the woman he continued to hold her hand. She looked so beautiful and so innocent. He worried for her--so fragile-looking and vulnerable. *Life truly can be painful,* he thought. Then he began to wonder how her husband had died: *Was it my army that caused his death?* he asked himself—suddenly feeling ashamed and guilty. (*It should be him here not me!*) He found himself speaking softly to her with words she could not possibly understand. And suddenly a stifled cry broke the still, stale air--and jolted the soldier from his contemplation. Near darkness prevailed all round, broken only by the light from some butter lamps and the moonlight piercing the partly-opened tent flat and fell upon the form of new life. The baby now delivered, its fragile tiny body lay wrapped in a soft turquoise-coloured blanket.

"Dawa, Dawa," implored the woman, as she held out her arms to hold her child.

As the soldier gazed at the face of the new mother, he could see sadness in her eyes--just before her outstretched arms flopped back down by her sides and her breathing grew shallow. She was slipping away. Child-birth had been too much for her small body. The soldier watched in horror as life seemed to drain from her eyes and as she forced one last breath, her head sagged lifeless back onto the pillow. The soldier felt an overwhelming sense of loss as he'd never felt before and wondered if this is what people called *love*. He felt bereft and alone and so very angry. Feeling a consoling hand on his shoulder, he rose to his feet.

"What good was *I*?" railed the sergeant, at himself.

"You were here for her," confirmed Lama Kunchen. "This is where you had to be. Life and death, birth and rebirth. You are part of this circle—here, now, and always."

But the soldier didn't understand. He was confused and in that moment wished he had the power to change the outcome.

"What now, for the baby?" he said in exasperation—now feeling an overpowering sense of helplessness.

"She is also part of the circle. She will be looked after," explained the lama, adding, "and 'Dawa' is a good name for this child. It means many things—it means the day on which she was born, and it means *moonlight*, and it describes someone who gives light and removes darkness."

The sergeant rose to his feet and followed the lama out of the animal tent. The light of the moon was just enough for them to see their way across to the other tent. But a yapping dog distracted the soldier and he lost his footing—tripping over one of the guy ropes he was trying so intently to avoid. And no sooner had he hit the damp ground that a strong arm was helping him back to his feet.

Chapter 6

"My God! How long have you been on the floor, sir?"

"I—I don't know. My head's a bit fuzzy," replied the old man. "I remember getting out of the chair to get some breakfast and got my foot got caught on the chair leg, and . . . "

Agnes' voice grew solemn. "It's the middle of the morning, sir," she said, lifting him to his feet. "Come on now--you look a bit pale. Let's get you to your warm study."

"I'm not completely *helpless*, you know," moaned the old man, clearly groggy.

"Sometimes I wonder. Sometimes I really do wonder," chided Agnes in mock exasperation.

Helping the old soldier back up the staircase and into the study, into his favorite armchair by the crackling fire she instructed him, "Now you sit there quiet and I'll bring up some hot tea and a sandwich. It's almost lunchtime now." It seemed no time at all to the old soldier before Aggie returned with a silver tray set with a steaming pot of tea and a plate of neatly cut ham and tomato sandwiches. Removing his whiskey tumbler from the side-table she set down the tray, poured him a steaming cup, and prepared to leave. "Will there be anything else, sir?"

"Don't go, Aggie . . . stay a while. Keep me company while I eat," said the old man. "Here, you have one of these lovely sandwiches you made." Since the master of the house very rarely asked for company, Agnes was momentarily caught off-guard. But after such a fall he could probably do with a bit of watching, she thought to herself.

"Very well, sir, but, I've already eaten," she resigns, taking a seat across from him. "Besides, you'll be needin' all them sandwiches to get your strength back."

After a few minutes of awkward silence the old man asks, "You never married, did you, Aggie? Oh--I hope you don't mind me asking!"

"No, sir, I don't mind," she replied. "No, I never married Alexander's father. Guess it wasn't meant to be. He's off away somewhere now. I think he joined the army. That's the story I've heard."

"I was married once, a long time ago," the old man confided. "It was when I was just coming out of the army. No family, though," he muses. "Joined the army when I was a wee lad. A bit too young, I suppose."

"Why's your wife not here livin' with you?" asked Agnes.

"We divorced. Split up. Married life was not for us. At least not to each other!" joked the old soldier. "Too set in our ways!"

"Hum . . . that's a pity," sighed the maid.

"I bet your grandmother has seen some changes round here over the years," he said. "She lives with you and your son, doesn't she?"

"She does that, sir," confirmed Agnes. "Been round here all her life. I believe she even worked *here*--here in the big house, I mean."

"Is that so?" said the old man, a question forming on his wrinkled face. But before Aggie can respond, the front door bell rings . . . and rings and rings as if someone is trying to pull it clean off its mountings.

"Excuse me, sir. I better see to that. Probably another one of them travellin' salesmen." With that Agnes left the room, leaving the old man to finish his lunch alone.

The old man sat thoughtfully for a moment. *When would Aggie's grandmother have worked here?* Before he can fully think this question through he hears more ringing: "Those bleedin' yaks!" shouts a voice behind him, "and their goddamn bells!" He could now hear clearly the sound of the bells that hung round the necks of the yaks as they laboured their way up the rumble-strewn paths. Paths both man and beast had to navigate on their way back out of Chumbi Valley.

"Look at all them yaks and donkeys behind us, Sarge," continued the voice. "Snaking all over the countryside, they are."

"Hardy beasts," replied the sergeant. "They've got as much right to go home as the rest of us.
Done a good job, they have, and we're *all* God's creatures," he said with a cheeky smile across his face.

As the column of returning soldiers and beasts wound its way up and out of Chumbi Valley, what vegetation there was gave way to rock-strewn paths and ever-diminishing clumps of hardy ground-hugging plants; an occasional gnarled and stubborn shrub or tree protruded at the path's edge, showing nature's defiance and power in the face of its own extremes. In addition to attracting local traders further back down on the plateau, the commotion and movement of the column had encouraged an entourage of curious birds ranging from the aloof and soaring vultures (effortlessly gliding high above on thermal currents) to the lower-flying, more adventurous ravens (the sheen of their feathers flashing the sun like knife blades) to the smaller, most obstinate crows--all intent on raiding the food wagons at any opportunity. As the terrain became more hostile the vultures began to lose interest, probably because they couldn't find enough warm air to allow their glided pursuit to continue. Then the ravens seemed to lose heart--leaving only a few determined crows to keep up the chase. But these birds too eventually gave up hope of a meal--flying off as if reluctant to leave the safety of the country and landscape they knew. All except one crow that was seen flying almost the full length of the advance column and back again, as if a general inspecting his troops. But then it too seemed to realise that there was nothing to be gained from following this strange procession of men and animals hell-bent on climbing ever-higher into the mountains. So it flew off ahead of the group and out of sight round a rocky overhang on the path.

As the sergeant led his men round the overhang he saw what would probably be the last standing bare and wizened tree he'd come across in this harsh and unforgiving landscape. A short distance away he could just make out two black figures sitting passively on one of its few remaining twisted branches. A moment later a third black figure alighted on the same branch, joining its friends and forming a trio of crows watching intently as the column passed; as if they were there to oversee the soldier's departure. As he looked back at the crows they turned their heads toward him and in that moment his thoughts flitted back to the crows he'd seen round the dying lama, and the crow caught by the vulture—forced to drop its bloody treasure.

As the path began to descend, the soldier's mind turned to his unsure footing on this rocky path; they would be descending back into Sikkim shortly, he knew. He shook his head, admittedly baffled by the country he was about to leave. He realised that this last expedition would be the pinnacle of his military career. His age was now against him. There were younger and fitter NCOs ready to take his place. After this he would be farmed out as a staff sergeant, no doubt, sent to some head-quarters somewhere. Never mind. The words of Lama Kunchen now echoed loudly in his ears: '*You are part of this circle—here, now, and always.*' He took strength from this and knew that the sights, sounds, colours, and spirit of Tibet were now within him and would be--no matter where he went . . .

"Come on, ma' bonnie lads," called an exuberant sergeant. "Lift your feet high, we've all still got a ways to go," he said as he led his rag-tag group of Sikhs, Ghurkhas, and Tommie's out of Tibet for what he thought would be the last time. But then the ringing of yak bells were drown-out by a louder and more resonant ringing:

The old man blinked his eyes. Forced them to focus. The silver tray was still setting on the small side-table next to him. All the sandwiches have been eaten, the teapot was empty and cold, and now someone else was ringing the doorbell. Ah—Aggie would get it.

Chapter 7

THE SOUND OF THE DOORBELL was soon lost beneath the sharp and staccato rattle of rain against the window panes. The afternoon sky had darkened to a dull grey, the best of the day passed. Now as his eyes blinked sharply against a flash of lighting--and again a few seconds later at the crack and rumble of thunder--he shivered. *It's going to be a wet and miserable evening for anyone caught out there*, he thinks. He's glad he's not one of them and returns his gaze to the licking flames of the fire.

For the remainder of the afternoon and well into the evening the rain pounds against the window; its sound hypnotic. So much so that he barely notices the *rat-tat-tat* sound against the front door. *Strange*, he thinks, *how can I hear knocking on the front door?* Then a sudden flash of lightning dazes him and when his eyes clear he's not in his study in the big house, but in the front room of his small house in Shimla, Northern India. An army accommodation he'd moved into when he was given a job at headquarters after being promoted to staff sergeant. The *rat-tat-tat* repeated. *Some poor sod's out in that rain*, he thought to himself, *better see who it is.*

As quickly as he could he got out of his chair and headed for the front door; opened it. And there before him stood a bedraggled figure dressed in Buddhist robes. The figure raised his head and slowly, to his surprise, he recognised the face of his friend, Lama Kunchen. Without hesitation he grasped the lama's arm and ushered him into the comfort of his home. Fetching a soft towel and gave it to his friend to dry himself. Then as he sat opposite the lama he looked into his face and smiled with affection, recalling their previous encounters.

"My dear, dear friend, how pleased I am to see you again, that must be almost a year since you were last here!" said the soldier, shaking his head in amazement. "How time flies"

"No doubt you are hungry, my friend. Can I offer you some food . . . something warm to drink?"

"Tea and a morsel of food would be nice," replied Lama Kunchen.

The soldier watched as the lama drank the tea he'd hurriedly brewed and ate some simple bread and cheese. He saw that the lama's face was older and a bit more world-weary, but still possessed that *knowing* quality. A quality that came with knowledge and experience. "You are looking well, Lama Kunchen," offered the soldier. "Still travelling, I see."

"Yes, and I still have some ways to go!" replied the monk with a wry smile. "And what of you, my Scottish soldier? Still traipsing the landscape?"

"Well, my travelling and soldiering days are mostly over," sighed the sergeant. "I'm behind a desk now, sorting and shuffling papers." Then as their conversion continued, the name *Dawa* was mentioned. Through quickened breath the soldier asked after her well-being, stumbling awkwardly, "Uh, so, how is she doing?"

"She is well. She is growing up fast and in the image of her dear mother," he replied.

"Does she have everything she needs?" asked the soldier. But as soon as the words passed from his lips he hung his head, realising that she *couldn't*. Her mother had died and surely a mother was much needed.

"My sister, Nola still looks after her," replied the esteemed lama. "She is well cared for."

As the evening progressed the conversation continued, but the sights and sounds of that night in the nomads' animal shelter when Dawa was born never left his thoughts. The image of Dawa's mother, the most beautiful woman he'd ever seen, again and again came to mind as it so often had over the years. He still felt the pain, the memories of that fateful night were a constant companion to him. As the storm outside raged, he could see that his friend was tiring. "I think we are both tired," suggested the soldier, "and a good night's sleep will do us both good. You are welcome to sleep in the spare room as usual."

"Most kind of you, my friend," said the lama. "Sleep will help clear our thoughts for a new day."

That night the soldier slept fitfully, his thoughts drifting between the lama and the child, Dawa. He knew in his heart and soul that he had to continue to help her and her people so the next morning he decided on a course of action. He rose to find Lama Kunchen in meditation so he quietly waited. At last the lama opened his eyes and smiled. The soldier took a deep breath before he spoke:

"I've decided that I still want—no *need*--to help Dawa and her family more, and this time I would like to entrust you with a small bag of money you can use to purchase whatever goods they need. It's not a lot, but I trust it will be of some help. Also, I would like to send along a small package, a present for Dawa. Please humour me by allowing me to do this. I feel an obligation to her."

Lama Kunchen thought for a moment and then in his direct and honest manner replied: "Tell me why you keep doing this for the child and her family?" *A strange question*, the old soldier thought. *Surely the why is obvious.*

"Because I feel some responsibility for her," he replied, himself not completely certain of his feelings. "I--I feel pained when I think of the circumstances surrounding her life. And as I am *'part of her circle'* . . ."

"You are *suffering?*" the lama then asked.

"I suffer all day, every day, when I think back to those times," the soldier continued, giving in now to his emotions.

"Ah," said the lama, "so you want to rid yourself of your suffering by way of money and gifts?"

Growing more confused the soldier thought, *Why should it be so complicated?!* Money, gifts--he was just being *kind*. But now the lama seemed to be questioning his motives. "No, it's not that," argued the soldier. "I'll always feel the suffering, the pain from that time in my life."

"Always feel the suffering . . . ?" questioned the lama with a knowing look. The old soldier shot him an uneasy glance. The lama continued. "So, you have decided that money and presents are good for the child?"

The soldier was now becoming anxious. Frustrated. He wasn't used to being grilled; his reasoning questioned. Falling silent for fear of showing and expressing his anger, he slowly but surely was growing angry at the lama for not understanding that he simply wanted to *help* the child. Lama Kunchen smiled and waited. The soldier finally spoke. "As before and because I have no children of my own, I believe I can do something *nice* for her."

"*Nice* for *her?*" further questioned Lama Kunchen. But then after a short pause he resigned, "Very well. I will do as you wish. I will take what you offer Dawa and her people."

Lama Kunchen thanked the soldier for his hospitality—making no mention of the gifts he bore. Bowing in farewell the lama turned down the path, leading his donkey. Moments later he disappeared from view. They'd agreed that it would be only fitting to meet as time and circumstances would permit to inform the soldier as to how the child, Dawa, was growing up. As he closed the front door behind him, thoughts of his time in Tibet played across his mind, but were soon forgotten when he heard a woman's voice.

"*What the*--Aggie, is that someone at the door again?" the old soldier called out. "Damn--am I the only one who heard it?"

Rushing into the room Agnes said, "The bell rang a while ago now, sir. It was another of those travellin' salesmen. We really need to get a sign put up."

"Oh, I see," murmured the old man, afraid to explain what he now feared to be true.

Something's not bloody right! he thought to himself. *My memory must be going!* As he tried to bring his thoughts into the here and now, his mind again drifted back to Lama Kunchen. The lama had visited him on several more occasions after that wet night in Shimla, he remembers, and on each visit he'd charged his friend with taking money and gifts back to the nomads, and, of course, something special for Dawa. He now vividly recalled one gift in particular: a beautiful turquoise necklace like no other.

What was it about that necklace that so concerned his friend, Lama Kunchen? The necklace was exquisite and unique—that was apparent.

A true work of art. It was made up of a configuration of large flat, highly-polished turquoise stones, each larger than the next, and set in its own silver setting. A series of five smaller stones hung down in a line from the centre of the necklace, with the largest and brightest turquoise stone at the bottom. Even Lama Kunchen was taken by such craftsmanship. He said that it was such an extraordinary gift that he had to seek spiritual guidance on what he should do with it so he travelled to Tsurphu Monastery to talk with his mentor and teacher, the Fifteenth Karmapa. (The Fifteenth Karmapa, said Lama Kunchen, was much travelled and wise in certain ways and knew many more things that most men could ever comprehend.)

As Lama Kunchen explained, upon presenting the turquoise necklace to the Karmapa, a smile of recognition spread across the great religious figure's face. The lama explained that it was to be a gift for a nomad girl from a friend, a Westerner, who knew the girl, having been present for her birth. The Karmapa smiled again and said that his friend must have been a soldier, and that he himself had met such a man many years before while on a difficult journey to Lhasa. Lama Kunchen did not question the words of the Karmapa, but asked what should be done with the necklace. Examining the necklace closer he said: "Just as I have mine, and you have yours, this necklace has its own path to follow. So has the soldier and so has the girl. Who are we but travellers on this path that may take this necklace with us?" It was only after meeting with the Karmapa that the lama fully believed the necklace should be given to Dawa.

The old soldier's memories of Tibet were becoming clearer now. It was after Lama Kunchen had told him of this episode with the Karmapa that he'd implored the lama to take him back with him to Tibet to meet with Dawa. He remembered their long discussions; his trying to convince the lama that he was still fit enough to travel, arguing that sitting behind a desk had not dulled his mind and body enough to prevent him. And after all, he knew what to expect. He'd been to Tibet before.

Chapter 8

AFTER HER BIRTH, DAWA HAD been taken into the family of her Aunt Nola; Lama Kunchen's sister, and raised in the nomadic traditions of her people. Through the years she'd learnt well the realities of the extremely arduous nomadic lifestyle; braving elements the likes of which most men found unbearable. Continuing their yearly cycle, the nomads now prepared to pack up and move camp, headed towards their customary fertile grazing land for their yaks.

Nola had grown to love Dawa with all her heart, but unlike her brother the lama, was much more reserved in manner. Over the years Dawa had often asked about her mother, wanting to know how her mother and father had died, and Nola had always tried to be truthful with the child. But even as Dawa grew older, Nola still found it difficult to explain the circumstances of her parents' deaths to one so young. Today as little Dawa helped with camp-moving preparations, she again asked her aunt to tell her about her mother. Nola replied as she had so many times before.

"Dawa, you are the living image of your mother. You have her small, slim figure and her dark piercing eyes. Even your dark straight shimmering hair is as hers was. Uncanny--you could almost be your *mother*--but ah, the *difference*, Dawa, between you and your mother is your temperament. It is that of your *father*; down to earth, always concerning yourself with everyone and everything, planning things and forgetting nothing. Is that enough information for you?"

(Nola had, in fact, become increasingly concerned about *how* inquisitive Dawa was becoming. So inquisitive that she'd imposed herself in the personal affairs of everyone in camp—to the ire of most—fond of repeating the day's events over and over again at the end of day with a superior tone of authority, and an unspoken expression of exasperation at the folly of others.)

Dawa nodded to her aunt and said, "But, how did my mother die. And my father?"

"Come on, little one, we have work to do," Nola said.

Seeing that she would get no definitive answer from her troubled aunt she would often resort to, "Aunt Nola, I have great love for my family and the other nomads, and I know I could solve their problems if they would let me. But they think I am too young. Why do you think this is so?"

Though Nola was bemused, she really didn't understand Dawa and was finding it harder and harder to withhold the truth from a child older than her years. "That's enough talk for now, little one. We all have our jobs to do."

Resuming her work—the careful packing of cooking utensils into wooden boxes--Dawa began to daydream of the special events associated with their yearly cycle of travelling camp to camp. New Year festivities and horse fairs were opportunities to meet and play with children from other nomad groups; to share traditional stories, songs, and join in playful games. But when with the other children, Dawa felt and acted superior to them. She knew this and, in fact, deliberately set out to teach them new skills; *her* skills. She wanted them to play *her* games *her* way and she took this superior role very seriously.

One event of the year she particularly looked forward to was the annual visit from her uncle, the Lama Kunchen. Once a year he would visit their camp, his donkey laden with goods and sometimes delicacies for distribution amongst hers and all the other families of the community, to use or barter as they saw fit. She greatly anticipated her uncle's visit to her tent where he would give her glistening trinkets and small gifts, sometimes made from strange materials she'd never seen before. Her aunt worried about Dawa and all these gifts. And one night while preparing last meal of the day, Nola lost her temper with Dawa.

"*Dawa*!" her aunt cried out in despair. "How many times have I told you *not* to look out of the corner of your eye! You look like you are watching out over your possessions! Nobody's going to steal them!" Exasperated, her aunt continued, "Why do you feel the need to hoard your possessions? *Look!*--you've even taken those small, unimportant stones you found outside and hidden them in that old box! *Stones!* Why do you feel you have to *hide* everything? This is not our way! We share, we are happy to share, and yet you are not! You have become greedy!"

But these words fell on deaf ears. The fear of losing--the dread of waking and finding all her precious possessions gone—consumed her:

"Why should I share my treasures?" replied Dawa defiantly, "they are *mine*! They have been given to me or I have taken time to collect them! So I have to keep them where I and I only know where they are!"

Nola stamped her foot impatiently. "But--it is not our way! No good will come of your greed-- for that surely is all it is! *Greed*!" lectured her aunt. But it was useless. Dawa had a way of her own and her aunt could only pray that one day she would see the wrong in what she was doing before it brought her harm. Exasperated, Nola turned her attention back to preparing the evening meal. Dawa sat taking inventory in her mind of all her possessions, hidden about.

As Dawa grew older she made it a habit to take some of her prized possessions along to the annual horse fairs to show them off to the other children, and took particular pride in her growing gem and precious stone collection. Once when Dawa was thirteen she attended one such horse fair with her cousin, and while he was busy with his friends drinking Tibetan beer, she approached a group of children who were playing games. As she neared, they stopped and glared at her. (They all knew too well what Dawa was going to say and do.)

"Look!" yelled Dawa. "Look what I've been given," she said as she dangled some of her precious trinkets in front of the other children's faces. "No--don't touch!" she cried as one of the girls tried to touch them. Then with an air of smug contempt she pulled her finery away from the other children and tucked them safely in the pocket of her blouse. Then with a flounce of her long black hair she turned her back on the group and swaggered off to find her cousin.

As always, the day's events at the horse fair eventually drew to a close. The nomads typically stayed a few extra days, camped out on the vast Tibetan Plateau: sometimes sleeping outside on the hard ground with a yak-skin cover to keep warm, lying near the dying embers of the dung fire they maintained during the day. Sometimes, depending on the weather, they would sit in their tents and be joined by many rowdy herdsmen and women drinking *thang* and singing and dancing the night away with abandon. Dawa loved this way of life and would always try to stay awake as long as she could, listening to the stories the elders told of their ancestors who were fearless and strong.

The annual fairs came and went—as did the seasons--and each year Dawa would go along, still showing off her fine trinkets and gifts. By her twentieth year she'd out-grown overtly teasing her friends with her possessions (though they still relished reminding her that she was motherless and fatherless) but now openly displayed them. *After all, these are special occasions and the perfect places to show off my special gifts?* she reasoned. These trinkets made her feel *chosen*; above all the others who didn't possess—and didn't deserve--such extravagant finery.

Just before her twenty-first birthday, Dawa eagerly awaited the arrival of her uncle, Lama Kunchen; sure to arrive any day now. He'd long made it a habit to visit the camp at this time of year and she was certain this year would be no exception. She'd been born in the Year of the Iron-Snake--according to the Tibetan calendar--or so she'd been told by her family. Now aware that her father had died before she was born and her mother had died giving birth to her, she found it difficult to imagine how her life would be any different with a mother and father, as she had been well-cared for by her many aunts and uncles. But it was the gifts her uncle brought her that made her heart sing and her feet dance and gave her ideas of what life could have been like with real parents.

The sparkling boxes, the jewellery, the beautiful silk clothes captured her imagination. And even though she was by now a mature--though headstrong--young woman, the anticipation of what her uncle would bring brought out a childish excitement, as there was always a different gift each year: the beautiful turquoise necklace; bracelets, earrings, and belts among other treasures. And she'd worn them all at one time or another with pride--at horse fairs and festivals and other gatherings. She now let her imagination run riot as she speculated as to what Lama Kunchen would bring her this time. And as she revelled in her own exuberance she laughed inwardly, thinking about what the other children and their parents must have made of her when as a young girl she sashayed round the camps and fairgrounds; quite the little princess be-decked in all her grown-up finery. And how as she'd matured into a lovely young woman, the young men would watch her from afar; none quite ready to engage with such a demanding and stubborn woman. They knew that her mind was usually elsewhere--wrapped up in talk of her uncle, Lama Kunchen, or her horses. She'd let it be known several years before that she had no intention of ever becoming a wife and mother and settling down. She craved *freedom*—even more than nomadic life could offer her! But that life was in her blood and she had no idea what she would do in the outside world or where else she could possibly live: the plateau, the nomads, and the animals were rooted deeply in her soul.

As much as she loved the presents her uncle brought her, she also loved *him*; he was a kindly man, always the life and soul of any gathering. He was generous, charismatic, and irresistible; some said that when he was round them his bravery seemed to banish any fears they harbored. Dawa thought he was so clever, he had so many stories to tell and always made time to sit and talk with her. She often asked him why he didn't want to settle in one place—not really understanding his need to be constantly on the move. His life both intrigued and frightened her; she needed the familiarity of her surroundings, the people and her possessions, all of which gave her security. Lama Kunchen spoke to Dawa of having to balance himself by implementing a routine in his daily life, utilizing meditation and exercises like yoga to calm his fiery temperament and emotional outbursts (that were his natural character), and to soothe his mind and spirit. Dawa often felt a strange calmness she could not explain after being near him.

Dawa believed that her uncle had far too much faith and trust in the unknown--and emphatically told him so. Lama Kunchen had grown to respect this aspect of Dawa's character; he admired people who stood up to him and questioned him--but he merely waved his hands and told her that he was there with her, alive and well, and that was all that mattered in the moment. What would happen tomorrow or next week--he couldn't control. And thinking and worrying about it wouldn't change what was going to happen. He had an active imagination and as a man of religion—but also a philosopher and astrologer—was always able to see new or alternative paths. But he also well understood why some individuals can see in only one direction.

Dawa shuddered and brought herself back to the present. There were serious questions she had to ask of her uncle. For one: *Why, through the years, was her community favoured by the lama above other nomads?* She knew this to be true from talking to young people from other groups when they met at festivals and horse fairs. Even though he was her uncle, this did not fully explain why he should do this; after all he was a teacher and mentor to many who lived out their lives on the high plains. And for another: She'd heard the elders talking furtively about the *Ying-gi-li* (the *English)* while looking in her direction and she suspected that her uncle, his gifts, and the English were somehow connected.

In the year that her hair was platted into three braids, she had asked her uncle during his annual visit why the tribes' people would talk about the English at certain times. She saw from his eyes that he knew something, but was reluctant to tell her. As she now pondered this from inside her tent she began to hear the drumming of the rain against the yak-skin of the tent sides; she peered out to see that the yaks and horses, apart from those tethered in their barn-tent, had already settled themselves down to weather the oncoming (and rare) downpour. And as she looked out further, across the flat scrub-land, she could just make out a figure labouring on horseback through the misty swirls of the driving rain, and recognised the silhouette immediately as that of her uncle, the Lama Kunchen. Now she would get the answers she needed about her parents, the English, and the annual gifts. Still, somehow deep inside she felt that she'd already worked it all out. She threw wide the tent flap and ran out into the all-engulfing rain to welcome her uncle--and what he'd brought.

Chapter 9

FIGHTING THE DOWNPOUR DAWA REACHED the corral of horses, rousing the slumbering Mastiffs that barked and snarled at all the commotion. Entering the barn she threw a saddle and bridle onto her horse. Slipping her foot in the stirrup she held onto the reins and pulled herself up and over the horse's back--and slotted her foot into the other stirrup. Nudging the horse's flanks and flicking the reins, the animal carried her out of the barn and into the storm. She pulled the reins to the right to steer him away from her tent and on toward the open plateau.

She'd prepared a fine meal of dried yak meat and *tsampa*, and a large tea pot simmered on the range inside her tent. (These were left unattended in her haste to ride out and meet her uncle.) There in the distance she now saw three figures: one was definitely her uncle, but the others she did not recognise. She dug her heels into her horse's flanks and he responded by breaking into a canter toward the approaching figures. Reining-in as she neared her uncle and his travelling companions, she could see that one of them was a man; and not Tibetan. She greeted her uncle with a bow of her head and a smile she reserved just for him. "Who is that?" she demanded. "Who is this pale-skinned stranger?"

"He is my Scottish friend," replied her uncle through the torrent. And instantly the words "Scottish" and "friend" began to echo round in her head, and somehow questions were now being answered: the hushed talk amongst the nomads of the *Scottish* soldier; her uncle's travels; the exotic gifts she was presented; her mother's death; her father's death. *Is this the man responsible?*

Dawa had never seen a Scottish man before but assumed that he was the *yingalee*--the English--the elders so often mentioned in hush whispers. She decided that this man had somehow made her an orphan. And the more she thought on this the more she felt beside herself with rage: she loved her uncle but in this moment she was furious with him for bringing this foreign man to her camp! Aggravated, she wheeled her horse round, dug her heels into his sides, and set off at a gallop back to her tent, with no explanation. Back at camp her head pounded as she tethered her horse and hurried back to her aunt's tent: she wanted to escape . . . to run from this evil man! Inside she sat herself on a large wool cushion and rubbed her hands together in frustration, asking, *why did uncle bring this wretched man to our camp? Is it to ask forgiveness? To explain how they really died?*

She recited a calming mantra--but her head was about to explode with rage. But at the same time she wanted the truth--and was bursting with intrigue to hear it. A moment later the flap of the tent was pushed back and her uncle stepped inside, the Scotsman beside him. Dawa kept her head bowed; she dare not look up for fear of releasing her anger. Lama Kunchen spoke softly to her in Tibetan, imploring, "Dawa, where are your manners? This man is my friend, and he is our honoured guest."

"I've heard the men and woman talking about a stranger from the West!" replied Dawa guardedly. "They speak beneath their breath as if I'm not meant to hear, but I know it's about my mother and father!"

"Gossip, Dawa, simple *gossip*," reassured her uncle. "This man has travelled far with me. No matter what you think you know, he is my friend, *our* friend, and a friend to you, too! I bid you make him welcome!"

As Dawa looked into her uncle's eyes she could see the truth of his words and her anger began to subside. "Very well, uncle," agreed the girl. "You always know best."

"This is the right thing to do, young one. You mean a lot to this man and he means a lot to you—as you will soon learn!"

Dawa tried to make sense of her uncle's meaning. Her thoughts racing wildly, she busied herself with preparing butter tea for their guest. "And, what of the other man who travelled with you?" Dawa asked, collecting the puzzle pieces; trying to delay the inevitable.

"He is our Sherpa guide. He is likely looking after our animals—and need not concern you."

The butter tea steaming, she could no longer delay confronting the stranger; this *Scotsman*. But as she stepped forward to present him refreshment, he reached into the flap of his heavy coat and produced a snow-white scarf folded in half lengthways which he draped across his outstretched palms. Dawa was taken aback. She looked at the scarf and then up into the stranger's wind-ravaged face. Being presented a *khata*, a white scarf such as this, as a gift, was a symbol of great respect. It represents the interdependence of each other. She looked anxiously to her uncle as if asking permission, but he only gave her a reassuring smile. Without further thought Dawa set the tea cups at her feet and allowed the stranger to place the khata open edges first around her neck. She gave the stranger a formal bow, then directing him to the cushions set closest to the fire she delivered hot tea into the stranger's hands. The three sat.

Initially there was only silence--save the whistle of the wind outside. The soldier could hardly look away: *Is this really the little baby I watched being birthed all those years ago?* Lost for words he now knew that Lama Kunchen was right. Sending money and gifts had not really eased any pain or suffering. Yet meeting Dawa now lightened the darkness that had long pervaded his troubled mind. Then--

"Oh--I almost forgot!" the soldier exclaimed, reaching again into his coat. "Here, Dawa, this is for you, too!" From within the folds of his coat the soldier had produced a small box wrapped in rich red paper and tied in gold-coloured ribbon. Words were lost on Dawa—as she neither spoke nor understood English--so her uncle took the small package from the soldier and passed it to her. As the girl looked upon it she said something to her uncle in Tibetan, with a cheeky smile.

"What did she say?" asked the soldier.

Lama Kunchen laughed and replied, "She asked if this is yet another present for her birthday!" The soldier looked embarrassed and then let out a heartfelt laugh. He looked toward the girl, who was now trying to suppress a laugh of her own, and nodded in agreement. With this exchange, the mood of the encounter changed.

The soldier was keen to ask Dawa about her childhood, while she in turn needed to ask what he knew of her mother and father--all the while, Lama Kunchen acting as interpreter. The soldier could see Dawa's mood change when he talked about being at her father's sky burial and at her birth, but seemed to understand and accept what had happened. Yet when he talked about the army and his fellow soldiers he could see anger colour her face and a look of incomprehension come over her. The two asked many questions of each other; the soldier's long-anticipated meeting with Dawa lasting well into the evening when a look of exhaustion appeared on all their faces. The esteemed lama suggested they retire for the night and get some sleep; time to allow their minds and bodies to rest.

The soldier slept well that night, as if some immovable weight had been lifted from him. He woke the next morning to find Dawa preparing tea and *tsampa*. She stoked the fire and added more yak dung, and once the tea and *tsampa* were ready, handed portions to the Scotsman and her uncle. Then she too sat on a cushion by the fire and began to eat. The silence was now a friendly one. The soldier smiled and stared into her eyes and it was as if he were looking into her mother's eyes that fateful day Dawa was born. Just sharing moments with Dawa the day before had released the soldier from much of his suffering and it was now as if he'd taken his first steps on the path Lama Kunchen had suggested for him. He began to feel an inner awakening. He discovered a genuine attachment to these nomadic people.

The rest of the old soldier's day was spent with the nomads as they went about their daily work. It was a decidedly hard life, but they never complained. He joined them as they herded their yaks round the best green meadows for grazing; watched as they offered prayers to the Dalai Lama and the Karmapa; sat with them as they enjoyed their evening meal round their fire--telling stories and laughing; perhaps at his own expense. Knowing that he'd have to leave the following morning saddened him. Somehow he felt welcome here as nowhere before. The nomads accepted him for who he was: a man, an individual, a being just like them, simply making his way through life. His sleep was the sleep of deep peace.

The following morning he rose early and before breakfast helped the Sherpa pack their animals for the return journey. Only the two of them would be returning to India as Lama Kunchen would be staying on with his family a few more days. After a breakfast of butter tea and *tsampa*, the soldier bid farewell to Dawa as best he could. It was not easy for him. He'd thought about her for all these years, had now only just met her, but it was time to leave her again. He knew he could never forget her and hoped she felt the same about him. They were, after all, inextricably *linked*. When it was time to depart, after Lama Kunchen had offered him words of advice about the return journey, their conversation was interrupted by Dawa shouting something in Tibetan.

"What is she saying?" enquired the soldier.

"She is asking you if I lecture you, *too!*" replied the lama, smiling.

Their conversation over, they shook hands and bowed deeply to one another. The soldier then looked to Dawa and gave her a deep bow as well; she in turn bowed back. He could see that she was clasping the deep red box in her hand and wearing the beautiful turquoise necklace he'd sent years before. But it was time to go. The soldier mounted his horse and waved for the Sherpa to follow. Riding out of the nomads' encampment with a heavy heart, he glanced back only once to Lama Kunchen and his niece; Dawa waved. The only sound he heard was the tinkling of the bells round the necks of the yaks being driven out of the camp and on to the next, best pasture.

Chapter 10

"THERE'S THAT BLOODY FRONT DOOR bell again!" the old soldier said, aggravated, patience thinning. "Blood hell--am I the only one who can hear it?!" (As well as ringing at the door, the bell was linked via a series of wires and pulleys to a smaller bell in the kitchen where the house staff could also hear it.) "Never mind! I'll get it myself!" Making his way out of his study, down the main staircase, and across the hall to the front door, by the time he reached it the ringing had stopped. Seeing the silhouette of a figure standing outside on the stoop, he opened the door to find an old woman standing there. A woman about the same age as he. She is small, pretty-faced, with ruddy cheeks and green-brown eyes. A familiar face--though he can't place it. He gave her a quizzical look.

"Hello, Donald," said the woman in a soft and lilting tone.

"Sorry . . . you have me at a disadvantage, madam," is all he could think to say as he scans his memory for help.

"May I come in?" says the woman.

The old soldier stood there racking his brain trying to comprehend why this woman seemed to know him. "Uh, *yes*--come in . . . *come in!*" he blurts out, standing aside.

With that invitation the woman walked over the threshold and into the front hall. "I've always wanted to do this, ever since I was a wee lass," said the visitor, with obvious satisfaction. (The old soldier is even more confused now.) Just then Agnes appears from the direction of the kitchen and lets out a gasp.

"Grannie! What are you doing here?! You can't just come here! Not this way!"

"*Wheesht*, girl!" scolded the elder woman, looking all round. "The master of the house shan't mind!"

The old man felt light-headed; dizzy. *What's going on? Have I finally lost my senses?* No--he's certain he's standing there in the entrance hall of his family home in the company of two women: one young, one old. "Look, here," he orders, pointing to the library entrance, "let's all go in and have a seat. Sort this all out." As he passed through the library door he could hear the hushed voice of Agnes scolding the old woman behind him. The two followed him inside.

"My, the library has changed!" opined the older woman, looking high and low.

"*Grannie*! Mind your *words*!" scolded Agnes.

"Now, now, ladies," said the old soldier calmly, "let's all sit ourselves down."

Once seated the old man looked across at both women and took in all he saw. There was familiarity in each face. He recalled Aggie telling him that her grandmother had once worked there. *This is likely her,* he thought to himself. He looked directly into the old woman's eyes for a sign from the past. His memory began to awaken: those cheeky, *greenie*-brown eyes. Those ruby cheeks. He remembered a lovely, fresh-faced girl from long, long ago. Stolen moments away from the stuffy old adults. A girl bounded by a starched white collar, white blouse, black skirt, and black patent-leather shoes . . .

"My God--*Lachina?*" is all the old man could say.

"Yes, Donald, it's me, Lachina," came the welcome reply.

Agnes didn't know what to do or where to look. Her grandmother had just called the master of this grand estate by his first name! And she'd dared come to the front door fully expecting to be invited in!

Seeing his house maid's discomfort the old soldier soothed, "It's all right, Aggie. Your grandmother and I are old friends. Old friends, indeed!"

"Aggie?" questioned the old woman jokingly. "Yes, Agnes, Mr. Cameron and I know each other," she said, her eyes fixed upon the old man. "I was just a slip of a girl working as a housemaid here--as you are now--and he was the rogue of the house. The old master's son."

Agnes had questions--*and lots of them*! But before she could get her thoughts in order her grandmother spoke with surprising directness:

"What happened, Donald?" she beseeched the old man.

"Oh, Lachina. My *father* . . . " he began with a tone of regret, " . . . he made it impossible. That controlling old man wouldn't let me be who I wanted to be! Maybe I was too young—I don't know. But the arguments—I'm sure you knew—got worse and worse. And I said some things I probably shouldn't. But he just wouldn't--"

"I thought it was *my* fault!" interrupted Lachina. "That I'd done something to make you get sent away!"

"Oh, no, it wasn't you—it was *me*!" he said, reaching for her hand. "After all that happened I was so angry that I just couldn't stay! I up and left and with a little persuasion from Cassels, I made my way south to Stirling," the old man explained. "And before I realised what I'd done I was in the army, and that was that. I was shipped off!" The old man then proceeded to pour out his life to Lachina and Agnes; Agnes now completely enthralled with his story. The story of a nondescript foot-soldier in the Gordon Highlanders rising to the rank of staff sergeant . . . his time in India and Tibet . . . his brief marriage . . . and then all of *this* (he waved his hand round the room to illustrate the sometimes overwhelming enormity of it all).

"When I left the army I looked for something to do with my time and discovered colour and light and energy," he explained—glancing recognition at Agnes. "It's amazing just how much colour plays a part in our lives, yet we don't yet fully understand it and take it for granted."

As Agnes' grandmother looked round the room, she now took in all the hues and colours of the glass bottles and fabrics and unusual tubes and equipment, then looked back at the old soldier and smiled coyly. "I remember when this room was a real library," she said, "though we didn't do much reading in it."

The old man laughed at this remark, his memories of the old house in happier times rekindled.

"What, between this room and my upstairs study, full of Indian and Tibetan memories, that's about the sum total of my life!" he joked. "And what of you, Lachina? What has life presented you these many years?"

"Well, I had to leave the service of your father," she answered; careful in choosing her words. "It wasn't long after you left. You see, I . . .'"

Seeing that her grandmother now appeared less confident than when she first arrived, Agnes urged her to continue. "Please, go on, Grannie."

The elder woman shut her eyes, took a deep breath, then said, "You see, I left to have a baby." (Both Agnes and the old soldier straightened in their chairs.) "It was a boy. Your father, John, Agnes." Lachina's gaze now fixed to the old man. She knew she needn't say more. The wistful look on her face was enough. The old soldier bowed his head and shook it pensively side-to-side, his hands clasped together in his lap, as if to prey.

A moment later he raised his head. "So we have a son? **A son, A Son**, Lachina"? "How old is he? Where is he? Wait a moment Agnes told me her father was dead some years back". My God, I never knew him, never saw him never even knew he existed..."I'm so sorry, Lachina. So *very, very* sorry . . ." was all he could say.

But why should he be sorry? Agnes asked herself. So why should *he* be sorry? But then she thought of her son, Alexander, and of her own untimely situation. And suddenly she knew: "Oh, Grannie!" she sobbed. "I never imagined . . ."

Looking directly at her master now, Agnes began to reason: "If my father was your . . . then I'm your *granddaughter*, and Alexander is your *great-grandson!*"

"Come, Agnes, see me to the front door," instructed the old woman, rising slowly from her chair. "I'm afraid I'm not as young as I once was."

"No, none of us can claim that," replied the old soldier with a wry smile. Oh how the circle of life turns," said the old man, looking to Agnes and then a somber Lachina.

"Here, Aggie, you help Lachina to the front door and we'll both walk her home."

"No, no!" insisted the old woman. "I got up here under my own steam and I'll make it back the same way!"

"But, I *insist*!" replied the old soldier--but could see in her expression that the old woman was having none of it. "Well, at least let Aggie walk back with you."

"Well, just this once," agreed the old woman.

"Off you go, then, Aggie. See that your grandmother gets home safely. I'll see you both tomorrow," decided the old soldier.

Looking directly into the old soldier's eyes, as if there'd be no other time the woman said, "I loved you, Donald. I never stopped loving you. I never met anyone who could take your place in my heart, and I love you still," she said as tears streamed down the creases of her aging face. Taking her grandmother by the arm, Agnes led Lachina out the door and down to the semicircle gravel driveway that made its way to the two stone pillars that guarded the entrance to Corbies Glen.

"Safe home," shouted the old man after them, following them with his eyes.

"We'll be fine so long as no crows are perched on those damn pillars!" Lachina shouted back. "Bloody damn *birds*!"

The old soldier thought for a moment and smiled. "Bloody damn birds, *indeed!*" he said aloud.

Turning and walking slowly back inside the house, the old soldier closed the door behind him. He paused. He felt exhausted. His mind was swimming. He knew he had much to consider. He quietly and quite deliberately made his way up to the solitude and sanctuary of his study.

Chapter 11

NEGOTIATING HIS WAY BACK UP the stairs proved a difficult task for the old soldier. Forced to stop and rest at the landing, he maintained a tight grip on the handrail. Light-headed and his legs about to fold beneath him, he heard his breath growing laboured. Gathering his strength he forced himself to press on, up the last few steps to the top. Shuffling into his study he only just managed to reach the respite of his high-backed desk chair before he collapsed.

He didn't often sit at his desk; this large dark-oak writing surface with black leather inlay. But today he felt lucky to have reached it. His favourite spot was the armchair by the fire, but today it's too far for him to reach. He sagged into the over-sized chair. His weight now taken off his tired legs, his breath slowly eased. Thoughts of Lachina and Agnes now fill his head: *I have to do something now before it's too late.* He feels responsible. And desperate. The image of the Tibetan girl from all those years ago now appeared in his mind--the one he'd showered with gifts to ease his consciousness. Now, the circle had turned. He must do the same for his own family.

An hour or so had passed before the old soldier returned his fountain pen to its place in the drawer, and pushed himself out of the over-sized chair. He'd done all that he could. Three pristine white envelopes now lay on the leather surface of the desk: one with the name of his solicitor on it, one addressed to Lachina, and one penned to Agnes. Satisfied, he slowly made his way to the fireplace, bent down and picked up two logs, and nestled them onto the smouldering embers of the dying fire. He fell into his favourite chair. He felt extraordinarily tired; his body ached.

The heat from the invigorated fire made him loosen his collar and as he did he felt the coral cord round his neck. His shaking hand reached up to touch the amulet against his no-longer youthful skin. For the first time since putting it on, he lifted the amulet up and over his head. He'd worn it next to his skin since the day it was given to him by the dying lama in Tibet, and he now held it tightly in his left hand. (Decades of time reversed in his mind.) Just as he gazed down at the amulet and wondered who'd take it from him, a tingling sensation moved up his left arm. A searing pain then gripped his chest and he saw a grey mist swirl round and round him that made him feel giddy and slightly sick to his stomach. His ears hurt as if somebody was clashing a pair of large brass symbols next to his head. He felt and heard his heart racing faster and louder--as he became the heartbeat.

As he surveyed the expanse of his room and all that had kept him company through the years, his eyes glimpsed what he thought was a flash of turquoise, indigo and black coming from outside his window; perhaps cast by the light of the moon. For an instant he wondered if it were possible—but *no*, it couldn't be. The crow was long dead. Lifeless and mounted it sat glaring out from its glass case in the hall. *But, I'd better check to make certain*, he thought to himself. And just as this thought occurred to him he found himself facing the dead bird; looking back at him. Now he was outside looking up into the branches of the tree that intruded upon his view from the study.

What--no crows roosting in the tree this afternoon? Where did they all go? he wondered.

Slowly he crossed the gravel driveway; there was no sound of footsteps. He reached the ornamental pond where the white of the lilies was picked out by the fading light of the afternoon and saw the soft petals stained with streaks of pink—and was held in their essence, safe and protected. He wanted to hold the beautiful flower in his hands yet found himself encased within its petals as he felt himself travelling faster and faster upwards. It was now the wild lotus flowers that flourish across the foothills of the Himalayas that he wanted more than anything to see again . . .

He traveled across the manicured green lawns of Corbies Glen. Stern and reproachful adult voices gave way to the familiar laughter and teasing of the children of his youth. He traced the path of light from the moon's lustre to the grey stone sentinels that guard Corbies Glen's entrance. With no effort he was now *free* of them; they drifted past him, just as they had that fateful dark night all those years ago. For a brief moment there is darkness and fear--soon replaced by a shimmering of grey stone that seemed to beckon him: a wall of white-peaked greyness that drew him closer to offer peace. He drifted over the whitened peaks and descended into another green; a green that swayed with the wind. A green of meadows and streams rough-hewn by nature--not man.

The moonlight was still with him. Offering solace and peace and leading him onward. Soon more colours filled his mind: the dancing yellows and oranges of a fire's flame; the *greenie*-brown of Lachina's eyes; the lustrous turquoise of a necklace. Still--more colours entered his consciousness: the gold and saffron of the Karmapa's procession; the deep rich red of Lama Kunchen's robe; the black sheen of crows' wings turned silver by the play of light that had now followed him from the gates of Corbies Glen to the mountains of Tibet and back. As the colours swirled and merged like mist, the turquoise colour grew brighter and shone through. His whole body, mind, and essence were bathed in turquoise and he began to feel absolute peace:

His aches and pains were no more.
He no longer heard the heartbeat.
There was silence.
He felt himself drifting . . . drifting between the blue of the sky and the turquoise sea of colour in his mind.

Memories of Corbies Glen dimmed into a darkness that once again encroached. This darkness had substance. Form.

A funny tingling had begun.
A heartbeat.
Pain and suffering.

Muffled voices were heard--as if from a distant room.

A gasp for air--the scent of burning juniper; the musty odor of animals.
A cry was heard, forced from new lungs!
A sudden chill was quickly replaced by the warmth of human touch-- all round.

Eyes that could see colour but not shape; a swirling black and the dark pink of magenta. The black offered her warmth, security, and belonging; the magenta, solitude, empathy, and a life of commitment. For a moment there was hesitation--but then the magenta was readily drawn into this new life.

The muffled voice then became crystal clear: "*Mthong, Dawa, bu mo!*" ("See, Dawa, it's a girl!")

Part II: Pembuti's Story

Chapter 1

(*MTHONG, DAWA, BU MO!*) "SEE, Dawa, it's a girl!" cried Anil as he gently lifted his new-born daughter from Jampa's arms and held her close to his chest. The baby's parents, Anil and Dawa, were nomads. Year-in, year-out they lived their lives travelling in a close-knit community just as their ancestors had, roaming across the high Tibetan Plain to pitch their tents where the grazing was best for their livestock.

Pembuti had been born, according to the Tibetan calendar, in the Year of the Iron-Snake, high up on the Tibetan Plateau in a tented animal shelter attached to the back of her parents' large black tent, in one such nomad encampment. Nomadic culture believed that the birthing process is *dirty* and therefore did not allow any birth to take place within their everyday living space. Thus, Pembuti was born in the space they used to shelter their animals from predators; away from the treacherous Tibetan weather. The Plateau was home to some of the fiercest weather conditions in the world: raging gales, blizzards, and freezing snow storms were not uncommon occurrences to be endured by man and beast alike.

There existed a strong, personal bond between all those who lived within their camp. The men, woman, and older children all helped and cared for one other, as well as their animals, each knowing where they stood in the social scheme of things. Their position within the *great* scheme of existence they left to their faith, a devout and reverential faith in the Buddha and his teachings, passed to them by monks and lamas, their wise and knowing teachers. There was much hardship and struggle for all who lived this nomadic life, but their faith served them well as the wheel of life turned as the cycle of seasons: the cold, harsh darkness of winter giving way to the youthful and bright expectation of new life in spring, through the warmth and comfort of summer leading into the sparseness and impending chill of autumn, to close the circle back to the steely sharpness of winter.

Twice a year the nomads dismantled their encampment, stowed it on the backs of yaks, donkeys, and cattle, and set off to find fresh pastures or shelter from the harshness of Mother Nature. This was their way; home was not one place. Home was their community, their family, and the bonds that tied them together as a people with a common aim. The bonds of blood, hardship, and friendship, looking out for neighbor and brethren: rare things in many societies, but to these Tibetan nomads it was how it was and how it should be. Such was the camaraderie amongst these simple people that everyone pitched in when it came time to move on.

The men would help dismantle each other's large hexagonal tents as if it were some kind of ritual; joking, no doubt, about the women in their lives--as most men do when left in secret enclaves and to their own devices. Most likely the woman were no less guilty of such indulgence as they stowed away yak-skin bedding, clothing, and kitchen paraphernalia, chatting and clucking to each other about the shortcomings of the men in their lives—and beds. The only innocent parties in all this activity were the children, untainted and as yet uncorrupted by the passage of time as they set about their given tasks, turning them into games. No doubt such gossiping, tale-telling, and childhood silliness would recommence when new pastures were reached; where beasts would be unburdened, tents reassembled, and a new encampment would emerge from the nomads' hard work and community spirit. Thus, such was the life Dawa's first child, Pembuti, was born into.

Jampa, Dawa's aunt, had stayed by her side throughout her labour, comforting and encouraging as the days and nights rolled into one. To Dawa it seemed like an eternity since the labour pains began; she'd been relentless, she'd screamed and cried as her heavily-pregnant but slim frame writhed round on the thin multi-coloured striped mat placed at the back of their animal shelter on the hard, stony ground. Dawa's cries were accompanied by the sharp gale winds outside as they whipped the black yak-skin canvas of the shelter. They caused the tent walls to billow in and out, creating a loud, almost drumming noise. And as the hours dragged endlessly on, Dawa, weak and exhausted, wondered how or even *if* she had the strength to give birth. It was these thoughts, as her labour pains intensified and tightened their grip that slowly exhausted her to the point that she began to lose the will to live. Lost in pain, fear took over, and she began to think of dying. Something she'd never done before.

Everything and everyone faded into nothingness until the thought of death came as a welcome relief. As her husband, Anil, stood leaning against the wooden stable partition a few feet from where Dawa lay writhing, he watched his wife transfixed, feeling helpless; knowing that as strong and formidable a man as he was, he could do nothing to end her pain. He winced as she winced, gasped as she gasped, feeling more and more helpless—having to avert his gaze as Dawa's small-but-sturdy frame seemed to be crumbling in front of his eyes. He cast his eyes towards the roof of the tent, trying to concentrate his thoughts on anything other than the despairing plight of his wife.

He considered the rugged stitching that held the yak-skin panels of the roof and tent sides together. The stitching was woman's work. He could see in his mind's eye Dawa sitting with the other women of the camp stitching and chatting, casting mocking glances at their menfolk as they got on with the heavy work of raising and lashing the timber poles and beams that would form the skeleton of each family's humble abode. Memories of good times filled his mind, when they'd moved camp; everyone chipping in to help. Everyone busy--even the children--knowing what to do and when to do it. A group of Mastiffs bounded round, caught up in the rush of activity, barking intermittently as if issuing instructions to the workers. Good days indeed, thought Anil; all that goodwill and support.

But where was all that goodwill and support now—now as his wife lay alone, racked by pain and fear, with only Jampa to comfort her? He shook his head to clear such thoughts; he was being selfish. He knew that most of his friends had been through the same experience and would help if they could. And knew they were saying prayers for Dawa and the new baby at that very moment.

His attention was now drawn back to the present by a gentle tug of his sleeve. It was Jampa. She'd left Dawa's side for a moment to offer Anil some reassurance. "Anil, do not worry, the way Dawa is now is normal for anyone in childbirth. It is just part of the birthing process," said Jampa, her eyes taking in his large frame clad in a heavy woollen coat tied round the waist with a brown leather belt. His sturdy black leather boots squeaked as he began to pace round the tent nervously. His long jet-black hair pleated, it trailed down the length of his back, almost to his waist. (Not unlike Dawa's hair except that her long brown strands were always split into two individual pleats at the nape of her neck that she swept up and round her head and pinned at the top with a beautiful turquoise clasp. This highly ornate clasp matched a necklace and pair of earrings, all of which had been presents from her Uncle Kunchen, a travelling lama.)

"I think Dawa is in need of a drink, Anil, so make yourself useful and fetch some thang." (*Thang*, a Tibetan beer brewed by the nomads, was consumed on birthdays and festivals and also used as a painkiller and relaxant.) Anil opened the flap of the animal shelter, stepped into the main tented corridor, and a few strides later was at the entrance of their black yak-skin tent. He pulled open the flap and walked toward the kitchen, located on the far wall of the tent, pausing briefly beside the fire crackling in the large cast-iron grate in the centre of the tent to warm his hands. All nomad tents had fires kept burning at all times as these fires were essential for keeping the family warm and for everyday cooking. Anil bent down and took some dried yak dung and juniper branches from the large basket beside the fire and threw them onto the dancing embers. He watched as the smoke slowly made its way up to the roof of the tent where a hole provided safe exit. Just for a moment, before the smoke reached the hole, he could see the twinkling stars of the night sky and felt comforted by such a normal sight. He looked away as the stars disappeared from his vision, obscured by the puffs of grey as they rose upwards.

When he had reached the kitchen he opened the door of the wooden cupboard and took out a container of *thang* and one metal mug. Quickly leaving the warmth of his tent, he returned to the animal shelter and passed the container and mug to Jampa. She then knelt down beside Dawa, lying stretched out on her mat, and cajoled her to try and sit up. With his help she pulled herself up almost upright; she leaned back and rested her head on some pillows Jampa had plumped up for her. Dawa's long brown hair, now badly matted with perspiration, hung loosely across the pillows. Jampa slipped her hand under Dawa's head for support while she put the mug of beer to her parched lips. As Dawa sipped, the sedative effects quickly began to take affect. After a few more swallows of the coarse liquor, Dawa's arms and legs had begun to numb. She felt the contractions of her baby struggling to be set free, but the pain was not there; the *thang* did its work. A short while later Dawa's ordeal was over as a stifled yet defiant cry broke the still and fetid air of the animal shelter. Jampa stood up and walked to Anil and gently presented the small and precious bundle tightly wrapped up in a soft turquoise blanket into his outstretched arms, bowing as she did. Anil had looked down and smiled, shaking his head in disbelief as the bundle let out another defiant cry. There, in his own powerful arms, was his new-born daughter, Pembuti.

As he gazed down upon the innocent face of this new life, a chill swept over him and through the tent. He turned to see the flames of the butter lamps flicker and fade from the sharp wind that had forced its way into the tent; the flames dancing at the behest of this uninvited guest. Instinctively Anil tightened his hold on his baby daughter. The shrill of the wind as it forced its way into every corner of the tent made Anil shiver, the noise reminding him of the screaming flocks of scavenging birds at the last sky burial he'd attended. Suddenly, stark images filled his mind: of frantic vultures, crows, and ravens fighting over the bloody remains. Anil snapped out of his daydream wondering, *Is this intrusive visitor to our tent an omen? This vision of gathering birds of carnage a forewarning?* No matter, he would protect his daughter. With his life. Nothing and no one would harm her!

Then just as suddenly as the wind had risen, all fell quiet within his tent. The only sounds were the gentle breathing of his wife, Dawa, who had slipped into a well-deserved sleep, and the shuffling of Jampa's moccasin-clad feet as she set about relighting the butter lamps that had blown out. Light was returning to Anil's world. The brightness of a new life was bathed in the warm glow of butter lamps. And all was well. He now had a family.

Chapter 2

THE MORNING AFTER PEMBUTI'S BIRTH, after all their customs and traditions had been fulfilled, Dawa and her baby daughter returned to the family tent, and for many days and nights after there was merriment and rejoicing within the encampment. Day and night, family and friends, adults and children alike would visit to pay their respects to Dawa, Anil, and Pembuti. They would all sit round the roaring fire chatting and laughing, the air filled with the sweet scent of juniper, roasted *tsampa*, and the sounds of gaiety. By the light of the fire and ever-lit butter lamps they recited special mantras and prayers, gave grain and water offerings to the Buddhist deities, and asked for protection and good Karma for the newborn Pembuti and her parents. Much *thang* was drank and much dried-cured yak meat and *tsampa* consumed, and it was a happy, joyous time.

As the days rolled one into another, Anil's love for Pembuti grew into a deep-rooted need to protect her. He loved to sit by the open fire with her on his lap and gaze into her eyes as he listened to her rhythmic, soft breathing. He loved it when she yawned and he could smell her warm milky breath, and he vowed to Dawa that he would always protect their precious daughter. Dawa was often moved to tears as she watched the large frame of her strong warrior husband nurture Pembuti with tenderness and softly spoken words of love as he cradled her in his powerful, muscular arms. He wanted to be with his wife and baby all the time, but there was so much to tend to. And on top of his own work—seeing to all his animals—he now had Dawa's chores to maintain as well until she could regain her strength--although some of their neighbors came in to lend a hand when they could.

Anil had always felt a deep empathy and respect towards his wife. How could such a small and delicate soul withstand such a hard and harsh way of life? He took comfort in knowing that she did indeed have *fire* within her! A sometime *raging* fire! If Dawa thought something was wrong or unjust she could let fly like the fiercest Kham warrior--with a powerful torrent of choice language and gestures!

Dawa's slim and slight frame was always clothed in a combination of several woollen vests covered by multiple baggy jumpers, and on her legs she wore long knitted stockings that were hidden by an ankle-length warm cloth skirt. Her outdoor garb was finished off with a fur-lined calf-length, ill-fitting yak-skin coat cinched round her middle with a leather belt. Her gloves and boots were also leather, made from yak skin, and they too were fur-lined. Dawa secured her long platted black braids, wrapped round her head with a striking jewel-encrusted hair clasp--choosing a different clasp each day from the beautiful collection brought to her by her Uncle Kunchen during his annual visits to their camp. But unlike Dawa, Anil's jet-black hair was scraped back off his angular, tanned face and then pleated into one long braid. His eyes were a dark brown set deep into his face, his thick bushy black eyebrows over-hung his thick eyelids, while his long wide nose was set in the middle of highly prominent cheekbones, and his fully shaped lips were, according to Dawa, wonderful to kiss.

Once fit enough, Dawa returned to her duties--besides looking after Pembuti. Each day after breakfast she would walk the mile to the nearest stream to fetch the water essential to their survival. Before setting off on her daily journey, Anil would hand her two large water containers and fuss over her to make sure she was wrapped snuggly. (Dawa's large eyes, almost black in colour, framed in her tanned heart-shaped face, were like magnets to Anil and when he looked at his wife he was drawn into their depths. Like precious gemstones they were at once deep and absorbing, yet bright and lustrous.) Once Anil was satisfied that Dawa would be warm enough he'd plant a kiss on her cheek and send her off. Then shouting after her to be careful he would stand and watch her figure fade into the distance. Women are such a contradiction, he often mused: soft, delicate and gentle, but also strong, determined and resilient--as if they are two completely different people. Anil smiled then headed towards the animal shelter. He now had to tend to his animals and make ready for his first journey to the pastures where his two hundred or so yaks grazed; he would check on their safety and health at first light.

Heading off in a different direction than her husband would, Dawa tread gingerly over the rough-going ground that was covered in gravel, scree, larger stones, and boulders that cluttered the non-existent path to the stream. Sometimes the ground, patched with snow and ice, was surprisingly broken up by clumps of blue- and violet-coloured ground-hugging flowers, clustered together like a tiny oasis in the barren and lifeless snow desert. The beauty of these rings of coloured life served as a fleeting distraction from the aches and pains she felt through the tough leather boots that pestered her ankles and feet. In addition to aching ankles and feet, the weight of the full water containers would pain her arms and hands on her long journey home. But Dawa always drew strength from knowing that water was necessary for their survival and as she walked she recited the mantras most dear to her heart. Once back at camp Dawa would take one of the containers inside their tent and fill the pots, ready for the day's cooking and tea-making, then take the other to the animal shelter for Anil to fill their animals' drinking trough. When Anil returned from the pastures she would serve a simple meal of buttered tea and *tsampa* and they would catch up on the morning's events—and camp gossip!

After lunch Anil would feed and water the animals then ready a horse and two yaks for Dawa, who would soon be heading out on the two-mile journey to the pastures north of their camp to collect the essential yak dung. Outside the tent Dawa watched Anil lead her team to her, saying, "I have filled the baskets with enough fodder for our animals on the plateau," pointing to the two wicker baskets that hung from the saddle on either side of the yaks. Dawa nodded to Anil as she mounted her rather irritable horse and took the reins. Dawa did not relish the task ahead; emptying these baskets was the easy part, but filling them with yak dung was time-consuming, back-breaking work. Anil handed his wife the long red-coloured ropes tied round the yaks necks. "Be careful on this horse! You're not at the horse fair races now!"

"Oh, stop fussing, husband!" she scolded back. "I'm a better horseman than you, and you know it!"

"I know, but this one gets a bit excitable at times," Anil counselled.

"Okay," conceded Dawa, "--I'll be careful! And *you* look after our little Pembuti!"

With that final remark, Dawa waved goodbye and with a sharp flick of her heels into the flank of her horse headed out of camp. Turning and looking back at her husband, she knew that most likely he'd join her later at the pastures once he'd completed his chores. But for now, horse and rider would wind their way across the stony ground towards the green meadows of the valley. To her relief, a few hours later after her back had nearly given out—bending and lifting the dung-heavy shovel up to the baskets—she saw a dust cloud approaching, horse and rider drawing near. Happy to see her devoted husband, he brought his horse to a rolling standstill and then jumped down and embraced her. "You've done very well, wife! You are surely tired. Rest for a while, while I continue." Anil smiled as he took the shovel and quickly began to add dung to the nearly-full baskets. "I will finish this and then we can head back to camp together!"

Dawa was most thankful for the love and support her husband gave her. She was indeed quite tired. An hour later the two retraced their steps back to their camp, where Anil led their horses back to the animal shelter. The two yaks with their full baskets of dung stayed with Dawa, who quickly began to empty them, piling the dung in high rows on the ground at the back of their tent so it would begin to dry. Today, like every day, Anil and Dawa would work from before first light to dusk, doing the jobs that maintained their way of life; a life of survival, faith, and camaraderie.

But, it wasn't long before Dawa began to see a change in her husband's mood. She worried as she watched him turn from a fun-loving, boisterous and cheery man, to a withdrawn, tired and angry man. And she worried as a tension began to grow between them. He would be short-tempered with her and cast rebuking looks for no apparent reason. His attention was focused on his work and there seemed little-to-no time left for her. As for Dawa, Pembuti got her attention too--as well as keeping the fire burning, the cooking, and the general household chores. And there never seemed to be time now for just the two of them: for Dawa and Anil. No calm to be with one another. Or was their no *desire*—Dawa wondered. Was this what man and wife become once a child comes along? Dawa had always warmed to Anil's touch; and he to hers. But now there was nothing: no closeness, no touching, no intimacy. Their feelings towards one another seemed to have withered--or were lost with Pembuti's arrival. Life had become a monotonous routine:

Each morning now Anil would wake as the first rays of light appeared in the dark pre-dawn sky. Quickly rising and throwing on his warm woollen garments, he'd stoke the smoldering fire--adding some dried yak dung and juniper branches--before heading out to the animal shelter. It would take him nearly an hour to feed the animals and clean out their shelter. Afterwards he'd saddle and rein one of his horses and two of his long, black-haired yaks, then lead them out and tie them up to the wooden rail set into the rocky soil outside their tent. Meanwhile, Dawa would prepare butter tea and *tsampa*, then tend to Pembuti; dress her in warm clothes then breastfeed her while the tea was steeping. As Dawa would sit beside the open fire nursing Pembuti, she always stared at the reds, oranges, and yellows thrown by the burning yak dung. And she'd listen for the familiar *clonk-clonk* just outside as Anil kicked his feet hard against the wooden post to dislodge the snow from his boots, knowing he would pause a moment before reentering the tent. (She had no idea why he did this. She thought, perhaps, he needed to gather his strength to face her and the child.) Today as he threw back the tent flap and entered, Anil saw that his wife was pouring him a steaming mug of butter tea and thought about the kind of life he now had. If only he could find a way to get back that part of his wife he'd lost.

Breakfast over, together they gave up their morning prayers at the altar set-up at the back of their tent, and recited their mantras. On the altar was a picture of the Dalai Lama, a *dorge*, a bell, and water bowls for offerings to the deities. This was now about the only time that Anil and Dawa became linked; by a mutual love and understanding of their beliefs, and it was in these moments that peace and tranquility became yet again part of their shared lives. Meanwhile, outside their tent a blizzard raged. But for Anil this was an acceptable inconvenience; he had to tend to his animals, and so he would. After prayers and mantras, he rose to his feet and headed for the door of the tent. "I will be off, now. Palden will be waiting for me," was all Anil offered Dawa as a goodbye.

"No--you do not want to keep your brother waiting!" replied Dawa in a mocking, resentful tone. A cold blast of thick snow rushed into the tent to chill their goodbye even more--as Anil dropped the flap, without turning round. The flap slowly settled into place as it fought against the in-rushing wind and snow.

Dawa's husband was gone for the day. And each day followed the next and the next . . . the same routine, the same conversation, drifting along day upon day with only Pembuti and their prayers between them. Anil tried to spend as much time as he could with his new daughter, mostly at night as they sat round their roaring fire in their tent eating and drinking before bedding down for the night. And he always took his baby daughter outside once their meal was finished to show her the night sky and let her breathe in the clear clean air of the Tibetan Plateau. He would hold her high above his head to get a good view of all the twinkling stars that shone so brightly like beautiful jewels in a setting of deep indigo suspended overhead like a blanket of wonderment. Anil and Dawa spent less and less time together: Anil had his animals to tend to, she her house work. They both tended to Pembuti.

Chapter 3

THE PASSAGE OF TIME TO the nomads of the Plateau was governed by the stars, the planets, the seasons, and the weather, and it was Dawa who one day reminded Anil that it was now time to take Pembuti to the nearest village to consult the local oracle. This was an important and ancient tradition—a rite of passage, as it were--amongst the nomads.

The oracle was a shaman, a holy man, who knew things beyond most peoples' understanding. A man who could provide insight into the otherwise unknown future. And it was necessary for parents to know what this holy man could foresee for their children. This journey to the village held a twofold purpose for Anil and Dawa: Not only would they consult with the oracle, they could trade for supplies needed for the next stage of their trek across the plateau, which would soon come round as the season was beginning to change and they would need to seek new pastures for their livestock. So after some discussion and planning, on a sharp and cold morning with a watery sun inching into a clear blue sky, Anil and Dawa prepared for their journey by packing warm clothes, food, water, and flasks of steaming hot butter tea. Panden, Anil's older brother, had informed the oracle of Pembuti's birth and arranged a day and time for Anil and Dawa to meet with him. This appointment aligned with the time the oracle saw as most befitting and auspicious to achieve the most conclusive consultation. Now that day had arrived and leaving the warmth of their tent Anil shielded his eyes from the morning sun's first rays.

Clasping the sides of his coat together and pulling them tight to protect himself from the icy wind, he circled round to the back of the tent. As he pulled back the canvas flap and entered the animal tent he smiled at his four horses, each of which had their own sectioned-off area with a water and food bowl. The horses all neighed, snorted, and puffed out plumes of misty air from their nostrils in greeting, knowing they were about to be fed. Anil set about mucking out each of the stalls, shoveling up the dung and refreshing their straw and water, then with a large round metal bowl, scooped out their food from the rickety, wooden container at the rear of the tent, and fed each horse individually. As he watched them eat he decided on the two he'd take; he needed to keep his family safe on this potentially dangerous eight-hour round trip. Tidying up the mess and tools he took two sets of reins, two saddles, and two sets of yak-skin saddle bags down from the wooden pole where they were stored. Once the horses had finished eating he bridled and saddled the two chosen--then led them out and round to the horse rail outside his tent, where he tethered them. All that was left to do was load the saddle bags with the necessities for their trip, so he headed back inside to find Dawa, who was busy tending to Pembuti's needs.

As he stood with his hands on his hips outside his spacious yak-hair tent, he inhaled a deep breath of cool morning air and let it fill his lungs. Looking over to his brother's tent, just a few hundred yards away, he heard the sounds of children. He watched as the flap of their tent flung open and his two nephews stepped outside, their faces blackened with mud and oil (done to protect them from the harsh rays of the sun). He watched as they squatted down and played with sticks in the dirt, pushing stones and earth round, creating thick plumes of dust, which did not seem to bother them at all.

There was a lot of activity coming from the other nearby tents as well: he saw rings of smoke coming from the holes in the tops of the tents, smelled warm *tsampa* as it filled his nostrils--as did the smell of burning juniper. Some of the men were now outside their tents checking the guy ropes, while others were feeding and watering their horses, ready to set off to the flat lands where their livestock awaited them. There were nearly thirty large black yak-skin tents in all, and all of them belonged to members of his family or close friends. There was a special bond between them all—as few extended families in other parts of the world would know. They looked out for each other. They *had* to. Their lives were mixed with harsh weather and poverty and no one could survive it alone.

Anil's eyes returned to the children playing and realised that they did live a very simple life. He then became aware of the children's laughter, their childish chatter, and hoped that his daughter would one day too be as happy. He pondered for a moment her birth and how this single event had changed his way of thinking and living. Instilled a larger view of life. A tug on his sleeve brought him back to the present. He saw the warm woollen multi-coloured blankets Dawa had wrapped Pembuti in to keep her cozy and warm. Anil nodded toward the waiting horses. A number of friends and relatives had now gathered round their horses and were offering their kind wishes, thoughts, and prayers for their safe journey and safe return. As Dawa prepared to mount, Anil took the baby and gave Dawa a leg up. She smiled as she took Pembuti from his warm hands and put her in the sling she wore round her shoulder, leaving the baby snuggled safely into her body. Anil walked round Dawa's horse and with a quick bounce--mounted his horse. With a jerk of the reins their horses turned and headed out of camp. Together they waved goodbye to their nomad friends, and with Pembuti safely swaddled into her mother, they set out across the Tibetan Plateau, away from the warmth of their yak-skin tent; away from the safety of their camp—their friends and family—and headed towards the village and their fateful meeting with the oracle.

There was a strange stillness about as they rode across the plateau--broken only by the crisp cracking of the hoar frost as horse hooves crunched through the frozen crust. As the horses rhythmically trotted on, Dawa became conscious of the colour contrast of the white-capped mountains against the deep-blue of the sky. And as she squinted at the sun's rays, which shone brightly into her eyes, she thought for a moment that she could see a rainbow; an arch of beautiful colours she could feel within her. She felt somewhat light-headed as she tried to shout ahead to Anil to tell him what she was seeing and feeling. But then the colours disappeared--leaving her feeling forsaken. She'd hoped to capture the colours and hold them forever with her, and wondered if this was a good omen for their visit to the oracle.

At last the village came into view, the smoke rising from the chimneys of the houses a welcoming sight. The horses picked up their pace; they seemed to know that their destination was minutes away. Here they would be fed, watered, and allowed to rest their legs a while. Carefully picking their way across the stony ground, Anil and Dawa rode side-by-side and chatted as they neared the tiny village. They were well known here; there were only twelve houses and a village store and they'd become acquainted with almost everyone. This store was where they often bartered their homemade butter and cured yak meat, trading them for ground barley, *thang*, and vegetables. At last the narrow dirt-track road widened out to where the first of the twelve two-story houses stood. This house belonged to Anil's cousin, who'd given up the nomadic life and settled down here with his wife who, although only in her mid-twenties, was expecting their sixth child. They both dismounted then Anil took their horses round to the back of the house to tend them.

The sides and backs of all the houses in the village were made of mud and stone supported by a wooden frame, while the fronts, at ground level, were enclosed only by a waist-high wooden slated fence with a wide wooden gate in the centre. This gate was large enough to enable their yaks and other animals to enter. This lower level was where they kept their animals, in a stable below the house that provided warmth when they were not out at pasture. Dawa hated the houses—and house living--much preferring her lovely, spacious tent. Although their animals lived near them, they lived apart from their living space. But here, the animals lived inside. And because of this, flies were everywhere. And the smell was not of dried yak dung and sweet juniper, but urine and rancid manure. Inside the lower level was a stone staircase that ran up the right-hand wall of the house and led to the one-room upstairs living area. Like nomadic life, there was no electricity, no plumbing, and no running water in the village, so like the nomads, village life had its own hardships. Dawa preferred her own hardships to theirs.

Once the greetings were over and the animals were tended to, Anil and Dawa set off for the oracle's house, stopping only to greet those villagers who'd come out to pay their respects. Upon reaching the oracle's house, Anil knocked loudly on the heavy wooden door. Dawa shifted her weight anxiously from one leg to the other--agitated that it seemed an eternity before someone came to the door. Lost in her own thoughts, Dawa jumped as the front door finally creaked open. In the darkness she could just make out an old stooped Tibetan man with a very weathered, ancient face. His worn and tattered woollen clothes caught Dawa's attention; his fur hat and leather knee-high boots were heavily soiled. He ushered them in, said nothing, pointing to a room at the back of the house.

He directed them to brightly-coloured but dingy cushions strewn across the floor, as he tended the many butter lamps setting on the table he used as an altar. He lighted some sandalwood incense from the flickering flame of one butter lamp and probed the clods of yak dung in the large open fire at the end of the room, with a long black iron rod. Beautiful red, orange, and yellow flames shot up from the dung as the sharp prodding ensured that it would give up more of its heat and light.

The old man then slowly backed out of the room, jerking the door shut behind him. Anil helped Dawa remove the sling from round her neck and she gently lifted Pembuti from it--while she slept on. Dawa gave her husband a sidelong look as she'd already begun to feel nervous; the palms of her hands were sweaty. She didn't know if it was the intensity of the increase, the heat of the fire in the small, stifling room, or her anxiety at what she was about to hear about her baby. But a mild panic began to set in.

As her mind drifted from one thing to another, three men entered the room carrying rolls of prayer scriptures, Dawa suddenly became mindful of her surroundings. She noted the piles of yak dung drying against the wall and the stack of firewood and thought to herself that the room was not really that much different from their living space in their yak-skin tent. The three sat down on cushions, crossed their legs, and began to recite the words written on the long narrow pieces of paper they'd unfurled before them. With the rhythm of the prayers a lightness came over her; she began to relax and her eyes began to shut. Just as they closed she heard the beat of a drum and the clash of cymbals coming from somewhere else in the house.

Anil, Dawa, their baby, and the chanting men sat in the stuffy room; warmed by the fire and the words of prayer. Then, unannounced, the oracle entered. He was dressed from head-to-foot in fine silk cloth; from an ornate and unwieldy headdress in part made of long soft black feathers, to flowing robes which spread out across the floor. The red sheen of the silk robe was intricately embroidered with multicoloured silk threads that formed swirling patterns on the surface. Round the oracle's neck hung a large, highly-polished metal disk which covered most of his chest; the flames from the fire casting an eerie reflection on its shiny surface. As the holy man sat on the one remaining cushion, Anil placed a small offering of money on the floor in front of him. The oracle then closed his eyes and slowly began rocking from side-to-side while at the same time shaking his head at an ever-increasing rate. A ringing clash of cymbals echoed round the room startling Pembuti--who woke from her sleep and gave a shrill cry before closing her eyes and returning to her slumber.

The oracle was not affected by this cacophony of sound as it slowly ebbed away--as if being absorbed into the bodies of those in the room and into the light of the fire and butter lamps; as well as into the walls of the room itself. Dawa watched as the oracle continued to sway and shake his head in an ever more frenzied manner and began to mutter words in a language she couldn't recognise. His movements became the fevered actions of a dervish, writhing round with arms and legs flailing as if in a torment of agony, his body contorted into a grotesque caricature of a man, with his face becoming almost unrecognisable. (It was as if he'd become a marionette under the control of some unseen puppeteer.) All this surreal activity had no effect on the oracle's attendants: they'd obviously been through this procedure many times before. Even Anil, outwardly at least, seemed to be unmoved by the activity unfolding before their eyes. For Dawa, however, what started as a feeling of unease was quickly escalating into something more: her pulse quickened, her face flushed--yet her skin was cold to the touch. She felt herself being drawn (albeit against her will) into the oracle's manic dance. Dizziness mired her thoughts. Now alarmingly disorientated: *Am I really in this small, dimly-lit room with the walls closing in on us?* The uneasiness intensified into sheer panic, the room becoming horribly stifling and oppressive. It was as if clammy hands were pawing at her to release Pembuti to their surreal clutches. *I have to get out of here!*

As hard as she tried to control her breath, Dawa could only fill her lungs with more of the same sour and fetid air that had pervaded the room. Anil and the other men appeared unaffected by all that was happening round them as they sat placidly watching the oracle unleash such oppressive and fearful energy. *Maybe*, she thought, *we are already under his spell! Out—I must get out of here before it is too late for me and my innocent child!* Just as Dawa strained to rise to her feet, the oracle gave out a plaintive, wailing cry, which echoed round the confines of the room and pulsated through her body like shock waves. And as his agonised voice subsided, so did his spasm-like movements (as if the puppeteer's strings were being cut, one by one).

As Dawa focused her eyes, she no longer saw the face of the robed man who'd entered the room: his eyes had changed from brown to yellow in colour. (She blinked as she wondered if this was just a reflection of the yellow flames of the glowing fire.) The black-feather headdress now seemed to have a life of its own as it took on the impression of the flapping wings of a great and powerful bird. This transformation suggested to her that someone or some*thing* else was now sitting across from her. The oracle had transmogrified and there was clearly another consciousness now present, apparently channelling through him. From this change, Dawa's mood of blind fear lessened, but apprehension still ruled her thoughts.

Suddenly the oracle lunged toward Anil--who instinctively drew the baby tight to him to shield her. Now the men, who'd been reciting prayers non-stop, moved forward and took the oracle by the arms to support him. Dawa noticed that they had red cloth wrapped round their hands. One of the men spoke softly to Dawa, requesting that she now ask her questions of the oracle. She nodded understanding but found that words would not come; her mouth was dry and she could barely catch her breath to expel that which she needed to say. Suddenly she found herself asking after the future for her daughter, Pembuti. Almost instantly, the oracle howled out a torrent of anguished screams--which filled the air round her as if there were hundreds of competing voices trying to communicate with her. The oracle then began to again sway side-to-side and it was as though he disappeared--with only the black feathers left swaying before her eyes. Then with a clenched fist he began pounding his chest and spoke in a hushed Tibetan voice:

"When the Year of the Earth-Ox comes round,
And the bang makes rings of smoke,
As the jewels hit the dust,
The body returns to the earth,
While the songbird's cry for freedom,
Is heard only by the flash of turquoise on black,
On the winds of time across the planes of existence,
Then the taste of defeat is in the mountains,
It will all come round again."

Still swaying side-to-side, he then threw out his arms towards Dawa.

In an instant, the stale and cloistering ether that had pervaded the room cleared, as if the oracle had commanded it to vacate. Simultaneously, Dawa felt a surge of electricity rush through her body that seemed to spark a *cleansing*; as if she'd been plunged into the icy chill of the turquoise waters of Lake Namtso, and yet, strangely, at the same time immersed in the steaming, sacred hot springs at Dezhong (these consecrated places she envisioned). This conflict of senses and emotion seemed also to still her mind—though trepidation and concern for Pembuti still remained strong. The oracle then slumped forward, swaying almost uncontrollably--the signal for the three men to pull him to his feet and help him out of the room, leaving Anil and Dawa alone with their baby—and trying to make sense of what had just happened. Together they slipped Pembuti back into the sling and Anil strapped her to him, then he and Dawa walked back down the corridor to the front door. As they were about to leave one of the men involved handed Anil a rolled-up scroll: Pembuti's astrological chart, which the oracle had recorded prior to their arrival.

Dropping it into Dawa's bag, they stepped out and back into their own familiar world.

They walked in silence as they headed toward the local market where they were going to buy much-needed provisions. But Dawa's thoughts were running wild; she had no idea what to make of the oracle's words—or the experience as a whole. She carried with her the memory of the oracle's almost inhuman gyrations and her feelings of unease, giving rise to an unwelcome foreboding of the future. Her nerves were raw from the experience: she'd expected a simple and straightforward traditional Tibetan ceremony. Such were her nagging doubts that she sought her husband's hand with her own, for comfort and reassurance that all would be well. She turned her thoughts to their mission at the market. Pembuti yawned and let out a cry and Dawa realised that it was way past her feeding time.

"Look Anil, we must stop. Pembuti needs feeding and we must eat also."

Heading towards his cousin's house it was decided that Anil would leave Dawa to tend to Pembuti, while he went off to make their purchases. Returning a short time later, they had a lunch of vegetables and rice then saddled their horses and readied themselves for their journey home. After regaling Anil's cousins with their extraordinary experience with the oracle they said their goodbyes and set off. Their path well-defined by the subtle glow of moonlight and distant stars, Anil and Dawa headed for camp laden with meat, *tsampa*, and tea, knowing that family and friends would be eagerly awaiting the news they brought.

The rhythm of Dawa's horse as it plodded along the trail back to camp allowed her to relax, and as she did she began to think of home; the warmth of their family fire, their everyday possessions always arranged comfortingly in the same place and order within the tent. Even though they moved at least twice a year, they always arranged their tent in precisely the same manner, and it was this *sameness* that helped Dawa resign herself to life of changing landscapes, and now with the arrival of a child, changing responsibilities. She was awakened from her daydream by Anil, who was now pointing and shouting that he could see campfire light in the distance. As Dawa strained her eyes, she too could just make out the warming reds, yellows, and oranges of the glowing fires that illuminated the boundaries of the settlement. Soon she would be back to the life she knew (and her prized possessions, now augmented by a beautiful baby daughter). The cycle of life of which she was an integral part could now resume in peace and harmony.

As they neared their camp and the colours grew bolder, Dawa heard Pembuti give out a soft cry as she began to wake from her slumber. At last they reached their own tent and a number of friends and family came out to greet them, helping Dawa dismount her horse. (They saw that she looked exhausted from this journey.) Her aunt took Pembuti from Anil and handed him the reins of Dawa's horse. Observing his broad and powerful form, Dawa was reminded of how lucky she was that *he* was her husband. He was her rock: he supported her, kept her safe, and went out in all weathers to tend to their animals in the fields. And he was fearless: she could count on him to fight for their very existence. She sighed. She was indeed fortunate to be his wife.

Dawa opened the flap of their tent and stepped inside, followed by her aunt, carrying Pembuti. She saw the fire still burning in its grate. (She was so glad to be home.) She smiled as she looked on the homey familiarity of the butter churn, the cooking pots, the storage baskets, and the earthen stove. She lighted the butter lamps throughout the tent and stoked the fire. Then she took Pembuti and allowed her aunt to retire to her own tent. As the flames took hold she took notice of the different shaped shadows now cast on the tent walls. Surprisingly, these silhouettes didn't provide the comfort they usually did, but became threatening forms that unnerved her. It was as if their movements were mimicking the jolting and jarring motion of the oracle as he went into his disquieting trance. She needed a mug of hot butter tea to soothe her nerves so she reached for the clay water pot and filled the heavy cast-iron kettle. Some *tsampa* would also soothe her, she decided, so she placed more yak-dung bricks inside the stove and placed the kettle on top. Then she went to the cupboard and got out two mugs ready for the steaming tea: one for her, one for Anil. She removed a few blankets from where they were stored--gently stroking the wheel of her treadle sewing machine as she passed. (It was one of her most useful possessions; a gift, of course, from her uncle the traveling lama.)

Dawa lit more candles and took Pembuti to her breast. She looked down at the helpless infant suckling, and smiled. She considered how fortunate she was to have all that she needed: equipment to cook and eat with, objects to offer her prayers to, her own private possessions to keep her amused, a husband and daughter to give her life purpose. After she fed Pembuti she rolled out the thin sleeping mats, the sheep-wool quilts, and the yak-skin pelts that kept them all warm at night. She put her nose to the blankets and welcomed their animal muskiness; it was a further comfort to know that she, Anil, and Pembuti would soon be safely curled up within them and they would keep them all warm against the extreme chill of the night. A moment later Anil appeared at the entrance of the tent. Dawa heard him and turned to smile.

"The butter tea is almost ready," she said, going to kitchen area and pouring the hot liquid into waiting mugs, and bringing them to the fire. A second trip brought bowls of *tsampa* for the two of them. They sat together by the fire and ate and drank in silence; both tired and the warmth of the fire made them even more so, especially after their long journey. (*So what if our marriage isn't perfect?* she said to herself. *We have something that goes far beyond simple attraction.*)

"So, what did you make of the oracle?" enquired Dawa of her husband.

"I don't really know," he replied.

"You must have some *idea?*" pressed Dawa.

"A lot of . . . it's just religious *talk!*" scoffed her husband, dismissively.

"It is about your daughter's future!" scolded Dawa. "Surely you not concerned about that."

"Of course," conceded Anil, "but what about *our* future; husband and wife?" he said, a harsher tone tingeing his words.

Dawa shrugged her shoulders and turned her thoughts to what the oracle had said. "He said something about the Year of the Ox, so something must happen in that year for Pembuti," she reasoned. "And something about black and turquoise. Maybe Lama Kunchen will bring me a very valuable present one day soon—even though I have not received anything in the past few years," said Dawa excitedly.

"Here we go *again*, Dawa! Trinkets, baubles, and goodness knows *what!* I do not understand your need for such *things!* You have everything you need, but still you want *more!* No good will come from this--it is not our way of life!" Anil reminded her.

Although Anil wanted what was best for his wife and daughter (and knew Tibetan life was extremely hard and sometimes special distraction was needed) he was unsure how all these expensive gifts fitted into their lifestyle. He could understand if Dawa sold or traded the gifts for food or needed items, but every time he made such a suggestion she flew into a panicked rage; refusing to even consider such a *ridiculous* idea! Anil also wondered what the point was in having such gifts if they were kept hidden. He watched as a scowl passed across his wife's face at his re-marks. (He did not like this part of his wife--not at all.)

After tea and *tsampa* Anil and Dawa were too tired to discuss further the day's events so they snuggled into bed, Dawa's eyelids slowly droop-ing, her thoughts revisiting their meeting with the oracle. Eventually they both fell into a deep sleep, but Dawa's was a troubled sleep--with dreams of strange beings flying through the air, wielding swords at each other. At each clash of these dazzling blades of steel the bright colours of these airborne warriors' outfits pulsed, sending rays of energy out-wards which then merged into a mass of black, forming the figure of a man. This eerily malevolent form seemed to sweep down and light upon Dawa, trying to engulf her in its blackness. Dawa suddenly woke with a start--her body drenched in sweat, her heart pounding savagely. She began to wonder if their visit to the oracle had been such a good idea.

Chapter 4

⟻

ANIL AND DAWA'S LIVES REMAINED dominated by a hard-but-necessary routine of work to eke out an existence, and religious devotion to feed their spiritual needs. As the first rays of the sun hearkened another day, Dawa woke up; her troubling dreams behind her. Still, this morning she felt particularly listless; *different.* She rolled up their bedding and picked up their mats and set them against the wall of their tent before joining Anil at their altar to begin their morning mantras. The couple knelt side-by-side on a coloured rug in front of the small altar at the back of their tent, and monotonously repeated their chosen Buddhist mantras.

The small and simple wooden table which served as their altar was adorned with Buddhist artifacts and items of significance to Anil and Dawa: rolls of handwritten Buddhist scripts, a book of Buddhist teachings, a burner for juniper incense, a few images of His Holiness the 16th Karmapa, a larger image of His Holiness the Dalai Lama, and several butter candles—lighted and extinguished several times daily. Next to the altar lay a box for jewellery and other valuables, a statue of Nämtose (recognized by the Buddhists as the god of wealth), a *dorge*, a bell, a few small silver prayer wheels, and a five metal bowls used for water offerings. All these items were integral to their daily prayers; for cleansing and purifying their home, their livestock, and themselves. As Dawa repeated the mantras she began to relax; she entered an hypnotic state and took in strength to face the coming day.

Life for all nomads was simple but hard. Dawa knew well their hardships but her family and neighbours all spoke of the benefits of such a free lifestyle; they had everything they needed and were free to choose. Dawa welcomed the hard work as it kept her body warm and active, and the daily mantras and meditations kept her mind occupied. The combined elements of nature fed her soul and gave her space to breathe in the tranquil energies that surrounded her. And Dawa loved the expansive terrain; it was her magnificent home. The land that fed their animals was the space that kept them calm and contented; kept their minds from intruding change. But at times she wondered what it would be like to live where she wouldn't have to work quite so hard.

Despite her acceptance of nomadic life, Dawa wanted more for Pembuti. More than the constant smell of yak skin, the buffeting winds of the desolate high plains, and the biting cold of the dark winter nights. Dawa's precious jewelry had alerted her to other ways of life—one, no doubt, far from the harshness of the wild Tibetan Plateau. And she wanted this for Pembuti, her precious daughter. Even so, Dawa was pure of thought, mind, and action, and like all nomads of Tibet, believed that she was living a life that was rewarding, even though she faced a climate of extremes and fought an almost constant battle with poverty. She knew beyond doubt that she lived at peace with herself and her surroundings, yet the material gifts she'd accumulated over the years had an undeniable hold on her. She'd come to place a value on them beyond her traditional values of the peaceful, simple nomadic life she led. Thus, the beguiling and glittering trinkets were her only source of inner conflict. Still, she knew she could never sell nor give them away. (They were hers and hers alone and they provided a window into other possibilities.) One day, she thought, the turquoise necklace and all her other trinkets would pass to her daughter. Maybe she would live a life where such things were fittingly appreciated and admired.

Today like every other day, after prayers and breakfast Dawa pre-pared herself and Pembuti for the freezing outdoors by adding layer upon layer of woolen garments to them both. Lifting Pembuti high into the air (who was busy gurgling and goo-ing), Dawa planted a warm and wet kiss on her small red lips before slipping her hat onto her vul-nerable, hair-matted head; her miniature handmade fur boots onto her tiny feet. Then she slipped her into a warm fur-lined yak-skin blanket sewn up on three sides to form a cozy pouch. This pouch was then nestled inside the sling Dawa would use to carry her close to her body. Once she felt her delicate little passenger was secure, she exited the tent, picking up two large, empty water containers--one in each of her gloved hands.

The ground this morning was slippery with ice and a soft layer of new-fallen snow. Dawa knew she had to be careful of her footing and that the journey to the stream would take longer than usual. She held on tightly to the large metal containers as the importance of fetching water could be a matter of life or death to her family—and their ani-mals. Fighting the freezing winds opposing her path to the stream, Dawa removed a jug from the belt round her waist, took off the top, and knelt down by the edge of the stream. Once glancing towards her sleeping daughter she began to scoop water from the stream into the jug, and then into the large containers. Once filled she secured the tops of the containers and began the long and more labourious journey back to camp. From time to time she's stop and rest--setting the heavy containers on the ground--and chewed on small bits of the dried meat she'd brought along. This gave her the energy she needed to continue the strenuous journey back to camp. And though she was exhausted by the time she reached home, she had still a day's work ahead of her. Dawa sighed. Without wishing her daughter's childhood away, she'd be glad when Pembuti would be old enough to share the everyday chores that seemed to comprise most of her and every other nomad's life.

And so day followed day . . . month followed month . . . and year followed year. Anil and Dawa seemed to settle for what they had and what they'd become. Gone was the intimate spark of their private time. They were growing old before their years; slowly ground down by the passage of time and nature . . .

Chapter 5

I<small>T WAS NOW THE</small> Y<small>EAR</small> of the Earth Mouse and as Dawa sat on her favorite cushion in their tent she stared at the flames twisting and licking
upward from the yak dung that glowed in the open fire kept lit in the
centre of the tent. Nine years had now passed since Pembuti had come
into their lives. Labelled the "wild and wise one" by the other nomads,
everyone loved Pembuti--with her striking and unusual-coloured brown
hair, her slight build, and her vibrant heart-shaped face set off by high
cheekbones and pouting ruby-red lips. For all this youthful and innocent beauty, the focal point of her features was her remarkable eyes:
glinting brown and black-specked orbs set on a pure white background
that seemed to reflect her thoughts and emotions. Guarding these were
long black eyelashes that fluttered as if attuned to her contagious smile
and apparent, wide-eyed acceptance of things round her.

Pembuti loved to sit and listen to the stories her elders told of times
gone by, and of their traditions and ancient ways. The elders saw in
her a very humble and innocent young girl who always lived in a sus-
tained state of wonder and awareness. For Pembuti, life was for living
with all its beauty and variety. She was always seeking knowledge and
information that she could store away for another time. But in addition to knowledge, she loved the beautiful jewellery her mother kept
hidden away from prying eyes even more. Taken out only on special
occasions, Pembuti took great delight in creating games round these

sparkling trinkets. And so it happened that Dawa saw the darker side of her daughter on one such day.

Meant only to revisit the beauty of her trinkets (as she sometimes did), Pembuti had grabbed at the box as Dawa brought it out from its secret hiding place, her precious jewellery strewn across the floor. In a flush of frenzy, Pembuti lunged for the sparkling pieces and gathered them to her breast saying, "No! These must be cared for! They must be *treasured*!" And when it came time to return the jewellery to the box, she reacted jealously--lashing out at Dawa in a blind rage--refusing to give it back: "*No!* You do *not* love them the way *I* do!" she said, holding the necklaces and bracelets close to her chest. And for the first time, Dawa saw an arrogant side to her daughter--coupled with an aggressive, stubborn, and demanding nature. And as she stared at her daughter in dismay, she recalled how as a little girl the other children had poked fun at her for being *different*. The fact that her dominant hand was her *left*--rather than what the nomads considered "normal," the *right*, made them wonder if being left-handed made her always have to be in control; resulting in an almost ruthless, competitive manner. (She *always* had to win.) Dawa had at first thought Pembuti's behaviour was just child's play--like her own at that age--but she now remembered other tantrums her daughter had thrown over the years when she lost at games or didn't get what she wanted.

Dawa had argued with Anil about it. But Anil saw his daughter's behaviour as a sign of power, assertiveness, and confidence. A sign of courage and leadership. He loved her fighting spirit and assured Dawa that she would make a great hunter one day. That she had the much-needed survival instincts to face the hardships of the Tibetan Plateau. That she was a true Khampa *warrior* at heart! And that in time he would teach her to ride and use the bow masterfully--for her own welfare and safety and that of others. It would seem, Dawa thought, that Pembuti was not going to be the thoughtful, family-oriented daughter she'd hoped.

But now, Dawa had a problem. It was she who was responsible, for the most part, for Pembuti's upbringing. Anil would expect her to ensure that their daughter grew up in the traditional way and so in turn, would become a good wife and mother. But if Pembuti continued with her uncontrolled and unprovoked rages, Dawa wondered how she could instill traditional Tibetan values in her—those passed down through the generations. And now, she feared for her daughter's future. She needed to teach Pembuti how to control her outbursts before it was too late.

Today was like any other day as mother and daughter set off to fetch their daily supply of water, except that Dawa knew they would soon be seeking new pastures and would need to pack everything up once again and move camp. Dawa had come to love and look forward to her daughter accompanying her to the spring each day; loved watching her slip off her leather shoes when weather permitted and dip her feet into the icy-cold spring and waggle her toes round. It reminded her of when she was herself a child. She watched with glee as Pembuti pointed at the water glistening and sparkling with the sun's rays on its surface, chatting wildly as the water separated into the colours of a rainbow. Dawa smiled at her daughter's seemingly boundless inquisitiveness:

"How do the beams of light bend and change direction?" asked Pembuti. "And how far down do those spears of light go? They seem to go on forever—don't they?! And, where do they go after that?"

Even so, Dawa did not have the answers Pembuti wanted and was glad when her attention was drawn to trying to catch the colours of the water in her cupped hands—becoming frustrated when she couldn't—and then laughing uncontrollably at her folly. Even the freezing touch of the water couldn't take away from that moment of pure joy. Dawa scoffed at her daughter's irrepressible laughter as she briskly rubbed her feet with a cloth to dry them. "Time to put your shoes back on, daughter. We have a long journey home and playtime is over." Sometimes as they walked back to camp Dawa could feel the weight of the heavy water containers in her gloved hands and knew that one day this would be her daughter's job. And that saddened her. She wanted so much more for her child.

As they continued along the well-worn path back to camp that day, Dawa decided that it was time to explain more about the mantras they recited three times each day. This was an understanding every nomad possessed. She began, "Pembuti, I think it's time to explain further about the mantras we recite daily." Dawa stopped for a moment and rested one of the water containers on the ground. Pembuti looked intently into her mother's eyes. "As you already know, the mantras are written texts we must all learn and abide by throughout our lives. It is through reciting these words, with emphasis on the syllables, that the meaning of the mantra comes into being. The sound created helps us focus our mind, which in turn helps our concentration. If we are able to empty our minds of all thoughts—which you will learn to do in time-- then this will allow endless new possibilities to arise. These possibilities mean that you will be able to better your life--your good fortune, your health, your wealth, and the physical, mental, and spiritual well-being for us all. This knowledge of mantras and calming of the mind has been passed down through generations of our ancestors, and I truly believe that daily chanting of mantras and prayers will earn us merit not just in this life--but future lives! This, Pembuti, is the life and beliefs we have been born into." Resuming their walk home, Pembuti believed her mother and understood what she was trying to explain. In short, it was as it was: their way of life was as it had been and always would be.

Once back at camp mother and daughter dumped some of the water into the animals' trough then set the containers in the kitchen area, knowing that they had more chores to do. But first they treated themselves to some *tsampa* and a cup of warm butter tea. Now amply fortified, Dawa and Pembuti left for the pastures where their animals had found some rough ground-stubble for grazing. Their job here was to gather up as much yak dung as could fit in their sacks--and they could carry. Pembuti's task, when they got back to camp, was to lay out the clods of dung on the ground outside their tent to allow it to dry out completely. An important and essential job, all their cooking and heating depended on a constant supply of this dried, organic tinder. Pembuti also had to ensure that there were always sufficient bricks of dried dung next to the fire and stove for quick use.

The next job of the day (and one Pembuti particularly liked) was the milking of the *dris*, the female yaks, which had to be done before her father took them out for the days' new grazing. She, like Dawa, would nuzzle into the flanks of the docile animals, drawing warmth from their furry bodies, and grasp the warming, milk-giving teats in her cold fingers. On really cold mornings, steam would rise from the sour-sweet liquid being squeezed into the milking pails. Such was Pembuti's enjoyment of this job that she would happily repeat the milking when, in late afternoon, Anil brought the yaks back from pasture.

Dawa showed her daughter how to process the milk into yogurt, butter, and cheese, and how to hang the cheese from the walls of their tent for storage, aging, and convenience. A few of the women in camp also taught Pembuti how to weave blankets and clothes. And when barley could be obtained, Dawa and Pembuti would grind it into flour to prepare *tsampa*—a job Pembuti alone would take over as she got older. But as she got older, she made it clear that she would much rather go with her father as he drove the animals to graze in the nearby pastures.

Like most nomad women of their camp, Pembuti (like her mother), seldom washed. Their ancestral beliefs considered washing an unhealthy and harmful practice, so Pembuti's face--like those of the other nomads--was always dirty. Today as they sat inside their tent as the wind howled outside, Dawa was helping Pembuti make a valuable, practical salve: "Pembuti, *concentrate*, please, and keep stirring the pot! We do not want the milk curds to burn! As you know, when it's cooled, this mixture will not only cleanse our skin, it will protect it from the harsh weather, and leave it looking soft and beautiful!"

"Well, I prefer to rinse my face in yak milk—but I will do as you say," Pembuti said, smiling mischievously. "But, I really *do* love the feel of the salve! It's so *soooothing*!"

"Well, this recipe was passed down from your grandmother's grandmother, Pembuti, and now you are old enough to make it yourself, and continue the tradition," said Dawa encouragingly.

"Well, I sure like it a lot better than the greasy layer of yak-butter and dirt we put on our faces!" laughed Pembuti. "It always makes me laugh when you do this since our faces then match our clothes--which are usually caked in dirt and dust from the plains!" Dawa smiled at her daughter and was once again reminded of how different Pembuti looked, compared to the other nomads of their clan. Secretly, many of the locals questioned why Pembuti's hair was dark brown with golden threads running through it—rather than black like everyone else. But apart from the colour, it was usual for a Tibetan girl's hair to be wild and unkempt—and in this regard, Pembuti was like all the others.

With the weather having improved over the past few weeks, Pembuti was now on a mission to sleep outside. "Please, please, can we sleep outside?" she pleaded with her mother. The high plateau could be extremely frigid—and they often, in fact, had snow in summer--but Pembuti, like her mother and father, loved to sleep out in the open. "I don't see why not, Pembuti, but I must check with your father first," replied Dawa. Anil was quite pleased with the idea saying, "A night away from the smoky air inside our tent is a very good idea! And a chance to be one with the universe!"

That night Pembuti lay on her sleeping mat curled up beside her dog, Mingma. As she turned and looked in all directions she could see for miles; the dark indigo sky that sparkled with a myriad of stars seemed to merge with the dark silhouette of the solidity of the Earth. The twinkling stars and shimmering moon cast their light upon the ground and sometimes she would see a star shooting across the sky and would wish that she could ride it--flying through the night as if she had wings. She remembered how she had on many occasions sent prayers up to the gods for good weather so that she could sleep outside as this was the only time she could share her mat with Mingma; he was not allowed inside their tent. Feeling warm and secure curled up beside him she would make up stories as they lay together, looking out over the expansive landscape. It never occurred to her that her beautiful dog did not understand a word she said. Even though he was the family's guard dog—an intimidating deterrent to fend off predators, both four- and two-legged--to Pembuti he was a big, warm, fun-loving bundle of energy and good-natured joy. With the warmth Mingma provided, the heat of the fire her father had lit, and the ambiance of the night's colours and sounds, Pembuti slowly drifted into a deep, peaceful sleep.

Chapter 6

PER TIBETAN CUSTOM, ONCE THE day's work was done, many of the nomads would visit friends and family in camp to catch up on the goings-on; share some *thang* and camaraderie. With everyone sitting comfortably round the fire they'd talk about many things--the weather, their animals, their way of life, what they needed to meditate on, and what mantras they should recite to help solve their problems. But it was when the elders' talk turned to the annual Tibetan horse festivals that Pembuti's attention became transfixed. Dawa, however, had heard these stories countless times before and preferred to dream about a life apart from that on the plateau. And as she gazed at Anil and their daughter engrossed in these tales, she thought back to the first of what would become a very significant yearly event; to the time her uncle, a traveling lama, had arrived for his annual visit to their camp bearing a beautifully-wrapped present brought especially for her; (along with money to buy provisions for her entire family, who were both delighted and shocked at such generosity).

As Dawa sat there by the fire she could see herself clearly, all those years before; how she'd jumped with joy at his yearly arrival! He was a link to the outside world and she loved to hear his tales of adventure. She remembered marvelling at his saffron and red robes. Then to her surprise, he handed her a paper-covered box tied with coloured ribbons. She remembered frantically peeling off the paper and screaming out with joy at the beautiful turquoise necklace that lay shimmering in the box—which she quickly removed and draped round her neck. And even as the excitement filled her heart, she returned it to the box and placed it on the altar at the rear of the tent. And she remembered that her uncle had walked toward the back of the tent to get his *chodom*, the small wooden table he used as his portable altar, just as she was placing the box on the altar. And having witnessed what Dawa had done, he did something he'd never done before: he raised his voice and demanded to know why the jewellery box had been placed there--his eyes boring into hers as she stood rooted to the spot!

Too frightened to explain that she wanted the jewellery to be protected and kept safe, she could only shake her head dumbly. (Secretly she'd recited her mantras each day thanking the deities for such beautiful things and asking them to keep them coming to her each year.) She watched as her uncle lifted the box from the altar, held it in the air reproachingly, then stared at it for what seemed an eternity before handing it back to her--nodding sternly in the direction of her bed. She took this to mean that she could no longer keep the box on the altar; that she had to keep it as near to herself as possible. Her uncle then prepared his own altar--adding his bell, *dorge*, water bowl, butter lamp, and image of the Dalai Lama to his *chodom*--beckoning Dawa to join him. Dawa realised in that moment that only those items sacred to their beliefs were permitted on an altar, but wondered why there was no allowance for things that *she* found important to *her*. She didn't like that there was no acceptance of the new, only reinforcement of the old.

As the years passed, her uncle brought her more and more gifts. And Dawa's desire toward these possessions only burned more feverish; she never wanted her prizes far from her. She felt fulfilled, whole, and complete with these objects round her. And as she sat now beside the fire she remembered how excited she became when his time to visit—always near her birthday—approached. How she'd dream of the gifts he might bring on his next visit.

But this inner *hunger*, this burning *desire*, in another way always seemed to unsettle her. As if she were heading towards an unattainable goal. And with each passing year, this made her feel more and more as if something were lacking. As if she'd mistakenly believed that her happiness was *dependent* upon these gifts. Yet once she'd attained them—there was no lasting satisfaction. No lasting feeling of joy. Still she kept her dream of fulfilling her desires alive by anticipating her uncle's next visit—and the next.

Dawa could now see that through the years she'd tried to look outside herself for the next thing that might bring her satisfaction. She watched other children and saw that in spite of their lack of expensive possessions, they seemed to have a serene, inner peace she lacked. They seemed content with very little and showed no desire to have what she prized most. And this baffled Dawa. No matter how many times she flaunted her gifts the other children seemed quite disinterested. And their disapproval of her demanding ways wasn't changed by the riches she possessed. There were moments when she wondered if the gifts had become a destructive element in her life. Obsessed with the *next* wonderful gift, she found it harder and harder to focus her mind during meditation. Her mind became prone to wondering.

Dawa now remembered the year the presents stopped arriving. It was the year the stranger arrived with her uncle and gave her the bright red-coloured box--which though intrigued, she'd refused to open. The visit when he'd given her the white scarf. Even now she was reminded of the great pain and anguish this visit had caused. Reminded too that the following year, Lama Kunchen did not visit the camp; stories circulated amongst the nomads that the stranger had done something to him. Of course, these fears were allayed when travelers brought news that they'd encountered Lama Kunchen further south, travelling with Akong Rinpoche. Dawa was mistakenly heartened by this; maybe he'd not forgotten her and her family but was on important religious business. Still, she thought to herself even now, she missed getting a gift that year.

As another year passed, Dawa was growing up quickly--but still took childish pride in her glittering trinkets. Lama Kunchen returned that year and confirmed that he'd been on a great pilgrimage (and had accompanied Köncho Samdrup) to the most holy of Buddhist sites: Lumbini (the Buddha's birthplace Bodhgaya (where the Buddha received enlightenment), Sarnath (where the Buddha first taught the Dharma), Kushinagar (where upon his death the Buddha attained *parinirvana*), and last stop, Dolma Lhakang monastery. (The nomads were enthralled by the lama's tales of the strange places he'd visited, the exotic animals and peoples he'd encountered, and the oppressive heat and humidity of the great plains of India. Of greater concern to Dawa, however, was the absence of any new gift. But all Lama Kunchen would say was to remind her of the impermanence of things. That his life and hers, and those of all nomads, must progress--

--Dawa's reminiscing suddenly interrupted by a tugging at her sleeve. It was Pembuti wanting to know more about the horse fairs. Dawa wanted to stay with her memories of fine, multicoloured gemstones, glistening silver and gold chains and sparkling necklaces, but she could not; Pembuti was insistent. The here and now demanded the attention only she could provide.

Their community eagerly awaited the coming festivals and there was much excitement about meeting other nomadic communities and participation in competitions such as horse or yak racing, archery, and games of chance. They chatted about their animals and the kind of year they'd had in relation to past years, as the festival was originally intended to celebrate a good harvest (though it more often served as a welcome respite from hardship). They broke their conversation to pray for the beneficial effects of a temperate climate during the coming year. On this night, eight elders were present, seated on cushions round the fire. A number of children were either curled up beside them asleep or playing games with stones at the rear of the tent. Silence reigned when prayer began.

By this time in her life, Pembuti had, of course, heard it all before. But the older she got the more she looked forward to these special events. In her mind she could still see even after nearly a year the previous festival's events: the hustle and bustle . . . the laughter and singing . . . people all dressed up in their finery. It was all part of the excitement. But she loved yak racing best. She could remember the competitors as they lined up for the competition; she saw how proud they all were to show off their riding skills and those of their yaks, with their colourful saddles and reins adorned in bright red, orange, yellow, green, and blue tassels trailing almost to the ground. And beside the yaks, the men all dressed in their finest Tibetan riding costumes. They looked so handsome in their dark brown riding breeches and billowing white tunics, with scarves of various colours draped across them. Some would wear broad-brimmed hats--which almost always blew off in the wind--while others braided their hair with white, blue, and red beads. (These sights were implanted firmly in Pembuti's mind—and nurtured almost daily.)

As she listened, she heard the elders discussing last year's yak race and how at the beginning of the race the start signal had gone off and all men had managed to mount their yaks--except one, who'd missed the animal's brightly-coloured saddle, tried to grab the reins (which were also adorned in various coloured ribbons), only to end up crashing to the ground where he lay stunned, flat on his back! Now roars of laughter filled the tent as they began to shout about the chaotic start, remembering how the late starters tried to steer their yaks round the stunned rider, while his mount had already set off toward the opposite end of the course—the rider shouting angrily for it to come back! Pembuti's cousin, Assam, was now talking about the end of the race and the ongoing argument as to who the winner actually was—as it had been a close one. Pembuti and the others had watched with great excitement as the winner, a rider from another nomadic society, was announced and received his *khata*, the traditional Tibetan white scarf, as well as a small sum of prize money.

Anil now began to brag a bit about the competitions Dawa and he had taken part in. He laughed as he told the story about when they were competing against each other on horseback, each of them showing their daring and horsemanship by leaning out over the saddle and picking coloured ribbons off the ground. They made a good team, Dawa joined in and agreed, recalling that their skills had left the crowd amazed and breathless. Anil looked mischievously at the other men, then at Dawa, then jokingly asked why so many of the women at the festivals huddle together like broods of hens, and what on earth they found to discuss!? Dawa quickly informed him (and the other men) that they were chatting about life on the plateau and all that had happened since last they met and, of course, the problems with their men!

Pembuti snidely recalled playing with the other children at the fairs--dancing, rope skipping, play fighting, and singing children's songs—though she had no real interest in other children. She considered them weak. Inferior. Her competitive nature drove her to win every game at any cost--and never once did any of the other children not let her have her way! With each passing year Pembuti wondered if or when she would be chosen to ride in the horse racing competition. She'd tried to show her parents just how good a rider she was, but it was as if they didn't care--and she begged her father repeatedly to allow her to train in the months preceding the races. She *knew* she could win: she rode with the best of them, with the skill of a horsewoman far beyond her years. Her horse obeyed her commands with agility and ability acquired only from countless hours of practice. And when they galloped across the plateau it was as if horse and rider were *one*. Her dream was that one day she would be the one to be awarded the *khata*, and afterwards be permitted to join in with the other men and women and perform their intimate popular dances and songs. Now on this night, as the embers in the fire glowed hot, Pembuti thought of an old traditional song called "Gingo," and as she began to hum it her eyes closed and she drifted off to sleep with thoughts of the colourful festivities in her head.

Chapter 7

In the years that followed, Pembuti grew into a beautiful young woman. And like the other girls her age, she became aware of her appearance and took special care to maintain it. Her long brown hair gave off a shimmering quality in the sunlight and was swept off her face and tied at the back with a scarlet ribbon. Her oval-shaped face was a soft brown colour with rosy-red cheeks--as yet unravaged by life on the plains. She had a pert, almost flat nose and when she smiled her upturned lips and white teeth brought a radiance to her face, and in particular, to her piercing dark carbon-flecked brown eyes. When she smiled she often tilted her head slightly forward, looking out from the tops of her eyes, giving an almost impudent and impish look--as if hiding some intriguing secret. True to Tibetan tradition regarding red-faced girls, Pembuti was fond of sinful pursuits and very stubborn, and took after her mother. There was an undeniable air about her that people were drawn to. She radiated an almost ethereal quality and was quite simply the outward picture of happiness.

Although the nomadic life followed a cyclical pattern attuned to the seasons, their religion, and their pastoral lifestyle (returning to the same campgrounds on their annual journeys), to Pembuti it was as if she were visiting each place for the first time. There was always something new to see. Then in the Year of the Earth Ox this enjoyable round of travelling and festivals changed. Instead of returning to the flat-lands of the

Plateau as always, the nomad community continued further east into the lush green of gorges, ravines, sweeping valleys, and mountains. Being so young, Pembuti didn't understand why her routine had been disrupted so she asked her mother. But Dawa only muttered something about *the Chinese* and told her not to concern herself with such things. The elders would. Pembuti just shrugged her shoulders; to her this would be a new adventure full of new scenery, new sights and sounds, and new people.

As they journeyed further and further east, the tracks and trails became more rugged and treacherous. Some of the pack animals, as well as people, lost their footing at times and slipped on the loose rocks and stones as the paths meandered round high crags and rock faces on one side, steep ravines with fast-flowing water below on the other. Sometimes at places along these paths the nomads would come across other groups travelling in the opposite direction. Pembuti watched as the elders of both groups met in serious conversation, gesturing wildly and pointing. From a distance she could just make out the words, *Chinese* and *fighting*, as they carried on the wind. All this *seriousness* was to her part of the adults' world. With her youth, she was more interested in the strange and wonderful sights and colours she encountered at practically every turn of the new track. For reasons she did not yet understand, she was drawn to the colours and light they shed; the varying shades of green as the light broke through the leaves of the bushes and shrubs; the yellow and pinkish-purple of the small petals of the ground-hugging plants; and the blue and grey as the sunlight cascaded off the sheer faces of the rough, barren rock.

At one such turn in the track, the ground fell away gradually into a large and relatively flat meadow. Set in the heart of the meadow was a series of strange-coloured tents lined in rows with a fenced-off corral of horses at one end, a short distance from the farthest tent. Pembuti's caravan abruptly halted and her father rode on to meet with the other tribal leaders at the head of the column of horses, donkeys, and yaks. Her mother pulled her close, gazed down at her with a reassuring but forced smile and told her that this was a *Chinese* camp. And it soon became apparent that the nomads' caravan had not gone unnoticed by those in the camp, as a group of about twenty Chinese were soon approaching at top speed on horseback.

As they reached the head of the caravan, where Pembuti's father had come to a halt, she saw that these men were all dressed in the same dull and unusual brown-coloured clothing and carried long dark-brown "sticks" across their backs. One of the Chinese men started shouting at Pembuti's father and the other nomad elders as if issuing instructions to them. He then waved his left arm in the direction of the caravan, whereupon some of the other brown-clad men made their way down the line of animals, pushing old men, women, and children aside and rummaging through their belongings. When one of the Chinese reached Dawa's horse, he began dismantling all the family's possessions, dropping the items to the ground. Dawa shook in fear as she watched the Chinese pull a yak-skin-wrapped package off the donkey—and immediately tried to wrestle it back. As she did, a turquoise necklace, a small red and gold-coloured box, and other glittering objects spilled out and onto the hard and dusty ground.

Suddenly, Dawa pushed the Chinese out of the way and bent down to pick up her prized possessions. And as she did, Pembuti heard a loud crack and saw the Chinese pointing the long brown stick at her mother. A moment later, Dawa was slumped in a heap on the ground, clutching the yak-skin bag, moaning lightly and barely moving. Pembuti saw small rings of smoke floating silently and slowly upward toward the brilliant blue of the sky; they looked almost like tiny clouds. Dawa knew that she was dying, and as the life drained from her body heard the words of her aunt Jampa that 'no good would come from collecting and hoarding all those trinkets,' and realised that her aunt had been right. They'd never really made her happy; if only she'd let the Chinese have them. In her final moments she realised that Pembuti would now inherit her "prized" possessions and the misfortunes they wrought.

Pembuti's father immediately recognised the *crack* as the report of a rifle. He, the other nomad leaders, and the remaining Chinese quickly galloped back down the line of the caravan and dismounted. Anil rushed to Dawa and found his wife lying motionless on the ground. Behind him a ruckus broke out--the nomads and Chinese men now shouting at one another--the Tibetans becoming more and more enraged. Suddenly all the Chinese soldiers stopped what they were doing and under orders from their leader, quickly remounted and galloped back to their encampment, leaving the nomads bewildered and in shock—with cries of revenge. Pembuti's father knelt down beside his wife, shook his head side-to-side, then dropped his head in defeat. He took his wife's head into his lap and rocked back and forth, cradling her. As he did, his mind drifted back to the day they met:

He'd been introduced to her at a horse fair by his parents, who'd chosen Dawa to be his wife. He had watched her, studied her, wondering what she was like. And immediately noted that she rode like an expert horsewoman; she mixed in with all the local boys and even acted like one. He was intrigued. Her stance, her style, her very *presence* attracted him. And when he became more settled in the idea he decided it would be a pleasure to meet this young, carefree girl. And within a few months he'd got to know her, visiting her most days. And he'd loved her ever since.

But as for Dawa, at first she'd been quite upset with her aunt--who'd told her what a fine husband this "Anil Sompa" would make! She did not want to marry *anyone!* And though Anil was older than she by some five years, she was slowly drawn to his strong and handsome face; his expert riding skills. He was quite tall, with jet-black hair cropped close to the scalp and braided into a long ponytail at the back, which sometimes lay casually forward over his shoulder. His skin was dark brown, still smooth and taut over his square-jawed and high cheek-boned face. His most striking features (which had all but mesmerised Dawa) were his eyes: an unusual light brown in colour with specks of amber laid in like mosaics. They seemed to make his whole, noble face light up and smile. In the Tibetan language "Anil" means *air* or *wind*, and to Dawa, he was like the free-flowing breezes that blew across the plateau . . . and had now drifted into her life.

She grew to trust him. Enough to confide in him. And to her surprise, she suddenly wanted to touch him; be near him. And one day while out on the plateau sitting on the grass, she leaned into him and tucked her head into his shoulder. His hand clutching hers she told him about the *English* and how they'd been involved in the death of her parents, leaving her to be brought up by her aunt. She told him of growing up alone, without a mother and father; and how she'd come to rely on her own company (and that of her horse). To this he merely smiled, lifted her face up to his, and then gently kissed her lips--brushing away her tears with his fingertips. For a moment she froze--but then slowly she smiled at him and understood that something had changed in her. A wave of joy spreading through her she realised that she never wanted this man to leave her.

Before Dawa met Anil, she'd never understood why people would want to be together. Why they'd want to be tied to one another; the inevitability of children further tying them down. But she now realised that men and women became attracted to one another and there was nothing they could do to prevent it. Dawa and Anil were married the following year. For numerous years they were happy just to be with each other but the one nagging doubt they both had was when would Dawa become pregnant? As time went on Anil became more and more angry that he did not yet have a son or daughter. So when after nearly fifteen years of marriage Dawa became pregnant, Anil and his wife were ecstatic. Dawa had a healthy pregnancy and Anil helped her as much as he could. When their daughter was born they called her "Pembuti."

Now as Anil sat on the ground holding his wife tightly to his chest, it was as if a black cloud descended upon him; he ached and now re-alised just how very much he truly loved her. He wished he could turn back time: He should have *demanded* that she get rid of all these childish bobbles and trinkets; told her that with his love she had no need of such meaningless *things*. As he clutched her lifeless body, he felt his own will to live begin to flicker. For the first time in his life he was powerless to affect change. To help his wife, the mother of their daughter. He sat lost in inescapable misery. With her final breath Dawa looked up at her husband—but could see his face only in her memory. As this picture faded from her mind she saw a flash of white skim past her. As she fol-lowed this flash of white it transformed into a black bird. Thus, the last thing she saw was a crow alighting a mound of rocks piled high, in a wilderness of vast emptiness.

Family, friends, and all the elders now surrounded Anil; his brother put a hand on his shoulder saying, "We must go now, Anil, we really must. I too am deeply saddened for your loss but for the rest of our peoples' safety, we must go! Let me help you up."

Anil and his brother carefully wrapped Dawa's body in yak-skin and placed her across her horse (beside her beloved possessions). Further along the trail, father and daughter had to say good-bye to wife and mother as they buried her body under a pile of stones, as they did not have the time to provide a proper Tibetan burial. Anil and Pembuti said their prayers for the dead and Dawa's safe rebirth, then continued on their way; broken. Dawa's death had changed everything. Pembuti and her father had lost the one thing that held them together. More so, now they knew that what other travellers had said about the Chinese was true and the nomads' journey could not continue as planned. They were now forced to disband the community and go their separate ways, to join other friends and relatives and, at all costs, avoid the Chinese.

Anil's heart and soul were filled with rage. And as a Khampa warrior, his blood boiled against the Chinese; he had to strike back and could not take his daughter with him. Pembuti--bemused by all that had happened—just wanted her mother back. Her father tried as best he could to explain to his twelve-year-old daughter why it had happened and what the outcome had to be. So with much regret he bade farewell to his nomad friends, then he and his daughter turned back--away from the pain and sorrow. And so Pembuti's experience with the new colours of the landscape--the greens, the yellows, the pinkish-purples, the blue and the greys—came to an abrupt end. The two would return to the familiar colours of the Tibetan Plateau, traveling alone.

After a few days the two reached the safety of a small village and managed to obtain lodging for the night under a roof and away from the night sky. Both Pembuti and her father slept fitfully, trying to come to terms with all that had happened. Pembuti awoke the next morning to a soft whisper in her ear and a hand pressed to her mouth; she lay still and motionless in the dark room as that hand pulled her to a sitting position. She then made out the face of her father, who laid his finger to his lips in a *shhh* gesture. Raising her to her feet he pulled her outside where their horses were tethered to a wooden stake. Silently he untied their mounts and gestured for her to climb up; which she quickly did and together they slowly and softly trotted out of town. Once on the outskirts he stopped and she drew her horse up beside him.

"Pembuti, there are Chinese all round this area so I am going to take you to safety, to nearby Ani Gompa, a nunnery where the resident nuns will take care of you until my return. It saddens me to say it but I feel I must ride and join my fellow Khampas to fight the invading Chinese. They have murdered my beloved wife—your loving mother--and many other innocent people. I have chosen to become a fighter and defend our homeland. I promise to return as soon as this task is finished, and together we will build a new life together." He then handed Pembuti, wrapped in yak skin, her mother's belongings, which she slowly unwrapped.

There in her hands was her mother's prized turquoise necklace. She carefully touched the large turquoise stones, feeling the cold of each stone as she ran her fingers over them. She then realised that this was the first time she'd ever held the large turquoise necklace without her mother present. Her thoughts drifted back to the day before they broke camp and her mother, sitting on the mat beside the fire in their tent, was focused on her trinkets. She had carefully wrapped them in the piece of yak skin with all the intent that this was the last time she'd ever see them. Pembuti had always dreamed of wearing the beautiful turquoise necklace but had never thought it would be under such dreadful circumstances. But as she gazed down at the necklace she became sick to the stomach and began to tremble, realising that her mother's attachment to it had led to her death. Had she not tried to stop the Chinese from taking the little bundle, she may still be alive. Surely, nothing was worth a life: especially that of her mother. And as she fingered the stones she felt a wave of intense emotion, as if she were touching her mother.

Images of her life now spun in different coloured circles in front of her, showing her various scenes from her past. As tears ran down her face she felt as though her heart was breaking. Her sobbing grew louder and louder and she vowed to herself that she would never feel pain like this again. With each cry of anguish, she hardened her resolve to never allow anyone to *ever* hurt her again. Grasping the necklace at both ends she strung it round her neck and firmly closed the clasp; closed her eyes, took a deep breath and held her head high, clutching in her trembling fingers the stones hanging from the centre point. She was going to survive, and no one would ever get in her way. And without realising it, the necklace became the focus of her new outlook on life: her "good luck charm," a magical amulet against anyone or anything that threatened her. The necklace gave her a sense of inner strength and power that she could do anything.

Pembuti knew that a nunnery would never be the place to fulfill her dreams, so even before they arrived she began to consider that the answer would lie outside the nunnery walls. Somewhere out there would be someone to shower her with gifts--as the stranger had done her mother. Someone would see her beauty and recognise her as someone *special*; someone who deserved all that life had to offer. She was going to be noticed; be *someone!* And she was going to pay back those who had killed her mother. One day she would have all this. A single tear slid down her cheek as she pressed the turquoise necklace to her chest and rode on, side-by-side with her father.

Chapter 8

As Pembuti and her father approached Ani Gompa north of Lhasa, her heart grew heavy. She had no idea what to expect. For all she knew she was going to be locked away and hidden from the outside world--*for who knew how long*. She'd lost everything--her family, her way of life, and soon, her father--and was exhausted beyond words. She wanted nothing more than to sleep. To forget.

As they neared, the first sight Pembuti saw was the colourful images decorating the low, level walls that surrounded the nunnery. A high wooden gate stood in the centre of the front wall that was firmly closed—causing Pembuti to wonder if anyone ever left the nunnery. Still, she smiled at the sight of coloured prayer flags strung along the walls that blew gently in the breeze, harmonising with the environment round them, sending out good fortune to all living things. She knew that the flags were written on by hand using natural coloured dyes and inks and on individual pieces of cloth attached to long pieces of string. She'd been told by her father that each colour represents one of the elements: blue--sky/space, white—air/wind, red—fire, green—water, and yellow--earth. He did in fact hang the same flags from their tent every time they set up camp, and always ensured that they were replaced when they became frayed and tattered, having sent their messages on the wind across the plateau. She now remembered her father replacing the old flags for the auspicious festivals and special religious occasions when visiting nomads joined her group and celebrated, ate, drank, told stories and recited mantras, and performed rituals that Pembuti had sometimes participated in and come to enjoy.

As she looked beyond the prayer flags she saw flocks of birds circling the roofs of the nunnery buildings, like eddying circles on calm blue water. The most adventurous, the crows, would perch themselves on the roofs and window ledges of the taller buildings, and even on the tops of the *stupas*. They seemed to be in control as if this were their territory and anyone else merely visitors. From the nunnery walls, prayer flags, and circling birds, her eyes drifted to a colourful scene behind and to the right of the nunnery where more prayer flags were attached to the tops of (and strung out like washing) long, thin poles spaced out in a wide tri-angle shape over a stream that rushed down a small gorge in the hillside. These had been placed there by the nuns to bring peace and balance to nature round the nunnery. Two lengths of painted red wood had been erected close to either side of the stream under the canopy of prayer flags, with a connecting bar above from which hung a yellow and red cylinder-shaped prayer wheel with a cogged wheel at the bottom that trailed into the water, and as the water passed over it, in turn rotated the large cyl-inder in a clockwise direction. The mantra *Om Mani Padme Hum* was inscribed on the side of the large prayer wheel, along with images of *da-kinis* (Tibetan deities). Pembuti's parents had shown her pictures of these *dakinis* and taught her this same mantra, thus as she looked at the prayer wheel she felt comforted by the familiarity of its inscriptions. Later the nuns would explain to her that the water touched by the wheel was said to become blessed and carried its purifying power to all life-forms in the rivers, lakes, and seas that it fed into (a concept she would like).

To the right of the prayer wheel Pembuti noticed an enormous rock with colourful Tibetan writing painted across it repeating the same man-tra, *Om Mani Padme Hum*. She was drawn to the rock's sheer size and the various colours used to inscribe the mantra. Her father reminded her that *Mani* meant "jewel," and *Padme* meant "lotus" and stands for *compassion*. He then softly said, "Pembuti, you must remember to practice your Buddhist traditions every day until you can find it in your heart to accept all that has happened to us in the last few days." But even as he said this to Pembuti, a knot grew steadily in his stomach as he himself had no such thoughts of acceptance. A fire of rage burnt fiercely inside him that could only be extinguished by exacting retribution on those who'd done wrong to his family.

Dogs began to bark as they reached the gates. Pembuti's father dismounted and came round to the left side of her mount and lovingly patted her left leg. He then looked up tearfully into her eyes; for an instant he wondered if he really knew her. For so many years he'd left Dawa to see to their daughter's upbringing, while he was busy tending to the animals and dealing with all the hardships of their life on the Plateau. And now he was leaving her behind. And he could not find the proper words; he needed Dawa to speak for him. His heart was heavy and now this: Pembuti was staring at him, her eyes trusting him, believing in him, yet he had no comforting words for her. He had to leave—and that's all he knew. He wanted her to understand--though he himself didn't understand. So he simply smiled and said, "Everything will be alright, Pembuti, you will see. The nuns are good women and they will look after you. I will return very soon, then we can be together again." But somehow he knew he wasn't convincing himself--far less his trusting and frightened daughter.

Alerted by the watch dogs, the gates of Ani Gompa opened and out stepped an old nun dressed in long maroon robes who introduced herself as Ani-Dolma. Anil approached to address her. "My name is Anil and this is my daughter, Pembuti. We were ambushed by the Chinese, her mother was killed, and I need to leave now to take care of new business. I was hoping the child could stay with you here at the nunnery until such time as I can return," said Anil.

Ani-Dolma looked at Pembuti and smiled, nodding her head in approval. "Yes, we will take good care of her, have no fear."

Planting a kiss on his daughter's head, Anil went back to his horse, remounted, and with only one final backward glance rode off to meet his fate. Pembuti stared at the old and heavy brown wooden gates in silence and wondered what her life would be like now (feeling as if she were being engulfed by the brown colour and subdued by the oppressive heaviness of the gates). She was now alone. No family or friends. She was scared and her stomach churned. Even the bright colours of the flags no longer provided solace. Still, she focused on the orange of the billowing flags; she loved the colour orange for it reminded her of the sunrise in the morning and the sunset at night; it warmed her, protected her, uplifted her spirits. But today it just seemed to magnify her feelings of shock and bewilderment.

Turning now to what Pembuti saw as an old lived-in face with a kindly and welcoming smile, she came back to reality. As Ani-Dolma stood looking up at her, she gently patted her horse on the neck and bade Pembuti to dismount. She then led her into the nunnery courtyard, the horse trailing dutifully behind. As Pembuti looked round she tried to take in the enormity of her new surroundings, but there was nothing to compare. Together they--Ani-Dolma, Pembuti, and her horse--walked towards the north end of the complex where she saw a number of *stupas* amidst painted rocks depicting menacing images. "I will tell you a little about our nunnery as we walk, Pembuti. We have been privileged by a visit from the Dalai Lama himself, who while here made the discovery of a self-arisen stone image of the Buddha amongst other rocks. This we will visit when we reach the lower temple," said Ani-Dolma. "In the meantime, that over there is a *stupa*. Do you know what a *stupa* is, Pembuti?" Pembuti thought she might, but shook her head *no*. "You see, stupas are mound-like structures that contain Buddhist relics and are used as places of worship. They hold a treasury of various objects such as jewellery and small offerings, and there are also mantras written on paper and rolled up into thin rolls and placed inside miniature clay stupas. A stupa is created by placing one layer of offerings, covering it with sand, then on that layer placing more layers until the entire space within it is filled. The *stupa* is the oldest-known Buddhist religious monument and it is said that the first was a simple mound of mud to cover the remains of the Buddha after his final state of being was set free from suffering." Pembuti nodded her understanding.

"A very important part of every *stupa* is what we call the 'Tree of Life,' which is a wooden pole covered with valuable gems and inside which we store thousands of handwritten mantras. We place this *tree* in the centre of the stupa during a special ceremony, while we hold colourful ribbons connected to it. Together, all the nuns make our most positive and powerful wishes, and we believe these wishes are stored in the Tree of Life and give energy to the stupa, thus empowering it to function for the benefit of all sentient beings." Pembuti listened intently, trying to absorb it all, and thought that if she understood the knowledge contained in the stupa then maybe her future might be set on the path she saw for herself.

"I know this is a bit much for you to take in so soon, but you have to start somewhere," said Ani-Dolma matter-of-factly. "I will now tell you about the fires of greed, hatred, and delusion." Pembuti nodded, her eyes widening. "These fires," she said, "are blown out upon death of the body, but only happens to those who attained complete *awakening*, otherwise the fires will still rage on." Immediately Pembuti thought of the fire that had always been kept burning in their tent, the smoke rising in billows out of the hole in the roof and out into the sky—day and night. If only she could have her family back, she thought, and now wondered if she'd lost it all through the fires of greed, hatred, and delusion Ani-Dolma spoke of, and if there was something she could do to fix it. As Pembuti came out of her daydream she heard Ani-Dolma talking about "enlightenment," and since she'd not been listening closely, decided this meant some sort of knowledge involving *light*.

At last they came to the building where Ani-Dolma said her horse could bed down. As they entered the wooden structure, Pembuti saw goats, sheep, and some donkeys in the large open area that made up most of the structure. Ani-Dolma pointed to a fenced-off area with a wooden gate at the far end of the building, and instructed Pembuti to get the horse food and water using a spare bucket. And when she'd finished tending her horse, she was to meet her at the main building just across a courtyard that opened out from the other end of the barn. Pembuti would have preferred to stay with her horse (sleep with him, curled up, safe and warm) but knew this wasn't possible so she did as told, promising to return as soon as she could to take him out into the wide-open countryside. She, like him, wanted to ride with the wind under the light of the stars and moon, as if it would carry her fears and woes off into the night time sky.

As her eyes adjusted to the bright sunlight of the courtyard, Pembuti could make out three separate buildings, one directly ahead and two others to either side of her: *Which one did Ani-Dolma mean?* The doors to the building to her left were the nearest so she decided to try them. (Besides, they were beautifully-painted and had large and inviting shiny handles draped in prayer flags beckoning her to turn them and enter.) Rotating one, Pembuti put her weight against the solid timber of the door and found herself stepping from the bright daylight into a darker scene. As she squinted to adapt to the dimness she could make out intricately-painted images on the side walls, set out in all the colours of the rainbow. And more. Pictures of gods, monsters, dragons, and people whose bodies and faces seemed to come alive in the flickering light from rows of lit butter lamps stretched out on shelves along the entire length of the walls. These lines of small dancing flames drew Pembuti's gaze to the far end wall where sat Gautama Buddha, his cherubic face and seated body picked out in lustrous gold paint. This was the largest and most impressive statue of the Buddha she'd ever seen.

The statue's presence seemed, almost, to fill the entire width and height of the wall, and his benevolent and compassionate smile brought lightness and calm to all surrounding it. Row upon row of lit candles were set out below the Buddha's feet, which in turn shed their glow onto other smaller statues of the Buddha painstakingly and precisely placed in individual alcoves so as to cover what remained of the bare stone walls. This dazzling display of yellow, orange, and gold played out by the statues and lit candles was dramatically interrupted by two figures placed at either side of the Buddha's feet: one a crystal-like white, the other a verdant green. Both, Pembuti recognised, were statues of the goddess Tara; White Tara the goddess of *compassion*, and Green Tara the goddess of *enlightenment*. Of course, it occurred to her, the nuns would revere female deities as well as the Buddha. This she realised must be the nunnery's temple and far more powerful than the simple *chodoms* and altars the nomads used to honour the Buddha.

Pembuti's eyes had by now adjusted to the subtle light of the temple and she began to take in more details of her wondrous surroundings. As she looked upwards she could see shafts of daylight play across the ceiling; light invited in through narrow slits cut at intervals near the top of the walls. These narrow openings also let in breaths of wind that gently swayed large *thangkas* which hung from the ceiling. These colourful sails of woven fabric told stories of the Buddha's life in images so that others might learn of his compassion and wisdom. Directly below two of these *thangkas* were two large brass gongs fixed by ruby-red cords into a heavy timber frame resting implacably on the building's stone floor; the wooden pommels for each gong hung impatiently on hooks on the frames' sides, waiting to strike the malleable metal and send a resonance of such power that might shake the entire building. Next to each of these impressive metal disks set a burnished copper trumpet, standing at attention, held in its own sparse-but-complete carved timber support (and like the gongs, waiting to send out its own unique resounding message of praise).

Pembuti stood in awe at the sights before her. Nothing the nomads had in their possession came anywhere near the scale of devotion the nuns made to their Tibetan deities and Buddhas. Even their written scripture rolls far outnumbered the nomads' own; the nuns seemed to possess scores of them, all neatly stacked in rows within open timber cupboards. And to finish off such an inspiring scene were a few basic wooden chairs and some colourful cushions laid out in rows on the hard and cold stone floor.

Pembuti's other senses now began to respond to the temple: she could smell and feel the sour warmth of the burning butter lamps, and the hint of extinguished juniper incense. The touch of the stone floor was *cool* rather than cold--as was that of the timber and fabric that she could reach. And she could sense something else: there was no sound, but also no silence! Whatever it was, it was pleasing to her ears as if innumerable voices were whispering lightly in tones of compassion and hope, making her mind feel peaceful and at ease, offering her inner strength and protection. This entrancing mood seemed to dwell and linger within Pembuti and the lightness she felt made her want to never leave this haven of peace. Yet somewhere in the recesses of her mind the voice of the old nun, Ani-Dolma, sounded--breaking the spell. She looked for the door she'd entered, ran to it and opened it, and stepped back into the glare of the harsh midday sun. She peered round the courtyard but there was no voice, and no Ani-Dolma.

Without direction or intent, Pembuti made her way to the next building on her left; the one at the far end of the courtyard. Unlike the temple doors, the handles on these doors were plain and uninviting, yet she turned one and stepped inside. This space, like the temple, was empty of people and by contrast had none of the colour, reverence, and inner warmth the temple had offered her. This building had bare mud and stone walls with regimented small openings to let in light. Rows of raw timber trestles and benches worn down by use were lined up along the floor. At one end was a separate room with an large, open doorway: but no door. At the other end, pressed hard against the wall, were a series of tall timber cupboards with their doors securely closed. Pembuti sniffed the air: there was a familiar scent to it so she walked toward the open doorway and peered in. There were ranges of tables, pots, pans, and utensils hanging from metal racks, and in the centre of the room, stoves. Indeed, the smell was familiar: it was of cold butter tea, cooked meat, and *tsampa*. This building was where the nuns cooked and gathered for their meals.

With nothing more to explore in the dining room, Pembuti turned and walked back out of the uninviting door: *Ani-Dolma must be in the last building!* she thought. As she made her way diagonally across the courtyard to the final set of doors, Pembuti noticed a detached stone wall, or rather, a stone *frame* round a long row of brass cylinder prayer wheels. These wheels had a spindle at each end that was securely attached at the top and bottom to the surrounding stone. As she approached the wheels her right hand instinctively reached out and brushed the cold, carved metal surface of the first wheel, and watched in silence as it turned. She then walked slowly down the line of prayer wheels, brushing each one with her fingertips in turn. Pembuti knew the wheels always turned in the same direction, reflecting the passage of the sun across the sky. This was also the same direction in which the prayers and mantras were written within the wheel. The spinning motion released the messages of the prayers into the world and helped the individual spinning the wheel see the channels, or *nadis*, through which the energy of their *chakras* flowed. Her mother had once told her that trying to become *one* with the motion of the wheel would move one forward with compassion and forethought on the path to enlightenment (though she had never quite understood what that meant). As Pembuti now pressed her hand against the cold metal of the wheels, she desperately tried to think and feel happy thoughts. She knew she was meant to send forth good thoughts to everyone and everything, just as the turning wheels were meant to send out theirs. But her emotions were raw and she found it difficult to summon the strength to feel kindness for herself--or for others. Still, when Pembuti had finished turning the wheels, she felt a calming energy that made her feel less anxious about her new surroundings.

"Good. So, you have been looking round, have you, Pembuti," a voice said. Pembuti looked out and saw Ani-Dolma waiting in the doorway of the last building, so she quickened her step to join her. "This building is our residence," she said. "Follow me and I will show you to your room." Entering through the heavy dark wooden door, Pembuti followed Ani-Dolma down a long narrow corridor. This was a two-story structure and at the end of the corridor was a staircase leading up to the second floor. Half way along the hall Ani-Dolma stopped at an open door. "This, Pembuti, is your room. Go inside," she said, waving her in. Pembuti saw that there was a single bed with grey woollen blankets draped across it, a small table with two lit butter-lamps, and a vertical opening in the wall which permitted a single beam of light entry. Through it she could see a sliver of the Dharma Courtyard. "I suppose you are not used to staying in a room of this kind, child . . . " Ani-Dolma said in a kindly, understanding voice.

"No, I am not. I-I am not sure I will be able to get used to this. Could I maybe sleep outside?" said Pembuti.

"I am sorry, Pembuti, but sleeping outside is not possible. But I can promise you that in time you will adjust. Everyone does! For now, take your time settling in and we will meet in the dining room. I am sure you must be starving. I will wait for you there."

Pembuti knew that there was nothing for her to do now but make the best of her new surroundings—though she felt trapped, to the point that she couldn't breathe. Pembuti had to be firm with herself; she had to take control of her mind and force herself to accept her fate for the time being. She had to resign herself to the fact that this was where she would stay until she could fly free and return to nomadic life with her father. With that she opened the yak-skin pouch and emptied her mother's precious belongings onto her bed. She touched the necklace round her neck. For the moment she was back in her tent on the plateau. The nunnery could wait . . .

Chapter 9

$\backsim$

THE NEXT MORNING AT BREAKFAST Pembuti sat beside Ani-Dolma. "Good morning, Pembuti, I trust you slept well."

"Yes . . . yes, I did," replied Pembuti, surprise in her tone.

"Well, it is time to start adapting to life here at the nunnery. You will be required to join the other nuns in their daily routine as they concentrate on their Dharma practice, which will include study, chanting and meditation, and you will also share in the responsibility for the maintenance and functioning of the nunnery itself. I will personally provide you with most of your general education, but you will also be given lessons in the Dharma texts by the most learned of our nuns."

Pembuti soon discovered that the daily routine began with what they called *puja*; expressions to honour, worship, and give devotional attention by bowing, making offerings, and chanting. These devotional acts were generally performed in the morning and again in the evening--and especially during communal festivals and days of observance. They were believed to aid the cleansing of the impure mind, which resulted in the individual experiencing inner calm and joy. On these special days the nuns would intensify their devotion to deepen their knowledge and express communal commitment to their beliefs. After *puja*, breakfast was served in the dining hall and once finished, she and a few other nuns had a work period devoted to cleaning individual and community living areas. Following this, classes in Tibetan writing and literature were held, after which a communal lunch consisting of rice or steamed buns with *dahl* (lentil soup), potatoes, or vegetables was served. (In accordance with Buddhist monastic discipline, no evening meal was served but Pembuti was permitted to save a portion of her lunch to eat in the evening if she wished.) After lunch was a rest period until her logic class started at 1:00 in the afternoon. Pembuti particularly enjoyed logical discussion; loved the idea that life was really simple and that solutions to problems were easily found. She was direct in thought and deed and was not afraid to say so in the same manner.

After logic, afternoon tea was served. Then she and the nuns were given time to study independently, most of which revolved round the basic logic texts, but also texts and prayers which by tradition were to be memorized. Each day they committed a certain number of lines to memory and recited them before the elder nun who served as their teacher, and sometimes before Ani-Dolma. Pembuti was also required to attend frequent recitation sessions with the nuns. More often than not, however, she lapsed into daydreaming: her mind empty and her eyes heavy, she would dream of her mother and father and their life together (before that terrible day) and long for her father's arms round her again. She wanted so desperately to be with him; for him to tell her that everything was going back to the way it had been. Because to Pembuti, the nunnery was suffocating. She doubted she could ever adapt.

To Pembuti, the unyielding walls kept the outside world out—but provided none of the imposing power and security of the great mountains. And while the smell of burning incense would sometimes relax and remind her of her tent out on the plains, it quickly grew stale and stifled behind the walls--unable to drift freely across the plateau. Pembuti craved the open spaces; she felt like a caged bird inside the nunnery. So late at night she would sneak out to the forest to recite the sacred texts aloud, where she felt an inner peace come over her, and most importantly, was awake in the moment: smelling the wondrous scents from the flora and fauna that abounded there. Pembuti felt free there.

Pembuti made time to talk with her horse every day, trying desperately to hold onto her past memories: of when she was free to ride across the open plain without a care in the world; where she was free from all the fear the Chinese (and now some of the nuns) had instilled in her. She'd grown up a creature of the wilds--carefree and in love with the world and all that was in it--but now felt herself a trapped animal. And she missed her dog Mingma terribly (he'd gone on with her father) and wondered if she'd ever see him again. The nuns (and Ani-Dolma) knew Pembuti would sneak out at night but only mildly chastised her, cautioning her against the dangers that lurked in the forest. But each visit further sparked ideas of how to find a way back to her old life, to her father, and those who were part of the nomadic life she'd known.

Every night before bed, when she should have been fast asleep, Pembuti would bring out her mother's collection of trinkets. She cupped the smooth gemstones in the palms of her hands, trying to absorb what energy from her mother they might still possess. The precious and delicate silver chains she entwined through her fingers; these strands of fine metal which held the ruby, emerald, and turquoise-coloured gems together also became links to Pembuti's past. The exquisite necklace would be ceremoniously hung from her neck; the large base gem she would press to her heart. Sometimes she would carefully position all the glittering bobbles on her bedside table (as if creating a shrine to her mother) but as she would drift off to sleep, thoughts of her mother and her jewellery would be replaced by visions of the *dakini* set round the nunnery; which seemed to come alive when she entered deep sleep. In these dream-visions she would be travelling across the sky, moving through space, becoming a sky-walker who could dance between the different realms of the stars with the lightness of air. Out there she was *free*: free of the physical confines of her bedroom, free of the nunnery walls, and free from outside influences. She was just herself. And in this free state she would encounter deities, apparitions, and fellow travellers.

One particular female apparition who appeared to her on a regular basis, Pembuti came to believed was her *protector*. She began to feel that she knew this apparition well. And she believed that while the apparition taught her from the sacred Buddhist texts about life and death, she also showed her how to separate her mind from her body, thus enabling her to continue to develop her true self and become one with the very core of her being. The apparition had told Pembuti that she must have the courage to protect these spoken teachings of wisdom, as they were hers alone:

In one dream Pembuti would long remember, she had the sensation that she were being covered in black feathers and hair--a dream which quickly turned from dream to nightmare with Pembuti waking up gasping for air and quite terrified. The next day during her lessons with Ani-Dolma Pembuti decided to share this dream. Ani-Dolma thought for a moment and then said, "Perhaps there is a legend that will be of comfort to you." Pembuti listened closely. "It is said that back in the Fifteenth Century as many as one-hundred thousand female Buddhas sacrificed their black hair to form a crown and offered it to the Fifth Karmapa as a symbol of his great accomplishments. As you may know, the Karmapa is a self-appointed incarnate lama who is the head of the Kagyu School of Tibetan Buddhism. Well, the Chinese Emperor Yung Lo, because of his teachings from the Karmapa, had become aware of a strange presence of power and energy round the Karmapa's head, which, to the Emperor, materialised as a black crown. The Emperor, so impressed by what he saw, offered to have a physical replica made so that others who were not so developed in their teachings could see this energy when they received a blessing from the Karmapa. Hence, a crown encrusted with precious stones and topped by a huge ruby was commissioned and presented to the Karmapa. Now the "Black Crown" signifies the Karmapa's power to benefit all sentient beings and has become the emblem of the oldest reincarnating Tibetan lineage, which is passed down through all Karmapas." Pembuti smiled. And while this story brought Pembuti comfort, she hoped this dream would never repeat.

Although Pembuti did well in many of her studies, she struggled to understand much of what the nuns tried to teach her about the *Dharma*, the Buddha and the Karmapas, and longed for something to take her from the daily routine. One day her wish came true. It was during the time of good weather that the nuns announced that they were going to embark on a special journey (a pilgrimage) to Heavenly Lake (Lake Namtso), and that Pembuti was to come along. This she thought would be like a holiday; away from the routine . . . the chores and the meditation . . . and a chance, perhaps, to just enjoy. Although for the most part the nuns lived in isolation, from time to time travellers would arrive at the monastery and bring news from Lhasa and places beyond--and the latest news was not good: the Chinese were taking over. There were stories of the Chinese Army killing innocent people--lamas, monks, men, women, and children--and because of these tales, Ani-Dolma was more determined that their pilgrimage should go ahead.

As Pembuti dressed for the journey, she decided to wear her mother's turquoise necklace under her tunic. Lifting it from the box she now kept it in, she began to run her fingers over and over the cold turquoise stones, trying to imagine herself as her mother when she was alive. Her father had told her that Dawa loved the necklace more than any other item she possessed, and Pembuti felt that her mother was still near when she handled it. So she decided to wear it on her journey to Lake Namtso. And as she placed the heavy necklace round her neck, she suddenly felt very grown-up and for a moment believed she *was* her mother. And she felt a closeness and warmth she'd not felt in a long time.

After much preparation and delegation of chores, the group of nuns (including Ani-Dolma) set off on a bright and sunny morning with just a hint of chill in the air. When Pembuti asked Ani-Dolma how long they would be away, she replied that it would take as long as it took; that she could not foresee what trials they may face along the way that could impede their progress. And after all, what was *time* anyway? She told Pembuti that it is the experience, the *moment*, that was more important for them to be awake in.

The journey progressed at a slow but steady pace to accommodate the older nuns, and took three days to complete. On the third day the flat plateau gave way to a rise in ground that gradually ascended up towards a range of snow-covered peaks. Ani-Dolma pointed to two peaks ahead and a pass running between them and calmly stated that this was where they were heading. It turned out to be an arduous climb which they took carefully; their feet picking out the safest route between the boulders, rocks, and scree that littered the way. The rough and treacherous ground caused many of them to slip--some even falling to their knees--but they quickly picked themselves up or were helped to their feet, silently trudging forward. As the group crested the pass, the Heavenly Lake came into view. Pembuti could not believe what she saw.

Her hands instinctively reached up to grasp the necklace round her neck, as she gasped for air--seeing below her the largest turquoise gemstone she'd ever seen! Its power washed over her in waves, giving off the most intense glow she'd ever felt in her life. The entire blue sky was reflected in it as were the snow-covered mountain peaks in the distance. *Is that a stone? Or is it some kind of giant glass mirror like I saw grown-ups look into at the festivals?* Ani-Dolma saw the perplexed look on Pembuti's face and smiled and said, "That is simply *water!* The clearest, bluest water in Tibet, bestowed upon us by the mountain gods! As yet pure and untainted by human hands." *Water?* Pembuti thought of the water and the waterwheel at the nunnery . . . the rushing waters of the deep gorges and mountain passes of her family's fateful last journey . . . even the meagre water they drank on their travels across the plateau. Those were nothing compared to the sight now before her!

As the devout group descended and the Heavenly Lake grew nearer, Pembuti could just make out ripples shimmering across the surface of this prodigious water. And as she watched it move it crossed her mind (for no explicable reason) that this *must* be where her mother had got her necklace from! The iridescent turquoise colour was drawing her closer . . . pulling her in . . . she had to get closer to it! To touch it— just as she could the necklace! She felt like running ahead but the path was steep and rocky and the ground beneath her loose and treacherous. So she moved cautiously, at the nuns' pace, taking in the majesty of the sight as they grew nearer and nearer. When they finally reached the water's edge Pembuti couldn't wait to *touch* the colour; she bent down, her heart pounding, and reached out to it. To her surprise, its surface easily gave way to her fingers--icy-cold like the snows of the mountains.

Suddenly awash in peace, Pembuti wanted to tell Ani-Dolma *every-thing*. Everything she felt. About her life. About the anger she now harboured. About her loneliness. About the attachment she felt to the necklace and how it brought her near to her dead mother. She wanted to ask how, even now, surrounded by such beauty, she felt such anger inside. Why it was as if a red mist enveloped her body that made her want to lash out at someone; especially the Chinese! She knew it wasn't like her to be this way--but had no idea how to rid herself of these feelings! She needed someone who could understand her. (All this she wanted to share with Ani-Dolma.)

When she stood up and looked out, all she could see was an expanse of blindingly-beautiful colours moving randomly across the lake's surface as the sun's rays danced across it. And as she looked out to the far horizon, all was blue; there was no separation of sky and water, it was all *one*. She knew of the separate elements of life—of earth, air, water, fire, and space--and their respective colours; she'd been taught this by her mother and father, and now the nuns. But here, air and water seemed to merge into one. Pembuti's thoughts were so transfixed by the waters of the lake that she at first failed to notice the rest of her surroundings.

She now noticed that other groups of pilgrims were walking round the lake, all in the same direction; some chanting mantras, others deep in contemplation, while slowly slipping their prayer beads through their fingers. The most dedicated prostrated themselves by dropping to their knees then stretching out their arms, palms down, stretched out flat on the stony ground with their face resting on the hard surface every few steps of their journey. As Pembuti's group joined this random procession of monks, nuns, and lamas they began their own clockwise journey and as they went, Pembuti noticed small *cairns* and various sized *stupas*, all with brightly-coloured prayer flags caught in the steady breeze. The flags were strung out in repeating sets of five colours (representing the five elements) and arranged from left-to-right in a specific order: blue, white, red, green, and then yellow. Blue symbolized the sky and space; white, the air and wind; red, fire; green, water; and yellow symbolized earth. According to traditional Tibetan medicine, health and harmony are produced through the balance of these five elements/colors.

Pembuti saw pilgrims there who were busy removing old and worn strings of flags, and replacing them with bright and fresh flags to carry their prayers on the winds across the lake and beyond. Ani-Dolma gave Pembuti a nudge--and with a slight shove, she moved forward.

Leaving the lake the group then proceeded on towards their destination and, after hours of walking, the monastery they intended to visit for the night came into view. Pembuti saw that the two large rocky outcrops near the monastery were draped with prayer flags and white *khatas*. Approaching the walls of the monastery, they gained entrance by ringing the bell and asking for refuge for the night. Once inside they finished the last morsels of their lunch and bedded down on the hard stone floor of one of the large rooms provided.

Pembuti woke before sunrise the next morning to the sounds of the horns and drums the monks used to call worshipers to morning mediation. Sleepily she pulled herself up from the hard floor; she felt sore and stiff. Her feet ached and as she sat down to look closer she saw blisters on her heels and toes. Her worn leather shoes seemed too small as she tried to pull them on. Ani-Dolma appeared and suggested that she leave her shoes off for the time being. Together they walked toward the main temple to join in meditation and prayer. And once inside the temple, Pembuti was amazed:

She smelt the rich incense as it burned in long flat wooden holders upon the altar. The altar itself was in the centre of the temple and at the back of it Pembuti noticed many small round metal bowls of water, as well as a large bell, a *dorge*, and images of the Dalai Lama and other lamas. There were richly coloured *thankas* that hung down from the walls creating a warm feeling of joy. Her eyes were drawn to the enormous statue of the Buddha behind the alter which was completely covered in a gold colour. The temple, to Pembuti, seemed to be a mass of vibrant gold, yellow, orange, red, and blue--all illuminated by beams of light that shone down from small slits in the top of the high walls just under the roof.

At the top of the isle on either side sat monks in a regimented line on brightly-coloured cushions, playing conch-shell trumpets. Pembuti watched as they blew into the shell openings (made by cutting off the spiral tips) and regarded the other monks who were clashing together small hand cymbals attached by string. (When struck they created a clear, resonating sound which began to calm and clear her mind.) She began to focus on her breathing as she'd been taught at the nunnery.

Ani-Dolma gestured for her to sit down on one of the cushions in the row near the back of the temple. After an hour of morning meditation and prayer, which the resident lama presided over, Pembuti felt herself in a trance. She felt relaxed and reluctant to leave. Ani-Dolma decided to leave her sitting, absorbed in her thoughts, for a while. She was so pleased that at last Pembuti had somehow managed to embrace the way of meditation.

After an unknown span of time had passed, Pembuti slowly opened her eyes. Although nothing had changed in the temple, it was as if everything solid was far away; as if there was an opaque mist in front of her eyes. She strained to bring back in focus the altar, the floor, and the walls. The mist gradually dissipated and everything again became clear. She stood and walked up the isle to the heavy temple door. Just as she was about to open it, the door opened inward: she stopped in her tracks, hands by her sides, motionless. There in front of her was a strikingly handsome monk. This man, she knew, was no ordinary monk. He was grandly dressed in the darkest claret robes she'd ever seen, lined with gold braiding. His tanned, olive-coloured round face beamed with radiance that touched her deeply. She was immediately overcome by feelings of joy.

As she stared at him she noticed his eyes drop to the turquoise necklace round her neck. He then raised his eyes to meet hers and gave a smile of recognition. He turned to the monk nearest him and spoke softly. With that the monk bowed and produced a white scarf, which he handed to the claret-robed monk. The monk held the white scarf in his upturned palms, said a few words over it, then turned and draped it carefully round Pembuti's neck. He stepped back and smiled.

Pembuti wracked her brains to place his face: it was as if she'd met him before, as if she already knew him. Just then one of the monk's followers whispered into his ear and ushered him past Pembuti, deeper into temple. (Their brief but enlightening meeting was over.) Excitedly, Pembuti descended the steps of the temple to look for Ani-Dolma and the rest of the nuns, and found them at the far end of the courtyard. Keen to tell Ani-Dolma of meeting the mysterious monk, she related what had just occurred and showed her the scarf, asking the elder nun if she knew who he was. Ani-Dolma confirmed what Pembuti had assumed; this was no ordinary monk but one of the most revered spiritual leaders of their faith: the 16th Karmapa himself.

For the remainder of the pilgrimage Pembuti joined the nuns circling the shore of the lake, her blistered feet healed with ointment the nuns had given her. As the nuns dutifully carried out their own meditations, Pembuti was deep in her own private thoughts; she kept going over in her mind her encounter with the Karmapa. On completion of the nuns' pilgrimage round the lake the group retraced their steps back over the mountain pass and toward the nunnery; all satisfied with the outcome of their journey.

Chapter 10

As HER TIME AT THE nunnery passed, Pembuti desired to be more involved with the ritualistic aspects of a Buddhist nun's way of life. She would sit in the temple and meditate on the beautifully coloured *thankas*, having come to appreciate their content and meaning. And she became more aware of the meaning behind the rites the nuns carried out. For example, the reason they bowed three times before the statue of the Buddha was to honour the Buddha, his teachings, and their devout community. Pembuti observed the nuns recite mantras and prayers as they made offerings. They would place seven water bowls in front of the Buddha statue, which were diligently filled--all to the exact same level--then emptied with the same patience and precision. This was practiced along with a plentiful supply of lit butter candles, flowers, burning incense, fruit, and purposeful use of a bell. As water is a staple of life, a pure sample is offered to show respect and reverence for life. Similarly, flowers symbolise their belief that everything is impermanent in the cycle of birth, life, death (flowers bud, grow, wilt, and re-grow), candles represent enlightenment and the sense of sight, while burning incense shows that the Buddhist teachings can be spread across the world just like the fragrant smoke it produces.

But despite her interest, Pembuti often struggled to understand all that was being imparted to her. So Ani-Dolma, a patient and diligent teacher, never hurried Pembuti, making sure she was given ample time to absorb all that was being said. And she'd explained to Pembuti that there was a tradition that any accumulated merits the nuns had gathered from praying and chanting were to be dedicated to all sentient beings. Pembuti questioned the reasoning of this practice: *Does this mean I will have to spend my free time gaining merits, only to give them away and start all over again?* (She hoped that anyone who received her hard-earned merits would look after them.)

Before her visit to Lake Namtso, Pembuti had watched the nuns create *mandalas*, the elaborate pictures and diagrams made from individual grains of sand—created, ironically, only to be destroyed after completion. This she could not understand. Now the nuns allowed her to help create their *mandalas*, teaching her how to take proper care to ensure that every detail was the best possible. They formed pictures of sky, forests, lakes, and rivers, as well as Buddhist symbols and deities. Everything was done with the utmost concentration, dedication, and focus of the mind. Creating these intricate designs could take days--even weeks--but the nuns stuck diligently to their task and placed each grain of sand with care and intent. This, Pembuti came to realise, was like reciting mantras and prayers, and all the other rituals they carried out; to teach them humility and ways of the *Dharma*. When all the nuns agreed that a mandala was complete, it would be scattered to the wind--sending its message from the nunnery out across the plateau. Its creation and destruction symbolised the transient nature of the physical form, and by beginning a new mandala, rebirth and the continuing cycle of life.

Ani-Dolma and the other nuns noticed a change in Pembuti following their visit to Lake Namtso. She appeared more settled and thoughtful, and to their minds, was progressing well with her lessons in the ways of the "Three Noble Truths," the teachings of the Buddha. Such was Ani-Dolma's confidence in Pembuti that she allowed her to begin accompanying the nuns on their regular visits to the local village. Daily life at the nunnery continued as it long had, with little disruption; the occasional traveller or visiting monk would bring news from the out-side world, most of which now concerned stories about the occupying Chinese. For Pembuti's part she became more resigned and accepting of the ways of the nuns and general life at the nunnery. Recognising this change in herself she thought it was, perhaps, just part of growing up. But her young and adventurous streak was still with her, and most apparent when she'd travel to the local village; the ideal situation to ex-ercise her independence, she felt.

On the mornings of these village visits Pembuti would wake herself bright and early and keen to get on with her morning prayers so that she could set off as early as possible. On one such visit, she met a hand-some and young Western-looking man. He was tall and slim with pierc-ing blue eyes, blonde curly hair, and an enchanting, infectious smile. From time to time the nuns put on shows for the villagers as a means of religious education, in return for food and supplies, and on this visit when the nuns commenced their performance, Pembuti sneaked off and made her way to the open-air market. And almost immediately, her eyes caught sight of a young man leaning against a market stall smoking a cigarette and laughing at something his friend (an older Westerner) had said. Pembuti became transfixed in this moment: her heart fluttered, she became nervous, and a tingling sensation came to her stomach. (She was unusually drawn to him.) The young man watched as she walked towards him--also becoming transfixed; he too felt unusually nervous at the sight of this dark-eyed, dark-haired Tibetan girl. Distracted, she dropped the basket she was carrying, and he rushed over to help her. While picking up her goods he looked down at her as she looked up, and their eyes locked. He asked her name. She didn't understand a word he said (having heard so little English) but she smiled back. Sudden Pembuti felt faint-- he held out his arms to catch her.

He is a charmer, she thought, and could not resist returning a coy smile and girlish giggle. He told her his name was William but that all his friends called him "Bill"--and that she should as well. He said he was known as the man who could beguile the birds from the trees--as he pointed to a group of crows circling above their heads—which she did not understand. She continued to smile at him as they walked together down the street, trying to find words to share. As an afterthought, Bill turned round and waved goodbye to his Western friend. Exchanging furtive glances and smiles, they continued to stroll round the market, occasionally stopping at a trader's stall where Bill would point to an object and in something resembling Tibetan would tell Pembuti what he thought it was. To her surprise, he sometimes got the name right. And when he didn't, she'd burst out laughing—and he'd follow. Nearby traders and shoppers took notice of what was passing between them--but Pembuti didn't care. She was enjoying herself. She had never felt like this before and the excitement only grew.

When their laughter would subside, they'd just look at each other. Often stopping to exchange knowing glances. Bill would touch her arm, caress her hand, sending tingles through her body that were both warm and tender. (Any guilt that sought to remind her she pushed to the back of her mind). Soon they were walking hand-in-hand beyond the marketplace, lost in each other's company, and Pembuti found herself at a house where she assumed he lived. As if in a trance-- she'd never been so overwhelmed by emotion--it all seemed so *natural*. She *had* to be with him. She'd spend the rest of her life with him; he need only ask. He led her into the house and through the first door on the right; into his room. Immediately they fell onto the bed, passionately kissing and holding each other; frantically undressing each other, their hands exploring each other's body before finally making love. For Pembuti, time lost all meaning . . .

Pembuti never wanted to leave that room. As she lay there nearly naked in his arms, she waited for him to ask her to stay forever. But as the shadows lengthened in the late afternoon, he gently shook her and pointed to her clothes. Pembuti couldn't believe that he just sat there in bed smoking a cigarette, watching her dress. She felt shame. She felt violated. Disbelieving of his now unfeeling attitude towards her. She'd foolishly believed that what they'd shared was special to them both. She turned her back and left the house--and never looked back.

Over the next few months Pembuti felt ill more and more frequently; particularly in the morning. She became listless and out of sorts. She was in love and in her mind had given her body, mind, and spirit to him. And Pembuti's state didn't go unnoticed by Ani-Dolma.

"Pembuti, I have been observing you. Am I right in assuming that you are with child?" Pembuti hung her head and nodded. "I am at a complete loss to know how this could be so," Ani-Dolma said, laying her hand on Pembuti's shoulder. Pembuti could only stare down at the floor in shame. She'd not for a moment considered the long-term consequences of a few stolen moments of bliss with the Scottish man. And now she'd have to tell Ani-Dolma the careless thing she'd done. As she did, she resigned herself to make this right. She had to find this charming man again.

Before the nuns' next trip to the village, Pembuti rehearsed what she would say to her lover; she had to tell him that she was pregnant. She would hold his hand to her stomach and he would understand that he had to save her; had to take her away from the nunnery to a place where she and her baby would want for nothing. So, during the next visit to the village Pembuti stole away from the nuns (as planned) and rushed to the house where he'd taken her that fateful day. Murders of crows and ravens perched on the surrounding rooftops were startled by the commotion caused by the arrival of the young woman--swooping down and almost touching Pembuti's head. As she approached, an old woman was sitting in a chair by the front door; a woman called Amo but known throughout the village and surrounding farms as a "seer" and medicine woman. As she gazed into Pembuti's eyes, all she could see was black; no light. She intuitively knew Pembuti's future.

Suddenly the old woman's heart grew heavy. Caught up in a vision, she sensed Pembuti's aching spirit. But she also knew with certainty that the pain she was now suffering was small compared to what was yet to come. Amo saw the wild child, the free spirit within her, and knew that Pembuti's heart would harden and that she would be alone for most of her life because of it. But while this would certainly come to pass, Pembuti would accomplish great things for her people even so . . .

Suddenly the old woman felt Pembuti tug on the worn sleeve of her dress—and returned to the present. As she did a mist passed before her eyes and she took a deep breath; she exhaled. She knew it was her time to move on to the next world. Just as Pembuti was about to ask after the young Scotsman, she saw in the old woman's face a strange urgency, and watched as a wide, vertical trail of coloured mist travelled outward and upward from the old woman's head—as she drew her final breath. Pembuti blinked to check her vision--but the mist had gone. Had she seen it, or just imaged it? Just then Pembuti noticed a foreigner coming out of Amo's house. She recognised him as the man who'd been with her blond-haired lover that day at the market.

Seeing the old woman now slumped in her chair, the man quickly rushed to her, knelt down and felt her wrist. He could not find a pulse. He turned to Pembuti and slowly lowered his head with a look of resignation on his face. He reached up and gently closed Amo's eyelids. Just then a younger woman came running out of the house and fell to her knees before the woman. She took out a string of Tibetan prayer beads and began to move each bead slowly in turn as she wept. Shaken and her legs about to buckle beneath her—Pembuti felt an arm steady her before she collapsed. She looked up to see a kind and reassuring smile. In broken Tibetan the man said his name was Alexander and then asked what she was doing at the house. The girl mumbled something about *the marketplace* and *nuns*, so he took her by the hand and, as best he could, told her he would help her find them. On the way he again asked her name and she reluctantly told him Pembuti, but did not volunteer more. He smiled and held her tightly as they hurriedly made their way toward the marketplace. There, Alexander spotted a group of nuns gathering their texts and *thangkas* after having performed to interested market-traders and buyers, which they did in exchange for food and clothing, per custom.

Alexander pointed towards the group and Pembuti nodded her agreement. As they walked across the open square he saw that one of the nuns had turned and was now walking toward them. He recognised her as Ani-Dolma, one of the senior nuns from the nearby nunnery. As they approached she acknowledged Pembuti and the Western-looking man leading her by the hand: knew him as "Alexander," the Scottish doctor. He had on occasion visited her nunnery to offer medical help when the nuns needed it. Ani-Dolma knew him as a kind and honest young man who had a passion for peoples' well-being, irrespective of age or social status. He'd been part of the Indian Medical Service and after his tour of duty with the British Mission had been asked by the Tibetan Government in Lhasa if he'd consider staying on and assisting in introducing Western methods of healthcare to compliment traditional Tibetan medicine. As a young and adventurous man of medicine who'd become enamoured with Tibet and its people, he was only too willing to accept. But as Ani-Dolma also knew, this had not gone down well with his wife, Fiona, a nurse who'd tried to adapt to a longer stay in Tibet but eventually decided to return to Scotland. Part of Alexander's work was now to tour the villages, monasteries, and nunneries in the outlying areas of the Lhasa region—within which jurisdiction the nunnery fell.

As Alexander and Ani-Dolma met, he released Pembuti's hand and gave a traditional Tibetan bow; she in turn bowed back. Ani-Dolma spoke a few words to Pembuti, who nodded and then joined the rest of the nuns. Alexander, still concerned about the young girl's plight, slowly and deliberately asked in his best Tibetan: "What do you think made Pembuti so upset? And why, do you suppose, she went to that particular house?" Ani-Dolma was at first reluctant to confide in Alexander, but knowing he was a compassionate man of medicine, decided to trust him. She drew near and said:

"Pembuti is with child, and she refuses to name the father. Knowing the anguish she is going through, I have not pressed her." When Alexander heard this he looked over to Pembuti, who was staring back at him from amongst the nuns. He could make out clearly her dark eyes and gave her a supportive smile. The old nun went on to say, "I have no idea why Pembuti would go to that particular house but I wonder if perhaps that is where she met the father. Perhaps he lives there."

Alexander thought a moment before he spoke. "Well, as far as I know the house belongs to the local seer, Amo, and her daughter, and I know of no Tibetan males living there. I did, however, have occasion to take a few days' lodging with Amo myself a while back, at which time I met another Scotsman, a younger, blond-haired man who called himself Bill, travelling across Tibet carrying out, as he put it, 'research into the flora and fauna of the region.' At the time I thought this an unusual occupation, and that the chap was most likely a bit of an adventurer and fortune seeker. But thinking us two kindred spirits, as it were--both a long way from home and in a strange land—I arranged for him to take the room next to mine." Alexander and Ani-Dolma looked at each other and immediately drew the same conclusion; Alexander's face turned pale. *"Of course!"* He now remembered seeing Pembuti with the other Scotsman several weeks before.

Alexander had practiced medicine in Tibet for a while by this time and was becoming familiar with Tibetan ways and culture, but still, it was comforting to spend time with another Westerner—which he'd come to see as a bit of a rare treat. Alexander now recalled their many conversations—a few taking place over bottles of local beer—in one of which Bill had said that he'd been, among other things, a chef with the British Trade Commission in Lhasa. He'd also confided that since there was nothing waiting for him back in the U.K., after fulfilling his responsibilities he'd decided to stay in the country and "seek adventure--and maybe his fortune," armed with just his "confidence, good looks, and a British passport!" According to him there was work to be had catering to rich Tibetan nobles and aristocracy who were keen to sample Western cuisine and culture. And while this had largely worked out for him (bragging of living one long adventure) Bill had wanted to get away from Lhasa for a while and ended up in this little village amongst the more traditional, and *poorer*, Tibetans. (Alexander had great doubts—which he kept to himself--that such simple people were ready for such a gregarious and forthright person as "Bill." In fact, as Alexander had considered, he was not at all backward at coming forward--to the point that unsuspecting villagers would find Alexander's camera thrust into their hands, Bill providing instructions on how to take a photograph of him and his new-found "best buddy"--Alexander.

The days Alexander spent with Bill went by like a whirlwind; everything had to be done *now*--as if there were no tomorrow. Thinking back, he now remembered one particular afternoon when Bill had taken to a young and very pretty Tibetan girl, recalling that the last he'd seen of them was when Bill waved back to him as he and the girl mingled with the market crowd. The following morning Bill said it was time to move on as he had work to see to back in Lhasa. He thanked Alexander for finding him lodgings and for his company, and then he was gone.

As Alexander revived his encounter with Bill (now regretting his befriending of the philanderer) he could hear Ani-Dolma's voice in the distance--which brought him back to the present predicament. Ani-Dolma had by now decided that it would be best if the nuns saw Pembuti back to the nunnery. Alexander nodded in agreement but given what he now suspected about the girl and Bill, asked if he could visit the nunnery on occasion to see how Pembuti was progressing. Ani-Dolma nodded a knowing look of appreciation. They both clasped their hands and formally bowed farewell.

Chapter 11

ALEXANDER CONTINUED HIS WORK, OFFERING medical advice and assistance to those who would accept it. (Many locals remained leery of Western medicine.) Knowing the ways of Tibetan society he knew better than to barge straight in; he would first seek out the local landowners or nobility who held sway over the people who worked their land, and gain their approval. Most agreed to his offer as it would show them in a good light towards their people and any visiting dignitaries from Lhasa. The further east he travelled, the more the talk was about the Chinese and what they were doing to the country--and less about pleasing Lhasa. Some landowners felt that the government was too wrapped-up in the business of politics to care about what was happening in areas like the Amdo and Kham regions. Still, in his private moments, Alexander's thoughts would centre on the pretty Tibetan girl, Pembuti; her plight, Ani-Dolma, and life at the nunnery. He grew curious as to how she'd come to live with the nuns, where her parents were, and what sort of life would she have after the birth of her child.

As promised, Alexander made regular visits to the nunnery to see the girl who was, at first, a little distrustful of him. This didn't surprise Alexander given the outcome of her previous experience with a Westerner. But slowly, after a few visits, Pembuti accepted him as someone who had her and her baby's best interests at heart; even allowing him to listen to her baby through the strange Y-shaped rope he put on her stomach and stuck in his ears. For Alexander's part, he began to warm to Pembuti and saw her as more than just another patient; he felt somehow responsible for her. But in a much different way, Alexander looked forward to his visits with her: He felt an excitement . . . an anticipation . . . a school-boyish rashness as if he had to see her to make certain she was still there. (Seeing her in his mind was not enough; he had to see her in person.) Thus, his visits to the nunnery were full of anticipation.

When he arrived at the nunnery and cast his anxious eyes upon her, it was always as if he was seeing her for the first time--her face subtly different each time. Still Pembuti, he noticed that she seemed to be able to change her expression and wondered if Ani-Dolma had noticed this as well. In her company he felt strangely comfortable with her, though not complacent or familiar. And there was no denying that a tension existed between them; he dared think of it as a *spark*. At times it became so overwhelming that Alexander had to leave her company (he was, after all, a married man) only to find that he couldn't stay away for long. Pembuti's round, girlish face with its dark, almond-shaped eyes and winsome-yet-playful smile was always with him.

During one of his visits to the nunnery, Alexander enquired of Ani-Dolma Pembuti's background and her reason for living amongst them. Ani-Dolma described Pembuti's early life, as that of a nomad travelling the plateau, and how that had all suddenly changed after her family's encounter with the Chinese forces: the senseless death of her mother and her father's desire to seek revenge. And, of course, Pembuti's subsequent abandonment (or so she felt) to life in a nunnery. Ani-Dolma explained that the best they could do for her until her father returned was to educate her in the ways of a nun's life, their faith, and prepare her for later life, to be a strong yet compassionate Tibetan woman. This they'd thought they were well achieving until the pregnancy. Ani-Dolma felt that she'd failed Pembuti and her father, who'd entrusted his daughter into her care, explaining that in all the years she'd resided at the nunnery, her father had never even sent word. She'd heard from visiting travellers that fighting in the eastern regions was still on-going between the Khampas and the Chinese, and for all she knew, Pembuti's father might well be dead. Ani-Dolma confided that she was not surprised that Pembuti had strayed on one of her trips to the village. She still had an independent streak and the nuns could only instill so much. Pembuti's only visitor was a venerable itinerant lama, Lama Kunchen, who was her great-uncle. But Pembuti had no female family members to counsel her.

Once Alexander learned the details of Pembuti's difficult life, his feelings for her only deepened: this was no ordinary Tibetan girl. Over the course of his next few visits he came to see beyond her striking dark brown eyes, into the soul of this young Tibetan woman forced through circumstance beyond her control to grow up faster than her years. Still, she'd somehow managed to retain the innocent and playful nature of a child. Sometimes when he spoke with her Alexander couldn't tell if she saw him as an authority figure, playmate, or if she was flirting with him. And before he realised it, Pembuti had become more than just a patient to him. And perhaps, he thought, he was becoming more than just a doctor to her.

As her delivery-date was quickly approaching, Alexander increased his visits to see her. On one such visit, after he'd completed his medical examination, he and Pembuti hit on the subject of their families. Considering that they'd grown quite close, Alexander was happy (even relieved) to tell her about Scotland; his life there, and about his wife, Fiona. (Alexander had become quite adept at allowing his thoughts of Fiona to be replaced by Pembuti.) When it came her turn, Pembuti recounted her tragic story, just as Ani-Dolma had told it, and he felt prideful that she trusted him enough to speak openly about her life.

One day as Alexander was finishing-up his examination and Ani-Dolma was fussing round the room, there came a knock on Pembuti's door. Before Pembuti could respond, the door opened and in walked an aged and distinguished-looking lama dressed in flowing maroon-coloured robes. "Good day to you all, my friends," he said; then regarding Alexander, "I am Lama Kunchen." Alexander watched as Ani-Dolma rushed forward, sunk reverentially to her knees, and pressed the lama's hand to her forehead. Lama Kunchen smiled and nodded to Alexander whilst bidding Ani-Dolma to rise to her feet, reprimanding her for being so *formal*. "Ani-Dolma, after all, Alexander and I are here in *your* nunnery! Mere men in a woman's world!" he said, humourously. When Pembuti realised that it was her great-uncle, her face lit up and she rushed to him, her arms outstretched. Lama Kunchen gently wrapped his arms round her as she snuggled herself into the billowing folds of his robes. At this touching show of affection, Alexander and Ani-Dolma quietly slipped out of the room, closing the door behind them, leaving Pembuti and her great-uncle to themselves.

Ani-Dolma knew that Alexander would have many questions for her, as well as answers to provide about Pembuti's condition. Walking together to the refectory, Ani-Dolma invited him to sit on one of the long benches that ran the length of the table, while she sat down across from him. A moment later an attending nun arrived with two mugs of piping-hot buttered tea. They sat quietly sipping the warming liquid, Ani-Dolma noticing the puzzled look on Alexander's face. "Tell me what is troubling you, Alexander."

"So, what of Lama Kunchen, Ani-Dolma?" Alexander asked; hesitation in his tone. "Pembuti seems to be very *fond* of him." Alexander knew of their kinship and had seen the tenderness between them, but still felt compelled to inquire as to the nature of their relationship.

"I know little about him, personally," Ani-Dolma began, "but I do know that he is quite old, quite wise, and known throughout Tibet for his teachings and wise counselling. He has, over the years, visited us many times here at the nunnery and has fascinated us with stories from times long passed, and about the strange foreign lands beyond the great mountains he has seen. He seems especially fond of Westerners—and has told us of those he has come across during his travels—and has made us understand that while many come here seeking fortune, not all Westerners are bad!" (Alexander thought he saw Ani-Dolma hide a grin.) "And he told us of the great world wars, the flying machines he has seen, and he was one of the first Tibetans to see a carriage on wheels propel itself! But most importantly, I reckon that his beliefs have only been strengthened by what he has seen and heard throughout his long life, and that his compassion for others is limitless. The only time I have seen sadness cross his expression is when talk turns to the Chinese. The last time he talked of such things he shook his head and said that he worries for things to come, but that the signs would appear to say that good and compassion will prevail."

Alexander seemed appeased at her description of the man. He then said, "Ani-Dolma, Pembuti's delivery date could be just days away, and I need to know what arrangements the nuns will be making." He knew from experience that traditionally, Tibetans had some unusual views on birth and how it was dealt with. "I can tell you that from my physical examination, I believe she may be carrying twins." Ani-Dolma's eyes widened in a startled expression (the first time Alexander had seen her taken aback by anything). He looked knowingly at her and said, "But you needn't worry. I'll handle that eventuality when it arises. What will be, will be," he said matter-of-factly. Ani-Dolma thought to herself that for a Westerner, Alexander displayed some wise Tibetan ways.

Just then, the refectory door opened and in walked the esteemed lama.

As Lama Kunchen approached, a broad and welcoming smile covered his face. Both Ani-Dolma and Alexander rose to their feet and bowed courteously before him, and he reciprocated. "I want to thank you profusely, Ani-Dolma, for taking care of Pembuti so well, especially now, given her current condition. Pembuti has told me all that has happened to her and how you and the other nuns--and now *you*, Alexander, who I believe is a Western doctor—have been so very kind to her." Addressing Alexander directly he said, "As you may already know, aside from Pembuti's father, I am her last living relative, her great-uncle, Kunchen Tulku Rinpoche. I have spoken reassuringly to Pembuti and told her that she is in very good hands here and that the nunnery is the best place for her at this time." He shook Alexander's hand and asked that he continue to care for his family. "It is now time for me to continue on with my travels, but I will be thinking of Pembuti and saying prayers for her."

"Lama Kunchen, have you received any news regarding the Kampa rebels in the East?" Ani-Dolma asked.

The esteemed lama knew she was referring to Pembuti's father. "I'm afraid there is little hope," he said, shaking his head. "Most of the rebels in the East have met great resistance from the Chinese. Of course, Pembuti need not know of this."

The lama bade Ani-Dolma and Alexander to escort him to his horse and donkey, who by this time had been fed, watered, and rested for the next stage of their journey. As the lama mounted his horse, Ani-Dolma signalled for the gates to be opened, and with a gentle word he encouraged his mount into a slow walk. His donkey, its reins tied to the horse's saddle, dutifully fell in line and followed in tandem. As the horse reached the foot of the slope leading to the next village, Lama Kunchen, without looking round, gave a flourishing wave of his right arm and was gone; the faces of Pembuti, Ani-Dolma, and Alexander framed in his mind's eye, where they would remain.

For reasons his own, Lama Kunchen had declined an invitation from Ani-Dolma to remain at the nunnery a while longer. When he reached the next village he was greeted, per custom, by its elders, who'd been made aware of his pending arrival. As always, they were happy to see him and hear news from his travels, and took comfort in his teachings and sage advice. And as he sat in the chair in the small room provided him, the esteemed lama slowly closed his eyes as if to meditate, reflecting back on his life. He'd enjoyed every moment of his travels; his life as a traveling monk had served him well. He'd always managed to stay fed, safe, and had received blessed teachings from some very wise masters. And through this had been able to impart wisdom to his fellow Tibetans, other Buddhists, and even some outsiders.

As his mind and body relaxed, his thoughts drifted back to Dawa and her daughter, Pembuti. His niece, Dawa, had died at the hands of the Chinese (all because of the jewellery and other trinkets she prized more than life), and he still felt ill-at-ease about his role in the whole affair. Had it not been for him agreeing to deliver the gifts to her on his annual visits, her path may have been quite different. She may even still be alive. But he knew that it was not for him to decide such things: that every effect had a cause and every cause an effect--which at some point would have to be accounted for. And as for Pembuti, she was still an innocent child who, like her mother, shared an affinity with the transient glistening baubles of vanity—particularly in the form of the necklace. Lama Kunchen took comfort in knowing that Pembuti had an inner strength beyond that of her ill-fated mother, beyond the need for possessions, which would see her through what was to come.

Now the lama's thoughts drifted further back in time. He saw his old friend, the Scottish soldier, long since gone from Tibet--in body but surely not in spirit. He then recalled his many meetings with masters and pupils, both the 15th and 16th Karmapas, the Dalai Lama himself, and all those wise men who'd helped shape his remarkable life. As his breathing became shallower, he could feel his meditation deepen; visions from his past became blurred, sounds became unrecognisable, as if all his senses, experiences, and feelings were merging into one: into a rainbow of coloured light which slowly transfused his whole being into one bolt of incandescent, pure white light. This bright light expanded and filled the room and an air of peace and acceptance prevailed over him. This light then seemed to dissolve the walls of the room in which he sat. He could no longer feel, hear, or even sense his breathing; it was not just the physical room from which he was breaking free.

That which had actualised its own feelings, thoughts, emotions, and experiences was fading, and would soon return to where it had sprung; yet the essence continued and became part of the whole. It knew nothing of fear for it had passed this way before and was better for where it had been, and was ready for where it must go. For it there was a short silence and then all that was heard was the rhythmic chanting of monks, the occasional beating of a large, sounding drum, and the mournful blowing of a conch-shell trumpet--broken then by the sensation of movement and being surrounded by everything--yet nothing. It set at the threshold primed (verily, anxious) to continue its journey and now heard the faint sound of two fast beating drums: each distinct but in accord. It must follow both, one journey on two paths. Senses slowly returned: the rushing sound of pumping blood; the sense of feeling and the boundaries of form. Then a thought of isolation and loss as the sound of each drum was lost to the other. Then followed the cold rasp of breath and two separate cries of life emerging . . .

Chapter 12

As Alexander had assumed, childbirth was not a common occurrence at the nunnery. When he arrived that evening, having been fetched from the local village by an excitable young nun, there were other younger nuns running round as if in a state of abject panic; entering and leaving the outhouse Pembuti had been segregated to when her labour pains began. The only calm amidst this storm of activity was Ani-Dolma, who stood at the entrance to the outhouse issuing precise instructions to those round her.

Arrangements for the babies' arrival had been made in accordance with Tibetan tradition. Offerings were being made and prayers said in the nunnery temple; word was sent to the local monastery for the lama there to offer prayers and readings from Buddhist scripture to assist in the birthing process. Since Pembuti's mother was dead and she had no female relatives present, Ani-Dolma and two elder nuns assumed that role. And in a most unusual break in tradition, Alexander was to be present to over-see the delivery; Ani-Dolma had permitted this at Pembuti's and Lama Kunchen's request--hence the excitable young nun's visit to the village to fetch him.

As Alexander entered the dimly-lit outhouse he could see Pembuti lying on yak-hair blankets on the cold stone floor, with one of the older nuns reassuringly holding her hand. Even now, his feelings for her were unchanged: he was desperately glad to see her, and the energy between them was apparent; even palpable. As Alexander sat down beside Pembuti, Ani-Dolma told him that the first twinges of pain had passed. They'd fed her small portions of *tsampa* and she'd consumed several cups of *chang*, which had apparently helped numb the pain. Pembuti gave a resigned and pleading smile as Alexander positioned himself next to her.

The slow passing hours of labour, broken by sharp and intensifying spasms, gave Pembuti time to reflect on her life. She was just fifteen years of age and about to give birth to not one child but two. She vowed that this would be the last time; never would she get herself into this kind of mess again. If only she'd considered then what she'd be experiencing now--her future uncertain, her dreams in tatters. *How could I have been so stupid to have given myself so thoughtlessly?* She reminded herself that it had been her dreams of escape, of being *somebody*, of finding a way out that had convinced her to do what she'd done with him. To lie with a man she hardly knew. Yes, she'd been *somebody* for those few impassioned hours; intoxicated by his smile, his infectious laugh, his sparkling blue eyes and strong, manly body that smelled of power. But at what sacrifice? Then in a flight of fantasy she now looked at Alexander and imagined that it could have all been so different if she'd met *him* instead. He was kind, caring, and gentle; he seemed to like for her for who she truly was. Even though she was pregnant to another man, he'd been there for her and she now began to wonder why.

Drifting in and out of consciousness, she imagined herself and Alexander together. He'd told her about his home, a country called *Scotland*, a long, long way from Tibet--but like Tibet in many ways. She saw them together there. There were the snow-covered mountains, the clear blue lakes (*lochs*, she'd have to remember to call them), the swift rivers that wound their way through lush green valleys. She imagined the cold winter mornings and warm summer afternoons. He'd told her that regretfully he had no children--but that was about to change . . .

Suddenly Pembuti winced with pain--and squeezed Alexander's hand hard. As her pain increased, she grew frightened, and begged him not to leave her. As her contractions intensified, it suddenly occurred to her that she--or one or both of her babies--could die. Though she'd witnessed this very process several times as a girl, she couldn't believe that through this agonizing pain would come birth. Then the crucial moment arrived and Alexander told her to bear down and push. She gritted her teeth and drew up her legs--and pushed with all her might. (She heard her own screams as if they were coming from someone else—yet felt as though she were being torn apart.) One of the nuns attending her mopped her brow with a soft cloth. Pembuti was exhausted and convinced she were dying. But then she heard Alexander tell her to stop pushing and the screaming in her ears receded; replaced with a hushed silence broken a few seconds later by a plaintive cry of new life wanting to be recognised! The old nun at her side squeezed her hand and told her that she had a daughter. But Pembuti barely had a chance to glimpse the baby girl before it was swaddled in a small woollen blanket and handed to Ani-Dolma. Then the searing pain returned.

Again Pembuti heard Alexander exalting her to push again--one last time! And as she did she let out one final scream--which tailed off and filled the room--replaced a moment later by a second plaintive cry of life. As the pain subsided she felt the old nun press her hand once again, telling her that she now had a son! Like the girl child the boy was wrapped in a small woollen blanket and handed to Ani-Dolma. Pembuti was exhausted, sapped, both physically and emotionally. Her thoughts did not turn to her babies but lingered in the fact that her ordeal was over; the pain had gone and never again would she experience such a thing. She felt a cool dampness as Alexander mopped her face, looked reassuringly into her eyes, and told her to relax and try to sleep. He and Ani-Dolma would look after her babies.

As Pembuti's eyes fell closed, Alexander stood up and went to help Ani-Dolma tend the two fragile specks of new life. Both, according to Ani-Dolma, were breathing normally and looked fit and healthy, her assessment making it obvious to Alexander that she'd been down this rocky road before. As Alexander made his own assessment of the newborns he confirmed that they did indeed appear to be fine, and by the lively sounds they were making their lungs were clear. Yet as he looked closer at them, he detected that aside from one being male and the other female, there were subtle differences--though he could not immediately ascertain what. *Ah, it's probably nothing*, he decided.

Pembuti woke after what felt like days; comfortable, warm, and at peace. And for a moment thought she was awakening from a bad dream. But her peace was soon shattered by the plaintive cry of a baby and quickly realised that what had happened to her was real. From the cozy warmth of the yak-fur bed she sat bolt upright and took in her surroundings. From the dim light of a few candles she could just make out the figures of two nuns: one busying herself, tidying the outhouse, the other bent over a raised crib, lifting a small, noisy bundle wrapped in a woollen blanket. The latter, now aware that Pembuti was awake, turned and brought the bundle to Pembuti; laid it on her lap and told her that this was her daughter. A few moments later the old nun returned with another wool-wrapped bundle, laid it likewise on her lap, and said that this was her son. As the old nun then proceeded to assist Pembuti to expose her breasts, the whole ordeal came rushing back: she looked down at the two round innocent faces peering out from their woollen cocoons and asked what she was supposed to do with them.

"Your babies need feeding," the old nun told her.

A look of terror filled Pembuti's eyes: "No! Take these things away! *Ani-Dolma . . . Alexander!*" she cried out.

Stopping her work, the other nun hurried off to find Ani-Dolma. Rushing to her side a few minutes later, Ani-Dolma told Pembuti not to worry, that the babies would be cared for a while longer while she regained her strength. "I've already sent for Alexander," she said, "so you just lie back, close your eyes, and rest. I know this is a lot to deal with, so soon."

Later that afternoon Alexander arrived and was met by Ani-Dolma just inside the gate, who explained that Pembuti had awoken and become quite agitated, but was resting peacefully now. The two then made their way quickly across the courtyard and into the outhouse. As if sensing his presence, as Alexander approached the sleeping Pembuti, she raised her head and held out her arms. As he sat down beside her she threw her arms round his neck and began sobbing uncontrollably. Alexander stroked her hair and spoke softly to her in Tibetan, his emotions welling up inside to the point that he wished he could lift her up and carry her and her babies away. When Pembuti eventually released her hold, Alexander stood up and went to the babies' crib. There as he looked in he gave a start, their distinctions now quite apparent: one baby had a tuft of dark hair, dark oblique eyes, and a soft, coffee-brown complexion; the other had long strands of fair hair, light bluish-grey round eyes, and a fair, pale complexion. His initial sense that the two babies were noticeably different was now confirmed: the baby boy was Tibetan, the baby girl was not. *She* had the features of a Westerner; an *outsider*. As Alexander turned, he saw Ani-Dolma sigh with resignation. They looked at each other. *What now?*

Over the next few days Alexander visited the nunnery daily to see how the babies and Pembuti were progressing. Pembuti was regaining her strength, but still trying to block out the babies from her life.

The nuns would help her wash and clothe them—and she'd feed them when given no choice--but without a mother to guide and support her, Pembuti was lost. They all feared a natural bond would never form. Ani-Dolma and Alexander feared much worse.

Chapter 13

WORD REACHED THE NUNNERY FROM the village that Lama Kunchen had died suddenly, a few days before. Now Pembuti had no one. There was still no news of her father who, if still alive, was thought to be fighting with the rebels in the east--though nothing definite was known. Pembuti was young, alone, and afraid, and as yet, unable to cope with all that had happened. Ani-Dolma kept the death of her great-uncle from her, deciding that she needed to first resolve the issue of motherhood. She'd also decided that Alexander should remain directly involved as Pembuti seemed to regard him as family. In any case, it was clear to both Alexander and Ani-Dolma that the twins could not remain at the nunnery. While it was of considerable concern that Pembuti could not seem to accept them, their very presence there would raise questions in the local village and attract interest from the Chinese, who needed little excuse to enter and ransack sacred places like monasteries and nunneries in the name of their ideology. While it was likely Pembuti would eventually come to accept the children as her own, that issue was secondary. The welfare and survival of the tiny siblings was now the primary issue. Ani-Dolma and Alexander knew that the boy could always find a home—many families would welcome another strong hand. But the girl; that was another matter altogether. She would grow up looking different, treated differently, and would eventually realise that. A free and peaceful Tibet would accept her as one of their own, but the ever-increasing number of occupiers would not.

As Alexander fretted over Pembuti and her babies' predicament, he couldn't help but notice that Ani-Dolma didn't seem to share his concern. In fact, the expression on her face was one of dawning realisation. During one of their frequent discussions, she told Alexander why. She recalled a conversation she'd had with Lama Kunchen during his last visit to the nunnery in which he'd told her of a Westerner he knew from his travels a long time ago. This Westerner, a Scotsman, no less, had asked him to deliver something very precious to Tibet each year, a gift for a certain young Tibetan girl. Lama Kunchen had told Ani-Dolma that perhaps a time would come when a Westerner would be asked to take a gift *out* of Tibet. At that time he entrusted to *her* a sealed letter to be delivered to the 16th Karmapa at Tsurphu Monastery. And while Ani-Dolma didn't know what to make of everything the esteemed lama had told her, having now seen the striking differences between the two babies, his meaning was crystal clear: he'd effectively left a set of instructions to follow!

Alexander did not, at first, grasp what Ani-Dolma was suggesting. (All his thoughts and emotions were wrapped-up in Pembuti.) Then the words "Westerner" and "out of Tibet" jumped out in his mind. Then like a bolt of lightning in a clear blue sky, he understood: he must take Pembuti and the babies away with him, to India. He could make his fantasy a reality! They could all live together in India! Then swept up in the emotion, Alexander suddenly blurted out his feelings for Pembuti to Ani-Dolma, and his solution to their quandary. She patted Alexander gently on the shoulder, as if to bring him back to reality:

"Alexander, you are a kind and compassionate man, and you've been a good friend to Tibet. But you cannot, nor are you expected, to bear the responsibility for all that has happened. You have a wife at home and a life beyond Tibet to consider. And Pembuti, well . . . you must put your feelings for her aside. Surely you know you cannot take her and her two babies into your world!"

But although Alexander was seen by most as a calm-headed and practical man (and how he thought of himself), he had, none-the-less, made the choice to come to Tibet to practice medicine—and allow his wife to return to Scotland without him. Therefore he must, somewhere within him, have another side; one attracted to adventure--even *danger.* Otherwise, why come to this remote and inaccessible country of strange customs, unique beliefs, and welcoming-yet-wholly-different people in the first place?! With his feelings for Pembuti now out in the open--and the lama's story echoing in his ears--he *wanted* to—no, *needed* to--protect them all: Pembuti, the boy and the girl. And there was also the letter for the Karmapa circling round his mind . . .

But then Alexander's practical side took hold: *What options are actually at my dispose?*

Alexander began to work out for himself what Lama Kunchen would have wanted. It would be best, it seemed, if the boy baby was left at the nunnery under the care of Pembuti and Ani Dolma. Pembuti's fate lay here in Tibet; with her father, if he returned, but probably not forever with the nuns. (Despite her efforts to fit in, she really didn't belong amongst them.) It was the girl-baby's fate that was of greatest concern. If he could not be with Pembuti herself, he decided, then he could at least be with her daughter. Take her out of Tibet and far away to safety. Alexander explained his reasoning to Ani-Dolma: by taking the girl baby he was helping Pembuti--and taking a bit of her with him. On hearing Alexander's plan, Ani-Dolma smiled with quiet satisfaction, certain that this was what Lama Kunchen would have wanted. Arrangements would be made, she said. Trading caravans moved south to Nepal and India and he and the girl baby could join one as common travellers, and not look out of place.

Over the next few days Alexander spent his time between the village and the nunnery, ensuring that his charges in both places were provided for: Pembuti and her twins in the nunnery, and the few patients who still required his attention in the village. He also sent word back to Lhasa that with the greatest regret he urgently had to leave Tibet and hoped that the authorities there would understand and be able to locate a suitable replacement. (It went against Alexander's nature to handle things this way, but then again, he was doing so many things out of character now.)

While Alexander tended to Pembuti and her babies, Ani-Dolma rode to the village and arranged for him to join a caravan headed south-west. Alexander marvelled at her resourcefulness. She returned with information that a large caravan was due to pass west of Lhasa in the not-too-distant future and that there was a young family in the village who'd gladly help him with the baby on the journey. As the day approached for his departure, Alexander's thoughts turned to Pembuti alone. Such an *innocent*, caught up in the ways of the harsh and often cruel outside world: What would become of her? He hoped that one day when she was older she would come to terms with what had happened and not think ill of him or Ani-Dolma, and understand that it was done with compassion, regret, and ultimately, *love*.

Apart from the baby, Alexander's travelling companions were a young couple: Assam and Nima Tsering, and their son Norbu. They were known to Ani-Dolma as very thoughtful young people; educated in Lhasa and concerned not just for their son's future but that of their country. They believed (as did Ani-Dolma) that both concerns could be best served by leaving Tibet and making outsiders aware of what was happening within their country's borders. Thus they were only too willing to help Alexander and the baby on their journey. One bright and clear morning soon after, they arrived at the nunnery ready to accompany Alexander and the baby girl on a momentous journey.

The courtyard of the nunnery was alive with activity that morning. Saddle bags were packed with provisions; some nuns hurried back and forth checking and double-checking that the pack animals were securely tethered to each other and that all bags, packages, and sacks were properly laden and evenly distributed amongst the beasts. Other nuns stood solemnly in a group fingering their prayer beads and in low voices recited appropriate prayers and mantras. All this commotion had raised a light cloud of grey dust from the courtyard floor that swirled round in tune with the movement of the nuns, the travellers, and the animals. The bright morning sunlight danced through this mist, broken up into unique colours which played off the shadowy moving figures, yet were trapped within the confines of the nunnery walls. At the heart of this surreal scene stood Ani-Dolma, motionless, with a reassuring arm round Pembuti's shoulder as Pembuti cradling her new born son pressed close into her side.

Alexander took a deep breath, straightened his back and raised his head. The first step was the hardest. As he walked he focused his attention on Pembuti; he wanted her image to be forever etched in his memory. "Pembuti," he said softly as they came face-to-face. She stood there wide-eyed, holding her son in her arms; asleep and peaceful. "It's time, Pembuti. And it saddens me so. I have come to care greatly for you and your children. And I want you to know that if things could be different, I can see myself living here in Tibet forever. This place . . . these people . . . and certainly *you*, are ingrained in my heart." He opened his arms and she came into him. He held her close. She was crying and he could feel his shirt growing wet, and he too wanted to breakdown. Gathering his strength he gently took hold of her arms and held her out in front of him. "Know this, little one. I love you. I truly do. And I will love and cherish your baby girl, *Ani*, always. She will live a beautiful life, this I promise you."

"I love you too!" said Pembuti. "I do not know how I will go on without you! I do not want you to go and leave me here all alone!"

"You will never be alone, Pembuti. I will think of you every day and you have your life here with your son, with Ani-Dolma and the other nuns to look after you." With that he planted a tender kiss on her brow, gazed lovingly into her baby boy's face, then turned and mounted his horse. As the gates of the nunnery opened the captive mist could now escape, leaving a clear picture of Alexander leading all his charge out and onto the road to Lhasa, Drepung, and beyond; Assam, Nima, and their son Norbu at his side. Turning, he saw Ani-Dolma and Pembuti waving a sad goodbye; both, he thought, in their own way, remarkable women of Tibet. He turned his attention to what lie ahead and never looked back.

Chapter 14

THE CARAVAN SET OUT FROM Nagchu, a small town some one hundred and fifty miles north of Lhasa, which over the years had traditionally been a gathering place for traders, nomads, and highwaymen. The town was the conversion-point of the old northern Silk Route (which ran east to west across Tibet) and the northern end of the Tea-Horse Road (which ran north to south) and had flourished for more than a century, making rich men of those prepared to deal with wily traders and the fearsome reputation of nomads from the Kham and Amdo regions. Trading in this manner, and on this scale was, however, slowly becoming a thing of the past. Modernisation brought on by the natural passage of time and hastened by the occupation of Tibet by the Chinese was making such a venture more of a traditional *event* than a commercial endeavour. The West's romantic notions of caravans were easily dispelled for those travelling in them: in addition to having to endure extreme weather conditions crossing the plateau, and the treacherous terrain of mountain passes, there was also random harassment by the Chinese military and raids by parties of reluctant Tibetan bandits made homeless and desperate by the occupation. Yet, some traders, merchants, and pilgrims still felt it necessary to continue such traditions; it was an act of defiance in the face of unwanted intruders and uninvited progress.

Alexander had been told that such a large and extensive caravan would not enter the city of Lhasa but rather skirt its western edges,

picking up traders and merchants as it passed on its way to Gyantse.
He'd been instructed to head for Drepung and Tsurphu Monastery. He
knew the caravan would come; it was just a matter of waiting. The oracle
in Nagchu had been consulted to determine the most auspicious day to
commence the great adventure, and news of its impending arrival would
precede it. The town of Drepung was close to Tsurphu Monastery, so
Alexander's party could go directly there to await the caravan's arrival.

The first leg of the journey south-westward was quiet and uneventful. Alexander began to get to know the Tibetan family better, and
they, for their part, were keen to know about him and where he'd origi-
nated. The small group of like-minded travellers passed north of Lhasa
almost unnoticed and continued on through Drepung. Once past
Drepung Alexander, Assam, and Nima checked all their belongings
to make certain they were securely bundled together, along with what
provisions they needed for themselves, the girl baby, and the animals
on their journey to Gyantse, where they planned to buy more supplies.
Alexander's medical bag was well-concealed inside a common yak-skin
bag, as well as some gifts and mementos Pembuti had given him for her
daughter. His personal documents he kept concealed in pockets within
his yak-haired coat.

He had to admit to himself that at times, from a distance, he looked
like a Tibetan trader--from his yak-hide boots and traditional baggy
cloth trousers and yak-hair coat--to his grimy and dirtied face peering
out from under his over-sized fur hat pulled down to conceal his far-
from-Tibetan eyes. No one had thus far shown any interest in him whatsoever since leaving the nunnery, so he felt safe traveling with a baby in
the large and moving trail of humanity that would be the caravan.

Now Alexander could just make out, coming from the east, a thin
brown line snaking its way across the plain between the clear blue of the
sky and the pale subdued green of the meadows blanketing the plateau

floor. Alexander, Assam, and Nima were each on horseback, with Ani carefully strapped across Nima's back—in typical Tibetan fashion. Their boy, Norbu, a stout and keen lad of about nine years of age was on foot, tasked with leading, cajoling, and otherwise controlling the pack animals. This task he'd relished since leaving his village, making him very much the young and adventurous trader.

As the meandering caravan followed the contours of the serpentine trail, the leading yaks were only a few hundred yards away, yet the caravan extended back as far as the eye could see. The leading traders pulled up their horses and ordered the yaks to halt at the foot of the slope. To the sounds of grunting yaks, the promptings of herders and the clanging of the bells round the animals' necks, the great lumbering train of men and beasts moved forward, shaking the very earth as they did.

As the line of pack animals comprised of yaks, *dzos*, mules, and donkeys passed by, Alexander could see that their saddle bags bulged with goods for trade and barter, and wondered what great treasures were contained within that would make men and women risk life and limb. All that was Tibet was passing before him: monks and nuns on pilgrimages to the great blue lakes farther to the south, well-dressed noble families intent on increasing their wealth, hardened merchants and traders who knew nothing other than this trading life, poor peasant families with little or no possessions looking for a new start. The musty and foul, sweaty smell of animals filled the air, broken only by the aroma of spices and dried meat to be traded, escaping from saddle bags.

Alexander spotted a small gap in the almost never-ending procession and motioned for his companions to follow him. Without fuss or objection they found themselves behind a party of monks and nuns, and in front of a group of Lhasa Newars. These Newars were renowned craftsmen and artisans from Nepal, allowed to set up businesses in Lhasa, and travelled frequently back home to trade goods. Alexander had come across them before on his travels around Lhasa and knew them to be friendly, and thought of them as foreigners like himself.

The caravan's progress was steady as it wove its way across the flat land. Conversation with other groups was polite and sporadic; the monks and nuns ahead concentrated on their devotions, but the nuns did take time to visit the baby girl and wish her well. The Nepalese traders to the rear were more forthcoming; they knew Alexander was not really one of them but took no exception as they were all fellow travellers. Talk was mainly about what kind of trading year they'd just gone through, their eagerness about returning to loved ones in Nepal, but invariably about the Chinese. They'd been looked down on by the more zealous occupiers as exploiters of the common people, but by and large had been left in peace so far. The caravan itself had attracted the attention of the Chinese military units based in the regions it had passed through north of Lhasa (and from Lhasa itself), but the Chinese officers were also pragmatists; they knew better than to impede the progress of such a large and significant Tibetan tradition. Also, the imposing size of this caravan had deterred any would-be bandit raiding parties. But that could change the further south and west they travelled and entered the more remote and rugged parts of the countryside.

As Alexander's section of the caravan passed through the Kamba La, the trail veered to the right and along the shores of the northern edge of Yamdrok Tso, one of the four sacred lakes of Tibet. The vast expanse of the lake was hidden from view further to the south, yet what could be seen was a picture of crystal-blue still water, reflecting back the late summer sunshine onto the barren grey and brown rocky slopes on the far side that seemed to slide directly into the water as if cutting through mirrored glass. Soon the monks' and nuns' journey would be over as they were travelling only as far as Samding Gompa, the Temple of Sacred Meditation; the only monastery with a female head. This monastery shortly came into view, perched on a hill on a peninsula which jutted out into the waters of the lake. The nuns' interest in the baby girl became clearer now, given the nature and destination of their pilgrimage. At the village of Nagartse the religious pilgrims took a smaller off-path to the south, taking their leave of those round them with thoughtful bows and good wishes, departing then for Samding Monastery. The pace and movement of the caravan was not disrupted by their departure; its slow but powerful momentum carrying it forward to the next obstacle: the Karo La mountain pass. But as fate would have it, passage across Karo La was not as formidable as Alexander had heard. The traders, merchants, and animals, in fact, took it all in stride.

As the caravan finessed its way across the high and sometimes daunting terrain, Alexander realised that the journey they were undertaking was not an obstacle in and of itself: he, himself, had simply made it one. To his fellow travellers it was just another journey, another set of circumstances to overcome in a long line of circumstances. And as the formidable procession rumbled on, clouds of dust rose and drifted across the flat landscape, thrown up by the innumerable number of hooves pounding away at the dry and fragile earth. Soon the town of Gyantse appeared on the horizon; or rather sight of the mighty *jong* (or fortress) which acted as its backdrop. This imposing structure set high behind the town and seemed to be carved out of the rock-face on which it set.

The town of Gyantse itself was in the process of being rebuilt following a near-disastrous flood the year before. Everywhere there was activity--from street traders trying to sell their wares to the still-moving caravaners--to platoons of Chinese soldiers riding round as if they were of some importance. There appeared to be no formal order for the travellers to halt, so every group picked their own spot to rest and make camp. Gyantse, like Nagchu and Lhasa, was an important stop along the caravan trail and for some traders, where their journey would end. For the rest it was a place to regroup and stock-up on supplies.

Alexander and his companions made camp with their new friends the Lhasa Newars, just on the southern outskirts of town.

Assam, Nima, and their son Norbu joined some of the Newars on a foray into the town's markets to buy what provisions they'd need for the final legs of the journey. Alexander thought it wise to remain with the caravan, with the baby, to avoid any unnecessary attention from both Tibetan and Chinese officials. So here he was, he thought, a young and proper Scottish doctor sitting with a group of hardened Nepali traders on the High Plateau of Tibet. *What would my professors and fellow students from med school make of me now--disguised as a Tibetan nomad, charged with protecting the life of a part-Tibetan, part-Scottish baby girl?*! he mused.

The infant had been of no bother, so far. She was being ably looked after by Nima, as if she were her own. Alexander's thoughts now turned to the baby: *Will she remember any of this?* The warm days and cold nights . . . sleeping under the stars? The lowing and grunting of mal-content animals? The scent of burning incense? The warmth and *too-closeness* of bodies--both human and animal--the smell of animal hair and hide? But then his thoughts were jolted back to the present by the sounds of muffled sniggering and chuckling; his friends, the Newars, having a good-natured joke at his expense as he sat there with the baby on his lap, babbling to her in a language that was neither Tibetan nor English. Just in time to save Alexander further embarrassment, his trav-elling companions returned.

The Newars had been quite helpful in securing good deals on the replenishing supplies they'd bought, and had also brought back news concerning the next stage of the journey: at Gyantse the caravan would split in two and proceed in different directions--one part travelling west along the old Silk Road to Shigatse, one heading south across the Himalayas and into Sikkim and India. Alexander and his group would join the latter. Although new travellers would periodically join the caravan, to Sikkim it would still be a lot smaller in size than that which arrived at Gyantse, and may attract more interest from the Chinese than before, as it headed for the border.

After two days' rest outside town, word reached Alexander that the southbound caravan was readying itself to leave. The Lhasa Newars were moving on to Shigatse, so goodbyes were said and best wishes exchanged for the remainder of each others' journeys. Some other familiar faces were part of this new caravan so Alexander and his companions did not feel like strangers.

As they resumed their southward aim, the landscape began to change. They were now approaching the rugged foothills of the Himalayas and the trail followed tumbling rivers and streams as they cut their way through green-clad gorges and valleys. Surprisingly, the caravan didn't draw the attention of the Chinese military as they left the flat plains for the mountains. However, the Chinese soldiers were well aware that trudging over and through these mountain passes was one of the worst details they could be posted to. And besides--Chinese garrisons stationed at the borders with neighbouring India and Bhutan could surely deal with a rag-tag group of Tibetan traders and merchants.

Due to the drastic change in terrain, the pace of the caravan dropped to little more than a crawl. Young Norbu Tsering earned his keep cajoling and prodding the pack animals with sticks as they apprehensively tried to find their footing on the rock- and stone-strewn paths. (The more stubborn beasts received a stinging reminder--a small pebble fired from Norbu's slingshot!) Without the Lhasa Newars for company, conversation amongst the travellers was limited; it appeared to Alexander that some of those now in the caravan would rather keep their reasons for journeying this far south to themselves. From his observations and their lack of pack animals, all were not just industrious merchants and traders.

The precarious lay of the land necessitated single-file travel, so communication was kept to a minimum--unless an animal or person got into difficulties. The meandering group passed the last of the crystal blue lakes, Bamtso, on their left. Further ahead to their left was Mount Chumolari, its snow-covered peak like a white sail set full against a clear blue ocean of sky. Plumes of smoke like snow drifted off its sides, forced from the security of the rock-face by the icy blasts of the prevailing winds. To the right of this magnificent peak was a gap in the almost continuous wall of grey rock. This was Tang La, the pass that would lead them into Chumbi Valley, and the last leg of their exodus from Tibet. The crossing of Tang La was arduous, but largely uneventful, with progress halted on two occasions to rescue mules which had lost their footing and shed their loads. Once over the worst of the mountain pass, stretched out before them was Chumbi Valley like a lush oasis of verdant greens and browns, compared with the slate greys and steel blues of the rocky terrain they'd left behind.

The caravan descended methodically into the valley, met by the sounds of rustling leaves, bird song, and rushing of water hurriedly tumbling over rocks and stones of the river bed. The bright pinks and reds of rhododendron bushes jumped out at the travellers, slowly giving way to the more subtle yellows and blues of the smaller--but no less vibrant--ground-cover plants. As Alexander took in these welcoming sights he realised that he could well be back in his native Scotland, taking in the view of the River Tay from Kinloch Rannoch and eastward. This landscape of rich colours and sounds would be a fitting memory of Tibet for him and his travelling companions, he thought.

Alexander's party, and the others, continued on through the valley in good spirits--knowing full well that most likely the final test was still to come: the Jelep La, the high mountain pass between India and Tibet in the East Sikkim District of the Indian state of Sikkim. Not so much for the severity and temperament of nature, but that of man: they would have to confront the last Chinese military outpost. If weather conditions in the pass were bad, it would work to their favor: the border guards wouldn't want to spend too much time out of their warm and comfortable huts. But were it fair, the guards might like the diversion of searching the caravan, as opposed to their usual tedious routine. Either way, Alexander must come face-to-face with the Chinese.

As the caravan climbed up and out of the valley, Alexander could make out the burning fires of the border guards' camp ahead. Then the stark brown timber-clad huts with their red and yellow-starred banners fluttering from the roofs came into view. Then as they drew closer, the movement of brown-uniformed figures preparing themselves for the caravans' arrival filled his field of vision. Soon the forward momentum of the caravan slowed and finally stopped as the lead animals halted at the border post ahead. By that time all riders had dismounted and were leading their horses. Alexander could not hear what was being said but saw a lot of arm-waving and finger-pointing. Some of the brown-clad soldiers then began poking and prodding the packs strapped to the backs of the pack animals. These men did not speak with any of the traders, this task left to one soldier in particular, most likely, Alexander thought, the senior officer.

The Chinese officer did not address every trader who passed him. Those he did stop bowed before him, and he courteously returned their greeting. He would then speak to them (presumably in Chinese, or maybe Tibetan), pointing his baton at the traders' animals. Sometimes the conversation seemed to get contentious; other times it was short and would end with a laugh, as if a joke had been exchanged between the men. Slowly the caravan edged forward and it was now Alexander's turn to pass by the officer in charge. As he did, two stone-faced soldiers approached, but barely gave him a glance as they passed to prod his pack animals. As Alexander looked out from under his fur-lined hat he could see the superior officer approaching.

The officer was a youngish-looking man; probably about Alexander's age. As he passed he nodded in acknowledgment and Alexander did likewise. At that moment the baby, carried on Nima's back, gave out a short--but sharp--cry; which drew the officer's attention. He regarded Nima then pulled back the baby's swaddling. The soldier's eyes gave a quizzical stare--then he looked up at the woman carrying the baby. Nima bowed her head deferentially but said nothing. The officer turned back and looked up into Alexander's face then said in a polite but matter-of-fact way (and in perfect English), "You must be a long way from home, sir. May you and your family have a safe journey" He then reached into his military coat pocket and withdrew a silver coin, went back to the baby and pressed it to her forehead. He then came forward and placed it in Alexander's hand—waving his baton as an instruction for the caravan to keep moving. Alexander clasped his hands together and gave the officer a deep bow, in response to which the officer touched his baton to the brim of his hat and carried on down the line of the caravan.

Alexander thrust the silver coin into his pocket, adjusted the reigns of his horse, and led his companions out of Tibet and forward toward India. About fifty yards ahead stood a group of turban-clad Indian soldiers, manning a road block. As Alexander's group approached them he fumbled inside the folds of his jacket and produced his British passport. Presenting it to the lead soldier, he pointed to Assam, Nima, Norbu, and their animals—but the soldier didn't take it. On recognising the British Royal Crest he simply saluted, nodded for the gate to be raised, and ushered Alexander and his companions into India.

For Alexander, all that had just happened was little more than a blur. As the caravan descended into Sikkim, Northern India, he was barely aware that some of his fellow travellers had turned off the trail and headed for Gangtok, while he and the rest of the caravan headed for Darjeeling. Time and time again he went through the events of that part of the journey (what had happened at the Tibetan border), but could never come up with a rational explanation. Such was his amazement that he would barely remember passing Kalimpong before reaching the outskirts of Darjeeling. The sight of this hill-station town was a welcome relief not only for Alexander, who had friends there, but also for Assam Tsering and his family, because many Tibetans who'd fled across the border since the Chinese invasion were now settled in Darjeeling.

Chapter 15

THE SERIES OF EVENTS ALEXANDER would later relate to his friends in Darjeeling about Pembuti, her babies, and his dramatic flight from Tibet, caught them all by surprise; to them he was a solid, reliable man not prone to acting on impulse. Yet here he was, in their midst, with a baby girl and a displaced Tibetan family in tow. But as Alexander knew would be so, all were made welcome to stay until their futures could be sorted out.

After much discussion it was decided that Alexander and the infant would make their way to Calcutta and to the Deputy High Commission there, to see about obtaining legal documentation for Ani. (Alexander and his friends knew that both the Indian and British authorities were sticklers for paperwork.) After speaking with Indian officials, Alexander explained to Assam, Nima, and Norbu, "You will all have to register with the Indian Government as refugees in Darjeeling. As for me, I cannot thank you enough, Assam, and your family for the help and support you've given me and Ani. We are all now strangers in a foreign land and most likely will never be allowed to return to Tibet. I must now make my way to Calcutta with Ani."

"Where is this place, *Calcutta?*" said Assam.

"It is a large city to the south, much larger than Lhasa, bustling with people, sitting on the edge of a great sea."

Assam looked intrigued, shrugged his shoulders, "I think that as we have come this far together, we should all complete the journey together." So after a few days' recuperating in Darjeeling, the daring band of travellers from Tibet, accompanied by one of Alexander's friends, boarded the Darjeeling Himalayan Railway and set off down and out of the hill country and onto the flat plains of northeast India. Again Nima tended to the baby, while her husband and son gazed wondrously at the scenes unfolding before them. As Alexander looked on from the relative comfort of this narrow-gage feat of British and Indian railway engineering, he could not help but be moved by the spirit and faith displayed by his Tibetan friends. These were not a people living in the past (and under tyranny) who needed freeing by the Peoples Liberation Army of China, they were an enlightened people who knew what life was for and were prepared to face adversity, good fortune, and the unknown, with equal resolve.

Time on the rail journey was spent answering all Assam's and Norbu's many questions, until the small train pulled into Siliguri Junction where they all had to transfer to a larger but more cramped train bound for Calcutta. As this train ploughed on southward, Alexander could see that Assam, Nima, and Norbu were becoming physically uncomfortable; the atmosphere inside the train was sweltering--thick and stuffy even with the windows open--and the temperature was climbing as they progressed. This was all new to his Tibetan friends, used to the clean air, open spaces, and cooler climate of their homeland.

Even for Alexander, arriving in Calcutta was a shock to his senses. Travelling the relatively quiet streets of Lhasa and surrounding towns and villages did not prepare him for the cacophony of ear-piercing noise common to this bustling metropolis. With little fuss, the party from Darjeeling headed for the offices of the British Deputy High Commission, the British Government office that dealt with all things related to West Bengal, Sikkim, and the other states in this part of the

Asian sub-continent. After providing their passports and a lengthy explanation of the situation by Alexander and his Tibetan friend, they were all shown into an anteroom to await their turn. Surprisingly, their stay there was short-lived, as a large highly-polished door was opened and a smartly-dressed official called them into a larger, more salubrious office skirted on three walls with bookshelves. (On the fourth hung a large portrait of Her Majesty Queen Elizabeth II.) In front of this wall set a large walnut-veneered desk, behind which sat a senior career diplomat with an array of papers and files open as if just having been reviewed.

At the official's prompting, Alexander and his friend repeated their stories; events spanning several months. The man sympathised with Alexander's precarious situation and understood the urgency of his requests: this was indeed 'a most unusual case,' he'd said, 'that would require considerable attention and thought.' In typical bureaucratic fashion, Alexander and Assam were told to return the following day when a decision would be reached. And though all this was a world away from what Assam and Nima were accustomed to, they seemed to take it all in stride. They were more concerned with the effects the stifling heat and humidity were having on their son, Norbu. Alexander assured them that in the end, all would turn out for the best.

The following day at the appointed time, Alexander and Assam returned to the Deputy High Commission's office Alexander had no great understanding nor insight into the workings of the diplomatic corps, but was greatly pleased by the outcome of this second meeting. In concise and efficient fashion, the child's name was immediately added to his passport, along with receipt of an official letter bearing the Royal Coat of Arms stating that he was the infant's ward and legal guardian, signed and sealed by the Deputy High Commissioner. A similar sealed envelope bearing the same crest was handed to Assam, which he was told contained information that would assist him and his family in settling in India. This was much more than Alexander had expected to accomplish in such a short space of time. (And like the incident with the Chinese border officer, he found it all a bit difficult to fathom.) Then just as he was about to thank the official for all his help, another suggestion was made:

"Oh, and by the way, Mr. Steward, you may want to contact the local agents of the shipping company, *William Thomson and Co.*, what we call the 'Ben Line,' about passage. If you like, my secretary can provide the agent's name and address, as well as call ahead to alert them of your arrival." So after a long and warm handshake of appreciation, Alexander accompanied Assam back to his lodging house, then set off to find the shipping office. Even without the written directions, the taxi driver knew exactly where to take him, and after a stop-start journey through the raucous streets of Calcutta, they arrived at his destination.

The offices of the shipping line's agent were on the first floor of a traditional whitewashed British Colonial office building. When Alexander introduced himself to the young Indian woman at reception, she said he was expected and showed him through to the main office. There a well-dressed Indian gentleman extended his hand and introduced himself as Mr. Bodasing, the Indian representative for *William Thomson and Co.* Alexander shook the proffered hand and sat down in the seat he indicated.

"Mr. Steward, I received a call from the British High Commission Office regarding the possibility of passage back to Great Britain for you and a baby," he said, smiling. "It so happens that the *Benmhor*, one of the Ben Line's merchant fleet, is making an unscheduled stop at Calcutta on its way back from Singapore to London. I believe it has something to do with a mix-up in crew rosters--which, of course, need be of no concern to you! At any rate, the British official indicated that he would be most grateful if you and your charge could be accommodated so I took the liberty to clear this request with *William Thomson & Co's* offices in

Edinburgh, who were only too happy to oblige! The steamer is due to dock in Calcutta in two days' time, so I suggest that you present yourself and the child to the port offices at the Hadia Dock Complex at 10:00 that morning," said Mr. Bodasing in his best formal Indian-English dialect.

Alexander returned to the boarding house to give his friends the good news. When he got there he found them suffering greatly from the steamy and oppressive heat of the city. His friend from Darjeeling could just about cope, but for the Tibetans, it was becoming debilitating. Also, the incessant noise, exotic odors, and constant movement of people and traffic were too much for them to endure. Their great adventure was becoming a nightmare: they needed to get back to the relative peace and tranquility (and milder climate) of Darjeeling. It was the closest thing they had to the atmosphere of their homeland, and they knew they'd be happier amongst their own kind. Alexander understood completely, so it was decided that the following day, Assam, Nima, and Norbu would return with Alexander's friend by train to Darjeeling. That evening Alexander treated them all to a traditional Indian dinner where they all reminisced about their journey across Tibet and into India, making light and joking about the trials and tribulations of the trip.

The following morning the group arrived at Calcutta Railway Station in plenty of time to catch the train back to Siliguri. Considering that Alexander was naturally a reserved Scotsman, saying goodbye to his friends should not have caused great distress, but on this occasion he found it extremely difficult to put into words his gratitude. Wading through his rampant emotions he told them what a profound honour and privilege is was to have met and travelled with such unassuming and compassionate people, whom he was certain would carry the ways and beliefs of their great country with honour. Assam thanked Alexander for his understanding and help in making their flight from their home-land possible, and for all that he'd done for them. He then pointed to the baby and smiled and said that Alexander was taking a little bit of

Tibet with him! Alexander ruefully smiled back then clasped his hands reverently in front of him and gave a most sincere farewell gesture to Assam and his family. Assam then reached into one of his pockets and pulled out a white scarf, laid it across his upturned palms, and offered it to Alexander. Tears welling up in his eyes, Alexander gratefully accepted this most precious gift. Unable to ignore his spilling emotions, he reached out and embraced Assam and his family. To him, these were truly remarkable people. The shrill of the conductor's whistle disrupted the emotionally-charged air surrounding the little group standing there on the station platform.

Alexander's friend ushered Assam, Nima, and Norbu onto the train and found them suitable seating. As the strain of metal-against-metal took hold and the hiss of escaping steam was replaced by the squeal and turning of train wheels, Alexander waved goodbye to his friends; his left arm sturdily holding Ani tight against his body. As the train slowly picked up speed the waving arms of his Tibetan family too-quickly receded from view. The train carriages passed in a speeding blur, taking his friends off to begin a new life.

Chapter 16

Alexander gazed lovingly at Ani and was reminded that he was about to start a new chapter in his life. He didn't sleep well that night, fully conscious that he was solely responsible for this baby girl--this tiny life--until he got her safely back to Scotland. The following morning he checked to see that he had all he needed for the baby; Nima had left him a list and detailed instructions. He then double-checked his bags to make certain his personal possessions and mementos of his time in the East were intact. And more importantly, that he had all the necessary documentation issued to him by the Deputy High Commission.

Right on time he arrived at the port offices at Hadia Docks and was shown into a waiting room. Already seated there were a young-ish Western woman and her two children, a boy and a girl, aged round three and four. The woman enquired if Alexander and the child were boarding the *Benmhor*. He nodded and said *yes*, that he'd been fortu-nate enough to have been granted passage on the steamer back to Great Britain. '*Good*,' the woman had said, she and her children would have company. She then introduced herself as Mrs. Gilfillan, her children as John and Ann. Her husband, she said, was the Chief Engineer of the *Benmhor* and they were travelling back home to Edinburgh with him. Alexander introduced himself and the baby and said he too was travel-ling back to Edinburgh, after spending a few years working as a doctor in India and Tibet. The Chief Engineer's wife thought it odd for a young Scotsman to be travelling alone with a baby, but didn't question it further; after all, it was now the 1950s and times were changing!

After a short wait, during which Alexander and Mrs. Gilfillan made polite conversation, the door of the waiting room opened and a young Indian lad popped his head round and politely asked if they would like to follow him, as he was to show them safely on-board. He told them not to worry about their luggage, that a couple of porters would come and stow it for them. Alexander's cabin was small but had all the necessities and comforts he and Ani would need. (It was, after all, a commercial vessel and not a cruise liner.) As he unpacked what items he and the baby would need, he began to think back to all that had happened, particularly his good fortune-- first with the Chinese officer at the Tibet border (who must have known who or what he was, and the child, yet did nothing), then with the British officials in Calcutta (generally, diplomats in these positions were stuffy and sticklers for rules and regulations, yet they'd provided their documentation remarkably quick), and then the willingness of the shipping company to give him passage on their steamer. And lastly, the engineer's wife, Ethel, had offered to help with the baby in any way she could. *What good fortune*, he thought. *But, was it really all just a matter of luck?* Even his meeting-up with the Tsering family in Tibet seemed to have had an unexpected, positive outcome.

The sea journey across the Indian Ocean was largely uneventful. The children, John and Ann, were fascinated by the baby and kept her amused most every waking moment, and Alexander was most grateful for all the help Mrs. Gilfillan offered. Alexander's interest picked up as the ship steamed up the Red Sea and then through the Suez Canal, past Port Said, and into the vast Mediterranean. It didn't seem long after that they were passing through the Straits of Gibraltar and into the rougher—and colder--waters of the North Atlantic. Soon the Bay of Biscay was crossed and the *Benmhor* entered the busy shipping lanes of the English Channel. Alexander's odyssey on the Asian sub-continent and the ocean waves would soon be over.

During the voyage, Alexander met with Chief Engineer Gilfillan on numerous occasions. He was a tall, dark-haired man well-tanned from all his travels; a man who was at ease on the floating world of the merchant marine, but who freely admitted was none-too-sure of himself on dry land. The engineer explained that when they docked at the company's berth at the Royal Victoria Dock on the Thames, he'd have to stay on board to oversee the unloading of the ship's cargo and inspect the engines and machinery under his purview. Thus, he would be most grateful if Alexander (if it were within his plans) could accompany his wife and children on the train journey north to Edinburgh--*at the company's expense, of course!* Alexander agreed as he thought it best that he get home directly with the child. So from Royal Victoria Dock to Kings Cross Station, Alexander's travel tickets were in the name, *William Thomson & Co.*

Mrs. Gilfillan thought Alexander looked unusually subdued as he sat looking out the carriage window, cradling the baby girl in his arms. And though clearly none of her business, she decided, she found it peculiar that no one was there to meet him and the child when they arrived in London. There had been a slight delay at *Customs* when they docked, and it appeared that the officials were more interested in Ani than Alexander. But he produced an official-looking letter as well as his passport, which seemed to satisfy their curiosity. Still, she thought it odd that he continued to travel alone.

As the train chugged its way north, stopping only at York, Newcastle, and Berwick, Alexander was deep in thought; stirring only when Ani required attention. Soon the familiar sight of Arthur's Seat came into view and the train slowed, rattling and clanking across numerous sets of points as it set itself to arrive at Waverley Station. To one last blast of hissing steam, the train jerked and jolted to a halt and passengers began to disembark. Alexander carefully stepped down onto the platform, tenderly holding his prize possession, followed by Mrs. Gilfillan and her two children, then a uniformed porter bearing all their luggage. Alexander thanked Ethel for all her help, then she and the children said their goodbyes to the baby. Alexander turned and followed the luggage-carrying porter to the nearest taxi stand. (Of course, no one was there to greet him.)

The taxi ride was just a short jaunt to the edge of the city centre. The cab pulled up in front of a solid stone-fronted terraced house. Alexander duly paid the driver, who'd quickly off-loaded his bags onto the pavement next to a black wrought-iron gate. Just then the front door of the house opened and a slimly-built, brown-haired woman dressed in a straight tweed skirt, cream blouse and patterned woollen cardigan, stepped out onto the lone front step. Alexander smiled at his wife and noted the scowl across her face. Crossing her arms she said, "So, you're *back*! And, oh . . . let me see . . . so it's *real!?* A *baby!?* What on Earth do you think you're doing bringing that child *here?* Have you completely lost your good senses?!"

"I'll explain later, but for now we're exhausted, and Ani needs fed," replied Alexander curtly. "There'll be plenty of time for explanations once we're inside!"

"Right, then you'd better come in straight away—*hadn't* you!" his wife shot back, turning and walking back into the house. Alexander struggled with the child and his luggage, maneuvering the latter up and over the front step and depositing it on the floor of the reception hall. He then shut the front door behind him. He was home safe at last. Home with his daughter, Ani.

Part III: Anne's Story

Chapter 1

Most decidedly, Edinburgh, Scotland was a nice place to live in the late 1950s and early 1960s. Rationing was a thing of the past; a throwback to the austere times of post-war Great Britain. So for Anne, sweets and toys would be in plentiful supply. Anne lived in a comfortable, stone-fronted terraced house in a well-established area just on the boundary of what could be called the city centre, in a house christened the romantic name, "Applegarth."

Anne's mother, Fiona, was a kind, round-faced woman, always busy doing *something*: if not cleaning or dusting, washing or ironing, she was tending the garden. And she was not one for venturing out of the house, preferring routine. Fiona always liked to look smart, loved tweed skirts and woollen jumpers best as they suited her slightly-on-the-plump-side physique. She wore practical, low-heeled shoes and her light-brown hair was short round her ears and permed by the local hairdresser once a month. There were always a set of pearls adorning her neck--even if she were staying home that day.

It was while working as a nurse at Edinburgh's Royal Infirmary that she'd met Alexander, her husband. She was a ward sister and he a young doctor doing rounds of the male wards. They'd struck up a friendship, a rapport, and one thing led to another and so they married. Soon after, Fiona gave up her nursing career. Alexander,

Fiona had thought at the time, was good for her. He was strong, confident, a leader; not that she couldn't *lead* (after all, she'd risen through the ranks, so to speak, to become a respected ward sister). And he could, at times, be a bit head-strong; impetuous, even. Like the time he came home from work to say that he was thinking he needed to expand his medical experience. Not just by moving to another department or another hospital, but by working abroad. And not just *any* abroad: he had *Tibet* in mind. But Tibet was a step too far for Fiona. Why not choose someplace closer? Somewhere she could accompany him?

Eventually Alexander wore her down. He'd take a position with the British Mission and Fiona would stay and look after Applegarth. His time in Tibet, he said, would pass quickly. They were still both young enough to do the things they'd planned to do together, and this was a *once-in-a-lifetime* opportunity--not to be passed up. But he'd stayed. And stayed. So here was Fiona in her tweeds and woollens tending house and garden until her husband returned from Tibet. Everything was on-course, routine, and in-place. That was, until the letter arrived.

Darjeeling
2 November, 1955

My Dearest Fiona,

I write to you with news of my travels throughout Tibet, with its snow-capped mountains, its barren flat plains, its colourful and rugged valleys and gorges alive with a wealth of fauna and flora. Its customs and traditions, its aura of serenity and peace. I feel as though I'm in a fantastic bubble and the outside world has receded in my mind to become almost forgotten.

I pray you receive this news well for it's with the most humble intentions that I tell you of this plight. I've been tending to a young pregnant Tibetan girl who subsequently has had twins, one a boy, the other a girl. Both babies and their mother, I'm happy to say, are doing well. Because of the girl's age, she and the baby boy will for the time being remain at the nunnery where she now resides. The baby girl, however, is a much different matter. She has blonde hair and blue eyes and the look of a Westerner, and seen as a foreigner. Although the baby girl may find acceptance by these deeply religious, even superstitious people, I fear for the baby's safety now with the Chinese occupation of Tibet.

More to the point, I've smuggled the baby girl out of Tibet and am now in India where I'll seek permission to bring her back to Scotland. Getting out of Tibet was a nerve-wracking adventure in itself, what with hiding in nomads' caravans and avoiding Chinese guards. But for the life of me I couldn't just leave this beautiful child to her fate in Tibet. I feel she belongs with me, with us, brought up as a Westerner, where she won't be persecuted for her appearance.

I'll sign off now and keep you updated on my progress. This will be such an exciting time for all of us. Imagine, us as parents!

Your loving husband,
Alexander

No matter how many times Fiona read and re-read the letter, she still couldn't make sense of it. The letter had arrived on a cold but clear late autumn morning, with just a whisper of snow in the air. It was an airmail letter postmarked: *India*. She and Alexander had a number of friends living on the Asian sub-continent so she wasted no time opening the letter to get their news. But as she sat comfortably in her favourite armchair scanning the letter, she grew increasingly confused by the talk of a *baby*, a *Tibetan girl*, and becoming a *parent*. At first she'd thought she'd opened a letter meant for another "Fiona." But it was clearly signed in her husband's hand: *Alexander.*

As Fiona struggled to make sense of the unusual letter, she let it slip from her fingers and drift languidly to the highly-polished timber floor of Applegarth's front room. Her eyes turned to focus on the sharp, cold blue of the sky glinting through the glass of the bay window; her thoughts now on the weather. *Yes,* she decided, *it'll likely snow today.* A shiver ran down her spine--but she wasn't cold. Inside herself a red heat was rising. *What did Alexander do?* She picked the letter up off the floor and slipped it into the bureau drawer, then went about her routine. Again and again her thoughts returned to the letter. That evening she took it out and read it again, this time as dispassionately as she could. The tone was so unlike him: he would have told her well in advance if he were planning to leave Tibet for India.

Over the next few days the content of the letter began to fester in her mind. Then just over a week later a telegram arrived from Calcutta, its clipped wording matter-of-factly stating that Alexander and the baby had gained passage on the merchant ship *Benmhor,* bound for London, and would be home soon. This message just fed Fiona's bewilderment; there was a constant knot in the pit of her stomach, squeezing her resentment of Alexander tighter and tighter. Too much to handle alone, Fiona decided she needed to tell someone. In desperation she decided to confide in her friend, Ruth, a bridesmaid at her wedding (a choice she'd since come to regret).

Both Alexander and Fiona were *famously* good friends with Ruth, and her opinion was valued by them both. Still, Fiona had grown distrustful of this overly-confident woman who she perceived as only *superficially* charming. And though often cold and aloof--and to Fiona, there was a haughty *air* about her, and it sometimes felt as though she were looking down her nose at her--Ruth was nonetheless a very practical woman. Sensible. But still, the wedding photographs continued to be a thorn in Fiona's side.

It was only after the wedding photos had come back from the photographer that she'd noticed it: In most of the shots it wasn't Alexander and herself standing together, but Alexander and Ruth! In some shots they were facing each other, smiling; and there was something about their body language that unnerved Fiona. There Ruth was--tall and slim in her dark turquoise pencil knee-length skirt that drew attention to her long, slim legs, her figure-hugging turquoise jacket with sparkling diamante silver buttons that framed her ample bust, and that tightly-cinched black patent-leather belt that showed off her slim waist--standing arm-in-arm with Alexander (the groom!) in his well-tailored black pin-striped suit. Meanwhile she, Fiona, was standing at least a foot away—like a mere *guest*--in her subdued beige skirt and jacket . . .

Maybe this isn't such a good idea, she second-guessed--just as the doorbell rang. Before she could answer it Ruth walked in and they greeted one another with a mock kiss on the cheek. Fiona gestured for Ruth to take a seat. "Coffee or tea, Ruth?" enquired Fiona.

"Tea, of course," replied Ruth. "You know very well that I don't drink *coffee*--it's absolutely *ghastly*!"

Returning a few minutes later carrying a silver tray with two china cups and saucers, matching creamer and sugar bowl with silver tongs, Fiona set the tray on the small side-table near Ruth. "Read *that*," Fiona said almost demandingly, handing her the letter she'd been keeping in her skirt pocket. Fiona watched as Ruth read the letter and subsequent telegram. As the two sat civilly in Fiona's spic-and-span lounge at Applegarth, Ruth let out a sharp gasp. Carefully slipping the letter and telegram back into the envelope, she laid it beside the tea tray and looked at Fiona:

"My, my!" Ruth exclaimed—almost in a hushed whisper. "Quite the turn of events, *isn't* it!" and Fiona thought she detected a tone of self-satisfaction.

"I don't know what to make of it!" replied Fiona. "All sorts of crazy ideas have been jumping into my head since I received them!"

Ruth leaned forward, reached across the low table and extended her left hand in a comforting gesture. "Now, now," she counselled. "Let's not jump to any wild conclusions here. We both know Alex is a sensible man. He's not prone to impulses--so there must be some good reason for all this."

"Yes, *maybe*," Fiona retorted with some indignation, "but it's all so sudden—and with no warning! A *fait accompli*, it seems! And to bring a baby back with him?! What am I supposed to do with a *baby*?!"

Ruth again reached out to Fiona. "I know what you're thinking--but not *Alex*. He wouldn't, he *couldn't*, do such thing."

"That's what I want to believe," sighed Fiona, "but now I'm not so sure."

Ruth guided the conversation to more mundane topics—the autumn, opera line-up, the next meeting of the Scottish Women's Convention--but Alexander's letter dominated both their thoughts. After the teapot had been emptied, Ruth clasped her hands to her knees and said, "Well, I must be going, Fiona. Got important things to do. Try not to worry. Alex is a good man. All will become clear when he gets back."

"I'm not so sure, Ruth," Fiona replied grimly. "I'm really not so sure."

After Ruth had gone, Fiona returned to the lounge. There next to the silver tea tray lay Alexander's letter—but she did *not* want to pick it up. What was the point? No matter how many times she read it, it said no more or less than the time before. It boiled down to this: there was going to be a baby in the house! All that was left to do now was wait for Alexander to arrive. Then, she decided, the child would go to the proper authorities. *There are special agencies for orphans like her!* That was her final decision—and she wasn't about to let Alexander talk her round!

Fiona drew a quick breath and grabbed the envelope, not daring to acknowledge it. Hurriedly she put it back into the bureau drawer: *Out of sight, out of mind*, she thought to herself. She then resumed her day-to-day routine as best she could.

Chapter 2

Iт was a cold and clear wintry afternoon when the squeal of car brakes drew Fiona's attention to the front window and a black taxi drawing up outside. Out stepped Alexander, cradling a package in his arms, while the taxi driver manhandled suitcases through the front gate. The day Fiona dreaded had arrived. She composed herself, straightened her outfit, and went to the front door. Taking a breath she opened it wide and stepped out onto the lone front step. Exchanging a few decidedly harsh words with her husband she turned and retraced her steps. In the front room she sat down in her favourite chair and waited. There would be no emotional reunion of husband and wife that evening. The atmosphere, in fact, lacked any warmth save that issuing from the blazing hearth.

"Hi, Fiona," he said, placing the bundle on the sofa. Fiona glared at him. "We got the overnight from Euston Station," he said, lowering himself into the opposite armchair. "It's been exhausting, but we're here." Fiona offered no reply. Alexander sighed. "I am sorry, dear. I know this must be awkward for you, but there was no choice, really. I couldn't just abandon this little thing. I just couldn't."

Words came now to Fiona. "Oh, Alexander, I really don't know if I can cope with this," she sighed. "What possessed you to take it upon yourself to bring this *thing*, this *baby* into our lives?"

Alexander lowered his head, Pembuti now flashing into his mind: her eyes, the softness of her skin, the beauty of her soul and the simplicity of life back in Tibet. He sighed. He already missed the East so badly and as he now looked at the four walls of their almost perfectly-square house—the house that had once held their dreams--he felt trapped; he longed for the freedom of the Tibetan Plateau. "It's not easy to explain and I'm really very tired," he offered, almost as an apology. "Can we look after this little thing first?"

Fiona could see the fatigue in her husband's face, and for a brief moment felt empathy. He looked frail and drawn, older than his years. "Okay, okay. I'll help you with her," Fiona conceded. "But all this needs sorting out," she said, gesturing toward the little bundle, "and soon."

The remainder of the day was spent getting their innocent little visitor settled in. Conversation between Alexander and Fiona was stilted; cursory and matter-of-fact. By the following morning Fiona's attitude had softened somewhat, the only real issue in her mind, *Is Alexander the father of this baby?* "Alexander, we really need to talk about this wee one," she said after the baby had been fed and changed and lay gurgling in the small basket Alexander had brought back from India. "I'm your wife. I deserve that." But Alexander wasn't listening, completely absorbed in Ani. Fiona grew furious: "If you could *drag* yourself away from the baby for a moment and answer my questions, I'd really appreciate it!" snorted Fiona.

Alexander turned to his wife and nodded, then turned back to the baby. "Later, we'll talk *later*," he said impatiently. But each time Fiona tried to bring up the subject that day, the baby needed attention. And so far he'd done everything for the baby himself--only asking that his wife do the laundry. Fiona grew increasingly incensed that her husband didn't even have the decency to address her concerns. So wrapped up in the baby, it was as if she no longer existed, and the anger started to burn away at her core. They avoided each other and spoke little. Several days passed before Alexander agreed to sit down and explain what had happened:

There was the birth of the twins at the nunnery . . . the situation with the invading Chinese . . . the caravan flight into India . . . and the sea voyage home. And, all this seemed perfectly feasible to Fiona; after all, she had friends in Asia and knew of the plight of the Tibetan people. Yet, two questions remained unanswered: What was Alexander's personal interest in this baby? And why had he taken it upon himself to bring her all the way back to Scotland? Surely the baby would be better off with her own people. Why subject the infant (and himself) to the hardships of a clandestine escape from Tibet, confrontations with the occupying Chinese, and the niggling bureaucracy of the Indian and British governments? These basic questions remained unanswered--Alexander intentionally side-stepping the answers.

As the weeks turned into months, Ani gradually became part of Alexander and Fiona's everyday life. Alexander petitioned the courts to adopt "Anne" and insisted that Fiona be named her legal mother. Fiona hesitated to have her name on the birth certificate as it mentioned nowhere that it was an *adoption* certificate. For all intent and purposes, she would be her actual mother, and Fiona knew she would never feel for the child as a mother should. Even so, she decided she could at least offer Anne a fine home, with more comforts than she could ever know in Tibet.

With Alexander now working as General Practitioner at a newly-established health clinic, Fiona became the dutiful mother; caring for the child's physical needs becoming her full-time job. (Emotionally there was a void.) Fiona felt left out of the bigger picture, robbed and cheated as she was a "mother" on paper only. She had not experienced the excitement and trepidation of discovering herself pregnant; had not had to adjust to the physical, biological, and emotional changes that come with motherhood; the awareness of another life growing inside her. And Fiona grew increasingly jealous of the bond between Alexander and baby. Finally, the obvious had to be asked point blank: "Alexander, a great deal of time has passed and the child is obviously here to *stay*. And I believe that if *anyone* were to leave, it would be *me*. So I ask you directly, is this *your* child? I deserve to know!" Alexander had been pouring juice for Anne and the question took him completely off guard:

"Da, juice spilling, Da, juice spilling . . . " chanted Anne.

Quickly tilting the juice container upright and setting it on the table, Alexander headed to the sink for a cloth to sop up the spill. "This is in really bad taste, Fiona.," he said, as if avoiding eye-contact. "In front of Anne you ask this question? She's old enough to pick things up, you know!"

"But, the child is always round! We have no time to ourselves anymore, and I have a right to know whose child I'm raising! If Anne is yours, just *say* so!"

Alexander was reaching his limit. Fed-up. Fed up with his wife continually bringing up Tibet. (Each time she did he wanted to grab Anne and run--run out of the house and straight back to a land of simple ways.) Fed-up with being a doctor. (Tending people who came to him whining of colds and coughs and aches—illness that in Tibet would be treated naturally; he blamed such ill-health on lack of fresh air and exercise.) Fed-up with this *civilized* way of life—this living in a concrete void . . .

"Alexander, I can't keep doing this," Fiona said one evening after the baby had been put to bed for the night.

"What do you mean?" asked Alexander

"*This*!" she exclaimed, standing up and pacing the floor. "Look at us! Look at this *place*! My house isn't a *home*—it's a bloody *nursery*! I'm not a wife, I'm a bloody nurse-maid!"

"Well, there *is* a baby in this house!" responded Alexander.

"Yes, there is!" shouted Fiona. "But not *my* baby! Is it *yours*?!"

The dam had burst. Fiona had held it back as best she could--for as long as she could:

"I get a letter from you! You're bringing a baby home—just like *that*! No discussion . . . no explanation . . . no consideration for the wife you left behind! Then you bloody well turn up with *that*!" she spit angrily, pointing up to the upstairs bedroom as her rant continued. "Now I'm stuck having to wash and clean up after you *and* your baby, Alexander! *Your* baby--not *mine*!" Fiona's face was drained of its usual vibrant colour as she stormed across the room to stare out the window. Alexander was stunned. He'd never seen Fiona so upset so he chose his words thoughtfully:

"Fiona, I've explained about Tibet, and the twins, and the political atmosphere there. What else can I say? What else could I have done but bring Anne here to Scotland?"

"You *really* don't get it—do you?" she said, turning to face him. "She's not *my* child! *We* didn't conceive her, *I* didn't carry her, and *I* didn't give birth to her! And I've asked you point-blank if you're the father and you refuse to give me a straight answer! Don't you see how this is eating away at me?!"

"Okay, okay, Fiona," Alexander agreed. "You're right--you're absolutely right! Maybe I should have given more thought to how this would effect you. And maybe part of me is still in Tibet."

"Part of you is still in Tibet? And just what part would that *be*?" she said—a sad desperation welling in her eyes.

"Fiona, I'm *here* now—isn't that what's most important? Even if I do have a few things to work through?"

"Alexander, it's been months!"

"Well, maybe if we got you some help with the baby! Maybe have Ruth come over and help once in a while," Alexander offered.

"*Ruth?*" Fiona said incredulously. "Of all people?! You can't *possibly* be serious!"

Alexander threw up his hands and stalked out of the room.

By now the sunlight was fading and the pale yellow of the street lights had given way to a deepening yellow hue. Neighbours' curtains were being drawn. Fiona reached out with both hands and drew the front-room curtains together. It was symbolic; enough for one day. Fiona retired to her bedroom while Alexander went to the second bedroom and the sleeping Anne.

Chapter 3

⟋

It was Saturday morning, his first weekend off in six weeks, and Alexander had succumbed to Anne's demands to be read *The Story of Cinderella*. She was now three years old and turning into a lovely, blond-haired, effervescent child. The two sat in his favourite chair beside the open fire in the front room. He was pleased to have his daughter near him; it certainly beat going into the surgery. In the kitchen Fiona had finished washing the breakfast dishes and Alexander now felt his whole body being jarred as she slammed dishes and cutlery. Before 9:00 that morning an argument had ensued and she was not in a good mood. He looked at the clock: it was only 10:00. He needed a drink but 11:00 was the earliest he could get away with it.

"Mum-Mum," Anne said, pointing to a picture of one of the ugly sisters.

"No, sweetheart, that's not Mum-Mum," he admonished, whispering, "and that's not a nice thing to say about your mother." Anne was just about to repeat her observation when Fiona entered the room and dropped heavily into the chair opposite Alexander, beside the fire.

"So, Alexander, we have you here on a Saturday morning for a change. Let Anne play with her dolls so we can have a few minutes."

Alexander gently nudged Anne off his knee saying, "Go play with your toys for a while, darlin', we can finish Cinderella later."

"No!" yelled Anne, stamping her foot. "We can finish it *now*— I want it *now*!" Alexander flashed a warning at his daughter, his look enough to make Anne turn and shoot Fiona a sour look. She left the lounge and headed for her bedroom in search of toys.

"Alexander, I think I've been more than patient about this. I know there's more to the story than you've told me and if you're not willing to tell me then--"

"Okay, okay--*fine!*" Alexander said, lowering his head. "I'll tell you the whole story." Alexander got up, went to the drink cart, and filled a tumbler half full of whiskey. (Fiona watched, bracing herself the worst.) Sitting down opposite her he took a gulp and began. "It was a chance meeting. I just happened to be at the market in a small village near Lhasa. I could hear a voice speaking English--with a Scottish accent, no less--rising above the hubbub of the locals. Of course, I looked about and spotted this chap trying to barter with a vendor, and having no success. He spoke no Tibetan and the trader knew no English. Anyway, I walked over and said to this fellow Scot that I would help. The chap spun round and let out a bellowing laugh and said, 'Thank god, a civilised man!' So using my best Tibetan I helped him buy a few necessities, at a good price." Fiona watched as Alexander stopped, raised his glass to his lips, and bottomed it before he continued.

"It turns out the chap's name was Bill Murray and he was a chef with some trade commission in Lhasa, and somehow found his way to my village. And what a *character*! He said he came from Perth and apart from cooking and catering he was a part-time musician. Played weddings and parties and that sort of thing round Perth--you know. So anyhow, we ended up spending the day together. To put it mildly, he wasn't slow at coming forward--but likable enough with it."

Alexander paused, got up, and poured himself another drink. Downed half before he sat back down. As he sat, Fiona noticed a troubled look on his face. He looked up at her then lowered his eyes before he continued. "He had nowhere to stay so I got him a room next to mine. Well, we spent all that week together—you know, it was nice to hear a fellow Scotsmen tell his stories-- and the next Saturday we needed a few things from the market so we went back. While we were there I ran into a group of nuns I'd helped on and off, treating a few of the sick they cared for at their nunnery. With them was a young woman--a *girl*, actually--of about fifteen. She wasn't a nun but was under their care. Had to do with her mother being killed and her father gone off to fight the Chinese in the eastern provinces."

Alexander had Fiona's undivided attention now. Perhaps the whole truth would finally come out, she thought, hopefully. She watched as Alexander looked wistfully past her and out beyond the lounge window--the whiskey glass set aside. "Anyway, the girl's name was *Pembuti*. A pretty little thing." (An unmistakable grin came to Alexander's face.) "Striking, likable, and a bit of a handful, according to Ani- Dolma, the head nun. She spoke almost no English, but it didn't keep her from striking up conversations with strangers. And she really stood out in that crowd!" (Again Alexander grinned— as if reminiscing fondly.) "Well, damned if this *Bill Murray* didn't take a liking to her! See, he helped pick up a basket of goods she'd dropped—and then just wouldn't leave her alone! Made her take him round and tell him the names of everything in the whole bloody market! And I guess--she fell for it! He was *young* . . . *handsome*, I guess you'd say . . . *charming*. And after making the rounds of the market, the two of them headed off on their own. The last thing I remember is him turning round and waving good-bye." (Alexander picked up his empty glass and examined it.) "Well, that evening Bill returned to his room in what I'd call an exceptionally *subdued* mood--and didn't really say much—which was quite out of character for him. The next morning he was gone—to Lhasa, I guess." Alexander gave a distant look and squirmed nervously in his chair. "So, that's *it*, then. This *Bill Murray* is the father."

"Fine! But what's *his* daughter doing in my house? And why the big *mystery?*" snapped Fiona.

"It's not as simple as that!" Alexander replied, getting up and revisiting the drinks trolley. "See, Ani-Dolma asked me to get involved—for the babies' sake. And then, Pembuti seemed to trust me in a way she didn't trust the nuns. And after I figured out that it was this *Murray* character—and if I hadn't arranged a room for him he may have just--"

"You felt guilty? Like you were responsible?"

"Well, yes--*no!* She was innocent, such a naive thing. And . . . she *needed* me! She was lost, a lonely little soul. Surrounded my nuns all day I—I think I probably reminded her of *him*. Me being a Westerner, Scottish, and all."

"And it was definitely this Bill? You aren't feeling guilty because you--"

"Now just a minute, Fiona! What are you suggesting? *Me?* You think it was *me?* You're bloody joking!"

"God, Alexander! She has blond hair and blue eyes! You fawn all over her! You brought her half way round the world! That's a huge sacrifice to make because you unknowingly got a lecherous chef a room!"

Alexander stumbled back to his chair—spilling his whiskey down the front of his shirt. "I could *never* do such a thing! What--to that innocent little girl?! *Fifteen years old*, Fiona! I looked after her, delivered her two babies, for Christ's sake! She needed help! Her babies needed help! I couldn't just *abandon* them!" Alexander ranted. "I was the only one who could help!"

"The *only* one?" Fiona said, clearly finding the idea preposterous.

"You just don't get it!" Alexander said, tilting his glass against his lips. "And you never will!"

Fiona sat in silence. She'd asked the questions. She'd never seen Alexander so defensive. So combative. Maybe it was the whiskey—but she doubted it. She got up and left the room, leaving behind a troubling wake of questions and answers—mixed with distrust and resentment. It hung in the air like a foul, suffocating odor. She slept alone in her room that night and for several to follow, while her husband slept next door with somebody else's daughter.

As time passed, Fiona softened, and Alexander's explanation seemed at least *plausible*. She doubted she'd ever know the whole truth but decided not to let it eat away at her. Life had to go on. Meanwhile, Anne was growing up quickly. Becoming more vocally demanding. Finally the adoption was formalised and Anne became Alexander and Fiona's daughter. Still, in her quieter moments, Fiona pondered: *What about this Bill Murray? Where is he now? Why didn't Alexander contact him?* And, *What does Ruth know? Does she know the whole sordid story?*

Chapter 4

Fiona watched as Anne grew into a pretty and often precocious toddler, always inquisitive, always venturing into places she was told not to go. And to Fiona she always seemed to get the better of Alexander with a twinkling of her soft-yet-knowing blue eyes and a radiant smile that lighted up her whole face. Fiona tried to discern her husband's features in Anne's little face, but could not. Yet her mind remained restless; searching.

"Da-Da!" Anne would squeal each morning, running in and waking Alexander and Fiona—now sharing a bed--at an unearthly hour. "Birds are singing outside, it's time to get up, listen I can sing just like them!" And to prove it she began to copy the birds' chirping.

"*Please*, Alexander, let me sleep!" Fiona growled. "I have a long day with Anne and I'm exhausted already!" she said, pulling the bed-covers over her head to block out the intrusion. Anne stared intensely at Fiona's blanket-encased form, unable to understand why anyone would want to stay in bed when the sun lit the sky and the birds sang their wake-up song. Hands on hips she flounced out of the room, following her father who was headed to the bathroom. While her father washed, shaved, and dressed, Anne would dance round the house waving her arms and tapping her feet as she sang at the top of her lungs. Fiona could only stick her head under her pillow to try and block out the noise.

Anne could remember little of her very early years. Why should she--stuck in a pram, staring out into space, the occasional strange face peering in? But it became a much different matter once Anne found her legs and her voice. Then there was no limiting her. Full of fun, bursting with laughter, and over-flowing with curiosity, her head of blond curls could be seen bouncing along as she skipped and danced everywhere she went; with so much energy, walking was too boring for her. And according to Alexander, the very moment Anne (or "Annie," as he came to call her) opened her mesmerising blue eyes each morning, it was as if everything was brand new that day.

Alexander came to believe that Annie had a special kind of *knowing*. That there was something that set her apart from other children. She would gaze upon people, flowers, trees, and everyday objects with an intensity that some people found a bit unnerving; as if she were looking through them and beyond. As if she could see something no one else did. Sometimes her mother would often have to nudge or shake her to bring her out of this reverie; Fiona's friends telling her not to worry, *She's only a child, she'll eventually grow out of it*. But for Fiona's liking, Anne was *too* inquisitive. Always asking *why*--why *this* and why *that*. And while her father delighted in trying to answer all her questions, Fiona found them annoying. Aggravating.

To Fiona's relief, Alexander did most everything for Anne. Cooked her meals, bathed her, read to her, and played games she liked. And except for when he had to go to work (when she became Fiona's responsibility) they were seldom apart. Anne would see him to the front door then run to the window to watch him walk down the garden path to his car, parked out on the street. She knew his every movement—the way he'd open the car door and get in; the way he'd slam the door with a squeak and a *bang* then coax the car to life with a splutter and puff of black smoke. She'd wait patiently until he glanced up in her direction, wave his hand, then drive off. But then she'd have to find something to do to occupy her time until he returned. But that was easy. To Anne, every-thing in her world was to be marvelled at--questioned and understood.

She took special delight in the colours emanating from things round her: the plants, the birds, the insects, and, of course, the people. She stared as if spellbound at the patterns these colours created as their ener-gies radiated outwards--a myriad of subtle and not-so-subtle shades and textures. She watched as these colours wove in and out of each other, blend with everything round them, then fill the air with their coloured energy (as if trying to communicate with her directly). And before long she came to understand that these colours and energies were convey-ing information that she should know; forming them into stories that needed to be shared. And when she tried to explain this to her mother, Fiona rebuked her for being silly. Told her to use her imagination for something *useful*.

All-in-all, Fiona eventually came to accept her lot in life: a du-tiful housewife and mother (still dressed in tweed skirts and wool-len jumpers) dedicated to washing, ironing, cleaning, and tending to her adopted daughter's needs. The only time she ventured far from the house was to go to the grocers or post office, or when necessary, take the bus to Princes Street to shop--with Anne in tow, or course. (Dreading the scene Anne would make on the bus, Fiona would delay these outings as long as possible.) It was one evening after one such outing to Princes Street, while Anne was playing with her toys on the floor at her father's feet, that Fiona asked Alexander a question: "Who or what is *Drakar*?"

"*Drakar*?" repeated Alexander. "Don't think I know that one. Why?"

"Well, we were on the bus today and *she*" (Fiona pointed down at Anne) "asked the conductor if the bus could take her to *Drakar*. It was obvious that it was lost on the conductor, 'This bus terminates at Kings

Road depot,' he told her, so I asked her what or where *Drakar* is and she told me that she lives there."

Alexander thought a moment and said, "Oh, probably just one of her imaginary worlds. You know—kid stuff."

"I reminded her that we live at Applegarth, but she insisted that *she* lives at *Drakar*." Fiona paused a moment then said, "It wouldn't be some *Tibetan* thing would it?"

"Not that Tibetan nonsense *again*!" snapped Alexander, shaking his head wearily. "I thought we were well past all that!"

"It's not *that* far-fetched, Alexander!" she shot back. "You've *been* to Tibet, she's *from* Tibet--I'm only asking! And how, exactly, do you expect me to get *past* it? Tibet is sitting right there!" Fiona concluded, pointing at Anne. Anne abandoned her toys and wrapped her arms round her father's legs.

"Now look what you've done! Dragging all this non-sense back up in front of her!" moaned Alexander. "You seem to forget, she's just a child!"

"Of course—don't even *consider* my side!"

"There shouldn't be any bloody *sides*!" he returned fire.

"What with refusing to listen to what she's told, and that nonsense about colours and lights, and now this *Drakar* business--I swear, she'll be the bloody death of me!" Fiona said, storming out of the room.

"Don't you worry, darlin'," Alexander told Anne. "Everything'll be just fine. Let's get you ready for bed. Daddy's got to go in to work early tomorrow, and we *both* need our sleep!"

Fiona found it more and more difficult to deal with Anne's continuing, rambling stories about birds and plants and people—their lights and colours--and took to banishing her to the relative freedom of the front garden, with strict instructions not to go out the gate. But this didn't deter Anne. In fact, as was often the case, her mother's words had the opposite effect as intended; they were like an oral invitation to proceed out through the gate and into other worlds. Invariably she would soon be skipping along the neighbouring streets, *la-la-ing* to herself, armed with a cheery "hello" for anyone she passed. Occasionally she would stop and compare other gardens to her own--and marvel at the colourful displays of flowers and shrubs, bursting out with their bright pinks, yellows, and blues, all set against the variegated greens and stark browns visible behind the coloured petals and flower buds.

As she stopped at one such garden, she could see a mass of darkish, glossy green leaves hugging closely the stone walls of the house. These leaves seemed to spread like a tapestry up the side of the house and round the sides of a large upstairs bay window. As Anne's eyes followed this trail of greenery she could see quite clearly a young girl standing next to a fabulous rocking horse, her arms rapped lovingly round its neck. *I must have a closer look at this wonderful plaything!* she said under her breath. With no further thought she opened the gate, skipped up to the front door, and rang the bell. After a few moments the heavy red door opened and a warm, smiling face beamed down at her. Before the woman could say a word Anne said, "I'm here to see the horse I saw up in the window. May I please?" Somewhat taken aback by this unexpected, if not peculiar request—yet taken in by the little girl's sweet and mannered demeanor--the woman invited Anne in.

"I'm Anne," she told the woman, pushing out her hand politely.

"Well, hello, Anne. My name is Flora." Anne nodded. "So, you'd like to see the rocking horse upstairs?"

"Yes, please," she said.

As Anne followed Flora up the staircase the woman told her that the horse had belonged to her daughter Edith, who was no longer with her, and that she just hadn't been able to bring herself to get rid of it. Once in Edith's bedroom, Anne stared at the bed with its silk magenta bedspread with sparkling sequins that glinted as the sun shone through the pink lace curtains—having never seen such a beautiful bedroom in her young life. There were Teddy bears propped up on the pillows and lovely colourful paintings of horses and other animals on the walls. Anne's feet felt as though they were sinking into the deep pile of the dark pink carpet, and there was the hint of a lovely fragrance in the air. Anne slipped out of her shoes.

The wondrous rocking horse was dark brown in colour with a cream hair-like mane, light brown leather bridle, reins and saddle, and sat proudly in the bay of the window. "Why don't you give her a try," Flora said. And although Anne had never been in the company of a horse before she instinctively knew what to do: she grabbed the reins in her left hand, put her left foot in the little stirrup, and threw her body over the back of the horse, her right foot immediately finding the other stirrup. Gently she nudged her body forward as if coaxing the horse to move. The mare responded by first rocking forward then back, then forward again; Anne's body quickly becoming attuned to the horse; her body rising and falling in rhythm with the animal's motion. As she spurred the rocking horse on she felt as if she and the horse could jump through the window--as if it were not there at all—and she would be *free*! *Free* as the wild wind to ride across wide open spaces, the soft flat and even ground below her. And as she became *one* with the horse she felt that she were flying; her heart soared, she was weightless and there was nothing near her except the horse beneath her. Flora watched with joyful glee as horse and rider rocked back and forth as one. The little girl was in a world all her own . . .

Anne slowly brought the horse to a halt and dismounted, patting its neck as if thanking it for a wonderful ride. Her curiosity then turned to the little girl she'd seen at the window, and asked Flora where she'd gone. Flora placed her hand to her heart and said that her daughter's heart had stopped beating, but that she was now at peace. She was laid to rest in the local cemetery where she too would be buried when her heart stopped. She said how very sad she was that she would never see her daughter again until she too passed on.

This confused Anne. She wanted to tell Flora that she was mistaken; that Edith was still there in her bedroom with her rocking horse and Teddy bears, but was too afraid to say so. Afraid she might not be allowed back to ride the horse again. Anne tried to imagine being buried under the ground: Is that really what happens when you die? But her love of the rocking horse soon made her forget the image of death Flora had painted.

Anne often visited Flora's house; Flora welcome it. It was nice to have a child's laughter and vibrant energy in her house again. Sometimes Anne would play with Edith and her toys; sometimes Flora treated her to orange juice and a biscuit, then read stories to her. But she always rode the rocking horse she now called "Jewel," gazing out Edith's bedroom window, watching the world go by on the street below. She noticed that everyone passing had one colour or another moving round them, and that these colours were vibrant in some people, dull in others. These colours moved and wove in and out, changing all the time. When people stopped to talk to one another on the street the colours grew longer and wider, moving faster and with more vibrancy. From these colours she would imagine what they were saying; sense what they were feeling—joy, love, anger, hate. Sometimes this outpouring of emotion made her feel uneasy; sensing that something bad was about to happen, but she could do nothing to stop it.

From her vantage point at Edith's window, Anne could see when her father arrived home from work. She'd watch him climb out, close and lock the car door, then amble into the house. Then right on cue, when he'd realise that Anne wasn't home as she was supposed to be, the games would begin: he'd rush back out of the house, stand on the garden path, and move his head side-to-side--a look of panic on his face. Then he'd race frantically up and down the street searching, stopping and asking people if they'd seen a little blond-haired girl. Meanwhile, Anne would ride the horse faster and faster, delighted that she was invisible to him and everyone else--except for Edith. Only when she saw her father's colour change from his usual vibrant yellow to a deep dark and murky green—and then to red--would she dismount the horse, say goodbye to Edith and Flora, then bounce down the stairs and out the front door. Then she'd wait until her father was looking the other way to skip up behind him and throw her arms round his legs, holding tight for as long as it took for him to calm down. Then together, hand in hand, they'd return home. He never knew where Anne had been--nor did he ask. The relief of finding her was enough. (Anne loved being invisible and in control of who and when anyone saw her.)

For Anne, life was idyllic. She had her father and mother to watch over her. She had the rocking horse to take her places far, far away. And she had her world of colours and lights and magical energy; her hopes and dreams. But just under the surface were those uneasy feelings some colours would bring. And as for her mother, Fiona, life was anything but idyllic. Anne was quickly becoming more than she could handle.

Chapter 5

As anyone from the outside could see, there was no real connection between mother and daughter. In cold and moody moments Fiona would describe herself as Anne's nurse. *After all, Anne isn't really my daughter,* Fiona would remind herself. No blood ties. No bonding. No shared experiences—in birth or in life. She felt no true maternal instincts. And even more disquieting was the closeness Anne and Alexander shared. What they had looked and felt *real*. Father and daughter, a natural bond grew day-by-day. And since Fiona only had Alexander's word for it-- his story about this Bill Murray and a naive Tibetan girl--and Ruth's constant prompting that Alexander wouldn't, *couldn't* have done such a thing—nagging suspicions continued to rear their ugly heads. Was Alexander Anne's real father? --she needed so desperately to know. But how to get at the *truth*?

This *Bill Murray* would know; *if* he actually existed! She knew Alexander's account by heart now--he'd repeated it often enough--by rote, it seemed. *Since this Bill Murray had come from Perth, I'll go there and find him!* she resigned. But she couldn't very well go to Perth with Anne in tow! Just show up on this Bill Murray's doorstep as say, "Here you are. This is your daughter! You take her—I've had enough!" Her only option was to ask Ruth to look after Anne while she took a day trip to Perth. First she had to convince Ruth—and withhold the truth. She'd tell Ruth she was going to Perth at Alexander's request, and it had to do with his medical work in Tibet.

"Oh--if it's for Alex," Ruth had said, "I'm glad to help. I guess I can bear Annie for a few hours or so," she finished with mock humour. But when Ruth arrived the next morning and Anne realised that she was being left with her and not going along with her mother, she flew into a screaming rage, stamping her feet and pulling at Fiona's skirt: "No--I *hate* her! I *hate* her!" But Fiona was determined to set off on her mission to Perth--with or without Anne's *approval*--leaving the house quickly to avoid further drama with Anne--and avoid Ruth's steely glare.

The train left Edinburgh Waverley on schedule and Fiona managed to find an empty carriage so she could have some peace and quiet to formulate her plan. The rhythmic *clickety-clack* of the train's wheels brought an element of comfort to Fiona as she stared out the carriage window. *Yes,* she thought, *this is what I should have done long ago!* Soon she would know the truth and the demons that had long haunted her would be forever vanquished . . .

Suddenly she was jarred from her tranquillity by the shrill of the train's whistle and jostling of its cars--from a smooth clicking to a hollow rumble as the track changed from solid ground to the occasional and hollow iron frame of the Forth Bridge. As she stared down at the flat and murky grey-blue waters of the Firth of Forth below, she knew the calmness was an illusion caused by the height of the bridge, and that as you drew nearer the surface the tumult and dangerous eddies could be treacherous. Fiona dragged her attention from the waters below and tried to work out what she would do: First she would check the Perth telephone directory for any "W. Murray." Then, as he had *supposedly* been a chef, she would visit or call as many restaurants and hotels as she could. Even just being in Perth was nearer the truth than just sitting at home in Edinburgh, she reminded herself.

On arrival, the directory listed twelve "W. Murray's," so she noted their full names, addresses, and telephone numbers in the little diary she'd brought. She then searched out restaurants and hotels round the city centre and laid out a course. When asked if a "chef called Bill Murray" worked in a particular establishment, sometimes the manager would give a suspicious look and refuse to divulge such information; sometimes she got a polite '*no*, but you can try *so-and-so's*.'

As the day wore on, Fiona was having no luck in her "restaurant-to-hotel" search, and time was running out; she had to get back and catch the train to Edinburgh. (At least she was now armed with some telephone numbers she could try from home.) Then just as she was about to ask a passer-by the quickest way back to the railway station, a poster in a shop window caught her eye:

The Bill Murray One-Man Band, now playing at the Fair City Hotel, it said. On it was a picture of a rather attractive blonde-haired man playing a guitar, and below that a contact number. Fiona suddenly remembered that Alexander had said that the Bill Murray he'd met in Tibet had said he was a bit of a musician. Her heart skipped a beat. She quickly scribbled down the details in her notebook and headed for the station.

As with the journey to Perth, the return trip to Edinburgh found Fiona's mind full of *what-ifs* and *buts*. And far from making things clearer, Fiona's discovery of a real "Bill Murray" only seemed to cloud things. What if the man *wanted* his daughter once confronted with the knowledge of her existence? What would Alexander *do* if she caused him to lose her? Maybe Perth wasn't such a great idea after all!? At last she arrived back home; exhausted. Upon opening the front door to Applegarth Anne, for once, seemed genuinely happy to see her.

"Mum-Mum!" she shouted. "Where have you been? I missed you! You've been gone for so long and *she* won't let me have a biscuit and I really wanted one!" she said, throwing a withering stare at Ruth.

"So . . . where exactly did you say you were going today, Fiona?" questioned Ruth.

"To a doctor's surgery in Perth. A GP there who'd worked with Alexander in Tibet. It had to do with some medical reports and records," Fiona replied convincingly--she hoped. (She'd always been a bad liar.)

"All a bit mysterious, if you ask me," frowned Ruth.

Fiona wasn't sure if Ruth was being cagey or had a genuine suspicion. "No, pretty standard medical stuff, really," Fiona assured her. "So, how did Anne behave while I was gone?" she asked, adroitly changing the subject—eliciting an instant scowl from Ruth.

"She really can be an unruly thing, *can't* she?!"

"She's headstrong, that's all," explained Fiona (somewhat surprised that she was defending behavior that she herself detested).

"There's *headstrong* and there's downright *rude* and *out-of-control*, Fiona!" Ruth was having none of that defense. "The child needs serious *discipline*!" she continued, staring daggers at Anne, "and lots of it! I'm sure *Alex* doesn't permit that kind of disrespectful behaviour!" Ruth said in her usual over-bearing tone.

"Actually, you couldn't be more wrong!" Fiona replied indignantly; intentionally lowering her voice to a whisper. "When it comes to her, she can do no wrong! I've tried my best to control her but Alexander constantly gives her her way!"

Ruth wasn't buying it—and it was clear. "Well, I think I've done enough *nannying* for one day," scoffed Ruth, with an exaggerated tone. "I'll leave her to *you*, Fiona."

"Thanks again, Ruth, I mean, for looking after Anne," said Fiona, following Ruth to the front door.

"Oh, I almost forgot," Ruth turned and said. "I don't know where she got it but Anne was playing with a jewellery box today. The contents sure didn't look like play things to me—so I'm guessing it may have belonged to you. One piece in particular, was an expensive-looking turquoise pendant. I tried to take it from her but she threw a tantrum and said it belonged to her. I think she must have put it back wherever she got it."

"Hummm . . . that's odd," thought Fiona aloud. "I don't know of any jewellery box with a turquoise pendant in it?"

Ruth just shrugged. "Well, I'm sure you'll suss it out."

For the next few days following her trip to Perth, Fiona went about her usual routine of housework and looking after Anne, while trying to piece together what she'd actually achieved and what she'd do next. It seemed that two sides were conflicting within her: one that had come to accept and love the little girl, one full of misgivings, doubts, and distrust. (Could Alexander not see that she wasn't coping well with all of this?) All that was left to her, it seemed, was Bill Murray in Perth. The key to this whole fiasco lay with him. So one evening when Alexander was out visiting friends and Anne had been put to bed a bit early, Fiona decided she'd make the call. But even as the phone rang out at the other end of the line, she was tempted to slam down the receiver. But then a voice answered. A woman.

Fiona asked to speak to Bill Murray. '*Hold on,*' she was told. Someone would go and get him. For much too long the line was just a cacophony of muffled voices and the clanging of glasses. Then: "Yeah--this is Bill."

Fiona's voice froze for a moment, then she blurted out: "Uh, Mr. Murray, have you ever been to Tibet?"

"Well, *yes*, yes I have," Bill politely but inquisitively replied. He'd worked there as a chef with the British Trade Commission a number of years ago.

Fiona pressed on: Had he met a young Scottish doctor there? Did he remember a young Tibetan girl called Pembuti? (She could sense a palpable tension on the line.)

"Uh, *yes*," he replied. He recalled a doctor called Alexander, but *no*, no one named Pembuti. "What's this all about?" he asked.

"I'm Alexander's wife, Fiona," she said. "Maybe he mentioned me." She then told him that her husband had brought home to Edinburgh a baby girl, with some story about twins born to this Tibetan girl. This Pembuti. And according to Alexander, Bill was the father.

"Hold on a minute, lass," the voice interrupted. "This baby—and this girl Pembuti—are you sure you have the right bloke?"

"Well, according to my husband, *yes*," Fiona said, feeling a certain sense of satisfaction at finally getting it out. "He said you spent some time with this *Pembuti* while you two were in Tibet? And a short time later this Pembuti turned up pregnant and--"

"--Whoa, now *wait*!" Bill Murray interrupted. "If I remember rightly, this Alexander, your husband, was a nice enough guy. But I don't know where he gets off spinning you such a wild tale! Yeah--I was in Tibet years ago, did a lot of things there. But I think I would remember any *twins*!"

"Well, he said you left Tibet before she knew she was—you know, maybe this wasn't such a good idea after all," Fiona flustered. "I mean, I thought you should know, but if you didn't--"

"You need to sort yourself out, lassie—and that husband of yours. I mean, phoning up strangers with story of babies and all that . . . " advised Bill from Perth—just before the line went dead.

Fiona's mind was ajumble now. Maybe she hadn't explained things clearly, but this Bill Murray of Perth really sounded as though he had no idea what she was talking about! No answers—just more questions!

Over the next few days Fiona's mind drifted from one of resolve and acceptance to one of dread: What had she done? If Alexander found out about her trip to Perth and the subsequent phone call—things would surely go from bad to worse. Hopefully, Bill Murray of Perth would simply forget the telephone call (if that were actually possible). But what if he *was* the Bill Murray Alexander had known in Tibet and decided he wanted to claim his daughter and just turned up unannounced on their doorstep? And even if he didn't, what if Ruth decided to confer with Alexander about the trip Fiona had made to Perth on his behalf? (The walls were closing in.)

As she tried to think things through to some logical conclusion, she knew that whatever the outcome, she would find no peace. And if there were to be any winners or losers from this sorry mess (which she now blamed herself for) then she must surely lose the most. Alexander and Anne would be lost to her, and she would find herself alone. But, she was growing tired. Looking after Anne was becoming more of a burden than she could withstand. And seeing Alexander and Anne playing happily together left her feeling distant and unloved. The closeness of father and daughter unnerved Fiona as it seemed to have replaced that of husband and wife. And the worst was yet to come.

One evening soon after, Alexander arrived home from the surgery earlier than usual. His usual affectionate exchange with Anne was cut short as he came directly into the kitchen where Fiona was preparing dinner. His face said it all:

"So! You went up to Perth!" Alexander stated rather than asked; a tone of indignation. "*Why?* Who do you know up there?" he said, suspecting full well why she'd gone.

Fiona was flustered; caught off guard. "Well, I just—I just thought I needed to get away, you know, a bit of a change," she stumbled.

"No, Fiona, I *don't* know!" Alexander pressed. He waited for her to confess the truth. He wanted to hear from her own lips that she didn't believe him.

"Okay--I had to find out for myself! About your true relationship with Anne!" Fiona blurted out—tears gushing from her eyes. "It's all very well for you to come home with this story about another man in Tibet—this Murray fellow--but I had to know that he actually exists! Can't you understand that?"

"What I understand, *Fiona*, is that my word wasn't enough!"

"I'm sorry, but your story--"

"And did you find this Bill Murray?" Fiona could hear the exasperation in his voice.

"Yes—yes I *did*," Fiona said, now looking and sounding sorrowful. "He admits to meeting you but completely denies the rest of your story!"

"*Story?* So, he convinced you it's a *story*?! Something I just *made up*?! Was that when you met with him?"

"No—no I didn't meet with him!" Fiona was floundering; felt herself drowning. "I—I only *phoned* him . . . from *here* . . . *afterwards*! I only wanted some confirmation to ease my--"

"Bloody hell! So, that's *it* then!" concluded Alexander. "You take the word of a complete stranger over your own husband! That about does it! Clearly, I should have stayed in Tibet like I had a mind to—and avoided this . . . *betrayal*!"

Fiona could see their relationship crumbling before her very eyes. "No--I didn't say I believed him over *you*! I just needed to know that he *existed*! Now I don't know who or what to believe!"

Alexander turned and walked into the front room to play with Anne, who was now shouting for attention—leaving Fiona standing there bewildered, in the middle of the kitchen amongst the debris of a day's housework. But, how did Alexander know she'd gone to Perth? *Ruth*, of course! It *had* to be bloody *Ruth*! Now *everyone* was against her! And now, Fiona had to do *something*. And she knew that whichever way she turned, a door would close--but another would not open!

Feeling that she must explain herself for the sake of everyone concerned (but could no longer rely on Alexander to listen), she resolved to write her reasoning and actions down on paper, hoping that someone would make sense of it; at the same time hoping that a little part of her guilt and desperation would be eased. After all, Anne needed to be told at some point in her life who she was and where she'd come from. Fiona could at least do that for her. The letter was written, sealed in an envelope, addressed and delivered to her solicitor on strict instruction that it was only to be opened upon Alexander's death. Why she'd chosen this route, Fiona herself could not explain. But this way, the matter of Anne and her questionable parentage would be resolved with or without her. She felt herself slowly drifting away . . . into a dark and empty place.

Chapter 6

In Anne's own little world, all was well. She had her own room, plenty of toys to play with, and sometimes her mother would even allow her to bring her toys downstairs to play with in the rear lounge, where the big bay window looked out over the well-maintained back garden. This garden--totally enclosed—with its mature hedges and trees on three sides, became Anne's secret adventure playground.

Besides the level and well-groomed lawn, there was a small rockery to the right of the kitchen door, and to the left a bed of long-established shrubs and bushes running the full length of the garden (fighting for sunlight with the perennial green of the hedge that overshadowed it). During the spring-to-summer season, an explosion of colours erupted from plants which had lain dormant during the winter months. Pinks, lilacs, yellows, and deep reds cast there entrancing light across the lawn, halted only by the sharpness of the low-set stones and contrasting boulders marking the rockery (as if protecting the shallow and delicate colours of the ground-cover flora that sprouted erratically between them). At the bottom of the garden was a small, green painted timber shed which looked as though it had seen better days; rusted door hinges and handle along with peeling paint were testimony to the passage of time. Adjacent to the shed was a raised vegetable bed where potatoes would struggle to emerge from their furrowed lanes and cabbages and carrots would vie for Fiona's attention. All this well-intentioned home produce was, however, overshadowed by the large palm-like leaves of ever-spreading rhubarb plants. Needless to say, rhubarb custard was a staple dessert for the family as was a well-stocked pantry of rhubarb jam. Anne loved the garden particularly during the summer months. She could lose herself in the make believe worlds that existed within the rockery, shrub bed, and vegetable patch.

When her father was away at work, and her mother unawares, Anne continued to visit Flora and "Jewel" to help pass the afternoons. Also, there were other families with young children living just down the street from Applegarth who Anne was sometimes allowed to visit or play with in the street—in the quiet hours of the day. But the children didn't like her loud, brash ways; nor did their parents, who saw her as a disruptive influence. Then one morning, quite unexpectedly, her mother announced that she was going to invite all the neighborhood kids to their house for a party. They would all be coming round that afternoon. But as it was to be a "surprise party," Anne was to wait in the front room while all the preparations were made. Anne was so excited she could barely contain herself.

To keep her occupied, Fiona sent Anne upstairs to put on her favourite party dress and pink patent-leather shoes; the ones with the neat little velvet bows on the top. But almost in the blink of an eye--Anne was back down stairs, asking Fiona if she could *Please! Please!* help. Her mother told her to wait in the front room until she was called, and not to get her nice frock dirty. So an anxious and excited little girl obediently waited with hands folded across her lap, feet kicking wildly, to be summoned. But before long, Anne's excitement began to turn to boredom.

When will my friends be coming? she asked herself. *Did they already sneak in the back door?* Every few minutes she'd get off her chair, walk to the big bay window and peer out through deep red floor-length curtains, hoping to see the kids arriving. But even as the pale winter sunshine and dusky late afternoon sky was replaced by the dull orange glow of the sodium-filled streetlights, no one came. The room now beginning to fill with dark shadows, Anne grew frightened, so she hurried to the door and tried to turn the handle. But it wouldn't turn. The door was locked. *What's my mum doing?* She pressed her ear to the door hoping to hear the excited giggled of her friends--or at least the sound of her mother busying herself with pots and pans in the kitchen. But there was nothing, no sound. All she could hear was the pounding of her own heart beating in her ears.

She needed to get out of the encroaching darkness--but her tiny arms couldn't reach the light switch next to the door. All sorts of thoughts raced through Anne's mind: Maybe her mother was very busy—and had forgot that she was still waiting in the front room. (But, why had she locked the door? Didn't she trust her to stay inside the room?) Or, maybe her mother had gone out to collect her friends. (But wouldn't she let her know that she was leaving her alone?) Soon, it wasn't enough to *imagine* what was going on, on the other side of the locked door; too much time had passed and she was getting scared. She seized the door handle with both hands and turned it with all her might--but it still wouldn't give! Flailing wildly against the solid timber panels of the door with her fists she screamed for her mother and father--but no one came!

She was trapped! All alone! She turned her back on the door and slumped to the floor, tears streaming down her face. Then two figures appeared before her, seemingly out of nowhere; as if from the very fabric of the room:

Through a gentle mist, her friend Edith appeared with a young woman holding tightly onto her hand, as if being led in Anne's direction. This young woman looked so beautiful with her long flowing, platted silver hair and translucent sparkling, flowing white robes. As

Edith's form receded into the background, the young woman knelt before Anne and placed a gentle hand on her forehead, then spoke to her in a pleasing and reassuring voice--though in words Anne could not understand. The soft touch of this strange and beautiful woman brought a warmth to Anne's brow which seemed to spread down through her entire body. As Anne tried to define the blurred contours of the woman's face, her attention was drawn to a beautiful necklace which hung from her neck' a ring of dazzling turquoise gemstones threaded through a shimmering silver chain, the largest and brightest stone set at the bottom as if protecting the woman's heart. Anne gazed wide-eyed into the stillness of the clear blue crystal and it seemed as though she were looking out over a placid blue lake reflecting an even bluer sky. But just then the peaceful serenity of this scene was broken by a tingling sensation in her eyes.

As Anne blinked, the turquoise was overpowered by a ball of red fire which seemed to grow larger as it engulfed the gemstone. This fiery orb exploded from the stone and bathed Anne in unspoken words of inner strength and confidence, assuring her that she would be safe no matter what was to happen. Then as the ethereal woman lifted her hand from Anne's head, she too receded back into the gentle mist from whence she'd appeared, the room slowly becoming a strange blend of solid forms and shadows cast by the false light of the street-lamps outside. And though comforted by Edith and this strange young woman's visit, Anne was still trapped; the room having now transformed from a place of safety and comfort to one of vulnerability and oppression. And then--a sickly-sweet odour filled the air; a smell that quickly made her feel sick to her stomach, leaving a sour, metallic taste in her mouth. Pressing her ear to the door once more she heard nothing. She began to breathe too heavily to remain standing. Then just as she dropped dizzily to the floor a familiar *chug* and *sputter* caught her ears. It was the sound of her father's car rumbling to a halt out front. *Oh, Da!* She got to her feet and made her way to the window:

As her father locked the car door and turned towards the house, Anne waved frantically--but he didn't seem to notice so she tapped on the window. Catching his attention he smiled and waved back. But when he realised that Annie was in the front room in the dark his expression quickly turned anxious. And as he quickened his step down the garden path he could see the frantic look on his daughter's face and the tears streaming from her eyes. As Anne rushed to the front room door to be rescued, all she could hear was her father coughing and the sound of feet on bare wood. Her heart fell as she heard his footsteps pass by her prison door and heard him shouting to her mother—*Fiona! Oh, God, Fiona!*--just before the sound of shattering glass and splintering timber filled the house.

Just as the afternoon had passed from an excited expectation of a party with friends to a frightening ordeal filled with panic, so the remainder of the evening passed in a procession of unreal sights and sounds which made no sense to Anne. She heard her father's raised voice, his hurried footfalls across the hall floor; the familiar, shuffling feet of the next door neighbour, Mrs. Thomson; an ambulance and police car's blue flashing lights bouncing off the neighbour's houses; a stretcher coming into the house and going out again; and finally, her father opening the locked door to the front room and giving her a big, hard hug--that strange sickly-sweet smell still lingering in the air like invisible fog . . .

"Oh, Da! I was so scared! So very, very scared!"

When Anne asked what had happened, all her father would say was that her mother had taken ill and had to be rushed to hospital. And that Anne would get a sleep-over at Mrs. Thomson's house because he had to go and see her. And that she was not to worry because everything would be alright. Anne followed Mrs. Thomson to the window so she could wave goodbye to her father as he got into the ambulance. Though it had been unsaid, Anne sensed a finality about what had just happened.

In the wake of the ambulance and police car's speedy departure, an empty house and strange silence only remained. But for Anne there was a lingering presence in the air like a memory of all that had happened, imprinted on the very fabric of the rooms. She shivered as Mrs. Thomson led her upstairs to collect her nightgown, slippers, and clothes for the next day. Excited to be spending the night in a new place—in a new bed--her thoughts were of her mother, Edith, and the kindly visitor who'd given her assurances.

The following morning Anne awoke bright and early with a start—and sat bolt upright. As she rubbed her eyes to clear the sleep she didn't recognise her surroundings; the bed felt softer and the curtains covering the window were blue and not yellow. And there was no flower-spotted wallpaper, just boring cream-coloured paint. Then memories of the previous day slowly filtered in—remembering now that she was at the next door neighbour's house because her mother had taken ill and her father had gone to the hospital with her. Quickly she jumped out of bed and was about to call for Mrs. Thomson when the bedroom door opened and in she stepped. Mrs. Thomson told Anne that as soon as she had a bit of breakfast she would take her home to her father; that there was a glass of fresh orange juice and a bowl of cornflakes waiting for her on the kitchen table. Anne quickly pulled on her clean clothes, scurried down to the kitchen, and made short work of all Mrs. Thomson had set out for her.

With the last spoonful of cornflakes, Mrs. Thomson nodded and took Anne's hand, leading her out of her house and back to her own. Anne frantically jumped up to reach the doorbell--but her diminutive size worked against her, so kindly Mrs. Thomson pressed the small, round green button and waited. A moment later the door swung inward and there stood Alexander; both Anne (and Mrs. Thomson) momentarily shocked by the haggard sight of the man. Anne looked round and past him trying to catch sight of her mother, but did not. He gently took his daughter's hand in his, thanked Mrs. Thomson, and told Anne that they needed to have a talk. Leading her into the front room he could feel the anxious tug of her hand so he told her not to worry. He would allow nothing to happen to her. Ever.

As Alexander sat in his usual chair by the fireplace, Anne stood in front of him, both her little hands clasped in his. When she looked into his face his eyes glazed over as if he wanted to look elsewhere. He said it had been very brave of her to stay with Mrs. Thomson while he went to the hospital. "I'm very proud of you," he said. But then he said that he had bad news. And that he was sorry. He said that Fiona had been so ill that even the doctors couldn't help her. Her heart had stopped beating. Now she was in heaven and would not be coming home again. But this was unthinkable to Anne. After all, he was a *doctor* and his job was to *make people well*! That's what doctors *did*! And if mummy was ill, why didn't he make her well? Why didn't he *save* her?

All Alexander could think to say was that sometimes accidents happen that are so serious that there is nothing anyone can do to help. Anne asked why her mother had to have an accident *so serious*--especially when she was going to have a surprise party?! Alexander pressed his daughter's hands tightly in his own, looked directly into her troubled eyes, and told her not to worry. That there would be plenty of other surprise parties. That they would be alright together--just the two of them. Pulling her near he hugged her warmly and said, "Mummy would want us to go on just as before."

That night as Anne lay in bed trying to fall asleep without a good night kiss from her mother, she snuggled down deep into her blankets seeking warmth they couldn't offer. Cold and alone she tried in vain to answer the unanswerable: How could such a bad thing happen to her mother in her own house? And why did her mother lock her in the front room and then just forgotten her? Her father had tried to offer explanations acceptable to a small and innocent child--maybe the door wasn't locked, just stuck from humidity--but found it hard to lie. The truth was more than either of them could bear. Then just as Anne felt that she could bear no more, she looked down to find her mother sitting at the foot of her bed:

As Anne jerked herself upright—an astonished look on her face--Fiona placed a finger to her lips, bidding her daughter *shhh*, and motioning her to stay put. Anne excitedly whispered how glad she was that she'd finally come home from the hospital—and started to get up to run and tell "Da." But then her mother told her that her daddy didn't know that she'd come back; and that Anne was not to tell him. It was to be their secret. She then heard her say that she should get a good night's sleep and that she would return in the morning to see her. As Fiona stood up and blew Anne a kiss, she faded into the shadows of the room. *Everything's going to be alright now*, whispered Anne. *Mummy's back!*

Chapter 7

As ANNE DROWSILY WOKE FROM a deep and pleasant sleep, the sharp rays of the early morning sun sliced through the small gaps that appeared intermittently through the drawn curtains, and sent a rainbow of colour to fill her bedroom. She squinted through sleepy eyes to see a figure again perched at the end of her bed. Fiona smiled ruefully at her daughter, seeming to reach out to hold Anne in her arms—but something was stopping her. And that kept Anne from reaching the comfort of her mother's arms as well. Anne could hear Fiona telling her not to worry, that she would return now and then to make sure that she was alright. "And remember," she said, "do not tell Daddy I was here. He wouldn't understand." Just then a beam of golden light penetrated the room through the open curtains, into which her mother disappeared. Anne sat and thought for a moment, the improbability of this encounter not registering to the four-year-old. To her open mind it was only natural that her mother should want to see her and look out for her—even after death; if that were where she was.

Anne hurriedly dressed and bounded off downstairs, ready to face a new day. When she got to the kitchen her father was already sitting at the table, coffee cup in one hand and a cigarette in the other, the latter adroitly manipulated between nimble fingers. Wisps of smoke spiralled upwards, forming an unruly trail of grey mist. Anne hopped neatly up into her chair and reached out for the glass of orange juice awaiting her.

As she carefully sipped from the plastic polka-dotted glass, she began to wiggle side-to-side and swing her legs forward-and-back. She beamed a wide and cheeky smile at her father; she was so excited, she knew something he didn't. And she was about to burst. She remembered well that her mother had told her not to say anything to her daddy about her visits, but it pained her to see her father so sad and thought it would cheer him up to know that Mum has not really died; not *really*. So in a matter-of-fact tone Anne blurted out that she'd seen Mummy last night and first thing this morning. Alexander could only look at his daughter with a wistful smile and gently shake his head.

"That's alright," he told her, "it's only normal to see your mummy in your dreams."

But Anne knew for certain that it wasn't a dream—and came straight out and told him so. "No, I really *did* see Mummy!" Her father just shrugged, nodded politely, and said it was time to get ready to go out. There were lots of things to see to. As Alexander stubbed out his cigarette in the ashtray, he watched Anne skip cheerfully out of the kitchen and into the hall to fetch her coat. *Such a wonderful imagination*, he thought. *What a shame that we all lose it at some point in life.*

The next few days passed in a blur. There were lots of visitors to the house, lots of telephone calls in and out, and lots of trips in the car to visit family and friends. Anne found all this activity exciting, seeing all these different people (and recognising all the colours they carried with them). She didn't mean to stare but was so intent on watching friendly and strange faces that Alexander on occasion had to tell her not to be impolite; that it was rude to stare.

Last thing each night and first thing each morning, Fiona visited Anne in her room, and they'd talk about the events of that day, or what Anne was planning for the next. Anne always begged her mummy to come with her, with Fiona saying that she couldn't *this* time; maybe the next. Sometimes Anne would mention her mother's on-going visits to her father, but he usually responded with an exasperated shrug and shake of his head, telling her that mummy was gone and would not be coming back. That Anne would have the chance to say a proper goodbye at the funeral.

The day of Fiona's funeral came and went. All Anne could remember of it were people dressed in black, the sombre nodding of heads, rigid handshakes between the men, and the occasional sobbing of some of the women. And she didn't really feel part of it. People were nice to her; they'd smile sweetly and sometimes pat her neatly-curled blond hair. Anne didn't know what the fuss was all about, *really*, her mother still came round. Why act as though she was gone?

Some evenings Ruth came to visit her father, and Anne was usually packed off to her bedroom. She had no idea what they talked about, or did, but she'd always tell her mother that Ruth had visited. Fiona would just nod. Then one evening when Ruth came, Anne was not sent upstairs but told to stay as her father had something he needed to talk to her about. He said that soon he would have to go back to work and although Ruth was willing to help look after her when she had the time, they'd need to find a nanny. Someone who could be there for Anne day or night—if need be. So for the next few weeks a procession of assorted well-meaning ladies came into Anne and Fiona's house. To a point, Anne tolerated—even humour--these women, but at the same time resented them for invading her world. She'd refuse to obey them and sometimes said to their faces that she, and her mother, did not like them in their house! By this time Fiona was not only visiting Anne in her bedroom, but anytime she was alone: in the kitchen, the lounge, or out in the garden. All this, naturally, got back to Alexander who by now was tiring of Anne's behaviour and insistence that Fiona wasn't dead. Sometimes he'd snap back at his daughter that she needed to accept that her mother was gone; that it was time to stop feeding her imagination with such outlandish ideas. Of course, Anne knew he was wrong and so ignored him.

For Alexander, Applegarth now held little more than painful memories. There was a perpetual coldness that always greeted him; just as when he'd returned from India with Anne, and the baby. Applegarth was no longer a home for the two of them so he decided that it was time to move house. Alexander explained to Annie that they were going to start a new adventure in a new house, and that there would be no more nannies. Instead, Ruth would be there to look after her. Ruth was going to be her new *mummy*. Anne was glad that there would be no more house invaders of the nanny type, but hated the idea of Ruth being there any more than she already was. She remembered how much she disliked being under Ruth's care in the past. Besides, why did she need a new mummy when she already had one? After much upheaval and the *to-ing* and *fro-ing* of wooden tea chests and crates packed with belongings wrapped in shredded newspaper, the new "family" said good-bye to Applegarth. Off to a bigger, more imposing house. There were no more nannies, but also no more visits from her mummy, Fiona. There was just Ruth.

The new house set at the end of a terrace of heavy grey stoned properties, with bigger rooms and higher ceilings than Applegarth. According to Ruth it was in a *better* part of the city. It took some time but Anne, her father, and Ruth made their imprint on this traditional stone-built Edinburgh house. Still, some things stayed the same; the yellow sodium street lights and white lace front-room curtains of their neighbours' houses. Conformity seemed to be following Anne. Then one weekend this sameness was broken by the arrival of Shuna, a cream-coloured Labrador puppy Alexander showed up with completely out of the blue. Unable to contain herself, Anne ran up and down the hallway clapping her hands excitedly: "Oh, Da! She's *lovely!* A puppy just for *me!*" As expected, Ruth's reaction was quite the opposite:

"What, Alex?" frowning as she spoke. "We really need a *dog*?!"

"Now, there's plenty of room," her husband defended. "It's just the three of us rattling round this place and she'll be good company for Anne."

"She's already got too-fertile an imagination as it is, Alex!" Ruth said, pointing disdainfully at the new arrival, "and this will just add fuel to the fire! Mark my words!"

"There's nothing wrong with having a mind of her own, Ruth. We shouldn't stifle the girl's creativeness," said Alexander.

"The girl needs *discipline*, not encouragement for her crazy imagination! Without discipline, God knows what she'll grow up to be!" Ruth warned.

Sometimes when Anne thought Ruth wasn't looking, she'd study her, trying to work out what kind of person Ruth was. (Clearly she was there to stay.) She was a tall woman with sharp, chiseled features who strode round in a quite dominating and self-assured manner, and spoke in the same severe way. Anne could always feel the icy blast that typically came from Ruth's glare when serving a harsh scolding for being *naughty* or *disrespectful*. (Of course, Anne had a completely different idea of what "naughty" was. And since her father usually let her off with just a word of admonition . . . .) Anne wondered why Ruth acted one way towards her when her father was there (kind, smiling and chatty) but quite another when he was out of earshot (cold and criticising; even threatening). This left Anne never knowing whether to smile and approach Ruth, or withdraw and keep out of her way. Anne and Shuna kept out of Ruth's way—as much as possible—Anne convinced that her dog disliked Ruth as much as she did.

While Anne would sometimes hear Shuna padding up and down the stairs throughout the night, she also heard new sounds in their new house. What sounded like footfalls, she became alerted to one particular step that would creak at exactly the same spot, but when Anne would jump out of bed to see who was there--there was never anyone. Not Shuna nor her mum nor dad—nor even a visit from Fiona. And the more she heard these footfalls, the more fear slowly crept into her being. When she mentioned this to her father he told her that all big houses creak and groan. That this phenomena was normal. That old timbers feel the cold and heat just as people did. That she should not to let her imagination carry her away. But Anne knew there was more to it.

Chapter 8

By the age of seven, Anne had already decided that she hated school; and didn't like her home life much better. To her, Ruth went out of her way to pick on her. To find fault and reasons to punish her. "Anne, do as you're told! Pay attention and stop daydreaming! And if you don't stop all this nonsense about seeing colours and secret visitors then your privileges will be taken away!" were the mantras. And each evening when Alexander arrived home from work he was met with Ruth's list of what Anne had done wrong that day. (There was never any mention of what she'd done right.) Anne found her escape at night in her bedroom; and in a most unusual way.

Once tucked in bed (always by her father), Anne would quietly slip out of bed and swing on the bedroom curtains, pretending she could fly away and be *at one* with the dark indigo sky and its twinkling stars. It thrilled her to cling to the long and heavy velvet curtains that reached from ceiling-to-floor, step back as far as she could, then swung out towards the window. And each time she did she recited her hope that she'd be able to fly right out the window and into that dark indigo colour; to disappear into it and become part of it. To her, darkness held no fear; it was a place of peace and familiarity. A place she'd been to before and would one day return. But with each swing she could succeed only in hitting the wood frame below the window--then dropping into a heap on the floor (a distinctive *thud* echoing through the house). She couldn't understand why her body was so heavy; why she couldn't leave it behind and just fly away . . .

But her curtain-swinging adventures were soon brought to an abrupt halt. One evening the nosy neighbour across the street (with nothing better to do) called Ruth to warn her that Anne was swinging on the curtains in her bedroom upstairs. She could see the upstairs front bedroom curtains flailing about quiet violently. Suddenly Anne's door burst open and there stood her new mother with her hands on her hips: "Just what do you think you're *doing*, young lady?! Get back in bed and stop this nonsense *now!*" she shouted (but not loud enough for all the neighbors to hear). Anne began to hate the nosy neighbour as much as she hated her new mother.

And school was no better. Chided for daydreaming, Anne became convinced that her teacher and Ruth were in cahoots--as she joined in the constant criticising and complaining. "You won't learn a *thing*, Miss McNaughton, by staring out the window! Get your head out of the clouds and into your geography book this instant!" *But, what's the point of a book filled with pictures?* Anne wanted to know. *Real* geography was out *there*; beyond the dour grey of the school playground and sharp coldness of the slated roofs of Edinburgh. It was *there* in the subtle and vivid greens and browns, the earth colours, and the wide-open spaces of Pentland Hills (that looked so close but at times appeared beyond human reach). But an unexpected respite from school and home was soon to come.

For her birthday that year her father got her a membership to a private swimming club where some of the local, more affluent children swam. Having watched others doing it, Anne was determined to learn to swim, and in no time was not only swimming but diving--passing every swim exam she took. But it was the trapeze and the rings that she most enjoyed, quickly climbing the steps leading to the platform, where she'd jump off and grab the trapeze that hung high above the pool, making it swing high into the air--then she'd curl herself up into a ball and maneuverer her legs up and over the bar until she was hanging upside-down by her knees. Then she'd swing upside down until straightening her legs and free-falling into the water below. Sometimes she'd stand on the trapeze while another kid would jump on, hanging below her. She so enjoyed the sensation of flying through the air, feeling free and exhilarated by the motion of the swing over the sparkling water below. This, she thought, was even more exciting than swinging on her bedroom curtains!

Just as enjoyable as the swimming club were the summer holidays. Though having to deal with Ruth most of the time, at least she was way from school for several weeks (and liked the idea that when she went back it would be like starting all over). She and Shuna would avoid Ruth as much as possible (sometimes holed-up in her bedroom closet or hiding in the garden) but at least Shauna could see the colours and lights that her father and Ruth couldn't. And joy of joys, for two of those summer holiday weeks they'd escape Edinburgh and head north, up A9 to the Highlands. It was real palaver to Anne; getting ready for the journey.

"Now!" Ruth would bark. "*You*, young lady, will pack your small suitcase neatly and precisely, and here's a list of all you'll need to take!" she'd say, handing Anne a neatly printed sheet of paper. "And I'll check it, so no mistakes!"

Though Anne would try her best to do as Ruth instructed, Ruth always found fault. The smallest thing--a wrongly folded skirt or missing pants or socks--would send Ruth into a rant, up-ending Anne's suitcase and forcing her to start all over again. *Who does she think she is?!* Anne would quietly seethe. *These are my clothes! My things! I bet she doesn't pack everything perfectly either!* Eventually, with suitcases packed acceptably, stowed away in the boot and Anne and Shuna settled into the back seat, the McNaughton family would set off. Alexander would drive--with Ruth clearly in control.

Out along Queensferry Road past the imposing red stone of Barnton Hotel, then out to South Queensferry they travelled. For Anne the adventure actually began as the car rumbled across the new Forth Road Bridge, the *b-dumm b-dumm* of the car's tires rolling over the joints in the bridge's carriageway like a rhythmic chant. As soon as they passed Perth, the landscape began to change; decidedly wilder. The light began to change and it was as though Anne could see further for longer. The soft greens and browns of the Lowlands were slowly usurped by the harder, sharper, more vibrant greens and darker hues of the Highlands. The fast and clear running waters of the rivers, the shear of the steely blue and grey of the broken rocks at the water's edge, and the imposing darkness of the distant mountain tops--all this was most inviting to Anne. She knew these places. She didn't know how--but she knew them.

After a while the road levelled out and the harshness of the high ground gave way to lusher greens, blues, and purples of flatter land. Fresher meadows and stiller waters (like sheet glass reflecting the blue of the hills and the sky beyond) were now the scenery Anne could see from her vantage point. They passed through the town of Aviemore then turned right, off the main road, and headed for Boat of Garten, their destination: a small cottage set off the beaten track and down a dirt track, rented for the two-week stay. As her father switched off the car's engine it seemed to give a sigh of relief; its job was done, for now. The doors were flung open and out bounced an anxious Anne and Shuna. *What an adventure this is going to be*! thought Anne. The fresh air, the clear sky, the open space, the tranquility. The stillness was quickly interrupted by Shuna giving the odd bark to show her excitement; this prompting Ruth to begin her barking:

"Anne! You're not done yet. You've got a suitcase to see to! Get it out of the boot and carry it inside!" A dutiful Anne gave a muted sigh and dark, sidelong stare towards her mother. Once inside the cottage, a proper exploration was made, Ruth assigning bedrooms: "You'll be in this *little* room," Ruth told Anne. "I'll be in shortly to see that all your clothes are neatly stowed away in that chest of drawers," a wiry finger pointing to a rough pine stack of drawers in the corner of the dimly-lit room. Anne did as she was told and nearly passed inspection, with Ruth unnecessarily smoothing a pink woollen jumper in the top drawer before pushing it shut. "There!" she said with obvious self-satisfaction.

Soon the smell of cooking filled the cottage; the air moist with boiling potatoes, steam-bathed vegetables and heavy with the aroma of sizzling meat. An evening meal of stew and potatoes was heartily eaten by all. They'd need their strength for tomorrow as it was going to be a busy day, Alexander had said before they'd dug in. And they should all get to bed early as they would be up with the larks and first light—Ruth added. So Anne was packed off to her room to snuggle under fresh bedclothes to dream about what adventures lay ahead in this mystical but comforting land; Shuna shown to her spot near the front door. "She is, after all, just a *dog*," Ruth had said.

The following morning they were all up and about by 6:00. When Anne shuffled half-asleep into the small kitchen, Ruth was packing a wicker hamper with sandwiches, a thermos flask, and food for the dog. "There's bread and marmalade on the table for you, and a glass of milk," was all Ruth said, not even turning to greet Anne good morning. "And don't dottle. Your father is dressed and ready and we want to get started."

"Where are we going?" asked Anne

"Never you mind," Ruth snapped. "You'll know soon enough. Just finish your breakfast and don't waste any more time."

Just then, Alexander came in. "Guess what! You're going to Loch Morlich, and I'm going up the Lairig Ghru," he said, smiling at his daughter.

"Going where—*what?*" questioned Anne.

"You'll see, they're *beautiful* places to visit!" Alexander promised.

The car re-loaded and forced to splutter back to life, the four nestled back inside. The dirt track was renegotiated and at the main road junction the car was guided out of the small village and towards Aviemore. As he drove, Alexander explained to Anne that Loch Morlich was like a big pond; a really *huge* pond; like Blackford Pond they sometimes visited in Edinburgh to feed the ducks--but much, much bigger. And Lairig Ghru was a mountain pass that cut across the Cairngorm Mountains just past Aviemore. He told her that this pass through the mountains was much too dangerous for little girls to climb, so he would walk it on his own—go on his own little adventure--while she would wait at Loch Morlich and have a picnic with Ruth. Anne and Shuna could explore the loch side and the woods until he arrived.

"But, I'm not *that* little, anymore, Da! *I* can do it!"

"'Fraid not, darlin'. Much too dangerous."

"But, aren't they just steep paths of rocks and stones, Da? And if you keep to the paths and are careful, you won't slip and fall," Anne argued. (She had, in fact, learned about this in school.)

"Where did she learn that?" Alexander whispered to Ruth, trying not to let Anne over-hear.

"Well, certainly not in *school!*" said Ruth at full volume. "Her teachers say she *never* pays attention to *anything* that goes on there!"

Alexander frowned at his wife then returned his attention to the road ahead, but not before catching a glimpse of Anne in the rear view mirror giving him an inside smile. As they reached the southern end of Aviemore, Alexander turned left towards the Cairngorm ski lift. A mile or so further along that road, past fields and trees, they soon came to a rough clearing by the side of the loch, where they pulled over. Everyone bounded out of the car; Alexander with a map and compass and walking stick, Ruth carrying the wicker hamper.

"Now you two--sorry *three*!" said Alexander, looking in the direction of the dog, "head off down that path towards the loch and I'll head out that way," he said, pointing toward a narrow path that had forced its way through a stand of old trees. Off they went on their separate ways.

"Come along, Anne! Don't dawdle! --And stick to the path!" was all Ruth had to say. "There's a nice little beach just up ahead where we can set the picnic out." Slowly the path gave way to some open ground leading to the loch side. Anne rushed to the water's edge--quickly overtaken by Shuna, who ploughed straight into the lapping water, shattering the placidity of a family of ducks who quickly made alternate plans.

"For God's sake! I swear, you're like bulls in a china shop, the pair of you!" scolded Ruth, who was straining under the weight of the heavily-loaded picnic hamper. Just as she reached the start of the rough sandy beach area, her strength gave out and the hamper slipped from her hands—crashing awkwardly at her feet. "You're really not much help to your mother, now, are you?!" shouted Ruth more in embarrassment than anything. (She hated for even Anne to think she was less than perfect.)

And maybe it was the all excitement or the rush of fresh air but Anne spoke before she could think: "Well, you're not my *real* mother!" she blurted out, wrinkling her nose jeeringly. "You're just a mean and nasty old *witch* like the ones I bet that live round here in the forest!"

Ruth took an aggressive posture and snapped back: "And you're just a rude and ungrateful little brat who doesn't *deserve* a mother! For two cents I'd drag you back to the--you wouldn't *dare* say that when your father's here, you . . . !" (Anne wrinkled her nose again and curled her lips mockingly.) "You know, you may be able to fool *him*, you little ingrate, but you don't fool *me*! Not for one *second*! You're a spoilt little--" she said, then catching herself. She didn't want to say something Anne could repeat to Alexander. Things were growing evermore strained between them.

For the remainder of the morning there was an uneasy truce between step-mother and daughter; Anne venturing off with Shuna, leaving Ruth to unpack the picnic hamper and get on with the book she'd brought. As Anne and her dog wandered round the edge of the beach, the full extent of the loch opened up before her, the beach outlining just a small portion of the water. The trees and shrubs that rambled down to the water's edge receded and gave way to a wondrous sight of still blue and grey water, mirror calm, that reflected the sharpness of the forest trees surrounding it that seemed to go on forever--only to be hemmed in by the blurred outline of the mountains beyond. Still, the colours, the light, the cleanness and innocence of it all was somehow familiar to Anne. This place was unspoilt; just *there*; unyielding, immovable, yet vibrantly alive. Moving only with the sun and the moon and the seasons revolving round it.

Anne and Shuna ventured further on round the loch; but still within sight of Ruth with her book and hamper. Every so often a small lightly-trodden path would offer itself for further investigation, deeper into the trees. Unable to resist the temptation, Anne would set off into the unknown with only the sound of her footsteps on the woodland floor, and Shuna's manic scurrying about in her ears. After three or four such ventures, Anne's peace was broken by a shrill and distant voice: Ruth was calling. Something about *picnic, lunch,* and *father*. Without fuss,

Anne retraced her steps back to the beach at the bottom end of the loch. When she got there her father was waiting, sitting next to Ruth, a map was laid out on the table cloth spread across the sand.

"You've not been gone long, Da!" said Anne. "It's only been a few minutes and me and Shauna wanted to explore some more."

"It's been over three hours, darlin'!" Alexander's said, smiling at the wanderlust in his daughter's sparkling eyes. "And anyway, I didn't get as far as I wanted. There was a rock slide on the path that made it too dangerous, so I turned back and took a short-cut here. Funniest thing though, there were these three crows sitting on the rocks, as if they were there to warn off passers-by."

"Not you *too*, Alex! Don't start with all that supernatural nonsense!" scoffed Ruth. "It's bad enough that Anne keeps dreaming up all that sort of thing without you letting her think it's *normal*! Now let's eat our picnic lunch before we miss the best part of the day."

Anne had to admit (but certainly not to Ruth) that she enjoyed the sandwiches and biscuits--topped off with a chilled glass of orange juice. Once everything was eaten (or given to Shuna or the nearby family of ducks) the cups, plates, and table cloth were put back into the hamper and the McNaughtons set off, back to the clearing and the suitably rest-ed car. Nearly there, Anne noticed some lovely white flowers floating just out of reach at the loch side. She rushed over to get a better look.

"Oh look, Da! *Padma, padma*! Look how *beautiful*!" she shouted to her father.

Alexander told her that they were called "water lilies" and that they were very delicate and liked to live out on the water away from other flowers and plants. Anne examined these unusual flowers more closely;

so peaceful as they gently bobbed up and down to the rhythm of the water. One in particular caught her eye, the one furthest out. It appeared to move with its own rhythm, differently from the others, and had flamed streaks of pink across its petals that made it stand out.

"Can I have one, Da, *please!*" pleaded Anne. "*That* one--that one out *there!*" she said, pointing to the pink-laced blossom beyond reach, her beaming face filled with desire.

"I don't know, Annie, it's a bit far out," Alexander said, not convinced that it was such a good idea to pluck it.

"Oh, please, please, Da!" Anne played on his tendency to give in to her.

Ruth gave Alexander a scowl as he bent down to undo his boot laces, sat down on the sand and tugged off his boots and then socks. Rolling his trousers up to his knees he offered an apologetic look back to Ruth. But no sooner had he taken a few tentative steps out into the water, the tranquility of the water surface was broken--the water lilies seeming to panic. Their bobbing up and down becoming more frantic as they seemed to try to scurry away from what they now sensed as danger. This was *not* what Anne wanted! Suddenly the comfort she'd felt from the placidity of delicate blooms was gone. She wanted to tell her father to stop; to come back out of the water. But it was too late. He'd already slipped his hands under the water and freed the single lily from its anchor. He held the delicate blossom in his hand like a priceless trophy.

As Alexander placed the flower in Anne's open palms, she burst into tears. The trophy was lifeless: no more a comforting white and pink-fused thing of beauty, it was dull and void of hope. Of life. Anne fell desperately sad. Such a waste, she realised. Alexander put his arm gently round his daughter's shoulders and brought her near; Ruth grimacing in disgust. The three made their way to the car, no words exchanged. Freeing herself from her father's hold, Anne turned and ran back. Alexander turned and watched as his daughter ran to the water's edge, bent down and returned the lily to the rocking waters. She doubted the flower wouldn't live, but felt that it was where it belonged.

Alexander watched as the sky darkened and threatened rain, the wind quickened and began to shout warnings through the trees. All this disturbed the calm waters of the loch, which began to tremble and appeared to scurry away from the wind--as if to escape its impending wrath. The mood round Anne, of the trees and the loch and the suddenly silent birds, seemed to close her in. The peaks of the greying mountains in the distance began to disappear in uncertainty of their continued existence. Gone was their solid backdrop to this place; their security.

"Quickly now, Anne!" came her father's voice through the snarling wind. "Let's hurry up and get in the car before the rain comes on."

The paths through the stands of trees were no longer places where friendly voices could be heard, but where grotesque characters reared up at each tree stump or gnarled top of protruding rocks speaking in rough and barbed voices. The comfort of Alexander's smooth and steady voice brought Anne back to herself and before long they were all scrambling back to the car as a sharp summer downpour engulfed the clearing where the car was parked. As the car turned and set off back down the road to Rothiemurchus, Anne looked back toward the loch. But it was lost; lost behind a curtain of lace-like rain.

The drive back to the cottage at Boat of Garten passed uneventfully—with little discussion. For once, Ruth didn't scold Anne for anything and it seemed they'd all enjoyed their day: Alexander on his interrupted walk, Ruth with her nose in a book, Anne and Shauna on their mysterious adventures round the loch side (and her harsh realisation of life and death). That evening the cottage filled once again with the smells of potatoes, vegetables, and meat, and once enjoyed, the family prepared for their visit to Alexander's mother, who lived in a next village.

Chapter 9

ANNE WASN'T SURE SHE COULD remember her grandmother. She had, apparently, come down to Edinburgh soon after her father had got back from India, but that was the extent of their familiarity. Her granny lived in nearby Nethy Bridge, in a stone-built, two-story house just off the main road, down a quaint and picturesque path. Not unlike Anne's house back in Edinburgh, it was quite an imposing structure for that area. When Anne, her father and mother got there, the reception and atmosphere were cool. Alexander and his mother were not skilled talkers so some neighbours were invited.

"I hope you don't mind, Alexander, but I've invited Malcolm and Patricia over. They're closer to your age and you have lots in common," announced Granny, blunt and to the point, Alexander quite aware that his mother preferred not to be alone with him. "And little *Anne* is it?" she continued, looking not at Anne but at her son, "will have company too. Malcolm and Patricia's children are in the back room playing. So, if you'll just show her the way, we can leave them to do . . . whatever it is kids do these days."

Alexander smiled and looked down at his daughter, took her hand and led her to the back room. There he opened the door and ushered his daughter in, the sound of the door opening bringing three children to their feet. They were all taller and older than Anne, and Alexander could see a look of disappointment on their faces at being confronted with a small girl, maybe half their ages. "In you go, darlin'," encouraged Alexander, "don't worry, you'll be fine. You all have fun now!" With that Anne took a couple steps inside and heard the door close behind her. For a moment there was an awkward silence—but only a moment--broken by the tallest of the three visitors:

"Hi, I'm Mary," said the first voice with an air of confidence. "And this is my younger brother, George, and my little sister Susan. Your name's *Anne*, is it?" Anne nodded. "Are you on holiday, too?" Mary asked.

"Where do you go to school?" George, the middle one, was anxious to know.

"In Edinburgh . . . and I don't really like it, much," answered Anne.

"Who does!" exclaimed Susan, the smallest and youngest.

"Don't be like that, Susie!" scolded her older sister. "We go to a good school. It's not up here, it's down in London."

With this short and stilted conversation the ice between the children was broken and soon the conversation turned to what they'd got up to since they'd arrived in the Highlands. Anne was surprised that they all had done pretty much the same things: walks by the loch side, trips to Aviemore, and reading indoors when the weather turned inhospitable. When Mary asked Anne what she did without her school friends to talk to Anne surprised them with her answer. "Oh, I talk to my dog, Shuna. And I talk to my other friends that live in the trees and the water."

The three shared a confused look. This brought a giggle from the youngest, Susan, and the other two just smiled curiously. It was obvious to them that Anne was still too young for sensible conversation about more grown-up, *teenage* things. "Well, we've been told to keep ourselves busy here in the parlour for the evening but so far we're all terribly *bored*," George volunteered.

Anne looked round the room; she so enjoyed the large log-burning fire. She looked at the old wooden breakfast table and counted six seats, then choosing the one at the head of the table and nearest the door, sat down and stared at the children. She noticed a green, tattered sofa to her left by the window (beyond which lay the front garden), and another door to her right. "Where does that door lead?" she asked the kids.

"Oh, that goes to the scullery, where the dogs are kept," George said. "The kitchen and pantry are also in there." Then as if on cue the door swung inwards and there stood a lovely young black and white collie who took one look at Anne, turned and retreated back to the kitchen.

"That's *Rob*," said Susan. "And they have an old blind collie called *Stan*, but he rarely bothers to get out of bed any more. Too old, I guess."

As the evening wore on and the conversation had gone from favorite toys to places they'd visited to school, the children got round to talking about ghosts; each one telling a scary story and trying to better the previous one. Then Mary brought up *Ouija* boards and how they spelt out messages from the spirit world. They didn't have a board there so Mary said they could made do with a glass and the letters of the alphabet written on slips of paper. So before long they were all sitting round the table with a glass tumbler set upside down in the middle of a circle of paper letters. George, who'd taken charge, said they should all put their index finger on the glass and concentrate. Anne wasn't sure about the whole idea and after just a few seconds took her finger off the tumbler:

"I don't know! I'm frightened!" Anne said, her voice quivering. "You mean we're going to bring dead people—like *ghosts*--here?"

"No, silly!" scoffed George. "Not *really*! It's just a *game*! *Pretend*! It'll be fun—you'll see!"

Anne was bemused. This wasn't like any *game* she knew about. "But, what if dead people—ghosts and such--*do* come? And they talk to us?" Anne wasn't convinced it was just pretend.

"Well, if you're too much of a baby . . . !" George said, getting annoyed. "And, why would a ghost want to talk to a little kid like you, anyway?!"

Though still not convinced she should be doing this, Anne put her finger on the glass, along with the other children. And for a short while, nothing happened; the tumbler just setting there in the middle of the circle. Then just as George let out an anxious giggle, the tumbler began to slowly move. At first, barely noticeable it slid first to the letter "A." Then "N," and then "N" again, coming to rest on the letter "E." George looked up and gave a startled look towards Anne.

"George! That's *enough*!" Mary said. "You're *pushing* the tumbler—so stop it!"

"Okay, okay!" apologised the boy, with a playful laugh. "Let's start again. I won't push it—I promise!"

The glass tumbler was restored to its position in the centre of the lettered circle, with all the children gazing upon it anxiously. Silent. No smirking or giggling. Only the strained look of four children's faces as they stared intently at the whiskey glass, its colours reflected from the flames of the burning wood in the open hearth, dancing through its faceted crystal. Then slowly, the glass began to move. Anne sat bolt upright in her chair—as did the others. Unlike with George's not-so-clever deception, the glass now moved faster than the four could follow it, as each letter was chosen by the glass. They all listened to the *wooshing* sound as the glass moved in small circles, gaining momentum, moving faster and faster, shooting back and forth across the table before their astonished eyes. Then the glass stopped dead--and there was hushed silence. All the children kept their fingers in place and stared, wondering what would happen next. Slowly the glass began to move again; quickly darting from one letter to another. Anne, her heart beating wildly, read aloud:

"B-L-A-C-K, it spelt *black!*" A second later the glass sprung back to life. By now Anne was feeling an overpowering sense of fear; she could sense a dark, black cloud above her. "We should stop playing this game--there's *evil* in this room!" she cried out. (They all laughed; after all, how could she possibly know what *evil* feels like at only seven!)

As if to demonstrate her warning, the glass shot across the table and stopped directly in front of Anne. Moving back to the centre, it then shot back and forth several more times, spelling out "DEATH," then "DOG," and then "MIDNIGHT." Anne felt her stomach clinch, now convinced that harm was going to befall *her!* Withdrawing her hand from the glass she leaned away. Then as if electrically repelled, the other three fingers were pushed off the whiskey glass--as the light faded from its patterned angles.

Anne jumped down from her chair and ran to the door, then followed her father's voice. Finding him with several other adults sitting round a table she rushed to him and said, "I'm *scared*, Da, really *scared!* They're playing a game I don't like! And I'm going to be killed at midnight by a dog!" Tears welled-up in her frightened eyes as she pondered death.

Ruth gritted her teeth, her eyes narrowing to angry slits. "Anne, leave this room *at once* and go back to your little friends! This is adult conversation and you have no business here!"

"No, I want to go *home*! I don't want to stay here anymore!"

Alexander tried to pacify his frightened daughter: "We'll be leaving soon, Anne," giving her a gentle cuddle. "Now run along and have fun, we won't be long." Ruth shot them both a look of disgust. Anne headed out of the room and back to the parlour, the last words she heard were from Ruth, "What an active imagination that child has! She really is a *handful!*"

"As I was saying . . . " her father said, resuming the conversation, "I don't want the house. Do what you want with it, my home is in Edinburgh and I have no intention of moving here and taking over another home. It's just not practical. Anne is in school and my work is there."

"So, what can I do with the house?" said his mother.

"Sell it. Sell it--get some money and enjoy yourself . . . "

Returning to the parlour, all the children mocked Anne, each one saying, 'Oh, running to mummy and daddy, baby, baby . . . ' they chanted. Anne sat alone on the sofa by the window, watching and listening to the tick of the clock on the mantleplace, following the hands as they moved slowly round its golden face, with midnight nearing. "Please come and sit with me," Anne implored of the other children. "I'm scared to sit by myself!" Just then the clock started chiming twelve. And the door from the kitchen slowly creaked open. Anne and the other children (who were all unnerved now by the atmosphere in the room) all held their breath—their hearts pounding in their chests. Then, the old blind dog Stan wandered in. And as if the old dog had only one direction to head, he rambled uneasily towards Anne. As he neared, the cold, life-less whites of the dog's eyes terrified Anne, her heart feeling about to explode. Jumping up she ran screaming from the room and across the hall to her parents--shaking and sobbing uncontrollably:

"We have no choice, Alexander, we have to take her home," said Ruth as she turned and addressed their host. "I'm really so sorry about her behaviour. Alex, get Anne's coat."

The journey back was made in a frigid silence, broken only by Ruth's harsh declaration: "Surely even you can see that she needs professional help, Alexander. Her special *friends*, the *voices*, the whole blood *lot*--we need to deal with this before it goes too far!" Alexander sighed and gave a resigning nod.

Immediately packed off to bed upon their return, Anne spent a fear-ful night alone in her room, eyes wide open, too afraid to sleep. She was convinced that she was being stalked by a black entity that meant her harm, and she had no idea how to save herself. And now, after hearing her parent's conversation, feared running to them to save her ever again.

The rest of that year's holiday in Boat of Garten was spent in and near the small cottage. And all too soon the small cottage was emp-tied of their belongings and meticulously cleaned and tidied by Ruth; left just as they'd found it. Suitcases deposited in the boot, Anne and Shuna occupying the back seat, the four begin their long journey back to Edinburgh. The car coughed and spluttered (like an old woman, Anne mused) but eventually gave in to the inevitable and trundled back down the dirt track, onto the main road, and through Aviemore--leaving Loch Morlich in Anne's memory. Back to lace curtained windows, musty classrooms, and the pangs of growing up.

Chapter 10

THE SCHOOL YEARS TICKED BY for Anne. But it was as if the more she was supposed to know, the less she actually did. Primary school gave way to the "big" school--yet the classrooms were much the same. More of them but they were all still musty smelling. Many smelt of books and paper and desks--with people's initials carved into them. Others had the sharp smell of glass and metal, with sliding glass doors, long benches with sinks, and high stools—ran by teachers in long white coats writing numbers and letters on a blackboard. But other than the bottles and vials of coloured liquid she saw lined up in science class, none of this interested Anne. (These meant much more to her than her teachers had imparted. A bigger purpose—she was sure of it.)

As time passed, Anne found her own little group of school friends. "Spirited kids," the teachers referred to them at Parents' Evenings (but had other *choice* expressions they used in the classroom, and far worse in the staffroom). By now, Anne had come to enjoy the gymnasium best. There she could move about, express herself, burn off all that teenage angst and energy. Sitting down and learning by rote wasn't for her. In those classes she'd just stare out the window. The Pentland Hills were there and she discovered that she could look beyond them to see in her mind's eye the Highlands, the Cairngorms, the Lairig Ghru and Loch Morlich. And of all the words she was required to learn and recite, none resonated with her more than these taken from ("My Heart's in the Highlands," by Robert Burns, a poem set to music.)

My heart's in the Highlands, my heart is not here;
My heart's in the Highlands, a-chasing the deer;
A-chasing the wild deer, and following the roe –
My heart's in the Highlands wherever I go.

These meant something to her. She'd been there, experienced it. That brought them to life.

Although Anne was growing into a fine and intelligent young woman, home life had changed little in recent years. With her father still working long hours at the doctors' surgery, Ruth was free to administer disdainful and haughty looks at will. Orders barked, requests never made: "You're *not* going to school with that skirt on, my girl!" was heard more than once. "I won't have people thinking I'm raising some sort of tart!"--she'd yell loudly but never loud enough for the neighbors to hear. "Tights!? You want to wear *tights*!" Ruth would question, making no effort to disguise her disdain. "I don't care if all your friends are wearing them or *not*! I hate to think what kind of parents they have, but as long as you're in *this* house you'll do no such thing!" No discussing, explaining, or reasoning. Just, 'Do as you're told!'

All this hostility set Anne to wondering what kind of woman Ruth really was, *inside*. What she was like growing up. What had happened to make her such an angry, controlling woman. She'd met Charles, Ruth's younger brother (a popular dentist with a private practice whose clientèle included a number of prominant Scotsmen), Ruth's older sister Frances (whose husband was a bank manager in Glasgow), and her oldest brother Ewan (who'd recently relocated to England due to his high-powered job as a civil engineer), and now realised how very different she was from any of them. Then one day she overheard a hushed conversation between Alexander and Ruth that caught her attention because at first she thought Ruth was referring to her own family. But then she realised otherwise:

"Well, she doesn't have our *genes*! *That's* why she behaves so oddly!" Then Anne caught the words *truth, letters, photographs*, and *documents*. *Who the bloody hell are they talking about?* she asked herself. *Her sister, Frances? But why be so secretive about it?* Anne then got the sense that it had to do not with Frances, but her. But how? Anne decided to find out what all the whispering was about. The bureau! That's where her father and Ruth kept all their important papers!

For the next few weeks Anne planned: the only way she could open her father's desk in privacy was to create an opportunity. She needed to be left alone in the house. So one morning on a day Anne knew Ruth would be out of the house (she routinely filled in as a receptionist at her brother's dental surgery) she feigned illness. Coughing and complaining of a sick stomach, she managed to convince Ruth that she should stay home from school. And since Anne had by now become a convincing actress, Ruth agreed that she *did* look poorly and rather than spread *who-knows-what* to her classmates, she should stay home. "Just stay in bed and don't get up unless you need to use the toilet! I'll be back as soon as I've finished at the surgery." Things were going just as Anne had imagined they would.

As soon as Anne heard the front door slam, she jumped out of bed and peaked through the heavy blue-velvet curtains to see the back of her mother striding down the street. Quickly bouncing down the stairs--her heart racing--she entered the study and noted exactly how far open the door had been, knowing that Ruth would notice if it was moved even the slightest. On tip-toes she then stood at the mantelpiece and the orange-coloured Chinese ornament setting atop it, exhaled hard and fished out the small brass desk-lid key hidden inside. Turning it over and over in her hands, pondering the repercussions of what would happen if her mother walked in, she waggled her head dismissively and unlocked the lid with a self-satisfied nod.

As expected, everything was neatly arranged within the bureau, so she made a mental picture of the exact placement: the wooden rack at the top of the bureau with letters inserted into small pigeon holes, the pens in their small glass cylinder, and on the bottom of the desk, neatly stacked light brown A4 files. Grabbing the first file in her hand she realised that it and the others were quite flimsy and knew that all the papers would fall out if she weren't especially careful. She gingerly lifted each to read the name her father had neatly printed at the top. After several she came to one labelled "Anne"--just as a painting fell off the wall behind her and hit the marble fire hearth below.

Her stomach lurching—fearing that she'd been discovered in the act--she went over to pick it up. It was one her father had painted some years before, a small colourful countryside scene; a green grassy meadow with huge white snow-covered hills in the background, with countless black birds nearly blotting out the sky. She'd always assumed that this was a place somewhere near Boat of Garten, where they'd been holidaying for many years now. (The birds appeared to be a great murder of crows hovering above--as if awaiting their opportunity to plunge to the ground *en masse*—yet resembled hawks circling their intended prey.) Placing the painting back on the mantel she thought for a split second that she could see a woman in the painting; confusing since she'd looked at this painting many times before and knew with certainty that there was no such woman. She looked again and to her relief—the woman was gone.

Heart thumping and holding her breath, Anne steadied herself and slowly opened the file marked "Anne." Focusing her eyes in the dim morning light she scanned the letter on the top of the pile. The letter, a formal declaration, stated that Alexander and Fiona McNaughton were now the "officially recognised" parents of baby "Anne *nee* Ani," and that a birth certificate for the child would shortly follow. *Ani? Does this mean I have a sister?* She then questioned the use of the "officially recognised" designation. Anne turned the letter over to reveal the next document, one headed from the Indian Government. This listed her father's name as well, and again the name "Ani."

The next paper was a letter her father had sent to Fiona from Darjeeling, India, which she quickly scanned and caught something about *twins* and *bringing back a baby girl*. But just as she was about to start reading deeper, a rumbling noise drew her attention from the letter; a noise coming from the chimney breast. All-of-the-sudden a cloud of smoke invaded the room through the hearth, a black ball of soot along with which came a blackbird that once free of the chimney flew round the room dropping soot everywhere as it searched for a way back out! Anne dropped the papers in her hand and ran to the window, unlocked it, and pushed it upwards. As she did, a gust of wind shot in. The bird, sensing freedom, flew right out--while the papers on the desk were caught in the breeze and now lay in disarray. Anne flew into a rightful panic as she noticed specks of black soot on the papers and this, she knew, would betray her antics to her father.

Slamming the window hard enough to break the glass, she quickly locked the snibbing then went back to the desk and began to tidy up--desperately trying to remember where all the papers went! Sufficiently satisfied, she closed the file with such force that the jar of pens fell over. Quickly up-righting the pens, she returned the file to its rightful place within the pile of files, then took one last long stare at the order of the desk. Satisfied that everything was reasonably in place she closed and locked the lid, then dropped the key into the jar. She then wasted no time running back to her bedroom, taking the stairs two-at-a-time. Legs shaking and heart pounding, she flopped onto her bed—what she'd just read spinning dizzily round her head—the words *officially recognised, Ani, Indian Government,* and *twins* adding to her confusion. One thing for certain, she had to get back into that bureau as soon as she possible could.

For the next few weeks, thoughts of *Ani* and the letter from India consumed her. At last the day arrived when she could return to the desk; Ruth was again going to work at her brother's dentist surgery. "When you come home from school, Anne, our neighbour, Mrs. Jackson, will let you in, and you'll only be on your own about two hours," was Ruth's parting instruction. "Make sure you do your homework and tidy your room before your father gets in. And do *not* get into any mischief!"

Once home from school Anne got Mrs. Jackson to let her in (Anne was too young to be trusted with her own key, according to Ruth) and wasted no time digging in. Quickly retrieving the key from the orange ornamental vase, she opened the desk lid. She knew the file names and her fingers quickly sifted through until she found the right one. This time she worked methodically; there was the document from India and behind that more papers. The first was a birth certificate. Picking it up she read: *Anne McNaughton, Father: Alexander McNaughton, Mother: Fiona McNaughton (nee Millar) 27.05.1955.* Rooted to the spot, Anne's brain tried to process this information. Shaking her head in confusion, she placed the certificate on the desk and picked up the letter from the Indian Government. Her eyes slowly scanned. It was a "Right of Passage" for Alexander McNaughton and child, Ani (McNaughton); the date, 30th November, 1955. Anne sat down and pondered aloud. "So . . . this must be *me*! I'm with Dad in India in 1955, a few months old and returning to Scotland." Quickly she filed through more pages and discovered a letter in her father's own hand. And certain phrases seemed to jump right off the page: *a young pregnant Tibetan girl . . . twins, one a boy, the other a girl . . . I've smuggled the baby girl out of Tibet . . . I feel she belongs with me . . . us as parents.*

"What the bloody hell? Why was dad writing to mum about Tibet? Why was *I* in India--if that actually was *me*? Am I this baby from Tibet?!"

Anne's head began to swim; and thought she would faint. Thoughts jumped in and out of her mind as she tried to process it all. A series of colours flashed before her eyes then cleared to show an image of Fiona, her mother. Then that sickly-sweet smell from the back of her mind filled her nostrils; her stomach became queasy. The sound of her struggling desperately with the front room door filled her ears. It died away—only to be replaced by the sound of her father crashing through the kitchen door. Shattering glass, splintering wood. Then flashing blue lights outside began to blot out the image of her mother. Yet, it wasn't her mother. Fiona *wasn't* her mother? *What the bloody hell's going on . . . really?!*

In a daze, Anne hurried to put everything back into the bureau. (She didn't know if it was in the correct place or not. And, what did that matter anyway?) She wished she'd never opened that bloody bureau! Anne locked it and replaced the key. Sick to her stomach she raced to the bathroom . . .

Chapter 11

THOUGH THE TRUTH WAS PAINFULLY apparent, Alexander never mentioned anything to Anne or his wife about Anne's venture into the bureau. And for a time, Anne stayed silent too--biding her time while feigning a willingness to follow Ruth's rules. She agreed to get her hair cut short (into a Page Boy style, per Ruth's wishes), agreed to wear sensible, practical clothes (of Ruth's choosing), and helped round the house (accepting vertible subservience). She decided to extend the courtesy and respectfulness she'd always showed her father to Ruth in hopes of avoiding questions about the desk—and what Anne may or may not have discovered in it. And while this ploy lasted for a time, what Anne now knew was eating her up inside. And allowing this woman--this obnoxious and controlling outsider—to dictate her every move was becoming unbearable. And rather than appreciate her efforts to be congenial, it seemed to Anne that Ruth was deliberately goading her into a confrontation. And one night it did end in a show-down. But not over the contents of the bureau; over power and ultimate control.

As it happened, Tracy, one of Anne's closest school friends, called early one Saturday morning to say that she and Moira, another friend, were thinking of going to the local youth club that evening. It was no big deal—or *shouldn't* have been. The youth club was organised by some of the more enthusiastic younger members of the local church and was held in the church hall. It was simply a safe place for the local teenagers to meet and let their respectable Edinburgh hair down. But Ruth had a different take on it. To her it was a place boys went with only one thing in mind: premarital sex with unwitting young girls. So she laid down the *Law According to Ruth*:

"You're *not* going to that youth club!" Ruth dictated, "and that's *final*! Tell her, Alexander, she's not to go!"

Anne's father gave Ruth a weary look and then shifted his gaze to his daughter. (The constant conflict between daughter and wife was wearing him down—and it showed. More and more frequently now after coming home from the surgery he'd skip dinner, slump down in his favourite armchair with a tumbler of whiskey, and gently nurse it through the evening until it was time for bed.) "It's only the local youth club, Ruth," he pleaded on Anne's behalf. "It's her friends from school, for Christ sake! You can't keep her from socialising with her friends!"

"Have you *seen* her friends?!" replied Ruth in mock horror. "The way they dress when they're not in school uniform?! Well *I* have! And it leaves little to the imagination! *Busoms--*" Ruth paused, but wasn't finished. "And it's not just local teenagers who go there, you know! There are girls--and boys, mind you--from less *desirable* areas, too!" she said, rolling her eyes derisively.

Alexander just shrugged. "We'll see later on today, darlin'."

That evening Anne got dressed to go out: nothing outrageous, what with her short *boyish* hair, baggy jumper and cord trousers--no one (she as certain) would even give her a second look. She popped her head round the front room door. "I'm off, then," she said to her father—not even acknowledging Ruth, sitting in the corner. "Won't be late."

"I told you earlier, my girl, you're *not* going *anywhere!*" barked Ruth. But her admonition fell on deaf ears as Anne was out the front door and shouting back:

"See you later, Da."

Ruth looked accusingly at Alexander and shook her head. "Whatever trouble that girl finds, Alexander, will be on you!"

Alexander got to his feet, went over to the drinks trolley, picked up the bottle of *Glenmorangie* whiskey and poured half a tumbler. "Why can't you just leave the girl alone, Ruth!? I don't understand *why* you have to pick on her so! It's as though you don't want her to have any enjoyment whatsoever! Remember *I'm* the one having to deal with what she saw in the bureau—not you!" he said—immediately realising that he'd said too much.

"What do you mean, '*saw in the bureau*'?" questioned a surprised Ruth.

Now wishing he hadn't let it slip, "She's been in the bureau. It was ages ago. I found some papers about her left out. I didn't mention it because--"

"That does it, Alex!" barked Ruth. "You didn't bother to tell me-- and now she *knows!*"

"What can she *know?* She's still too young to put it all together," Alexander offered as an explanation.

"Too *young?* Are you *blind?* She's hardly a little girl anymore, Alex! She's almost a woman!" Alexander grimaced and rolled his eyes. "And you better *not* be planning to tell her the whole truth! I don't want to hear about Fiona--those times are in the past and should be left there! I've been much more of a mother to her than *she* ever was—yet she treats me horribly!"

Alexander flinched and gulped downed his drink. "Listen, don't bring Fiona into this! You think I don't know how wrong all that went? I live with that every day--and so must Anne!" he snarled uncharacter-istically. "It's no bloody wonder she's the way she is! The death of her mother like that . . . and now what she must have seen in the bureau . . . and you--you putting her down at every bloody turn! There's more to being a parent than barking orders!"

Clenching her teeth she said, "I've done my best for her--and *you*! Sometimes I think you only married me to get a child-minder and house-maid! And just where would you—and *she*--be now if I hadn't been there to step in and help with your little Tibetan *princess*!" Ruth was in full steam now—and Alexander knew it was time to back off. "Just wait till she gets home! I'll teach her manners about prying into other people's private business—even if you don't have the backbone to!"

And teach Anne she did. That evening as Anne walked through the door, Ruth met her with a swing of Shuna's leash across the face. "You ungrateful *brat*!" she screamed. "After all I've done for you and this house! You've disobeyed me for the last time!" she ranted, raising the chain to strike her again. Desperate to get away, Anne scrambled--in-stinctively raising her arms to protect her face as blood ran from a gash above her eye and cheek. Startled by the uproar, Alexander jumped up from his chair and dashed out to see his daughter cowering in a corner of the hall, just as Ruth landed a second devastating blow—Anne's skull now running red. Alexander tore the leash from Ruth's hand and shoved her aside—letting Anne run upstairs to the bathroom. There she sat on the toilet seat with her head in her hands, sobbing, blood collecting on her clothes.

At this moment, Anne hated her life and everyone in it. The constant battle with Ruth was draining, and she wondered why her father would let the abuse continue. And suddenly, she felt that something inside her was missing. Long seen as *different* by most people, she now believed that she *was*. But as she sat there on the toilet seat she suddenly felt that she was not alone. She looked up. On the small bench across from her was a swirling grey mist . . .

At first she didn't trust her eyes; she focused and refocused. And as she did the mist took on the form of a man. Anne became transfixed. She could still see the bench clearly, while at the same time the man-- as two over-lapping objects. The man wore translucent white flowing robes. As her eyes tried to adjust, there was a strange silence, then the crackle of electricity in the air. And as her ears strained to separate noise from sound, her body suddenly felt light--as if she were weightless--then everything faded round her; the bathroom disappeared and she was face-to-face with the man. Though his lips didn't move, she heard his words clearly:

"Anne, I appear to you now in the image of the Christ to tell you to accept that you are different. And that I am ever with you. Never give up on yourself. Times are difficult now but one day you will understand why it had to be this way." Anne smiled as the man slowly faded into the grey mist--then suddenly felt as though she were being dragged backwards down a long tunnel; her ears slowly becoming aware of the distant sound of banging as she flew through space and time lost measure. A banging on the bathroom door. Suddenly pulled back to the here and now, her eyes focused on the walls round her, wondering if she'd just imagined the whole scene. The banging persisted.

Her senses wakening, Anne unlocked the bathroom door and found Ruth standing there, arms folded across her chest, her face contorted and red with fury. Anne waited calmly for the verbal onslaught--or even worse, the blow that would come from this dark figure blocking her way out--but to Anne's surprise, Ruth said nothing, simply turning and walking back down the stairs. There was no sound from either of her parents for the remainder of the evening.

Things quieted over the next few days, as if a truce had been declared, but the tension in the house was palpable. Days passed into months and the school terms came and went until it was clear to Anne that she'd had enough. (The incessant cold shoulder and tongue lashing and silence was painful and deafening.) Anne's last school term finished without any fanfare, Alexander and Ruth painfully aware that she was no star pupil; as was Anne herself. Ruth was all for forcing Anne to go to one of the advanced education institutes in the city to get better qualified—but Anne wasn't having it. She wanted to get a job, earn some money; move out and get the freedom she longed for. And besides, her best friends Tracy and Moira already had jobs.

Anne had grown to be a presentable and well-spoken young woman, and managed to get a job at a well-known Edinburgh clothing store in Shandwick Place in the city centre, as a shop assistant. She liked it there. She met interesting people and broadened her long-term horizons. And to the surprise of all the staff at the shop, it was Miss Jones, an elderly and unapologetically cantankerous spinster who instilled fear in all who worked under her, who Anne connected with. Ironically, Miss Jones showed a motherly compassion towards Anne, and Anne in turn managed to make Miss Jones smile--and sometimes, even laugh. Fast friends, they often travelled together on the same bus home from work. On one such trip Miss Jones told Anne about her sister June who suffered from *elephantiasis*, and that she was her only caretaker, explaining:

"I never married. But there was this one handsome lad, I still think about sometimes!" she confided, smiling. "But, well, things changed and it never came to much."

"Why not?" asked Anne out of intrigue.

"Well, both our parents died in a car accident and I had to look after my sister," she said, her eyes lowering in a moment of pained resolve. "There simply was no one else to do it."

How very sad, Anne thought. Losing both parents and having to sacrifice so much for your sister. And that set Anne's mind to thinking about her own parents. Who are they--*really*? Papers and official documents in a bureau . . . babies, twins, Tibet, India. Two mothers, Fiona and Ruth; one father, Alexander. The more she thought she knew for certain, the more questions that formed in her inquisitive mind. And for now, Miss Jones was her confidante. Someone she could talk to about Ruth; how very domineering and hostile she'd always been. Yet as of late—she couldn't care less if Anne was alive or dead if she couldn't control her.

"Your life's been hard, no doubt, lass, but mark my words. One day you'll understand what it's all been about. You're a bright one! I can see you writing a book--maybe two or three!"

"Really? You know, I was at the bottom of my English class at school!" laughed Anne, pondering the absurdity of writing even a single book. Still, something resonated with Anne, even though writing a book was far beyond her imagination. Miss Jones simply smiled.

But then one morning Miss Jones didn't report for work; which was highly unusual. And she didn't clock in the next day or the next. Then one of the managers came round and told the staff that Miss Jones was ill and was taking a leave of absence. Worried, Anne asked if she could visit her--after working hours of course--when someone else from the shop was going. So one evening she accompanied one of the store managers to Miss Jones' residence. There they were both shown into the house by a woman who Anne assumed was her sister. (The woman had great difficulty walking, was immensely overweight, with legs the size of tree trunks.) But gone was the bright and lively Miss Jones Anne knew from the shop; replaced by a dull and lifeless grey form in a room where even the sharp and beaming light streaming through the window couldn't disguise the inevitable. There was heaviness in the air; an oppressive atmosphere as if something or someone was just biding their time . . .

"Come closer, dear," beckoned Miss Jones. Anne inched closer. "Now listen, you keep that wonderful spirit you've got! Force them to see your true colours!" she told her. Anne fought back the tears. "I know all you see here is dull and empty, but there was colour and light here once, and there will be again. That's just the way of things," mused Miss Jones. "And deep down, I'm sure you know that. Never lose faith, dear. *Never!* You'll get there, I promise," she said, squeezing Anne's hand. Then a look from her sister told them that it was time to go. The two said their goodbyes and followed Miss Jones' sister to the front door.

"Thank you for coming," her sister said, smiling. Looking at Anne now, "I know she really likes you and thoroughly enjoyed your visit. It meant a lot to her."

For the next few weeks Anne went about her work as best she could. She was moved to the coat department; just temporarily, until Miss Jones returned. But Anne knew she never would. A few days later the staff (including Anne) was summoned to the meeting-room and told the sad news: Miss Jones, who'd been a stalwart of the store for twenty-five years, had died. Taken by cancer. More than anyone there--Anne was devastated. A kind, lovely woman like Miss Jones taken from her; the unfairness of it all began to eat at her. Inside, she raged against the world. There was no one to share her pain.

Chapter 12

GONE NOW WERE EARLY EVENINGS at the local youth club with school chums, replaced with late nights at pubs, discos, and popular nightspots in the city centre—often with veritable strangers. Anne had money in her pocket so it seemed only natural that she move up to the social and drinking scene. Only one of her friends, Tracy, was old enough to *legally* get into these places, so she always led the way. Other friends soon became well-versed in reciting, with supreme and believable assurance, false dates-of-birth to any barman or doorman who'd ask, and those not immediately taken in by the fluttering eyes of a group of attractive, older teenage girls. One such favourite target was a disco called The Chameleon.

No one was quite sure how it got that name, but some of the regulars said it was a businessman's haunt at lunchtime and weekdays that was transformed into a disco, drawing younger crowds on weekends—thus, a *Chameleon*. Name aside, Anne and her friends liked going there. It was sophisticated and not too big (like the major dance halls elsewhere in the city centre), and if you didn't know it was there you'd likely walk straight by it, as it was down a flight of steps and into the basement of a military regimental club. And as the girls discovered upon their first venture, the main obstacle to getting in was "Shug," the doorman, a big man whose ample frame nearly filled the small vestibule which was the entrance to the club. But his imposing presence wasn't to dissuade young and attractive girls from coming in, but to let the young men know who was ultimately in charge. So Anne and her friends had no problem sidling in, fake ID in hand, mature expressions across their faces.

Once inside, The Chameleon was a world apart from the local church discos. It looked small and compact, but was surprisingly spacious. Just off to the right was the bar, and further round were an inviting array of plush seating and tables. Straight ahead from the entrance was a small-ish timber-boarded dance floor, and beyond that, next to the back wall, was the discotheque booth. It too was small and compact, with the customary bright neon lighting fronting it. And finishing off the setting to the left were more sitting booths and tables, which took up the entire length of the wall. This was a proper club: no jeans or T-shirts here. Young men dressed in sports jackets and flannels, or three-piece suits and proper leather shoes--with matching self-coloured ties, top- pocket handkerchiefs, and Brogues for those wanting to make the ultimate fashion statement. For the young ladies it was crushed velvet dungarees, short tight fitting dresses or skirts with colour-coordinated tops, tasteful jewellery, small handbags, and smart high platform shoes (some to daring heights). Yes, The Chameleon was *the* place to be on Saturday nights—and Anne *loved* it!

One Saturday night Tracy and Anne stood at the Chameleon bar, sipping their blue lagoons.

"Do you think we will still be friends when we are old, and still drinking blue lagoons"? Laughed Tracy.

"We will always be friends Tracy, true friends, I can just see us when we are old reminiscing over our younger life as we sup our cocktails in some new and upcoming bar. But in the meantime check out that guy over there" said Anne as her eyes homed in on a young man attempting to lean nonchalantly against one of the pillars that skirted the dance floor. Good looking, tall with longish fair hair, he was quite smartly dressed, and there was something about his eyes. A pint in one hand and a lit cigarette in the other, he seemed to be part of a group who flitted between standing round the bar and poised at the edge of the dance floor. He stood there by himself. He caught Anne's eye-- but she wasn't sure if she'd caught his. As the DJ finished one record, the dance floor cleared, ready for the next one. Most of the young women, and probably the young men as well, had certain songs they liked to dance to and the next one was a dance-floor favourite by Rod Stewart. Anne liked it and took to the floor prepared to sway her hips alone, when almost immediately she felt a tap on the shoulder. She spun round to find her good-looking guy smiling down at her. "Would you care to dance?" he asked.

"Yeah, sure," Anne replied—trying her best to be coy.

When the Stewart record played out and the next one started, Anne and Rob, as the young man had introduced himself, were still dancing. She'd learned that he was training to be a Quantity Surveyor with a firm in the West End. And there was no denying it; that *spark*. They'd both felt it. Anne now had her first proper boyfriend.

Working at the clothing shop and spending time with Rob passed for a normal teenage life to outsiders. They'd meet on Saturday nights to go out together, usually to The Chameleon. Wanting to see more of each other, Anne would go to Rob's house on Friday nights and listen to records in his bedroom, and he would come to her house most Sunday nights—their rendezvous invariably interrupted by Ruth barging in and saying, 'Isn't it time for Rob to go home,' an accusing look on her stern face. To Ruth's self-satisfaction, Anne and Rob suffered teenage fickle, their romance running hot and cold. And before long the two went their separate ways. Then, something else in her life was going wrong. Or, was it?

Over the next few weeks Ruth, quite uncharacteristically, suddenly had little to complain about. And while Anne was at first thrilled at her new-found independence, it suddenly occurred to her that Ruth was different in other ways, too. She noticed that what had begun as an occasional cough had now become a chronic hack. And Anne suspected the worst.

"Da, Ruth's not well," she confided to her father. "I think you should examine her—or make her see her doctor." Anne could not understand why she, herself, would want to save this wretched woman, but something deep inside was triggered at the thought of her step-mother's life force fading away.

"Oh, it's just something that's going round," her father assured her, "half the staff at the surgery have it." But Anne wasn't convinced, and somewhat surprised that her father didn't recognise it as something more serious. A week later Anne called Ruth's doctor and asked him to make a home visit to check on her Mother's health. After examining Ruth the doctor called an ambulance. As with Miss Jones, Anne felt a dark boding about her step-mother's condition. Death sent her signals, she was coming to believe.

Later that night after visiting his wife in hospital, he returned home, he was rightfully flustered. Why had Anne—and not he, a trained doctor—recognised the telltale warning signs? Ruth's condition was indeed serious. Knowing he'd now be dividing his time between the hospital and the clinic, Anne was given a house key for the first time. She'd be able to come and go as she pleased; her first real acknowledgement of adulthood. She'd essentially be in charge of the house—and the prospect thrilled her immensely. She cooked for her father, did the cleaning and laundry, and began to grow more self-confident. Though she sometimes wondered if there weren't more hidden family secrets (something was still not making sense to her), she was filled with new-found power. (The fact that is came with ridding the house of Ruth was her secret guilty pleasure.) In the weeks that followed she worked during the day, tended to the house and her father in the afternoons, and went out most nights. Her new world was filled with plenty of attention, *Bacardi* & *Coke*, and cigarettes. *I could definitely get used to this*, she said. It was one night after coming home from The Chameleon that things took another decisive turn. As she locked the front door she noticed that the light was still on in her father's study, so she pushed the door open thinking to switch it off. There she found her father sitting at his bureau with his chair turned away from her. Anne could see a half-empty glass of whiskey in his hand. On hearing the door squeak open, he said:

"You'll have seen some of this," Alexander said with a tone of inevitability. "It's all about you."

Anne looked curiously over her father's shoulder and saw papers strewn across the open shelf of the bureau top. Here was the truth laid out in bold black and white. "I knew you'd been in my bureau, Annie— and I don't really blame you. I know I've skirted round this for far too long." Alexander shuffle "the truth" round the shelf with his free hand. "It was all *this*," he said with sorrow his voice, "that killed your mother. Well, *Fiona*. I guess you figured out some time ago that she wasn't your *real* mother."

"Yes, I worked that part out, Da," Anne replied, her party spirit quickly fading.

"Yes, it surely killed her . . . " Alexander pressed on, self-blame in his voice.

"Please don't torture yourself, Da. After all, Mum was ill," Anne said. "Her heart just gave out, what with all the work and the worry."

Alexander let out a soft chuckle. "Heart gave out?! Yeah--that was the story, now, wasn't it!" he spat. *Bloody hell!* She put her head in the damned oven, she did, and turned on the gas! That's the bloody truth of it! She just wanted *out!* *Away* from the bloody deception I created!" Alexander's shoulders began to heave ever so slightly and Anne could hear gentle sobbing. But then her sensibilities took over: *What? My mother killed herself?!* Guilt overcame her. *No matter how it happened, I was part of this!* "And there's more!" Alexander spit angrily. "And you're going to hate to hear this—but it needs said. I'm not your *real* father!"

The words echoed through Anne's head as if from a great distance. What had she heard? The man sitting there beside her was not her father?! No! There must be some mistake!

"Sit down, Anne, before you fall down," Alexander said softly. Anne lowered herself into the high-backed chair across from the bureau.

"But, *Da* . . . I don't understand! You're my *father*! I mean, we're so alike in so many ways!"

"I delivered you, but I'm not your father," interrupted Alexander. "Let me try and explain." He lifted his tumbler to his lips and poured the remainder of the amber liquid in. "See, I was working in Tibet. Your mother, uh, Fiona, was here in Scotland. I did some medical work for a group of Buddhist nuns there and one of their charges, a young Tibetan nomad girl, got herself pregnant. And being the only doctor for miles, I delivered her babies. You and your brother. You were named *Ani* after the abbess of the nunnery who looked after Pembuti. Pembuti was your mother. I don't know what name was given to your brother." Though still reeling from Alexander's revelation, Anne listened intently, trying to piece it all together.

"You see, times were quite difficult in Tibet then. The Chinese had invaded the country. So in order to protect you and your brother, it was decided that the best thing to do was to smuggle you out of Tibet— bring you back here to Scotland." He looked earnestly at Anne and said, "Fiona, I thought, would be a good mother to you. But that's not the way it turned out. I—I know I could have, *should* have, handled it better, but . . . " The room fell silent as his voice trailed off.

"But--I don't look like a *Tibetan*—do I?" queried Anne, in a tone as if to reject all that her father had just confessed. "I mean, I've seen pictures! This woman, Pembuti . . . and the monks. I look nothing like them!" Head swimming she slowly rose to her feet and told Alexander that she was going to bed. Crossing the study and leaving the room, she left behind a certain sense of finality. How could she ever look him in the eyes again?

Lying in a heap on her bedroom floor Anne felt nothing but anger. *Rage!* And it was as if she'd known this anger all her life (and all-too-often, it was all she had). And this anger burned inside her like a raging fire about to burn out of control; burn a hole through the wall or through someone--if she'd let it! Yet, all Anne had ever wanted was to love and be loved and to fit in. To be at peace with the beautiful colours flowing round every living thing. But now this mounting fury threatened to destroy all those beautiful colours, leaving her with pain that hurt in a way she couldn't name; pain that filled every part of her mind and body and soul. And the source of this fury had a face: *Ruth*. *Ruth* needed to be eliminated from her life. Withering away on her deathbed, Anne prayed for her quick and painful death!

Shocked and betrayed, Anne felt lost and alone. Now, she truly was *different*. No connection to anyone or anything. She was a living creature with no roots. And she wondered about her *true* mother—this lovely, Pembuti--and began to create a mental image of a wonderful, kind and caring mother who—*no doubt*--had never wanted to give her up. But unbeknownst to her, as she did, she became fearful: *fearful* of being on her own, *fearful* of love, *fearful* of life--

Relationships are out!--thought Anne. She had to become self-suffi-cient; *hardened* against the pain! For so long she'd longed for the truth and now that she'd met it, it was too harsh to bear. Hard and cold, the truth had shattered her world to bits.

Chapter 13

AFTER A SEEMINGLY ENDLESS SLEEPLESS night, Anne was completely drained from crying. During the night a transformation had taken place: A steel shutter had closed tight round her heart. The pain was overwhelming; the sense of powerlessness frightening. She was convinced that it was all Ruth's doing—all part of a malicious plan to get her claws into her father that began with driving Fiona to suicide. Silently she repeated the same words over and over again: *My dad's my dad. I know no other. This other man—whoever he is--means nothing to me.*

Anne went into work, but couldn't concentrate. Her head full of thoughts and pictures of her father and Fiona . . . and this Tibetan woman, Pembuti . . . and her brother . . . Anne made it to morning break but once in the staff room, burst into tears as she sat alone in the corner. Not knowing how to help her, one of her colleagues called her department manager (a sour stern-faced middle-aged woman) who decided it would be best if Anne went home. "Take some time off, dear," she told Anne. When she arrived home the house was empty; emptiness that resonated hollowly through her whole being. She felt herself an empty shell.

Nights out now became wilder; more careless. Drinking, smoking, boyfriends came and went--none of them taken seriously. Life of the party. To compound her agony, Ruth had a "miraculous recovery" and returned home from hospital--after Anne had convinced herself that she was now the woman of the house and Ruth was no longer needed (or wanted). Ruth's presence immediately undermined the congenial understanding she and her father were building.

And though for the sake of her father (who she now saw as a victim) Anne sometimes joined them for meals, the scene was nothing short of surreal; sitting opposite virtual strangers. Still, Ruth sat there with her haughty air of self-importance as queen of the roost. The bare truth out, Ruth now owed Anne nothing—and Anne knew it. And by association, Alexander owed Anne nothing. And if Ruth pushed her husband hard enough she could be shot of this unruly teenager once and for all.

A decisive point was reached one evening soon after when Ruth attempted to dictate Anne's social plans, refusing to allow her to pass in hallway while on her way to wash and dress to go out. Blocking her path, she repeatedly provoked and threatened her, goading Anne to over-react. Taking the bait, Anne shoved Ruth out of the way--causing Ruth to stumble backward into a table leg and cut her ankle. Later complaining to Alexander--in quite exaggerated terms--that Anne had violently attacked her (and was, in her opinion, "in need of psychological observation"), he was just about to discuss the matter with Anne when she announced that she was moving into flat with a friend. "It's all been arranged," Anne coolly stated to them both. "I've got to get away from here. --From *you!*"

"But Anne, are you *sure?* Really *sure?*" Questioned Alexander, sounding truly concerned. "You're still so young, and you have everything you need right here."

But Ruth was not going to let her well-laid plans be ruined: "Just let her go, Alex! She'll find out soon enough how lucky she was to have us! Wait till she gets a dose of the real world!"

Alexander could see a steely, resolute look in his Anne's eyes. Her mind was made up. So Anne was off--off to a small tenement flat just on the border of the city centre. No more prying eyes from Ruth; no more monitoring her every move; no more violent confrontations. She was in charge of her own life.

The new Anne decided it was time to quit her job at the department store, and took a job in the Pension department of a Civil Service office. It was simple administrative work--fetching and carrying files—and was certainly no *career* opportunity for Anne--but it paid well. Anne couldn't fathom why anyone would want to spend their adult lives stuck behind a desk (any desk) while the whole world was turning just outside their office window. This job—like any other-- was a way to make some cash; and nothing more.

There was so much to consider with her newly-claimed freedom—and Anne wanted to experience it all. Every waking hour should be filled with excitement—and there was no time to lose! One of her new friends from the office managed to get her a part-time waitressing job in the evening at a city centre pub called The Bandwagon. Anne liked the hustle and bustle of the bar; the excitement of serving drinks to--and flirting with--any eager male customer who caught her fancy. She'd come to realize that she was an attractive and vivacious young woman, and that she loved the attention! But boyfriends were meant to be teased and tormented, and she liked the control and power she could wield over them. And without realising it, Anne's behavior was being fueled by her increasing use of alcohol and nicotine (and occasional marijuana).

Before long the lure of an easy office job waned for Anne, so she moved on again, this time as a receptionist at a driving school. But still, the partying continued, gaining a reputation as a wild, crazy, *fun* loving girl. Her new work mates soon noticed that while she always had room for another drink at lunchtime, she never seemed to eat, asking: "Don't you ever eat?"

"I ate something yesterday, I think . . . " Anne replied, "or maybe the day before. Who knows!?"

For Anne there was no tomorrow—and today was running short of time. It wasn't just living *in* the moment, it was living *for* the moment. And each moment had to be better than the last. As no surprise, the driving school moment didn't last long.

While on holiday in St. Andrews with Amelia, a new friend, the two liked the east coast city so much that they took jobs as chamber maids at one of the more elite hotels there. A new adventure, a new moment, Anne felt she was living the high life—the backdrop, the stunning views across the Old Course and the sands of West Beach. But this type of job was seasonal and usually short-lived—which didn't bother Anne at all. (She didn't even have a short-term plan--let alone a long-term.) But when the hotel manager offered the two jobs at one of the hotel chain's London branches, they packed their bags and trooped off to the bright lights of the big city.

In the blink of an eye--three years had passed. Three years of what? --Anne could barely remember. Except that she'd met Graham. With Rob just a waning memory, Graham stood out as *different*. Or maybe it was just timing, or biology. And though barely acquainted, they moved in together. He could look after her—as Alexander once had. But Graham was *not* Alexander. Anne discovered that he'd been married before and had fathered five children--to five different woman! A control fanatic, he watched Anne's every move—and it was like Ruth all over again! Finally, when he set up his own driving school and pro- ceeded to give certain female pupils lessons that had nothing to do with *driving*, Anne went back home to Alexander (and Ruth). And though

Anne was now a grown woman, Ruth resumed treating her as she always had--like a child; even barging into Anne's bedroom each morning ostensibly to make sure Anne was up and getting ready for work (and taking perverse pleasure in finding Anne sleeping nude). Before long, the pressure threatened to blow--just as it had in the past.

Anne took a job at a telephone answering service, kept mostly to herself, but spent most evenings with friends; anything to keep away from Ruth. But one particular evening, things took a decidedly different turn. Ruth had been working more regularly at her brother's dental surgery and had insisted that both Anne and Alexander be present to hear about an incident that had taken place there. As they all sat uncomfortably at the kitchen table, Ruth excitedly explained that a group of monks had arrived at the surgery—but not your typical Christian monks in black robes and hoods. Rather, Asian monks wearing maroon- and saffron-coloured robes. And they were from Tibet! She said:

"They were like the ones in your old photographs, Alex!" Ruth explained smugly. "You know, your photos of Tibet and India?" Anne looked at Alexander and saw his apprehension as Ruth continued. "Well, they all seemed to be most deferential to this one particular monk—subservient, really--who according to the interpreter, had a toothache and required treatment. He said they'd been referred to us, although by whom was never disclosed. Well, you have to imagine, they all filed in, bowing and scraping, except the one with the toothache." Anne found herself quite intrigued and was glad she hadn't ignored Ruth's invitation. Alexander's look of apprehension was replaced now with one of curiosity.

"So, in went this head monk and the interpreter into the treatment room, while the others stayed out in the reception area. But, not sitting down on the seats like normal people, just standing there with their hands clasped in front of them like statues—one or two occasionally lifting their heads and smiling. Eventually the treatment room door opened and out came the two monks, all big smiles, followed by my brother."

"So, Charles treated his toothache, is that *it*?" queried Anne. A withering look from Ruth stopped Anne before she could say more.

"If you'll just let me *finish*!" scolded Ruth. "Well, as the interpreter was directing the monks back outside, this head monk gave me a little smile and then said something to the interpreter--in Tibetan I guess. The interpreter turned to me and said that the *Karmapa* was most intrigued by the lovely turquoise necklace I was wearing. You know the one, Alexander."

Anne looked at Alexander, who had an incredulous look on his face which was lost on Ruth--but not Anne. Before Alexander or Anne could respond, Ruth rattled on, looking directly at Anne: "It was that necklace of *yours*! You know, the one you keep in that precious little box of yours and used to make such a fuss over when you were a little girl! Well, needless to say, I was taken aback! What a strange thing for a monk to comment on, I thought. Well, I said that it belonged to my stepdaughter and I had just borrowed it," Ruth said. "Then I said, 'what a coincidence. My husband, who's a doctor, worked in Tibet about twenty years ago, and here you are in my brother's surgery!'" Neither Anne nor Alexander said a word, and just looked at each other. Appearing not to notice, Ruth resumed her tale.

"The interpreter looked most surprised at what I'd said and excitedly relayed it all to this *Karmapa*. He just smiled, took a pamphlet or something from the interpreter, wrote something on it, and told the other monk to place it on the table beside the magazines--for Charles's patients to see, I suppose. And before I had time to thank the interpreter, he bowed and followed the main one out the door." Looking to Anne now, she said, "And, what do you think of *that* then?"

Though Anne was nearly speechless—taken aback that Ruth had directed a question to her—she nonetheless felt that this story should mean something to her. And she could see that it registered somewhat with Alexander, too. Anne had expected some more catty remarks from Ruth about jewellery and finery and Tibet, but now sat silent instead. She'd regaled them of her little adventure and it now appeared that was the whole of it.

"Uh--are you staying to supper, Anne?" Alexander asked, looking hopeful.

"No," she said, getting up from the table. "I have something else to take care of."

Upstairs in her room Anne reached under her bed and pulled out her precious box; still nestled just where it had long been. (Ruth had apparently put it back after borrowing the necklace.) It surprised her now that she'd not taken it with her when she'd moved out. Inside were the turquoise necklace and other special gifts—just as she'd left them. Lifting out the heavy necklace, Anne cradled it in her hands. Hung it from the middle finger of her right hand to see the facets catch the fading light. As she studied it she reminded herself that nothing would be right until she found her true roots. Found out who she really is. But even pleasant memories from her childhood (like her precious jewellery box and all that it contained) could not save Anne from the viciousness of life with Ruth.

Chapter 14

Now REGRETTING HER DECISION TO move back, moving out became inevitable. No longer step-mother and step-daughter, their rows were woman-to-woman: personal, up-close, and intense. A collision of generations, beliefs, and lifestyles—with Anne's now fueled by regular use of alcohol and nicotine (and pot when it was around).

Anne moved into a flat down in Leith, keeping her job at the telephone answering service—as well as her carefree nightlife. After working late one evening at the telephone answering service Anne suddenly had an overwhelming feeling that she must go for a drink at a local pub -The Circus Bar. Persuading her work colleague that they still had time for at least one drink before final orders were called, the pair hailed a taxi. A five minute trip and they had arrived at their destination. As if on automatic pilot Anne headed to the far end of the room and squeezing between throngs of people she finally reach the bar. Waving a ten pound note in her hand to attract the bar man's attention she was momentarily distracted by a soft male voice whispering in her ear. "Could you add a coke to that order, so hard to get served here, I would be happy to pay for your drinks as well" said the young man. Anne smiled at this man and nodded in agreement. Suddenly without warning a brawl broke; people began pushing and shoving—with flying glasses shattering into the bottle gantries. The man who had asked Anne to order him a coke now threw his jacket over her head and she was spirited away to a safe corner. Anne's White Knight was a young man named Calum. Uncloaking her, he said politely, "Best if we get out of here. What d'you think?"

"Sure, why not," she replied; a bit stunned, but pleased.

"I know a quieter—and *safer*--place up near Haymarket. A friend of mine owns it," he said.

Once out in the street, Anne got a better look at her rescuer— and her pleasure only increased. He came across as confident, but not pushy or arrogant. And he was quite good looking. Conversation was easy between them and before long, Anne felt at ease in this young man's company. A short jaunt in Calum's yellow *Mercedes* brought them to the pub he'd mentioned where they were greeted by Calum's friend Ian, the owner. Quickly caught up in conversation and stories (and lots of drinks), time flew by and the sun was cracking the sky by the time they left. Anne was dropped off outside her Leith flat and left with an invitation to return to the bar the following weekend for a special party.

The week passed uneventfully, work at the call centre slow. Come the weekend, Anne decided to go out with her old friend Tracy that Saturday evening. All week she had argued with herself as to whether to meet Calum or not. It was only after they'd arrived at Mad Dogs, a popular cocktail bar on George Street, that Anne suddenly realised she did want to take up Calum's invitation. Convincing Tracy to change their plans and come along with her to the party, from that night on, Anne and Calum were inseparable.

Unlike young men Anne had known in the past, Calum acted genuinely interested in what Anne had to say. And talked to her intelligently. And as never before an attraction grew—feeling safe and never just a "past-time" as she often had with other men like Graham. Before long Anne moved into a flat in the city centre with her friend Moira, evenings and weekends the two going their separate way: Anne with Calum, Moira with her boyfriend Charlie. As their relationship blossomed, Anne would take advantage of every opportunity for Calum to spend the night at their flat. Over the next year, Anne and Calum were a popular "couple" in the club scene.

Almost a year to the day, Anne decided to make an appointment with her doctor, complaining of stomach pains and constant fatigue. A simple urine test confirmed it: she was pregnant. Two months. *Pregnant?* Sure, she and Calum were having sex—and a lot of it--but a few years before she'd been diagnosed with a condition called *endometriosis* and told that unless she conceived within six months of beginning sexual activity, she likely never would. Yet—here it was! Breaking the news to Calum, he suggested they marry, and Anne agreed. Keeping the pregnancy quiet, they announced their wedding. To Anne's surprise, Ruth actually seemed happy that she was getting married—especially to someone of Calum's social standing; a respectable businessman and man of means. But Anne was suspicious of her well wishes, convinced that she was scheming about something.

As with most families, announcing an engagement and plans to marry was the easy part. The hard part; agreeing on the details. And though Ruth nearly derailed the entire ceremony (and Anne nearly called the whole things off several times) over choice of church, type of service, and selection of bridesmaids, the wedding went ahead. A time for families to gather, reminisce, and look to the future with optimistic eyes. Harsh words and ill feelings were put aside for the sake of the bride and groom; even Ruth spoke in glowing terms of how happy she was for her daughter—though Anne believed not a word of it. (Had Ruth been aware that Anne was already pregnant, the wedding may not have proceeded at all.)

For Anne the future ahead was motherhood; something she'd never really considered but now would have to deal with. Family and friends were supportive, their kind sentiments accepted for exactly what they were: mere words. *It's not them having this baby*, thought Anne, *it's me! My body, my side-tracked life.* The remainder of her pregnancy dragged by and, after twenty-one hours of excruciating pain, a son was born. The name "Daryl" was eventually chosen after much debate over familial obligations. For reasons Calum couldn't begin to fathom, Anne had at first insisted on the name "Drakar" for their son—with no idea where the name had come from. "It just appeared in my mind," Anne told Calum.

The question now was: What to do with this helpless, new arrival? Oh, there were textbooks debating breastfeeding vs. bottle feeding, and instructional handbooks on nappy changing and advice on practical parenting. But no matter how hard Anne looked, she found no books on how to manage the emotions and moods brought on by the strange little intruder now in her care. And leaving the maternity ward, Anne felt that she was now on her own; *completely* on her own. As if on cue, Ruth offered plenty of unsolicited baby *dos* and *don'ts*—but her advice was promptly ignored by an obstinate Anne. Calum did his best to help, but day in, day out, it was mostly Anne and baby Daryl.

Before long, Anne came to believe that if she loved her son (which she truly did) he would die. And as badly as the first few weeks went, over the next four months it went from bad to worse. At just seven weeks, Anne became convinced that Daryl was seriously ill—though there were no obvious signs. She didn't know *how* she knew--just that she *did*. A few days later Daryl developed a high fever and after waiting four hours for a doctor to visit Anne took her baby directly to The Royal Hospital for Sick Kids, in Edinburgh. There he was misdiagnosed with viral meningitis and remained in hospital for more tests. Anne *was* convinced that there was something very wrong with her son. The doctors and nurses grew steadily more annoyed with Anne's round-the-clock observations and assessment of her son's condition. Still, every prediction Anne made proved true.

Anne's greatest concern was that she could see Daryl's stomach growing larger. Yet when a nurse placed a measuring tape round the boy's waist, his measurements remained constant. Three days later the doctors informed Anne that Daryl was not producing vitamin K, the vitamins required for blood coagulation—her fears about her son's condition now vindicated. And though Daryl's blood stabilised a few days later, the following day he was rushed to the operating theatre, having developed a bowel disorder (where one section of the bowel had telescoped into the next) and in need of immediate, emergency surgery. Now what Anne had intuited was evident to everyone: Daryl's stomach was now quite visibly distended, having expanded some four additional inches.

Over the next few months Daryl was repeatedly taken to the doctor for one ailment or another—each ailment only becoming apparent a few days *after* their visits (Anne sensing each well in advance). An ear infection that would not clear up after several visits to the doctor (and changes in prescription) finally resulted in Anne demanding to see a specialist who, upon examining Daryl, told Anne that her son had been misdiagnosed and given the wrong medication (adding that if she hadn't followed her instincts and sought his expert advice, Daryl would most likely have lost the hearing in the infected ear). But Daryl's struggles with illness weren't over. Suffering a seizure due to running a dangerously-high temperature, he was again hospitalized— this time diagnosed with a serious urinary tract infection. At seven months old Daryl began to walk, and soon after this while on a family holiday Daryl managed to unlock the door to the swimming pool. Within seconds he had fallen into the pool. The noise alerted Anne who rushed to his rescue. Anne administered the kiss of life to Daryl as they waited on the ambulance.

Anne could take no more of it.

Slowly becoming more exhausted, Anne grew fearful and filled with dread over her son's health and daredevil antics. She began to lose rational thinking.

Meanwhile, Calum's business and social life was taking up more and more of his time. *Yes*, he provided well for his wife and son but Anne felt alone. Finally Calum hired a nanny. Though not ignoring her duties as mother, Anne began to resent her husband's absences and fell back into some of her old ways, unwinding with the help of alcohol—and a cigarette was always in her hand.

Ruth grudgingly accepted that Anne had a right to bring Daryl to visit Alexander—his "grandfather." But if she couldn't dictate childcare, Ruth had no interest in the child whatsoever. Anne worried about Alexander's health, now retired, he spent most of his time at home with Ruth, increasingly more dependent on whiskey and cigarettes. Anne would berate him for not minding his health, but he would point out that she still drank and smoked—and was being hypocritical. Soon, coughing spells let to occasional nosebleeds, which got worse. Diagnosed with a heart condition a short time later, Alexander was told that he required valve replacement surgery. And though the doctors pronounced Alexander's surgery a *success*, Anne wasn't convinced. Seeing that he had no colour (no visible energy whatsoever) she feared that something else was wrong. When she and Calum brought Daryl for his weekly visit, Alexander wasn't in his favourite chair as usual.

"Where's Alexander?" she asked Ruth.

"Alex had to go back into hospital last night," was Ruth's matter-of-fact answer, "just for some more tests. No big deal."

"What!?" exclaimed Anne. "And you didn't think to contact me?!"

"Now, don't start your petty dramas with me--and don't go rushing into see him! You'll just get in the way!"

Grabbing Calum by the arm she said, "Come on, take me to the hospital, *now*!"

"You heard what your mother said. He's just in for tests! You can't just go barging into the hospital—getting in the way!"

"Getting in the way!? For once, just do as I ask! Neither of you have a bloody clue what's going on here! He's going to die--I know it! And I've got to get there, with or without *you*!"

Calum knew that reasoning with Anne was not an option. "Okay, I'll drop you off at the hospital and wait outside for you while you see your father."

No time for niceties with the nursing staff, Anne demanded to know what ward Mr. Alexander McNaughton was in. Though well past visiting hours, the young nurse could see from Anne's face that this woman was in no mood for formality, so she pointed Anne in the direction of the stairs: up to Ward 35. Taking the steps two at a time she could only hope that she'd get there before it was too late. When she reached Ward 35 she encountered a tired looking, middle-aged man in a white lab coat: "Doctor, how is my father?" Anne blurted out. "Mr. Alexander McNaughton?"

"Ah, yes, Alexander McNaughton. And you are?"

"His daughter, Anne De—I mean *McNaughton*."

"Oh, I see, Miss McNaughton. We've run some tests and we think there may be a problem with the replacement heart valve. His condition is being monitored and we've scheduled more tests, but he's stable and resting for now. You can come back during visiting--"

"*Stable?* I'm sorry, doctor, but I think you're mistaken! I don't believe he's *stable*! I'm quite certain he's going to die!" said Anne.

Used to dealing with distraught family members who dwell on doom and gloom, the doctor smiled and said, "He's in that room there, number 122, if you'd like to visit," turning away to continue his rounds.

Opening the door, Anne found Alexander lying on a bed connected to dozens of wires and tubes. He looked quite calm and peaceful but Anne immediately noticed the greyness of his pallor and the lack of energy round him. Anne sat on the bed next to him and clasped his hand in hers. "So . . . you're back in here, again," Anne said in a mock-scolding tone.

"Just more tests, darlin', that's all," replied Alexander. "Routine stuff."

"You should have told me you were going back into hospital," Anne chided (wanting to add, *since that bitch of a wife of yours wouldn't think to*).

"There really wasn't time, but it's really just a precaution," Alexander said as a comfort, knowing he was telling a white lie. The two just sat there in the stillness of the moment and for once in a long while there was peace: no stress, no worries, just connected as they once were. In this silence Anne began to hear the most angelic music, soft, clear, crisp notes that resonated deep within her. For a split second she wondered if there truly were such things as angels. Finally, "Guess you'd better get going, young lady. They'll be coming for me shortly to take me for more tests, and you need to get back to that wonderful boy of yours!"

Anne kissed Alexander on the cheek and went to the door. As she passed through she turned and wagged a scolding finger in his direction, then closed the door behind her. Once in the hall the tears began to flow. She was more certain than ever: the man she'd long known as her father was dying. Outside the building she saw Calum sitting in his car, tears blinding her eyes. "He's going to die, I just know he is" cried Anne. "I can take Daryl to stay with my mother for a few hours, but you will need to help me get his clothes from the house. I'm not going to miss my football game." Replied Calum.

As she unlocked the front door and stepped inside the phone was ringing. "Is this Miss Anne McNaughton?" the voice at the other end enquired.

"Well, sort of, that is my maiden name, but--"

"This is Sister Ray here at Ward 35 at the Royal Infirmary. I've been trying to reach your mother, Mrs. Ruth McNaughton? But I'm getting no reply," continued the voice.

"Is it my dad? Are you calling about my father?" Anne asked, afraid of the answer.

"Yes—yes I am. I'm calling to inform you that Alexander McNaughton was just sent for emergency surgery. It's hospital policy to let the nearest of kin know, you know . . . just in case there are complications."

"Yes, I understand," she said coolly (though her heart was breaking). "I'll locate Ruth—uh, my mother—immediately." Replacing the receiver she threw some clothes, and other essentials for Daryl into a bag and handed it to her impatient husband. He threw her a look as he left the house.

Then she began looking through her diary to find the numbers of Ruth's friends. After calling several unsuccessfully—and about to give up—her friend Doris said Ruth was having lunch at the Braid Hills Hotel. Before she called the number Anne dialed the local taxi company and ordered a taxi. Taxi ordered she dialed the hotel where she prayed her mother was.

"Yes, I'm trying to reach a Mrs. Ruth McNaughton. Could you please check and see if she's in the restaurant? It's urgent."

"Yes, okay. Hold on. I'll try to find her," the voice replied.

Silence followed by an abrupt voice: "Ruth McNaughton here."

"Ruth, it's me," gushed Anne. "Dad's in emergency surgery, and you need to get there as soon as possible."

"Why can't you just be sensible for once and let the doctors and nurses do their jobs?!" Ruth scolded. "When will you ever--"

"You don't understand," Anne shot back. "They tried to reach you at home and couldn't, so they phoned me. You've got to be there in case there are complications."

But Ruth was having none of this. "You and that ridiculous imagination of yours! I swear, you're such a *child*! Now, act your age and do *not* call me again!"

"But--don't you care about dad?" said Anne sharply. "He's going to die—I'm certain of it!"

"Don't I *care*--why you nasty little hypocrite! Don't talk to me about *caring* for your father! A caring daughter *you* are!" she said bitingly. "Swanning off to live in dingy flats all over town--then down to London with some bloody womaniser! And then you get pregnant before you're married! No wonder Alexander's in the hospital! You're the biggest heartache he has! *You*, you--!"

"You're a horrible, horrible woman! You--" and with that the line went dead. Anne screamed and slammed down the receiver.

Grabbing her bag Anne ran out of her house slamming the door behind her. Happy to see the taxi driver idling in the driveway she opened the door of his taxi and jumped in. "The Royal Infirmary Hospital," she said, suddenly feeling cold and empty. She knew in her heart she'd never see her father again. Jumping out of the taxi and rushing through the emergency room doors, she ran to the reception desk. "Mr. Alexander McNaughton," was all she could manage to say. "His surgery . . ."

"And you are?" the woman asked.

"Anne. Anne McNaughton. His daughter."

"I see. If you'll have a seat, the doctor will be here to talk with you." But Anne was already certain of what the doctor would tell her. A few moments later, a graven-faced man in his mid-forties approached. Anne stood nervously.

"Miss McNaughton, I'm afraid I have some bad news. Mrs. McNaughton, uh, Ruth, your mother, has already been informed. Your father died on the OR table. There were serious complications and there was nothing we could do. But I can assure you, he died peacefully." Overcome with tears, Anne sat for a moment before making her way back outside where she hailed a taxi. Once home, she had but one phone call to make:

"I hope you're happy now, you worthless piece of fucking trash," was Anne's parting remark to Ruth. "You destroyed a family and killed a good and decent man. I hope there's a special hell for trash like you!"

Chapter 15

ALEXANDER MCNAUGHTON'S FUNERAL WAS A dignified and substantial affair. Friends, neighbours, distant relatives, and former medical colleagues all turned out to see Anne's father off. Ruth remained stoic and unemotional throughout the whole of the proceedings--exchanges between Anne and Ruth perfunctory and stilted. Anne had lost the one thing, the one person, who was a constant throughout her life. Despite his part in deception, he'd always been there for her; quietly supporting her, a buffer between Ruth and her.

The impact of losing her father was far greater than Anne could have imagined. Her life now focused wholly on Calum and Daryl, abject loneliness was about to set in. Loneliness aroused by a voice from the past. When called to her father's solicitor's office, Anne was presented a most-unexpected bequeath: a letter addressed to her from Fiona. The letter spoke with a voice overburdened with loneliness and confusion. It set free the words of a young woman trying to come to terms with a baby not her own; a distant husband, an imposed life, and abject desperation. And it told of her *real* father, living in Perth, who wanted nothing to do with any of this. It spoke of a distraught woman who saw but one way out: suicide.

Anne read the letter again and again until it spoke as clearly as if the writer were sitting there beside her. Then other voices joined in; Alexander and this woman she knew as "Pembuti." And once they started, neither she nor Calum nor Daryl could keep the voices at bay. She tried to stifle them with family life—then alcohol and nicotine. But they wouldn't be silenced. Then marijuana was enlisted when she could find it. Slowly withdrawing deeper and deeper within herself, it didn't help that Calum was very rarely home and Daryl was gaining his own independence. She began to wonder: *Am I to suffer the same fate as Fiona? Or become a cold and calculating woman devoid of feeling like Ruth.* Amidst this confusion, another dark cloud appeared overhead. To her horror, Anne found herself pregnant again. With hesitation she informed Calum.

"Well, that's wonderful!" Calum said, having always dreamed of many offspring.

"*Wonderful*?! Are you *insane*?! Can't you see that I can barely cope as it is?!"

"Ah, you'll be just fine! You'll see!" he said, heading for the door. "You did it once, you can certainly do it again!"

"No--" Anne began to protest--but Calum was gone. Anne broke down in tears. Alone.

As the months passed, Anne became resigned to her pregnancy, vowing to have a different attitude towards motherhood, and found an unexpected happiness within herself during the final months. The day finally arriving, she was admitted to hospital in good spirits. The following day a baby girl was born; a daughter Anne named "Tara." At first insisting the baby be called "Adel," Calum finally gave in. Thus they became a family of four.

In the ensuing months, Daryl and Tara demanded so much of her time that Anne became exhausted. And before long the pressure awakened the troubled past she'd thought she'd escaped. Growing ever desperate, she felt she had no control over her children and had no idea how to be a mother. How to *love* them and yet *discipline* them—as a mother must—was beyond her. Making the pressure even more unbearable, Anne and Calum decided it was time to go their separate ways. So they parted. The house was sold and Anne found a new place to call home for Daryl, Tara, and herself. But the new house came with a very disturbing problem: *ghosts*. (*Ghosts* that made no end of noise, dimmed the lights, slammed doors, and made dishes fly off the shelves). So after only two months, a new home was found, with Anne devoting her attention to improvements and renovations. And although Anne felt that her life was finally moving forward, it was not in the direction she would have preferred. Because in her quieter moments, Fiona's and Alexander's deaths still haunted her; as did Ruth's heartless attitude. And the whispering voices were still in her head, making her question who and what she was, and what she should do next. By outward appearance, those round her saw Anne as emotionally and physically strong, but inwardly, the foundation that held her up was crumbling; the ground beneath her starting to quake. And whether it was the voices or the breakup of her marriage, a day arrived when she no longer wanted to put on a brave face. She wanted to be alone.

Over the following months Anne grew more and more introverted; going out less and less, visited by fewer and fewer people, until finally she became house-bound. Losing the will to control her life or her children, she spent more and more time in bed until one day she simply didn't get up. Now bed-bound, Daryl and Tara were essentially on their own--Daryl always getting into trouble (even involving the police), while Tara was content to just wile away the hours alone (talking and playing with the little creatures she'd meet in the garden).

By this point, Anne was smoking upwards of forty cigarettes a day, had begun smoking marijuana regularly, and was washing it all down with glasses of red wine and *Bacardi* rum. Less and less able to see life objectively, Anne began to shut down emotionally; lacking the motivation to do anything. Calum had by this time hired a new nanny to take care of the children—who Anne hated, but accepted as she had no energy to look after the kids herself. One day not long after she woke with her heart pounding wildly against her chest and became convinced that she had a heart problem—that would very likely kill her. As Anne lay in bed staring out the window, she watched as snowflakes fluttered down from the sky, leaving a white frost across the ground. But this beautiful scene gave her no comfort as her heart continued to race with no apparent cause.

Convinced that death was near, for the next several weeks she lay in bed unwilling to eat or sleep, allowing herself to grow weak. Unable to convince her to see a doctor—even for the sake of the children--Calum at last called one in who, after examination, diagnosed Anne as having a virus affecting her heart, curable with simple medication. But as the days went by, even with medication she only got worse, so the doctor was called again. This time attributing her symptoms to food poisoning, he prescribed a soft diet and continued bed rest. Over the next two weeks Anne grew weaker and weaker and more despondent—certain the doctor was wrong. *Death is coming.* Then as if she'd toppled into a dark, indigo tunnel (somewhere in the recesses of her mind), she felt herself falling—falling into a bottomless pit from which no one could save her.

Slipping in and out of sanity, she began to pray to God for help--her mind racing with thoughts that made no sense; overtaken by terrifying hallucinations. Unimaginable fear gripped her--though her fear had no face nor form. *Isn't death the ultimate answer—and my destiny?* All the while her heart would suddenly race out of control--a runaway train ripping down the tracks to nowhere. Realising now that Anne would surely die if not hospitalised immediately, a lifeless, emaciated Anne was taken by ambulance. (Calum saw a strange smile appear on Anne's face as they sped through the city streets. In her mind she'd died and was being taken to the morgue.)

Waking in her private room, Anne was confused. Alone and afraid. Her heart still racing, she realised that death had not come. And there was a certain sense of disappointment; of failure. Over the next few days, Calum, Daryl, and Tara visited almost daily, but it was Tara who was first able to reach Anne. Reading aloud a letter she'd written, Anne was suddenly brought back to the present by the haunting words, *I love you Mummy, please come home.* Tears bursting, Anne suddenly realised that she'd never even considered her children loving or missing her. And she felt shame. When Calum and the children left, Anne collapsed into uncontrollable sobbing; tears that wouldn't stop. When a nurse came in a few minute later to check on her, the woman saw a chance to reach the despondent woman. She approached Anne and said, "Dearie, d'you know what happens if you keep putting rubbish in a wastepaper basket that's already full?" Anne looked curiously across the top of the white hospital bed clothes and thought it an especially odd question to ask. "It'll overflow, honey. It'll overflow!" Anne began to think clearly for the first time in months.

What had Anne been putting in her *emotional* wastepaper basket? *Everything and anything!* Her emotions were overflowing and there was nowhere else to put them. And to make room she would have to go back home, get well, and get on with her life. That evening she convinced Calum to take her home and back to the children. Calum reluctantly agreed. Against doctors' advice, Anne signed herself out.

But, reclaiming her life wasn't as easy as she'd thought. Finding ways to not let her emotions overwhelm her was something she'd always failed at. (And was the root of her deep-seated anger.) She thought to focus on what made her happy: she was a mother, had been a housewife, and had worked at several different jobs. But in truth, she hadn't been happy for longer than she could remember. *So, what the hell's missing from my life? What am I really searching for?* The break-through answer came from the most unlikely of places:

"Bloody hell--snap out of it!" Ruth yelled at her, standing in the doorway of Anne's bedroom. "Your kids need you—and here you are lying about feeling sorry for yourself! You—with everything to live for!" Walking to the window, Ruth threw open the drapes and let cruel, harsh light enter the room for the first time in months. "Now, get up and do what you know you need to do! You have responsibilities—so own up to them!" Ruth's words were hard to take and lay heavy on Anne's mind but brought a realisation Anne had herself lost sight of.

As Ruth hurried down the stairs and out the front door, Anne pulled herself out of bed and shuffled barefoot to the armchair by the window; she sat down. She watched vacantly through partially-open eyes as Ruth walked to her car and got in. She saw Daryl playing in the street beyond and Tara fiddling out in the garden. And as she sat there the fog that had set in weeks before suddenly began to dissipate. She had a decision to make: whether to choose life or death. If she wanted to live she had to change the habits that had brought her to this—no more drinking, smoking, and especially, no more smoking marijuana. But is that what she wanted?

Closing her eyes for a moment she then took in the state of her body. Then her room. Looking out her window again she then noticed her white *BMW* parked outside. (She'd completely forgotten that she's bought the car that to her spelled *freedom*—now realising that it hadn't provided that at all.) It then occurred to her that freedom isn't a destination, it's a state of mind. And that's what needed to be changed. For the first time in months she saw an opening through the fog.

Chapter 16

Now open to making the necessary changes, Anne did her best to reconnect with her children—and make up for time lost. Meanwhile, new avenues of interest opened up. After reading an advert in the local newspaper for aromatherapy treatment, Anne met Brigid, a woman who'd trained in various natural health modalities. Upon meeting, Brigid understood Anne, offered her counseling, natural remedies, and taught her meditative exercises. Anne soon began to feel better, more *alive*, and wanted to know more about Brigid's work, so she decided to take some of her instructional courses. During one of these weekend workshops, Anne came across the world of colour and energy (a world that had intrigued her since childhood, but understood little about.) After much discussion as to what it was, Brigid produced a bottle filled with two coloured liquids. When Anne first observed the colours—contained like lightening in a bottle, as it were--she knew that this was what she'd long been searching for. The understanding of what she'd experienced since childhood. No thought to destination--this path of illumination was enough for now.

Brigid brought colour and light and energy to life for Anne—broadening her perception as nothing ever had. Real and comprehensible, these concepts had form and substance and played a part in everyday life. They shape and effect us all—as they had Anne--yet are taken for granted by most. Once explained and given a practical dimension, Anne's life suddenly became clearer. It was as if lights, or perhaps beacons, now lighted her new path. Anne felt a sense of belonging that had always been lacking from her life.

Through Brigid, Anne was introduced to Vicki Wall, a colour therapist of some renown. Posing rhetorical questions like, *Why do people use the expression "green with envy"?* And, *Why do people say they get the "blues"?* Vicki's interpretation and teaching of the meaning and individual's choice of colour was another step forward on Anne's new path. And perhaps most significantly, this world of colour made sense to Anne as nothing else ever had. It struck an intuitive chord. It somehow provided insight into others and herself that she'd always *sensed*. And becoming more aware of why people craved material things, the idea of having the best of everything receded in her mind. She came to understand what drives most people to become who they were, and how they react to the world round them. And as these realities became clearer, her own past was revealed to her and she began to understand what had led to her nervous breakdown. Now—*at last*--she had the tools and understanding to unravel her own life, and the means to change and find her true self.

Behind the barely ruffled curtains of Edinburgh's gentile suburbs, Anne's house became a haven for the unusual, the different, and the alternative thinking. Such ways did not suit the starched lace-curtained houses of suburban Edinburgh. The idea of rebelliousness amongst the coffee mornings, the power dressing, and the *BMW*s and *Mercedes* of the affluent terraces of Auld Reekie no doubt struck her neighbors as unusual. But for Anne it meant more than the latest fashions, newest car, or best-manicured garden. Add to this mix the newest member of Anne's family, an exuberant Irish Setter puppy they named "Candy"-- and a mid-terraced townhouse was not the place for Anne and her extended family to grow.

For Anne, everything now had a purpose; as if everything was some-how interconnected and nothing happened randomly. Life—and the whole world, for that matter--as it moved on was driven by cause and effect. Happenstance and coincidences were just intricate patterns yet unrecognised, one just had to look in the right places to find them. And like a jigsaw puzzle, one had to create order of the seemingly chaotic ar-ray of little pieces--and that took patience, concentration, and purpose-fulness. And with each passing day, more pieces of Anne's own puzzle began to fall into place.

It was a Saturday morning a few months after Candy's arrival that as Anne sat sipping her morning coffee in her favourite chair by the fire she suddenly said: "New plants for the garden!" And in that moment she decided to finish her coffee and head out to the nurseries to see what was available. The children were away for the weekend with their father so Anne hurriedly grabbed her coat, bag, and car keys and headed out the front door. Her white *BMW* looked somewhat dingy—she'd been ne-glecting it, she thought--as she plonked herself down on the seat. As the car roared to life she was reminded of how much she still enjoyed this car. A few minutes after setting off towards the city centre she began to daydream; something she often did. Today her driving and dreaming took her on a number of wrong turns that eventually brought her to a parking space miles from where she intended to go—to right outside the Edinburgh Solicitors Property Centre on George Street. Remembering that she'd actually set out to buy plants, she wondered how she ended up here.

Jumping out of the car she paused for a moment, a bit dazed, then scratched her head as she considered whether to go inside. (*But, why would I?*) Then with no further thought she headed towards the ESPC front doors. She pushed her way inside. There she saw six long isles, each with wooden display boards on either side with photographs and details of all the properties for sale. Suddenly driven to look further, she slowly wandered down the first isle. Nothing caught her eye. Reminding herself that this was sheer madness—that she was supposed to be plant shopping--she suddenly became aware of a soft, compelling voice in her ear. A voice telling her to look at the property on the top shelf at the end of row five. "What the hell?"--Anne said aloud, instantly turning round to see who'd spoken--finding no one there. Curiosity now getting the best of her she walked back towards row five, counting as she went: "One, two, three, four, *five*." At row five she looked up to the top shelf and walked to the end of the row. There she saw the particulars of a property called "Gowd Yettwye Estate," situated in the village of Auchendinny. The photograph of the house immediately drew Anne in. Fascinated by the look of the house and the surrounding land, she began to read:

Gowd Yettwye, a three-hundred-year-old estate house, four large bedrooms, lounge, dining room, and two bathrooms. A unique opportunity has arisen to purchase this property which includes twenty-one acres of arable farm land, fields, stable blocks, and forest in the heart of Roslin Glen, twelve miles south of Edinburgh, and includes the meandering River Esk that runs through its boundaries. In need of renovation.

Now, Anne was more than intrigued. She'd never heard of Auchendinny, a village twelve miles from Edinburgh, but something urged her pick up a copy of the property details. Tucking the notice under her arm she rushed through the large glass doors and drew a breath; smiled and hurried to her car. Butterflies in her stomach and her heart jumping, she had to view this property *now*, the garden could wait. She headed out of Edinburgh.

Anne followed the directions and found it relatively easy to find Auchendinny. As she descended the downgrade towards her destination she turned left and found herself on a narrow tarmac; a road that changed into a muddy dirt track flanked on either side by very tall evergreen trees. Anne now saw, looming slightly ahead and to her left, two magnificent ten-foot-high black wrought-iron gates with weathered gold print: *Gowd Yettwye.*

Anne noticed that the gates were in desperate need of a fresh lick of paint, and as she hopped out of her car to open them further, she heard the creaking of the hinges move with slow, stiff resistance. A seven-foot-high black wrought-iron fence in the same motif as the gates, with huge six-inch spikes protruding from the tops, went right round the boundary of the car park, stables, and house, giving the overall impression that Gowd Yettwye was a stately, private home, and welcome to only those invited. Anne proceeded through the gates and saw a staggered row of pine and oak trees leading up a wide, curved driveway past a wooden stable-block on her right and opposite a concrete stable-block on her left. She followed the road as it curved to the right, and there in front of her now stood a most impressive house.

Parking at a forty-five degree angle to the house, Anne jumped out and walked toward the very old, long wooden building flanked by ancient pine trees. Peeking in through the grimy, single-glass windows, she realised that this had been a stable--and her excitement rose. Her eyes then swept across the car park to a large barn and she could suddenly imagine chickens; a childhood fantasy was of owning a farm when she was older. As Anne approached the main house she counted the mammoth oak trees, nine in total, then seven stately pine trees—as well as five pink-blossom trees, three white-blossom trees, and at the front door a huge Rowan. (Anne recalled her father telling her that the Rowan tree was renowned for its powers to ward off evil. It was thought to protect the house and the people within from malignant forces.) Anne took a long, deep breath. She felt as if she'd come home.

Suddenly, vibrant reds, pinks, and lilac rhododendron bushes, and the deep reds of the peony roses that drooped with the weight of their heady flowers drew her attention. These had been planted in earthy borders, with neatly-cut grassy edges. Wild life was the exception to any formal invitation, coming and going of their own free will. There were at least fifteen large black crows making a haunting, screeching noise from their sharp black beaks as they hung onto the telephone wire that ran from Gowd Yettwye to the main pole set beside the dirt-track road. When the crows were not balancing on the wires they would swoop down onto the grass, hop then stop, repetitively pecking at the grass while their beady orange eyes looked out from their small heads; their heads darting side-to-side, making sure there were no predators round. Their presence added a sinister feeling that there was something strange and eerie behind the large black gates.

Gowd Yettwye was constructed of cut sandstone, with huge chimney stacks rising from the bold red roof. And although some three-hundred years old, the sandstone still glistened in the sun (and seemed almost alive as if it somehow retained all the secrets of those who'd lived in the house before). As Anne approached the main house she marveled at the magnificent old and dark, wooden front doors. She reached for the large, round brass door handle and gave it a turn. But as expected, the door didn't budge. Excitement mounting, she now wanted to make certain that nobody was about so she took hold of the brass door knocker and gave a *ra-ta-ta-tat* on the door; the noise echoing loudly round her. Again, no response. Anne peered in through the dirt-caked windows right of the doors. Pressing her face to the glass she could see through the complex of cobwebs to the centre of the room where an old, hard pine dining table with eight wooden chairs tucked into it stood. On the right wall stood a Welsh pine dresser and she could just make out some china fairies, crystals, and other ornaments on its shelves. On the wall facing the dresser was a large fireplace round which was an intricately-carved wooden mantel piece. On the hearth a large basket filled with curing logs set, a wrought-iron coal scuttle, tongs, brush, and shovel. "This is exactly what I've been searching for all my life! I've got to have it!"

Anne walked down the path at the side of the house and just as she rounded the corner gasped with pure delight at the panoramic view across Rosslyn Glen. The land sloped away from the house down to the bottom of the valley where she could see a river meandering its lazy way through fields on either side. The fields then rose up on the opposite side of the river, revealing acres of bright green pastures with numerous horses idly strolling, heads down, eating sumptuous-looking grass. A wave of deep-seated peace had come over her as she first set eyes on the property, and now that she'd experienced the postcard scenery, she nearly wept with joy, vowing to acquire this property, no matter what.

Anne's desire to own Gowd Yettwye, however, was not equal to the challenge of sorting out the cold and hard legal and financial aspects, which she left to her lawyer. A month before she was to close on her new home, a previously-enthusiastic buyer for her current house developed cold feet--and backed out of the deal, so Anne decided on an alternate course, instructing her lawyer to arrange a bridging loan from the bank. However, the day before she was to secure Gowd Yettwye, she contacted her lawyer to make certain he'd arranged the money, only to be informed that he'd forgotten. Informing her that he couldn't possibly arrange such a sizable loan now, under this timetable. In a blind panic, the first person to come to mind was Brigid. Anne called her and explained her extreme dilemma: that she had just twenty-four hours to raise £125.000 to purchase her new home. With no hesitation, Brigid told her to meet her at her natural health clinic in one hour. Once there she said, "Okay, let's focus on raising the £125,000 you need!" Closing her eyes a moment she asked, "Who do you know at Allied Irish Bank?"

Anne thought a second and replied, "Allied Irish Bank? Uh, *nobody*."

"Think, Anne," Brigid encouraged. "You *do* know *someone* who works there!"

With valuable time ticking away, Anne ran it through her mind. Smiling, she shouted, "Wait! Yes, I *do* know someone there! A man called Stewart! He used to date one of my friends!"

"Call Irish Allied Bank, *now*! And, you'll get your money!" said Brigid with a tone of certainty.

Although Anne had no idea what he did at the bank, she quickly dialed the bank--only to be told that Stewart had gone. But the girl offered to provide his telephone number. Taking the number Anne immediately called him and told him her problem, and of the urgency. He told her he'd meet her within the hour. Arranging to meet at her current residence, Stewart did as promised:

"Nice to see you again, Anne, after so long," Stewart said, smiling. "I've brought the paperwork for your mortgage and bridging loan, so all you need to do is check the forms and sign."

"*Really*? That's *all*?" (Anne was thrilled but staggered.)

"That's all! I have more paperwork to sift through but I should have a contract for you in, say . . . an hour? How's that sound?"

Anne was reeling--and couldn't believe it! True to his word, within the hour Stewart had arranged the mortgage and bridging from Bank of Scotland, and equally amazing, the lawyers selling Gowd Yettwye had omitted the "late-penalty" clause, meaning Anne would not have to pay a *per diam* penalty. Of course, now she'd have to sell her old property. However just at this point the property market took a nose dive and over the months no buyer could be found for her old house. Anne now spent time each day visualising Calum purchasing and living in her old house. He she believed was her only hope of avoiding bankruptcy. She broached this subject with him from time to time. In the beginning he had flat out refused to sell his house and buy Anne's old house but to Anne's amazement out of the blue one day he suddenly agree to take it off her hands. When he put his house on the market it sold immediately. (Now she was free of the burden of the bridging loan.)

In the past, Anne would not have given a second thought to all this coming together as it had. But now with clearer perspective, she knew that it was all inextricably linked. (Things happening now were being affected by what she'd done before—even if not apparent.) Though she couldn't explain it, this was how her life was now unfolding, leading her along her new path, and she believed that buying a new house and moving to Auchendinny would subsequently have a bearing on where this path would take her. It wasn't as if she were planning a future with deliberation; she knew it would unfold for its own purpose and through time would reveal itself.

Chapter 17

Tara was seven and Daryl eight when they moved into Gowd Yettwye, and at first found it a rather strange environment; away from the concrete jungle where they'd been so restricted. Having never been allowed to explore the streets (only allowed to have friends round to play in the garden and taken everywhere by their mother) now they could roam freely across the countryside. And this was pure joy to them! Before long they made friends with the local villagers and their children.

Anne had missed cooking and now with her new healthy dietary interests took to cooking for the neighboring children (who came in droves), who loved the house, loved being in Anne's company, and of course, loved her food--spicy hot and vegetarian, something most had never tasted. And believing that Gowd Yettwye was a very special place, a place of beauty and tranquility, Anne decided that she should create a natural healing centre there, based on her insights into colour, energy, and spirituality. This she knew would help people cultivate their own sense of purpose and well-being. She could also teach chakra energy training and meditation. Thus with singular determination, she decided to build a space to accommodate such a business. Her vision then expanded to exemplifying a holistic way of living—including growing her own organic fruit and vegetables. But her lack of experience, as well as a wrong choice of builders, proved daunting, the cost of renovation quickly escalating beyond budget.

Anne decided that the name "Gowd Yettwye" didn't quite suit her—or her vision. (She'd be spending half her time just telling friends and family how to spell it!) Also, her new direction into light and colour and holism convinced her that she should reach out to those who needed it; to show them how it could change and enhance their lives. The name "Drakar" popped into Anne's head, as she'd always had an affinity for that name. Thus, Gowd Yettwye became *Drakar.*

The sun was shining as Anne woke to a new day at "Drakar." She and her children had by now settled well into their new country life. The day before, Anne had been digging in the garden and noticed a reddened swelling of her right hand: the telltale signs of a bug bite. She'd chosen cards from her colour pack and through their meaning had begun to suspect that something wasn't quite right with her health so she decided to call the doctor and make an appointment. But when she arrived at the surgery, instead of showing him the angry bite, it was as if unseen hands raised her blouse and bra. She found herself asking the doctor about the fact that her breast nipple had become inverted. He examined her and told her there was nothing to worry about--after all she was only thirty-four and appeared to be in good health--but referred her for a mammogram nevertheless. Remembering that Calum had kept her *Bupa*, a private healthcare plan, she called him for the particulars and made an appointment for the following day. Things then took a dark turn.

Anne's mammogram revealed a tumor attached to her nipple. It was then immediate surgery, radiotherapy, and medication to save her life. It was hard for Anne to fathom that at just thirty-four years of age her whole world was threatened--just as she was learning how to care for her children—and herself. They were so young. Who'd look after them if she didn't survive this? Alone, the tears flowed. She cried as never before. But this malaise was short-lived as Anne decided that a new way of treatment befitted her new approach to life and sought the advice of one Dr. Mary Morris, a well-known naturopath who'd worked for over fifty years as a researcher in the field of natural health and holistic medicine. Dr. Mary Morris was also a qualified medical doctor but preferred to treat patients with holistic remedies.

At Dr. Morris' request, Anne was seen by a leading researcher in the field of energy medicine, who happened to be visiting Edinburgh at the time. During this consultation the scientist told Anne the precise location of the tumor *via* use of an energy scanner the scientist had himself designed. He then proposed a regimen of specific energy-field treatments to help restore her energy to a healthy *vibration*. The treatments were infinitely successful. Following these treatments, Anne decided to train with this scientist.

Anne's intuitive ability in using these modalities widened soon after when her new puppy Aurora, (Candy's offspring) became lame. The vet could only suggest that Aurora's leg muscles had been damaged by over exercising, and offered no treatment. At this same time, an artist friend was staying with Anne, and one evening Anne stumbled upon one of her natural intuitive gifts.

"Mind if I borrow your paints?" Anne had asked Simon that night.

"Not at all," replied Simon, "always happy to encourage budding artists!"

Anne began to randomly paint on a large white sheet of art paper. As she looked at what she'd created, all she saw was a mass of shapeless colours that all merged into each other. This image brought back memories of her art teacher: 'Too messy, Anne! Why don't you draw what's before your eyes!' Anne had always argued that what she saw is what she drew. Frustrated at her inability to paint a "proper picture," she decided to throw this painting into the open fire—and put away forever any thoughts of painting.

"Anne, stop!" Simon drew closer and pointed. "Wait a minute! Look closely at your painting. What do you see?"

"*Nothing!*" replied Anne. "A bloody *mess!*"

"Wait. Look here! You've drawn the shape of a dog curled up in a ball. It's exactly how Aurora is lying there at your feet."

Anne looked from Aurora to her painting and now saw what Simon was seeing. And as she studied the image her eyes were drawn to the splash of pink colour corresponding to the area of Aurora's back. Excitedly she said, "Simon, this is amazing! If this picture *is* of Aurora, I've painted her aura colours! The pink is the energy seeping from a gap in her auric field! It's seeping from this gap because it's her back that's damaged--not her legs!"

The next day Anne took Aurora to Bruce, a friend who treated humans and animals with a specific form of massage. Anne didn't show him her painting nor tell him of her findings. By a method called "dowsing," however, Bruce found a trapped nerve in Aurora's back at the exact location as the pink splash of colour Anne had depicted in her painting. Miraculously, after just ten minutes of concentrated massage, Aurora was running round the room with no trace of lameness. Somehow, Anne had managed to translate what she'd intuitively sensed into something tangible, visual, and explainable.

Chapter 18

On a cold, wet and windy day, Anne opened her door to a rather bedraggled, wet blond-haired woman who Anne guessed to be in her early thirties. Inviting her inside, Anne discovered that "Lily" was most intrigued with Anne's knowledge of light, colour, and auras, and having heard about the natural healing centre Anne was developing, decided to check it out for herself. Lily told Anne that she was a practicing Buddhist, as well as being involved with natural curatives, massage, and meditation. Little did Anne know that the day Lily arrived at Drakar was the day her life would make one of its major changes. After much conversation, Lily made a suggestion:

"You should come down to Samye Ling with me some time."

"And what would Samye Ling be?" Anne queried in an almost mocking tone.

"It's a monastary, a Buddhist Centre down in the Borders," Lily said. "They do things a bit differently down there--a lot like you're doing here," she said. "You'll fit right in!"

"Oh, I don't know," shrugged Anne. "Organised religion is not *me*."

"No, no--it's not like that at all. It's not some 'true believer' cult thing. They're just ordinary Tibetan monks who have a different outlook about life," Lily persisted.

The word "Tibetan" struck a chord with Anne, and Lily could see that.

"Ah--got your interest now, I see!" Lily said, unaware of Anne's personal connection to Tibet.

"Well . . . sure. Why not! You arrange it and I'll come along," Anne agreed.

After Lily left Drakar that day, Anne thought about her timely, *coincidental* visit. Here was yet another connection--and perhaps another step along her new path. It could be something--or nothing--but it deserved looking in to. Anne no longer went in for second-guessing outcomes and knew that matters of the spirit required an open mind. For the next few days Anne went about the business of the healing centre, but thoughts of this *Samye Ling* were never far from her mind. A few days later an anxious Lily phoned and confirmed that she was going down to the Borders the following Tuesday and would stop by about 9:00 a.m. to pick Anne up. (An anxious Anne began to imagine what would come from that visit.)

The following Tuesday came round and Anne, for a change, was ready on time; the kids packed off to school early. Lily's battered old *Ford* Fiesta sputtered to a halt on the gravel driveway outside the front door—and appeared to die. (No need for Lily to sound the horn.) Anne was out the front door and sitting in the passenger seat before Lily could get it started again. "Good morning! Ready when you are!" said Anne.

"Okay, okay," agreed Lily, shocking the engine back to life and putting the car in gear. "Say, you'll never guess! I managed to get us a meeting with the Rinpoche himself."

"The *who?*" questioned Anne.

"Akong Rinpoche," tutted Lily. "He's one of the founders of Samye Ling. A *tulku.*"

Anne thought it best not to ask too many questions, and just enjoy the journey--though Lily's driving left a lot to be desired. Not long into the journey, Pebbles and then Innerleithen were successfully navigated—to Anne's relief. On the long and winding narrow roads that had to be negotiated, the two women relaxed and made light conversation. After the road flattened out (following the undulating humps and hollows of the sheep farms) it followed the ever-flowing waters of a narrow river. There was something especially pleasing about the movement of the water to Anne, as if sensing that the old river was on the same new path that she was. Lily had decided to fill Anne in on a few details about Samye Ling when a sharp smack rang through the little car—and Lily jammed on the breaks, bringing the car to an abrupt halt.

Their hearts pounding, Lily and Anne made a quick assessment of the car to see if anything looked amiss. Nothing was apparent until a smudge began to appear in the middle of the windscreen. "I think we hit something, Anne," Lily said quizzically, "a bird I'd guess!" The smudge now took shape as a clear imprint of a feathered body. Reactively, both women turned and looked out of the rear window, their gaze settling upon a black rag-like object on the road behind them that seemed to flutter in the slight breeze.

"Looks like a crow or something!" said Anne. "Think it's had it, so we better move on so as not to block the road."

"A crow!" Lily replied with a reverential tone. "Can't just leave it there! We'd better take it with us."

Anne looked quizzically at her friend: surely she was *joking*! And she was just about to say, 'take it with us?' when Lily jumped out of the car and hurried back to where the bird was lying, now motionless. Gingerly picking it up, she returned to the car and carefully placed the lifeless body on the back seat. "We'll take it to Samye Ling. Akong Rinpoche will know what to do with it," Lily said with certainty. Anne gave her friend a troubled look, now wondering what she'd let herself in for by coming to this *Samye Ling* place.

Less than ten minutes down the road Anne could see a gold dome forcing its way through the top of a stand of tall pines. It looked quite out of place in the natural setting--but somehow comforting to see. Just as the brightly coloured dome disappeared, the car followed a dip in the road and Lily guided the car through a beige-painted stone archway and past a regimented array of lit tea candles. A moment later she came to a jolted stop outside a white-washed façade of an old country estate house. "Quick, Anne," instructed Lily, "you nip inside and get a box or something to put the bird in."

"*Me?*"

"Sure. Just go in through those doors."

Now resigned to playing along with the unfolding drama, Anne got out and strode through the heavy wooden door, blurting out a somewhat garbled oration about a dying crow on the back seat of the car. A young, bald-headed monk quickly rose from one of the chairs set round a table in the middle of the room, and gestured for Anne to follow. He went to a large cupboard next to the door, reached in and pulled out a shoe box, then headed out the front door with Anne hurrying along behind.

"Ah! Dhargey!" exclaimed Lily as the monk approached the car. "Quick--the bird is on the back seat!" The monk bent down and peered through the side window. "If you don't mind, we need a cup of coffee after the long ride—and now, *this*--so we're off to the tea room."

Dhargey nodded and smiled. "I'll see to the bird and maybe catch up with you later," he said, giving them a small bow.

Given no time to take in her surroundings during the bird incident, after the monk had gone Anne got her first real glimpse of these new surroundings. It was pleasant—though it looked a bit ramshackle--but there was a distinct stillness about the place. A placid atmosphere that seemed to envelope Anne and offered a sense security; as if she were in a safe place, like home. Lily tugged anxiously on Anne's arm and said they should get a well-deserved cup of coffee, then led the way between two near-by buildings. The building to the left was busy with the chattering of voices and clinking of plates, dishes, and silverware; a dining room of sorts, thought Anne. The building to the right was a smaller version of the white-walled one Anne had entered upon arrival. But unlike the other, it was silent; no activity within, only an uninterested peacock strutting round a paved patio at its entrance. Ahead stood a timber-clad chalet-type structure bearing a painted sign saying TEAROOM. As Anne passed under the sign she noticed open ground beyond a massive tree set a few yards past the end of the building.

"What's down there?" she asked curiously.

"It's a stream. And beyond that some farmers' fields," answered Lily.

"Can I have a quick look? I promise I won't hold up our coffee break too long."

Lily led the way round the tree and down a small flight of earthen steps which led to the bank of the shallow but fast-flowing stream. On the bank Anne saw a stone *cairn* erected to her left, set some distance away from the bank, out in the clear running water. Beyond it another fast-flowing stream joined the main one at a right angle. Ambling along the bank Anne could feel a growing sensation of well-being and inner-strength welling-up inside her. Like a faint pulse of energy washing over her, its source seemed to be centered round the confluence of the two streams. This, thought Anne, is a very special place. She just knew it to be true.

Anne felt a tug on her arm as Lily interrupted Anne's musings with a gesture of raising a cup to her lips. Anne nodded, smiled, and followed Lily back up the steps and into the tearoom. Ordering two cups of black coffee—which were set before them within seconds—the two women took seats opposite one other at a low, wooden table. The colours of the tearoom were bright but not gaudy--yellows and dark reds (like the monk's robe), interspersed with the light and dark browns of the natural furniture. (One thing it wasn't was a traditional British tearoom! Anne thought with relief.) The calm and reassuring atmosphere that greeted Anne upon her arrival was now with her in this welcoming, little room. As they sipped their coffee, conversation wasn't needed. Being there, together, seemed enough. Lily remarked:

"We'd better keep an eye on the time."

The meeting with Akong Rinpoche fast approaching, Anne drained her cup and followed Lily out of the tearoom. Lily led them straight past the two primary buildings, round a corner to the right, to a wide path that ran past a low-standing stone wall with a mass of dense tress on the left, behind which was concealed a rise in the slope of a small hill. To the right a red-brown brick wall extended upwards about two stories in height. Her eyes drawn upwards, Anne saw rows of beautiful, multicoloured bricks at the head of this wall, interrupting the same-ness of the brown brick assemblage. Beyond the coloured bricks Anne could see exotic carvings where the walls gave way gracefully to the roof. She'd seen this motif before, she thought to herself. Her father had shown her photographs he'd taken in Tibet showing buildings with similar carvings: Tibetan Buddhist temples. Thus here, deep in the remote Scottish Borders, was a Buddhist temple; a little piece of Tibet. Lily beckoned Anne to keep up as the path began to rise round the grove of trees behind the low wall, then made almost a half-circle before revealing what was a traditional family bungalow—with nothing exotic or Tibetan about it. Inside, Anne and Lily were greeted by Clare, who obviously knew Lily already.

"You're next," Clare confirmed in a hushed voice, then disappeared down the hall.

"Okay," confirmed Lily with a nod, sitting down in one of four chairs lined up along the wall. Lily then slipped off her shoes and gestured for Anne to do likewise. By the time they'd both slid their shoes under their chairs Clare reappeared and signalled that it was time. Anne had no idea what to expect. Clare pushed open the first door on the left and waved Lily and Anne in. Anne attempted to consciously take in her surroundings but a feeling of excitement quickly overwhelmed her. All she saw was a large room set with mismatched furniture, storage boxes and piles of papers strewn across the large oval table. Proceeding, Lily and Anne approached a small oval-faced man seated at the far side of the room, who rose from his armchair and shuffled forward to greet them.

As the two women neared, the man reached out to take their outstretched hands, then gestured for them to sit on the two seats prepared for them. Anne was enthralled by this man: tan skin and wearing maroon monk's robes, he had lived-in Eastern features, and there was an indescribable presence about him. Not in his stature nor mannerisms, but something subtle that touched Anne in a most profound way. Lily introduced Anne as a friend who desired to meet the Rinpoche. This wasn't exactly the truth, but it compelled Anne to show the Rinpoche some photographs of Drakar and her natural healing centre:

"I'm not sure if this would interest you," said Anne politely, "but these photographs are of a healing centre I'm trying to establish. A centre for alternative ways of healing and helping people."

The Rinpoche took the photos and scanned them with interest before handing them back to Anne. "I will be the overseer to your project, and I grant you a dharma centre" replied the Rinpoche. "Come back and see me when you have written out a plan for your centre"

"Uh . . . oh, thank you," said Anne, dumbfounded, not knowing how to respond.

Seeing that the meeting was over, Lily bowed to the Rinpoche—as did Anne—the Rinpoche returning the gesture. Once outside, Lily immediately admitted that she didn't know what to make of it all. Anne was even more baffled--but felt a sense of achievement even so. Lily suggested they go to the temple and think on their meeting with Akong Rinpoche, and Anne agreed. Anne followed Lily back down the slope, up the steps, and into the temple courtyard. Several wooden chairs were set beside the big wooden doors of the temple, along with racks for storing shoes. Again Anne followed her friend's lead and removed her shoes before following Lily inside, where another row of chairs set along the back wall; choosing two they sat down to take in the amazing view before them.

Just past the row of chairs set a large golden figure of a sitting Buddha, surrounded by numerous smaller figures of the Buddha, each in its own glass case and ranked by size, from ceiling to floor, and extending to the far end wall. Working back from the largest Buddha, Anne noticed rolled-up scrolls on shelves against the side walls, large drums and bronze horns, and other richly-coloured Buddhist paraphernalia and artifacts. The styling of the ceiling and uncluttered walls was amazing: bright and colourful exotic images of the East set out with their own meaning for those who understood them. The barrage of colour and detail was too much for Anne—a Westerner--to take in, her senses reeling and her heart pounding wildly. Despite the assault of colour and light, the atmosphere was warm and calming, inviting all who entered to relax and reflect.

Anne thought it strange that there was no one else in the temple yet there seemed to be a chorus of voices whispering all round them; not distracting Anne, but helping her free her mind to go within and find meaning to her meeting with Akong Rinpoche. And soon Anne was free of all thought, her mind empty, and was floating *somewhere*--conscious that she was sitting in a Buddhist temple, yet she wasn't. She was inside her own mind and there was no past and no future, only that moment to be experienced. Then Rinpoche's words overtook her thoughts: a project to be overseen. Work to be done. Then with no concept of time, Anne came back to the present, to the warming images of the temple in the here and now. A convergence of past and present, she now had to look to the future. Lily motioned that it was time to leave.

"I don't know about you," Lily said as they put their shoes back on, "but I could sure use another cup of coffee." Still in a bit of a haze, Anne nodded and let Lily lead the way. Back at the tearoom they found the monk Dhargey talking to the young woman working behind the counter. After an exchange of greetings, Lily asked Dhargey to join them and he duly accepted. As all three sat round a table sipping black coffee, conversation turned to Anne's meeting with the Rinpoche.

"Are you sure he said '*Dharma Centre*'?" said Dhargey with obvious surprise. "He is going to grant you a '*Dharma Centre*'?"

"That's what he said," interjected Lily before Anne could speak. "A Dharma centre. It surprised me too!"

Anne, meanwhile, had no idea what all the fuss was about.

"That is a great honour!" commented Dhargey. "And after your very first meeting with him--and you not being a Buddhist—that makes it even more remarkable! You must be someone quite special to him!"

"Well, I don't know, really?" questioned Anne, her eyes darting between the two of them. "I have to put some plans together and present them first," she said, far from appreciating the gravity of it all.

"But still," Dhargey went on, "For him to even *offer* it means he has great respect for you. It is an honour or great significance."

The conversion then tailed off onto more mundane things before the monk excused himself, as he, like all resident monks, had chores to tend to. Anne and Lily exited the tearoom into the bright noon-day sun, and headed for the car. Once seated and belted in, Lily coaxed the engine awake and drove back out through the arched entrance, turning right and onto the road back to Innerleithen, Peebles, and then home. Anne turned and looked at the empty backseat. Neither she nor Lily had remembered to ask Dhargey what had happened to the crow. But Anne somehow knew that it would be alright. It would be where it was meant to be.

Chapter 19

Life at Drakar after Anne's visit to Samye Ling continued as before. Visitors came and went in a kind of haphazard sequence. Anne knew well that there was no real structure to the healing centre; thus it lacked direction and focus. Most disconcerting, minimal income meant that she and the children were living hand-to-mouth. Had she taken on more than she was capable of handling? Was Drakar one step *too* far, *too* quickly, along her new path? Her motivating grace, however, was that Akong Rinpoche and Samye Ling were behind her, and her visit there had left an indelible impression on her.

Anne was determined to put together a formidable plan for the Rinpoche. So much so that she enlisted the help of Calum, her ex-husband. As a successful businessman, he provided her with some valuable insight she could apply to her intended business, which she committed artfully to paper. Confident in her plan, Anne contacted Clare, the Samye Ling secretary, to arrange another meeting with Akong Rinpoche. This time she would drive herself--and take the kids along. On the appointed day, new business plan in hand, they all bundled into Anne's aging *Volvo* Estate and set off. Daryl and Tara (and even Aurora and Candy) were uncharacteristically well-behaved on the long drive.

It may have had a lot to do with Anne babbling on about Buddhism, monks, and Samye Ling, but the now-familiar gold dome that rose above the pine trees came into view a lot quicker than Anne expected. This time as she turned off the road and beneath the stone arch there was no injured bird to tend to; only two kids and two dogs to keep amused while she met with Akong Rinpoche. Fortunately, as she brought the car to a halt outside the main house, she spotted Dhargey coming out the front door. She waved to get his attention, a look of recognition quickly spreading over his gentle face. Anne could see him straining to see who was in the car with her—expecting Lily, no doubt. As she turned off the ignition, he approached the car.

"It's Anne, isn't it?" he said with some confidence as Anne got out.

"Yes, you remembered!" replied Anne, pleased that she'd made an impression.

"Well, how could I forget someone who was granted a Dharma Centre!" Dhargey said with a glint in his eye. "What brings you back?" he asked.

"Well, I still have to present my plans to the Rinpoche," she said. "And I've brought my children along to see this spectacular place."

"If you like, I could show them round while you're meeting with Akong," offered the monk with a small bow.

"That would be most kind of you," replied Anne. So Daryl and Tara were herded out of the car and introduced to Dhargey, and warned to be on their best behaviour. Anne decided it would be safe to leave Aurora and Candy alone in the car with a window down for the short time she'd be gone, then made her way up the sloping path to the building where Rinpoche held audience. Clare was busy rearranging the chairs outside the meeting room as Anne approached.

"Oh, good, Anne!" Clare exclaimed. "Right on time! You're next!"

Anne hurriedly slipped off her shoes, just as Clare opened the door to show her in. The room was much the same as she remembered it: nothing religious or pious about, yet it had a supremely peaceful and calming atmosphere. Feeling the same sense of excitement as on her first visit, Akong bade her welcome and held out his hand to take the papers she clutched tightly. He gestured for her to sit down while he went back and sat in his over-sized armchair. After a few minutes deliberating, the Rinpoche spoke:

"These are good plans, but not the *right* plans," he said, handing the papers back to Anne.

Anne didn't know what to say. She couldn't very well ask him *what* plans he wanted; she knew that was up to her to work out. (That was how it was done.) Anne thanked the Rinpoche, the two bowed, and she quietly left the room. Though a bit stunned, she didn't feel annoyed or let down. On the contrary, she came away with greater resolve to succeed; to see this thing through. Akong Rinpoche was a wise and wholly spiritual man, and his words had to be deeply considered to understand their meaning, Anne decided. And the fact that he believed in her was motivation enough to believe in herself.

Before returning to the car, Anne decided to visit the temple and try to empty her mind to gain perspective. Just as she reached the temple steps, Dhargey was coming out, followed by Daryl and Tara. Anne thought they looked appropriately impressed. "Oh, I was going to go in for a few minutes," said Anne.

"No doubt a wise idea," replied Dhargey, smiling. "I'll take these two to the tearoom for a drink and a biscuit or something," Dhargey said, holding both children's hands. "They well deserve it, they have been so well behaved!" (Anne thought he was surely being kind.) The three turned and waved a casual good-bye.

Once inside, Anne could feel the spirit and voices of the temple wash over her. She knew they would help her find the way to fulfill Akong Rinpoche's wishes. But this time she couldn't free her mind to hear what they had to say. Maybe she was trying too hard? Perhaps not hard enough? After a few fruitless minutes, Anne left the temple and made her way to the tearoom. It was time to check on the dogs, no doubt about to get into mischief. Rounding up Daryl and Tara she thanked Dhargey and headed back to the car. Dhargey could see by Anne's expression that she had much on her mind so decided not to burden her further with his advice. He wished them a safe journey home.

The journey back to Auchendinny in the old *Volvo* was quiet and uneventful. It seemed everyone had much to think about; the calming influence of Samye Ling effecting them all. No sooner had they returned home, the phone rang. It was Norman, an old friend of Calum. A bit of a high-flyer in local business circles, Norman had recently begun to search for something different. A new direction. "I tried to reach you earlier but got no reply," explained Norman from the other end of the line.

"I've been down in the Borders most of the day, at Samye Ling," Anne replied.

"*Samye Ling*?" questioned Norman. "What's that?"

"It's a Tibetan Buddhist monastary, a centre near Lockerbie," she informed him (now feeling a bit of an authority).

"Wow, that's weird!" exclaimed Norman, clearly amused. "You'll never guess who I had a dream about last night! The Dalai Lama!"

Anne's mind leaped a couple steps. Confounded by what Akong Rinpoche had told her and the fact that her visit to the temple hadn't achieved anything, she considered that perhaps Norman was now part of the solution. "You know, I'll be going back sometime soon," Anne told Norman, "if you'd like to tag along. And actually, you may be able to help me with something I've been struggling with. I need to put together a project plan for the Rinpoche and don't seem to be able to put my ideas properly on paper."

"Sounds intriguing," enthused Norman; excitement in his voice.

A few days later Norman dropped by and reviewed the plans Anne had already put together. His business savvy helped Anne greatly, but it was his openness to thinking "outside the box" that proved most useful. New ways of looking at things might lead to what Akong was looking for, they decided. After bouncing ideas back and forth over the next few weeks, Anne and Norman agreed that the plan they'd come up with was the best they could imagine. Anne arranged another meeting with Akong Rinpoche.

Anne wasn't sure what Norman would make of Samye Ling—and was somewhat wary that his expectations might exceed the reality. She knew that not everyone *got* Samye Ling. (Either they were ready for it-- or they weren't.) But for Norman, this visit was exactly what he needed. His spur-of-the-moment phone call to Anne and the help he'd given her on the project outline suggested new opportunities for him. Opened his mind to a new path. So when the long-awaited day arrived, he got to Drakar nice and early, with plenty of time to review what Anne would present to the Rinpoche. With Daryl and Tara visiting their father, the two set out while the sun was still low in the morning sky.

Time seeming to just fly by, it seemed just minutes before Anne turned off the road and drove through the archway, then pointed to

Akong's business centre: the tearoom, dining hall, main office, and the temple. (The winding path up the hill was now like a familiar backyard trail to Anne.) As she opened the front door, she and Norman were greeted by Clare, who asked them to take a seat as the Rinpoche still had a meeting to conclude. At the last moment—much to Norman's delight—Anne asked him to accompany her to the meeting. Norman followed Anne in removing his shoes and sliding them under his seat.

For the longest fifteen minutes Anne could remember, they just sat in the hallway in silence, exchanging impatient glances. Anne wondered what Norman was making of all this--and what Akong would make of her latest plans. (*Surely* she was getting closer to the right answer!) Clare eventually reappeared and ushered them into Akong's inner sanctum. Anne introduced Norman and they both sat before the Rinpoche as he promptly took Anne's new plans and looked them over. Unlike the previous time, he seemed to study Anne's outline with much thought. Anne and Norman looked at each other anxiously and smiled. The Rinpoche then slowly raised himself out of his chair; his expression neither one of satisfaction nor displeasure.

"These are indeed very good plans," he said matter-of-factly. "I see that much consideration has gone into these. But sometimes there are other reasons for work and effort. There is more to be done here."

Anne approached and took the presentation from his out-stretched hand. "Thank you," she said. "I will continue the work." Anne bowed, turned, and walked toward the door with Norman following. Once outside they put their shoes back on, neither speaking. Remembering that Norman had expressed a desire to see the temple, they proceeded back down the hill and made their way there. Inside, there were several monks conducting a prayer session. The chanting was mesmerising, interrupted only by the banging of the large bass drum and the deep bellow of the ceremonial horn. Enthralled by the sights and sounds, Anne and Norman sat a couple seats apart at the back of the temple, deep in their own thoughts; deep in their own mysteries. The haunting sounds permeated every corner of the temple, but for Anne the sound was round her, only the vibration, the feeling and meaning of the prayers finding their way into her body--but not her thoughts. As before, her thoughts struggled to find the inner message within Akong's words.

Leaving the temple, Anne and Norman leisurely made their way to the tearoom for a cup of coffee and a biscuit to fortify them for the return drive. Clearly in another world, Norman was unusually quiet as they sipped their coffee. Anne sought to invade that world. "I'm beginning to wonder if I'll ever figure out what I'm supposed to do, and what project he wants to oversee," said Anne, a clear tone of desperation. But Norman could only nod as he too was taken aback that their master plan wasn't better received. Coffee finished and questions still unanswered, they made their way back to the car; climbed in. Silence reigned as they passed through the arch and onto the road to Edinburgh.

Arriving at Drakar just as the sun was dropping behind the western skyline, Norman got out and walked to his own car, parked where the gravel drive met the green of the front lawn. "Sorry to love you and leave you," he joked, "but the trip took longer than I thought, and I'm late for a meeting back in town."

"Oh, no problem, Norman," Anne replied. "Thank you so much for coming along. I hope you enjoyed yourself."

"Yes, I did—very much!" concluded Norman.

"Would have been better if our plan had gotten his approval, but . . . "

"Still, it was a wonderful experience!" Wanting to leave her with a positive spin Norman added, "And when it comes to business, where there's *one* brilliant idea, there's always another!" Anne smiled.

Norman got into his car, started the engine, and headed back down the gravel drive out of Drakar. He could see Anne waving goodbye in his rearview mirror. *What now?* Anne asked herself as he disappeared down the dusty road. *What the bloody hell does the Rinpoche want of me?* A few days later, Anne thought she had the answer.

Upon answering the telephone, Anne thought she recognised the voice at the other end. But *no*, it couldn't be! *Yes*, the voice confirmed, it was Akong Rinpoche calling! He said that someone from Samye Ling would contact her in a few days to arrange a visit to her healing centre. (Anne took Rinpoche phoning her himself as genuine *progress*.) True to his word, a few days later a spokesperson phoned to explain that a party of monks would visit (on such-and-such day) and requested that she provide them with refreshments. With no thought whatsoever, she gladly consented--"Yes, yes, of *course!*" As she hung up she thought, *This could be the breakthrough I've been hoping for!*

On the day of the visit, Anne was more than ready. Everything had been cleaned and cleaned, again and again. The doorbell rang. She went to the door, held the cool knob in her hand, took a deep cleansing breath and reminded herself: *If life boils down to a few decisive moments, this is surely one of them!* She opened the door to find seven monks and two Scottish Buddhists standing there, hands folded. After an exchange of greetings and respectful bows, they proceeded inside.

Anne gave them a full tour of Drakar and the "Natural Healing Centre," the grounds and all around the estate house. Little was said during the tour but there were plenty of head nodding and knowing looks as she explained what she was trying to do with the "Centre."

Admirable seemed to sum up the general consensus. Anne then led the group into the dining room for tea or coffee, finger sandwiches and biscuits. As the afternoon sun began to search its way into the cozy, firelit room, Anne was thanked for her hospitality and the delegation departed, giving nothing away about what they thought of her future or the healing centre. No doubt she would hear from someone in due course, Anne told herself.

But she didn't. Days, weeks, and months rolled by--but not a word came from Samye Ling. Akong Rinpoche had apparently abandoned her project. She'd done all that she could--but it just wasn't enough. She couldn't live up to his expectations. Maybe she hadn't understood what the Rinpoche was trying to tell her. Maybe she'd been expected to provide yet another version of her plan during the delegation's visit. Or maybe, it just wasn't meant to be! Things unfold as they will and the future cannot be forced or controlled—that's the law of the universe! Every development has its own energy and will show itself when it's time. (Perhaps Anne's only intended link to Tibet were the faded documents once in her father's bureau which now lay hidden away in her own locked desk.)

Chapter 20

As FATE WOULD HAVE IT, a chance meeting with the mother of a friend of Tara's named Belinda resulted in bringing a much-needed secretary to the Natural Healing Centre. The morning after the delegation from Samye Ling had visited, Anne was sitting in her office chatting with Belinda over coffee, Belinda having asked about the previous day's events--which Anne was only too-eager to share. Belinda was quite impressed (confessing that she herself knew nothing about Buddhism), telling Anne, "I told Graham about this Buddhist delegation from Samye Ling and he asked me to ask you if you could find out what happened to a monk he rescued from a very bad car crash here in the village when he was a fireman. He said it was one of the worst crashes he'd ever attended--and it still haunts him! One of the passengers, a nun, was killed outright! It happened down by the little bridge just as you leave the village," said Belinda. Graham was Belinda's soon-to-be ex-husband.

"Wow," said Anne, "that's tragic, and *really*, quite curious! Lily told me that one of the monks who visited yesterday had survived a horrendous car accident here in Auchendinny a while back. Apparently, Akong Rinpoche had insisted he be part of this delegation." Anne was about to discuss the incident further when the shrill of the telephone interrupted their conversation. Belinda answered. A moment later: "Anne, a girl is on the line wanting a colour reading with you. She just read a book on colour by Vicky Wall and heard that you do colour readings. Tomorrow at three?" Anne nodded. Replacing the receiver Belinda announced that the girl would be accompanied by two monks from Samye Ling, who she was giving a lift to Edinburgh.

The following day when Anne answered the door, to her amazement, there behind the young woman who'd called, stood Dhargey, along with his friend, another monk she'd met at Samye Ling. "Brought you a cake," announced Dhargey by way of greeting, gasping when he realised that it was Anne's house they'd stopped at. "Wow, you live here? I didn't know it was *you* we were coming to see!" He threw his arms round Anne.

The young woman smiled and raised her eyebrows in a question. "So . . . you two know each other?"

"Well, actually, we *all* know each other!" laughed Anne. "Please, come in!"

As they entered the house, Anne pointed to a picture on the shelf in the lounge that held a special place of honour, a painting of the White Tara. Dhargey had given this deity picture to her on a previous visit.

"It looks so . . . *right* there!" said Dhargey. They smiled at one another. Suddenly a loud bang on the large lounge window made the group jump and turn. "Oh, I see!" said Dhargey. "So, even here crows go out of their way to get your attention! But at least they do not give up their lives!" he laughed. Anne smiled, fully aware of his meaning. "You know, Anne," he continued, "have you ever worked out why Rinpoche offered to be your overseer?"

"No, not really," she replied, "It's still a mystery to me."

"Well, this may be a useful clue," said Dhargey. "Buddhists believe that the crow represents a reincarnate lama. So in your case, the crow that flew into the car you were traveling in sacrificed its life to deliver Rinpoche a message. I would consider that as the crow was taken to Akong Rinpoche your presence was linked to it, then he then realised had to take special heed of you. And this he *did*, didn't he?!" Dhargey said, giving a knowing smile. Before Anne had time to reply, Dhargey continued:

"You know, I was just wondering, Anne. I am going on a special pilgrimage to Tibet with Rinpoche, and to do this I must rely solely on donations, and I was wondering if you would consider contributing."

Anne took a measured breath. She desperately wanted to donate, but money was so tight. Even so, she heard herself say, "Yes . . . yes I will. Would £100 be okay?"

Dhargey bowed his head and said, "Oh, yes, thank you! If possible, I will need it within the month as I leave in four weeks."

"No problem. I'll post it to you."

"Also, if you could include a photograph of yourself with the money? I will put it in the Book of Prayers at Jokhang Temple."

"Great!" said Anne (at the same time wondering what Jokhang Temple was).

(When the time came for Anne to send the money, it was last minute and the only photo she could find was one of herself and her dog, Aurora, so she sent that. And though it would be several years before she saw Dhargey again, it would be much sooner that she received proof that he had in fact reached Tibet. And brought along her photo to Jokhang Temple.)

The Natural Healing Centre limped along (like a sick patient for whom Anne couldn't find the proper curative). She'd long thought Samye Ling was the medicine it needed, but that possibility had come and gone, it seemed. Thus it was quickly becoming a weighty millstone round Anne's neck, threatening to take her down. The income from visitors and what courses she conducted were not paying the expenses, so she now had to look in other directions. Subletting was a viable option--as was turning it into a guest house or bed & breakfast. But nothing stuck with Anne. Her commitment to working with colour and people still led her to believe that that was where her life was meant to go (and increasingly convinced that Tibet and her childhood must play a part--*somehow*). Then one day, Tibet returned to her life (so to speak). An old friend, Frank, came to visit Drakar. He'd heard that Anne was running an holistic and natural health centre and was curious to see what it was all about. So he turned up unannounced—with Anne thrilled to see him after so many years:

"I'm just back from Nepal and managed to get into Tibet for a few days," he said excitedly as Anne led him into the front room. "You know, with the Chinese military and all that . . . ." Anne turned and nodded. "And you'll never guess who I saw there!" he said with special excitement in his voice. Anne gave a blank look. "*You!*"

"*Me?!*" queried Anne. "I don't understand. How could *I* have been in Tibet?"

He smiled, knowing he was playing a little trick on her. "Well, sort of! It was a picture of you and your dog!" Frank said. "You see, I was visiting Jokhang Temple, what they call the 'House of the Buddha,' and inside this temple is a very large prayer book where people from all over the world add a photo or a message or a prayer, and then mantras are said over the book as a way of blessing. The blessing is given by a very high-ranking lama and is said to bring abundance of blessings to the person named. Anyway, there was a photo of you—right there--clear as day! I had to do a double-take! So, how did it get there? There must be a story involved!"

Only then did Anne remember giving Dhargey the photo. "I gave a photo to a Samye Ling monk going on pilgrimage there. He said he'd place it in the temple—but frankly, I forgot all about it!" Anne said, remembering how doubtful she was of it actually reaching Tibet. "But how *strange*! You, there, and my picture! What a coincidence!"

"Yeah—maybe it means something replied Frank. "Anyway, how are things with you and the healing centre?" Anne told Frank about all the trials and tribulations of trying to keep the centre open, their conversation then turning to reminiscing about old times and old friends. "So, how are Daryl and Tara these days?" Frank wanted to know.

Realising now just how much time had passed in her life, Anne said, "Well it's hard to believe but both have children of their own, all grown-up now!" replied Anne.

"No! I can't believe that! That's *crazy*! It seems like only yesterday that they were just kids!"

"You're telling me! Seems like only yesterday they were crawling round the floor getting into all kinds of mischief!"

Frank raised his eyes to the ceiling and smiled. "I remember some years ago, Daryl telling me he wanted to run away from home. Wanted to run off to the Highlands of Scotland and live in a cave and just write and play music all day! What a spirit that lad had!" Anne nodded and smiled proudly. "Oh by the way, did you know there's a well-known cave in Tibet called 'Drakar'?" said Frank—happy that he'd remembered to bring this to her attention. Anne raised her eyebrows, momentarily taken aback. "Yes, there is!" laughed Frank. "Just like the name of this house! They say that was where Milarepa, a very famous yogi, began to practice his Buddhist teachings." Anne felt a momentarily stunned by Frank's revelation as an ice cold chill ran through her body.

Trading old memories one-for-one, the two old friends chatted on until dusk, when Anne and Frank finally bid farewell. "Do let me know if you make any return trips to Tibet!" Anne said—partly in jest.

Chapter 21

DESPITE ALL THAT HAD HAPPENED between them, for the sake of Alexander, Anne still kept in touch with Ruth, who was now living in sheltered accommodation. Anne tried to arrange her periodic visits for Sundays, when she knew that Ruth's brother Charles would be there as well, so that conversation would be easier. On one such Sunday when Anne arrived, Charles and Ruth were deep in conversation—and Anne nearly chose to make a quick exit. But then she realised that they were reminiscing about how Ruth had sometimes stood in for Mona at the dentistry, Charles's usual receptionist.

"Anne, how very nice to see you!" Charles said. "Incidentally, after you mentioned your trips to Samye Ling and to see Akong Rinpoche, I remembered something that you might find of interest. The tour programme that the monk gave me that day in the office."

"Oh, I remember! It was when all those monks turned up—one with a bad toothache!" Ruth said.

"That's exactly right!" replied her brother. "Quite a bit of excitement that day!" Turning to Anne he said, "Anyway, I thought you may like to have this!" Pulling the yellowing paper from his inside jacket pocket he added, "Not like I have any use for it!"

Anne thanked her uncle for the programme and without thought, tucked it straight into her bag. As usual, before long, conversation between Anne and Ruth became heated—old ugly issues coming to the surface--so Anne thought it best to leave. Saying her goodbyes she headed out to her car and set off for home. As she drove south, the grey stone and concrete of the city was soon behind her, replaced with the greens and earth browns of the countryside. As traffic calmed, Anne's thoughts turned to how Tibet had now come back into her life; firstly with Frank's visit, and now the pamphlet her uncle had bestowed. "What next?" she murmured aloud. That question was soon answered.

A few days later Anne received a call from Norman, anxious to visit Drakar and catch-up on how things were developing at the healing centre. Anne said she'd be happy to see him so the following week, Wednesday, Norman arrived about midday. Anne welcomed him into the lounge and offered him tea (knowing that he didn't drink coffee anymore), and soon their conversation turned to Samye Ling. Anne explained that she'd done all she could and had now lost interest. And since nothing had come of the monks' visit to Drakar, it had become clear that her path did *not* lie in that direction. Thinking he may find the tour programme a curiosity, she went to her desk, withdrew the document and handed it to him. (A bit worse for wear, Anne confessed that she'd actually used it as a drinks mat before realising its potential value.) A round ring stood out prominently like an artist's watermark:

"This is really very interesting," offered Norman, inspecting the document closely. "It's the tour programme of the Sixteenth Karmapa's visit to Scotland in 1974, and it looks like handwriting here--see Anne?" he said, pointing to what appeared to be script. "I'm no expert but I would have thought this *Karmapa* would have used a seal rather than sign it himself. That could be significant." Anne pondered his observation—but was skeptical. She'd been down this rocky and meandering road before: the promise of a Dharma Centre, fruitless visits to Samye Ling trying to satisfy Akong Rinpoche—which had come to nothing. Still, in the back of in her mind she wanted to believe that it all amounted to *something*.

"You know, you might want to take this to Samye Ling and let this Akong Rinpoche take a look at it," Norman said, pointing out a card in Anne's hand she'd not yet played. But Norman could see that Anne was more than just hesitant. "If you don't mind me saying, Anne, can you really just let it go without using everything at your dispose? I mean, what have you got to lose?" Anne saw the reasoning of it: In for a penny, in for a pound . . .

So once again Anne set off for Samye Ling—with Norman again tagging along--Norman informing Anne that while she meets with the Rinpoche he has some business of his own to discuss with Clare, the secretary. Anne couldn't imagine what that *business* might be, but proceeded straight away--the familiar gold dome and stone arch soon coming into view. As she passed through the door into Akong's meeting room, the programme clutched in her fingers, Anne found that little had changed. She was greeted by the same placid atmosphere of calm and peacefulness she'd encountered on her first visit. She approached the Rinpoche and they exchanged greetings and pleasantries as always. Choosing to avoid talk of the monks' visit and the ill-fated Dharma Centre, Anne simply said she'd brought something for him to see, and hoped that he could shed some light on it. Anne leaned forward and placed the pamphlet into Akong's outstretched hand. No sooner had his eyes set upon the document that he leapt out of his chair and gave out a loud shriek--which sounded round the room and echoed through the building, and took Anne utterly by surprise:

"*Where did you get this*?!" demanded the Rinpoche.

Taken aback and nearly afraid to speak, Anne said, "It--it was given to me by my uncle . . . a retired dentist. He treated a monk for a toothache many years ago and was given this in gratitude."

"I was *there*!" said Akong, clearly shocked. "*I* was the Sixteenth Karmapa's interpreter that day!"

"What a coincidence," said Anne, still unsure why he'd reacted so.

Akong Rinpoche looked at Anne, clearly not believing in coincidences. "Do you know what this document says, Anne?"

"Well, no, not really . . . " replied Anne, trying to remember what Norman had said.

"This is a message of thanks, dated 1974, and signed by His Holiness." Handing the pamphlet back to Anne he turned and walked away; apparently having said all he planned to say on the matter.

Anne, quite confused by the Rinpoche's reaction to the pamphlet, thanked him and left the meeting room—shaken. As she pulled the door closed behind her, Norman met her in the hall.

"What was all that about!" he asked, his eyes wide. "I could hear the Rinpoche from down the other end of the hall!"

"I wish I knew!" Anne answered, her face now flush. "The mere sight of the pamphlet just set him off! I never imagined that *anything* could make him react that way!"

"Well, it definitely means *something* for him to go on like that!" observed Norman.

"Oh, I don't know," replied Anne, rolling her eyes. "I've misread him before," previous meetings coming to mind. Anne dropped the pamphlet back into her bag; out of sight, out of mind. Though the peace and tranquility of Samye Ling was still there for Anne, the atmosphere had somehow changed. Her confusion only multiplied.

When Anne reached home, the tour programme was put back into her bureau drawer. There were other, more personal issues to deal with. For one, Tara had now had her second baby and had moved out to live with her children's father. For another, Daryl had also moved out, to live with his girlfriend and their children. Everyone was growing up and moving on, it seemed, except for Anne. It was as though she was just marking time. In the past few years Candy had died--and then Aurora— leaving Drakar empty. The once imposing estate bubbling with excitement was now just a rambling and creaky country house. Nothing left for Anne, she needed to move on. But where was her path leading now?

Chapter 22

THE ISLAND OF CYPRUS, SOUTH of Turkey, was most definitely a change for Anne. And before long she managed to fit in with some of the ex-patriots who lived in the small village where she'd rented a traditional style cottage. A woman named Barbara, for one. Her story was that she'd moved to this small Mediterranean community to get over a rather unpleasant divorce. Both Anne and Barbara instantly hit it off and knew that their lives were intrinsically linked. Many, like Anne, seemed to be escaping former lives. But selling everything in the U.K. and running off to Cyprus (of all places) did not sit well with Daryl and Tara. Even so, here Anne was, sitting in the little café Barbara ran, regaling her of her own trials and tribulations. The change of pace and scenery invigorated Anne. It felt like a new start. The indigenous olive groves, the goat and sheep herds, and the lighter, earthy hues of the landscape appealed to Anne's aesthetic and emotional sensibilities. And through contacts made at Barbara's restaurant, Anne was able to develop a small following in colour readings and therapy, and now, face-reading.

While out one evening with friends, Anne found herself attracted to a tall and slim, grey-haired, handsome man with piercing blue eyes called Hector. Hector had worked for most of his life in the medical sector, but was now retired. Slightly older than Anne, they instantly hit it off, a relationship soon developing. Hector was intellectual, practical, owned his own house and was very much in control of his life. Anne thought he was what she needed—at least for now. He paid her attention and initially made no great demands of her.

Confiding in Hector of her health problems in the past (and her brush with cancer), Anne mentioned that she'd received a free health check with her car insurance policy, and though the policy was due to expire in only a few days, didn't intend to claim her free health check, saying, "I don't really need another health check, Hector, I've only just had one. And I had a routine mammogram just last year."

"But it's free," reasoned Hector. "Why not take advantage of it?" While Anne felt fine and had no cause to worry, she did as Hector suggested. Thus, she was devastated when the mammogram showed a small lump in her left breast. A biopsy was sent to the lab for analysis and Anne was told to prepare to have the breast surgically removed. When the test results came back, the news was not good: the tumour was diagnosed as a Grade 4 and as it was apparently attached to a muscle, more tests had to be run. A review of previous mammograms from Scotland revealed that the tumour had, apparently, been there for quite some time. Her medical consultant questioned how she'd lived so long with an active Grade 4 tumour—yet showed no overt symptoms. The consultant decided to send a biopsy to a specialist in London for a second opinion. Meanwhile, Anne discussed her condition with her friend Samantha, an author who lived in London, who immediately got in touch with her friend Nigel, a cancer specialist in Edinburgh. Something, so it seemed to both Anne and Samantha, didn't add up.

"Anne, I just spoke with Nigel and he's quite confused," Samantha said over the phone. "He can't understand the grade four tumor diagnosis. With a grade four, he would expect you to be deathly ill, and hospitalised. He suspects the tests are inaccurate and said that you should be re-tested. And it so happens that he's having dinner in Paris on Saturday with one of the world's top breast cancer specialists, who's living in Cyprus. He'll pass along your name and contact information and will ask him to look into this." For the first time in weeks, Anne was optimistic. The fact that she had no symptoms was a good indication of mis-diagnosis.

Anne knew her medical consultant had been trying to reach her all week-end, but she was mentally exhausted and couldn't face any more bad news. At her appointment with him on Monday, however, he told her that he'd been trying to contact her to arrange a consultation with a particular specialist to discuss treatment. Anne told him what her friend Samantha had learned, including the details of the meeting being arranged with an expert in the field. Upon hearing this, her consultant looked at her strangely and said: "The specialist I was arranging for you to see had dinner in Paris with someone from Scotland on Saturday." A quick phone call verified that it was the very same specialist Nigel was arranging for her to see! Meanwhile, Hammersmith Test Labs sent back the lab results: It was a "Grade 3" tumor—not Grade 4! And somewhat miraculously, further tests showed that the cancer had *not* spread to her lymphatic or muscular systems as first suspected. In fact, minor surgery and routine medical follow-up were the only treatment necessary! (In just a couple of weeks, Anne was good as new.)

Soon after, Hector asked Anne to marry him, and she agreed. But before long, his character flaws began to surface: He became aggressive, bullying, had a controlling and demanding attitude, and drank far too much alcohol. So after many heated arguments, Anne left him-- and Cyprus--and returned to Scotland. One of the first people she met upon her return was her old friend Norman.

"So, how was Cyprus?" Norman asked, clearly happy to see her.

"It was okay," replied Anne, "but it wasn't really *me*--if you know what I mean."

"I sure do," affirmed Norman. "Sometimes you have to test-drive a new place to know for sure whether you belong or not."

Anne then asked Norman what he'd been up to over the last few years. "Nothing much, really, just scratching out a living as usual. Oh, by the way," he said curiously, "whatever happened to that old tour programme you showed the Rinpoche? Did anything ever come of that?"

"No, I've still got it, somewhere," Anne said with a sigh, "but nothing ever came of it."

"You should really have followed up on that," Norman scolded. Anne gave Norman a skeptical look, but he pressed on saying that perhaps there was some other question she should have asked, adding, "I met with him not long ago, you know. Had some ideas I wanted to consult him on. And I asked him about your last visit to Samye Ling and that tour programme business."

"Oh?"

"Indeed. And he said something most interesting. That it was '*unfinished business*' with you."

"'*Unfinished business?*' Well, what does *that* mean?" shrugged Anne—clearly confused by the suggestion that there was more to come.

"Well, just go down there and ask him, silly!" scolded Norman. "That old piece of paper must mean *something*, going by his reaction when he saw it!"

Over the next few days, Anne mulled over what Norman had said and concluded that something had brought her back from Cyprus—and it wasn't just the cancer scare or escaping Hector. So, why not give the Rinpoche situation the benefit of the doubt and follow it through? Ringing up Akong's secretary, Clare, she made an appointment (just like old times). This time she was determined to get to her truth once and for all. She began formulating the questions she intended to ask.

Gone now was the rattling old *Volvo;* died years before, coming to its final laboured stop, never to be revived. Arriving in her rattling old *Jeep,* Anne delighted at the sight of the golden dome as it peered over the tops of the tall pines, just before she drove beneath the stone arch. As if it were only yesterday, the path up to the Rinpoche's house was second-nature, as were the seats outside the meeting room. Once inside, she realised that nothing had changed; that air of peace and trust was there to welcome her as it always had. Akong Rinpoche greeted her and gestured for her to sit, asking why she'd come. Anne explained that she'd spoken to their mutual friend Norman and he'd said that there was "unfinished business" between them. Anne asked the Rinpoche directly if it had anything to do with the signed pamphlet.

"Ah, yes. The tour programme," nodded Akong Rinpoche.

Remembering Norman's advice, Anne pressed on: "Tell me, this tour programme. What does the handwriting say and what is its significance?"

The Rinpoche appeared to display a look of relief; as if he'd been waiting for these very questions. "It means many things. It was a grateful thank you to your uncle for his great help. The signature is there, *fixed*, in an ever-changing world amongst the impermanence of all things. This makes it a rare relic to the Buddhist community."

Anne was impressed, and rightfully relieved. The Rinpoche had said much more than she'd hoped. Nothing to lose, she took a breath and pressed harder.

"Tell me, what should it say to *me*? And what should I *do* with it?" she asked, now feeling the weight of this singularly important document.

Akong Rinpoche paused for a moment then spoke. "I am afraid I cannot say. It is not for me to decide. Only His Holiness the Seventeenth Karmapa can answer that," he said as he gazed at the tour programme held in Anne's hand. "Perhaps you should yourself seek him out in Dharamsala, in India, and ask that question of him."

Anne realised that she now had her answer, and knew Akong Rinpoche could say no more. Thanking him for his words and advice, she bowed and left the room. Feeling that a visit to the temple may shed some light on Rinpoche's pronouncement, she made her way. Once inside the temple, she felt its subtle energy pervade her mind and body; her mind suddenly clear and sure as never before. Her next step was certain. She would go to India. But how? And when? There was only one person Anne could consult: Norman. He often organised trips to and from India—and had, in fact, been the topic of conversation when meeting with the Rinpoche. She phoned him and asked him to come round for a visit.

"You see!" said Norman, pleased with the results of his advice. "If you ask the right questions, you get the right answers!"

"Okay, okay—no need to be smug about it!" joked Anne. "So how, exactly, do I get to India?"

"Here's the contact information for a travel agent in Delhi," he said, handing her a piece of paper. "He'll help you make all the arrangements." Anne nodded her head in appreciation. Norman then smiled broadly and said, "Now, I don't know if it's luck or fate, but as it turns out, *I'm* going to India myself in October! I'm sure we could meet up— if you can arrange to be there at the same time!"

Anne could only smile, considering the reality of *coincidence*s. "I don't want to make the trip alone, so I'll think on who I can ask to come along."

"Well, let me know when you work it all out!" Norman said enthusiastically. "Oh, and make sure your passports and other travel documents are up-to-date."

Norman left Anne mulling over just what she'd agreed to. *Yes*--she'd been abroad before, countless times on holiday, and had lived in Cyprus. But this was different; a step into the true unknown. A step towards getting to the truth: truth she wanted to know—yet fearful of what she might discover. The signed tour programme had been the spark to reignite her connection to Buddhism and Tibet, and from everyone's reaction to it--from Norman to Akong Rinpoche--it seemed to hold great meaning. Yet, it held no real meaning for Anne. All she had was a heart-felt feeling that she should follow it and Akong's suggestion that an answer lay with the 17th Karmapa.

But who (*in their right mind*) would want to go half way round the world on the strength of a scrawled signature on a faded Buddhist tour itinerary from the 1970s? To Anne's surprise, her son Daryl was keen to go. His personal relationship had disintegrated and had left him at a bit of a crossroads in his life. Maybe, like his mum, he needed a new path. Mother and son talked it over and it was agreed: Anne and Daryl would travel together to India.

Chapter 23

Travel arrangements booked and paid for, there was no going back for Anne. Rummaging curiously and wide-eyed through her father's bureau seemed a lifetime ago; when she'd stumbled across papers revealing a baby girl named "Ani" and references to India and Tibet. It stirred memories of Fiona, and her letter, and of fathers--real and maybe imagined. Anne's whole life—her very existence--now seemed focused on a yellowing sheet of paper signed by an enigma who'd travelled across time to be part of her new journey. A journey that continued when she and son Daryl boarded the Edinburgh-to-Heathrow Shuttle.

On arrival at Heathrow, they had just enough time to navigate the bustling throngs as they sought the best route from the domestic terminal to international departures, for the long haul to New Delhi. Soon they were through the departure lounge and ticket gate and onto the aircraft—and into the air. Minutes drifted into hours as they rode the bumpy air currents *en route* to the vast unknown. Sleeping helped pass the time, but the length of the flight was at the very edge of Anne's endurance for air travel. (She made it—but *just*.) Once off the plane they retrieved their baggage and cleared customs without a hitch. Outside, a culture shock awaited Anne and Daryl—as even the tooting car horns sounded different. Then a barrage of strange sights and sounds and smells that were India washed over them, almost immediately cleansing them of their Western senses and sensibilities. They both felt an urgency to adapt *quickly.*

There was a two-day stopover in Delhi, and after Anne acclimated herself, she could see that Westernisation of the East was not far off. Corporate logos and branding, steel, glass and concrete monoliths stood boldly, draping the *real* India in a somewhat familiar facade. But all of this spice-scented metropolis could not be absorbed in just two days, so Anne and Daryl took the standard tourist fare in the time available--which passed all-too quickly. A regional flight to Dharamsala had to be negotiated which, after some trepidation, was managed. No multi-engine jet for this type of commuter flight. Instead, a small turbo-prop craft operated by *Buddha Air* was in order. And if Anne and Daryl thought Delhi was a journey into another world, then Dharamsala was *unworldly.* Like stepping back in time--as if Anne were back in Scotland as a child on holiday with Alexander and Ruth--the mountains, the tree-covered slopes, and the cool fresh air. Even the geographic names were familiar: *McLeodganj* and *Forsythganj.* What was incongruous, however, were the buildings--gold- and red-roofed structures with upturned eaves. Dharamsala was a town filled with Samye Ling-like temples!

The accommodations arranged were comfortable--if basic--and located in the McLeodganji district. After a night adjusting from the three-star Delhi hotel to an almost trekkers' hostel bed, Anne and Daryl set off by taxi the following morning to the Karmapa's residence. It was a dusty ride to the monastery, the car bumping and swaying listlessly along the dirt-track road, slowing down for the occasional cow, or, individual wandering carelessly on the road. At last they arrived at their destination. The taxi driver told them he would wait for them to return.

Anne and Daryl climbed the stone steps leading to the monastery. At the top they skirted round the right-hand side of the massive structure and entered through the open doors, which were flanked by two armed guards. Anne strode purposefully towards one of the guards and asked to see His Holiness the 17th Karmapa. The guard tried to dismiss her, telling her to come back the next day, but she stood her ground, saying, "I have an important document to show him. I have come all the way from Scotland." Momentarily, a monk appeared and demanded to know her business. "Dr. Akong Tulku Rinpoche from Samye Ling in Scotland has charged me with coming and meeting the Karmapa to show him this document," she said, knowingly stretching the truth. The monk asked to see the document but Anne refused, saying, "It's only for His Holiness the Karmapa's eyes," employing a hint of melodrama to emphasize the gravity of the matter. At first told that an appointment took weeks to arrange, she was miraculously given one for the next day.

The following morning, Anne and Daryl arrived at the monastery and explained that she had an appointment to see the Karmapa about an important document. This official, like the one the day before, reached out his hand as if see the document. As Anne attempted to explain that she'd been through this vetting process the day before, the guard whispered something into the official's ear and Anne and Daryl were ushered without further word to the very front of the long queue of waiting people. Shortly after, a monk instructed them to ascend the stairs. At the top, Anne and Daryl were shown into a large anteroom. Anne had no idea what to expect; *Maybe it will be like Samye Ling*, she thought to herself. Like Samye Ling, as soon as they passed through the door, the atmosphere changed; as if *charged*. There was an energy, a palpable electricity that pervaded everything. It was both intoxicating and soothing. As Anne tried to adjust to this atmosphere, she realised that she was in the presence of the Karmapa, seated just a few yards away. She bowed deeply. The Karmapa gestured for her and Daryl to a take a seat. Anne could see a young man sitting low to the floor; to his right, an elderly man sat. Anne blinked and squinted as luminous colour energy swirled round the room. The Karmapa nodded to Anne to begin.

"I brought you this tour programme," Anne began, holding the document in her extended hand. "It is signed by His Holiness the Sixteenth Karmapa, who left it with my uncle, a dentist who treated him for a toothache when he visited Edinburgh, Scotland, in 1974." The Karmapa smiled and held out his hand to receive it. Anne returned the smile and delivered it into his waiting palm. He looked closely at the paper, then passed it to the monk sitting to his right. He asked Anne how the programme had come into her possession so she related her story and how she'd met Akong Rinpoche, who'd ultimately suggested that she come to India and meet with him. Anne then took a measured breath and asked, "I was wondering what you think I should do with it. It seems to carry great importance and I wish to do what is called for."

The Karmapa smiled and nodded. "Print this tour programme in a book for all the world to see," he replied, gesturing for Anne to come forward and reclaim the pamphlet.

Anne said, "And what shall I do with the actual document?"

"It is yours to keep," he replied, his smile broadening.

Meeting over, Anne and Daryl exited the room. And whether it was the intoxicating atmosphere, the powerful energy, or the Karmapa's own presence—they both began to laugh hysterically much to the surprise of those people waiting in line to have their audience with the Karmapa. Both Anne and Daryl knew that something wonderful had just occurred. Needing to collect her thoughts, once downstairs Anne sought out a chair in the waiting room and sat down--her thoughts whirling dizzily round her head. She mused at the Karmapa's suggestion that she put it in a book--of all things?

It now occurred to Anne that she'd found the project Akong Rinpoche had long alluded to. It slowly dawned on her that the signature on the mysterious programme *did* mean something to her. It meant something to the Karmapa; had meant something to Akong Rinpoche; as it had clearly meant something to the Karmapa in 1974. Now Anne's past and present were distilled into one meaning: a book for all the world to see! *But, what kind of book?*

Anne now believed that the words His Holiness the 16th Karmapa had written on his tour programme in 1974 were leading her; directing her towards an incredible journey of unimaginable importance. And, as if a bolt of lightening had hit her, she knew clearly what her next move would be: Tibet she must seek. The Tibetan people and the land was her destiny.

Chapter 24

BACK HOME IN SCOTLAND, ANNE began to plan a trip to Tibet. Her old friend Norman had paid her a visit and suggested she contact Tom, a man who lived in a small village near Inverness in the Scottish Highlands. Tom organised sightseeing and Buddhist-linked trips to Tibet and had done so for many years. This, Norman said, would be a safe and relatively easy way to travel to a country inherently fraught with difficulties and official obstacles. Anne quickly contacted Tom.

"I understand that you lead tours to Tibet?" Anne said decisively.

"Yes, I do. Have done for many years. The next one will be organised a couple of months from now. Are you interested in joining my party of fellow travellers?"

"Yes, I am--as well as my son, Daryl."

"I'll email you all the relevant forms and the itinerary, so make certain you read everything carefully, fill in all the details, and send everything back to me with a copy of both of your passports. I'll need that as soon as possible. And by the way, this trip will include a couple of nights stay at Kopan Monastery in Nepal, before venturing into Tibet. At the monastery we'll participate in daily meditation sessions, and visit several Buddhist holy sights."

As Anne replaced the receiver, she felt elated. She was going on an adventure--perhaps the adventure of a lifetime! She was finally going to have the opportunity to unravel the mystery of her birth--back on her home soil. And if she really tried, perhaps she could even find her mother and her long lost family! And she wondered why she'd never considered taking this action before! She was beside herself with pure joy at the prospect of finding her true family.

With new-found excitement and the future panning out before her, Anne decided to visit Akong Rinpoche and share the news from her visit with the 17th Karmapa in India (particularly since it had been at his urging). As she entered the Rinpoche's now familiar room on the day of her appointment, she immediately felt a new sense of peace. She took in a deep cleansing breath, felt her shoulders give in, and smiled as she saw Akong sitting in his usual chair. He stood up and smiled, then gestured for her to sit opposite him. Anne felt lightheaded; intoxicated by the high energetic vibrations of the room; the noise of the silence almost deafening. Nearly bursting--her heart pounding and her spirit soaring--she excitedly began to tell Akong the latest chapter of her story:

"I met with the Seventeenth Karmapa as you suggested," Anne said; her excitement apparent. "And the meeting was so *amazing*! -- *Indescribable*, really! When His Holiness saw the tour programme he suggested that I put it in a book for the whole world to see. But the thing is, I have no idea what the book should be about--although obviously it would have to do with Tibet, and Buddhism, and finding my own roots." The Rinpoche nodded, sensing that there was more. "And because of this, I have decided to visit Tibet!" Anne smiled, knowing that Akong would be pleased since Tibet was his homeland. She was most definitely prepared for his reaction to her good news.

"A *book*, you say . . . yes a *book*," Rinpoche said, nodding his head agreeably. Then he smiled and said ponderously, "Why would you go to Tibet?"

"I'm rather certain that my mother is Tibetan, and I would like to try to find her before it's too late. And if I'm to write a book about Tibet then I need to get the *feel* of the country. To stand on the land and understand the people, the culture, the fauna and flora . . ."

The Rinpoche's face turned grave. "No! I do not recommend you go, Anne! It is much too dangerous! If you go asking questions this could bring you great harm!" said Rinpoche firmly.

"But, I've already booked the reservations!" Anne pleaded.

"I can only suggest that you *do not go*! Even the walls have ears in Tibet!" replied Rinpoche, disapproval in his tone.

Neither reaffirming nor acquiescing, Anne dismissed herself, bowed, and left the room—shaken and half in shock. So certain that he'd be pleased by her decision to go to Tibet, she had once again left without his approval. What was she missing?

The day finally arrived for Anne and Daryl to meet Tom and the other nineteen members of their travel group at Glasgow Airport, for the first leg of their journey to Nepal. They flew first to London, then after a short delay, boarded the *Boeing* 747 that would deliver them to their final destination. And after a long, tiring flight and jostling bus trip, they arrived exhausted but safe at Kopan Monastery, a Tibetan Buddhist monastery near Boudhanath, on the outskirts of Kathmandu, Nepal. There they were led single-file into the dining room where officials were taking all their travel information and collecting passports.

Form-filling and photocopies of their insurance and passports completed, Anne and Daryl were finally shown to their small room. Daryl grumbled that the room was not what he'd expected--having only two single beds and an *en suite* toilet. He headed for the shower, only to find it only sprayed out cold water. *This*, he grumbled, *is not my idea of an ideal holiday!* But his ill-mood did not affect Anne as she knew that this journey could well change her life. This journey to Tibet was going to shed light on her ancestors, their way of life, and the ultimate meaning of the Karmapa's signed tour programme. But unbeknown to Anne, despite her best-laid plans, this was not to be.

The next morning after a breakfast of boiled eggs, cereal and fruit, Tom distributed an itinerary of the day's events. Daryl was furious that he was expected to participate in group meditation—*like all the rest!*--and was to join the others in the monastery meditation hall in an hour. But after considerable cajolery on his mother's part, Daryl agreed to accompany her and soon they were both sitting cross-legged in a half-circle before Tom who sat at the head of the group. After explaining what they were about to do, Tom asked everyone to close their eyes and breathe deeply and to clear their minds. But this calm was short-lived as suddenly the door swung open and there stood a nun; the only nun in this monastery. Her position was as secretary and overall overseer to the smooth running of the monastery.

The nun walked directly to Tom and whispered in his ear. Tom looked directly at Anne and Daryl, then nodded his understanding. Anne felt uncomfortable and nudged Daryl, raising her eyebrows in a questioning manner. Tom then motioned for Anne and Daryl to follow them out of the room. Outside, the rays of the sharp morning sun momentarily blinded Anne.

Tom said, "It has come to our attention by way of the Chinese authorities that your son (he pointed to Daryl) is believed to be a journalist and has therefore been refused entry into Tibet."

Anne looked at Daryl--who returned her confused expression. "But, that's *absurd!*" cried Anne.

"Wait. There's more," informed the nun. "And because you are on a *group* travel visa, the other members of the group cannot travel to Tibet either." Tom lifted his hands to cover his anguished face.

"Oh, my God . . ." was all Anne could say, the enormity of the situation suddenly hitting her. She knew that for most of the group this was a holiday of a lifetime, and in some cases, had taken years to save up for. She felt shattered. Overwhelmed. Angry and frustrated. "I just don't understand," she said, shaking her head. "A *journalist?*"

Looking directly at Daryl now, the nun said, "The passport number you sent when you booked this trip is not the passport number that you entered Nepal with, Master Demarco."

"Oh, Lord!" said Anne—her eyes wide, her mouth twisted. "Daryl, remember when your old passport had somehow gone into the washing machine, after I'd sent a copy to Tom? Well, because of the water damage, I ordered you a new one! I just assumed that the new passport would have the same number as the old one—and I never thought to check!"

"Well, obviously *not,*" replied Daryl, a bit put-off by his mother's carelessness.

Anne now felt her world falling apart, her dreams of returning to her homeland and finding her past, in pieces. She burst into tears.

All efforts were now undertaken to persuade Chinese authorities in Nepal to allow Anne and Daryl to travel. At first they said Anne could travel alone; but she refused to leave Daryl behind. She was then told that this was not her decision to make as the group depended on her going for their own passage. Finally, after a monetary sum was paid to Chinese officials (a sizable bribe), Anne was told that she and her son could travel to Tibet the following day. Anne was elated; her dream was about to be fulfilled. But that dream turned to nightmare just hours later . . .

About 4:00 a.m. while Anne and Daryl slept, they were woken by a knock on the door. A groggy Anne opened the door to an exasperated Tom: "No way can you travel, I'm sorry to say! Chinese authorities in Tibet have refused you entry! They said that if you board the plane you will not get off--rather you will be returned immediately to Nepal!" A dejected Anne looked to her son with tears in her eyes, unable to find meaningful words. A few hours later Anne and Daryl waved a fond fare-well to their group, who were now heading for the airport to catch their flight bound for Tibet.

Although Anne and Daryl found an alternate holiday in Nepal, nothing could make up for the sense of loss Anne now felt. Her dream of finding her mother and the sensation of feeling the vibrant energy of Tibet beneath her feet were gone--replaced with a void of emptiness. She wondered why she hadn't taken the Rinpoche's warning more seri-ously, and now began to feel that perhaps in some way it was fortuitous; that maybe something bad would have happened to them if they'd suc-ceeded in reaching Tibet. She'd long known that the Rinpoche was a wise man, but now realised just *how* wise he was. Thinking back now to their last meeting, she remembered how Akong had smiled and said *yes* to the book . . .

Indeed, Anne still had the book to consider.

However, this book was now put on hold because of the death of her Uncle Charles. A subsequent meeting with her uncle's old and dying secretary became the catalyst for Anne's visit to Aviemore. While clear-ing out her uncle's former home, Anne had found photographs of herself from childhood, as well as pictures of her father, Alexander, his mother, and a large stately house.

For weeks after her uncle's death, Mona, her uncle's former receptionist, had crossed Anne's mind. She'd not seen Mona in over twenty years and wondered why she now felt an urgency to contact her. But she just couldn't seem to get the aging woman out of her thoughts. Finally Anne gave in and tracked her down, arriving unannounced at the nursing home where Mona now resided.

After the usual pleasantries, catching up, and talk of their shared sadness at losing Charles, Anne told Mona about her involvement with the Karmapa and how her uncle had given her the document with the signature. Mention of the Karmapa led Mona to ask:

"Well, you know, deary, that reminds me, but did you happen to come across that Kalumpa fellow's dental records? When your uncle closed down the practice we did toss out some of the old records—you know, people we knew would not be needing them . . . well, most had died by then--but I would not be surprised if that Kalumpa's records are still there. That is, if that sorta thing interests you," said Mona. "When I visited your uncle the last time, I guess that was about five years ago now, he asked me to sort out all those old records—but I never got round to it. So they might still be there. And I do, of course, remember your mother telling everyone what an amazing experience that Kalumpa fellow's visit was!"

"*Karmapa*," corrected Anne.

"What was that you said, deary? Something about the Kalumpa?"

"I said, it's pronounced *Kar-ma-pa*."

"Well, *Kalumpa--Kramoppa--*or *whatever*—Ruth said he was a lovely man!"

Anne knew that while she'd been sorting through her uncle's things she'd never come across any such records, and had torn through more boxes of paperwork than she could count. There was only one more cupboard left--the cleaning supplies cupboard—and thought she recalled seeing a box in there. So she called her daughter Tara and together they went back to her uncle's house, pulled out the large box, and began to search through it. The first thing Anne came across as she opened the lid was a small box wrapped in shiny red paper and tied with red ribbon. Setting the box aside they discovered that beneath it were a number of dental records that appeared to have been separated from the others. Taking one pile each, Anne and Tara began to sift through them. Finally, Tara shouted that she thought she'd found what they were looking for. Indeed, there they were, the Karmapa's dental records, including his address: Dharma Chakra Centre, Rumtek Monastery, Sikkim. How close Anne was to never knowing of the existence of these records! Anne knew she'd never have checked the box had Mona not suggested it—and gave a silent *thanks*.

Because it had been her intuition that had led her to now possessing the Karmapa's dental records, Anne followed another powerful urge; to trace her grandmother whom she'd visited when she was a child, living just outside Aviemore. A few days later she drove to Aviemore and headed straight for the public library, where she began to research local history and much to her surprise found an old newspaper clipping pertaining to her grandmother: *Agnes McNaughton, local of Dulnaine Bridge, is left lifetime residency of Corbies Glen by the late Laird Donald Cameron. Agnes, a former maid at the old house, has declined this offer. The house has subsequently been left in trust and will remain unoccupied until such time as the trust can find a suitable occupant.* Anne then traced her grandmother's obituary: *Agnes McNaughton beloved mother to Alexander died . . . .*

On a cold and crisp winter's morning, Anne decided to visit the house in the photograph--more than just a little intrigued. As she swung her car into the driveway she noticed large pillars with eagles on top, and a living black crow under one of the eagle wings. She smiled. As she drove up to the house she saw on her right a pond and there in the middle her favorite flowers: water lilies. Hearing the gravel crunch beneath her wheels she drove round the half-circle drive and stopped her car at the front door. She sat in her car for a moment taking in the details. She could imagine a young girl coming here each day to clean, all those years ago. She wondered about her life and the goings-on in the house and wondered why on Earth her grandmother hadn't accepted the offer to live here. She stepped out of the car and slammed the door, and made her way up the steps. Pressing the brass doorbell she waited, anxiously. At last the door was opened by a young woman in her twenties.

"Yes, how can I help?" the young woman politely asked.

"Well," said Anne, suddenly realising that she hadn't properly prepared, "you see, my grandmother used to work here as a cleaning woman, and I saw it mentioned in a newspaper clipping that the late laird's will had provided for her to live here for the rest of her life--but she declined. So I—I guess I am just curious to see where she worked, and could have lived. Sorry . . . I hope I'm not imposing."

"No, it's no imposition at all," the young woman said, smiling broadly, extending her hand. "My name's Kyla. I'm staying here for the time being as I am doing an inventory and assessment of the house for the factors. Come in. Interesting, you say your grandmother worked here?"

"Yes, for many years."

Upon entering the large and spacious foyer, the first thing Anne noticed was a large black crow in a glass-domed case set against the far wall. She felt as if its eyes were set on her—and felt slightly un-nerved—yet drawn to it. Everything round seemed to look old, antique, as if nothing had changed in many years. She hesitantly approached the glass-enclosed crow.

"He's a fine little fellow," said the young woman, "but a little *scary* for my tastes."

As Anne focused on the glass-encased, rarefied black bird, a beam of sunlight shot through the hall window, sharply striking the crow and illuminating its inky, black feathers. And as she examined it more closely saw feathers composed of deep tones of shimmering tur-quoise-- intermingled with the black--immediately reminding her of the turquoise necklace she owned. She thought of the Buddhist belief that crows are incarnate lamas--and of course, thought of Tibet. And as she did she suddenly had a vision of the 16th Karmapa's picture on his signed tour programme. As she turned back to face her hostess, Anne saw over the woman's left shoulder a gold-framed painting on the wall of a man who could pass for her father. Anne suddenly felt light-headed—horrified that she was about to faint and make a spec-tacle of herself. The room began to spin, her knees buckled, and she dropped lifeless--right into arms that caught her just before she could hit the floor . . .

The next thing Anne knew she was sitting in a large armchair, propped up against a large cushion, watching Kyla search through jars of herbs on a bookshelf. Hearing her stir, Kyla turned and handed Anne a glass of cool water, then resumed her search. As Anne sipped the cool liquid she sensed a familiarity about the house, though she couldn't quite put her finger on it. There were lots of artifacts from Tibet, and images of the Dalai Lama and the Karmapa, so she attributed her sense of fa-miliarity to her involvement with Samye Ling and the knowledge she'd acquired about such items. As Anne began to come round, she realised that she was indeed in a very unusual room. Sections of the large bay window had stained glass instead of clear glass, which sent shafts of coloured light bouncing round the room. She then noticed pendant crystals hanging strategically throughout, and followed the bands of colour they emitted. *This is home*, she thought. *Here she was amidst the world of colour and energy she so loved.*

"Feeling better?" Kyla asked.

"Yes, much. Thank you," Anne said. "This certainly is an interesting room."

"Not particularly my taste," Kyla said, "but if you appreciate a meeting of two old worlds, this is the perfect house for you."

"So, it's for sale?"

"For rent. But because of the particular restrictions of the late Laird's will, we've had ongoing problems finding a tenant." Remembering then why Anne had come, Kyla said, "Say, what was your grandmother's name?"

"Agnes McNaughton," replied Anne with a smile. "My father was Alexander McNaughton."

"You may be of some help to the factors," Kyla said, thinking aloud. "They've had difficulty finding anyone related to Agnes—uh, Mrs. McNaughton. I take it you married?"

"Yes, I did marry, but I divorced."

"Hummm, you know, it just occurred to me that if you're a direct descendant of Agnes McNaughton, then I need to inform the factors, as it may have some bearing on the future of the house. Say--why don't I show you round in the meantime!"

"Oh, I'd love that!" Anne said. "What about tomorrow? I need to be heading off soon in search of a B&B for the night."

"Listen, there are plenty of extra rooms here, and I'm sure it would be alright if you stayed the night. After all, you may have some claim on this house! Let me inform the factor's office of your arrival and your relationship to Agnes and see what they say."

Anne couldn't believe her luck and readily agreed, thrilled at the prospect of spending more time in the house her grandmother had once worked.

After speaking with the factors, Kyla offered Anne a room on the first floor, a lovely room facing the front of the house. As Anne gazed out at the ornamental gardens outside her window, the colours resonated with her soul and brought a sense of peace. With two hours before dinner she unpacked her small travel case then decided to take a leisurely stroll round the grounds. Leaving by the front door she headed for the lily pond she'd seen. There the tall rushes swayed in the gentle breeze, the pink and white lilies bobbed up and down on their dark green leaves as the wind gently rocked them. She sat on a bench a few feet from the water's edge, took a deep breath, and closed her eyes. Within a few moments her body became light and she felt as though she were floating. The silence became louder, the cawing of crows becoming lost in the distance as she lulled into a deep meditative state . . .

When she awoke, she had no idea how long she'd been sitting there. She felt cold as she slowly opened her eyes. To her surprise, a crow was perched on the other end of the bench, looking directly at her. "Hello," she said. (She'd become used to the appearance of crows in her life--ever since that day she'd been party to killing one on the way to Samye Ling Monastery. Now they seemed ever-present. And while she'd once found that troubling, she now welcomed their company like old friends.) Standing up and stretching her arms towards the sky, she began to make her way back to the house. As she glanced up at the large windows of the house she saw what looked to be a face—not that of Kyla--staring back at her from behind the clear-but-dusty glass and wondered if there were ghosts residing in this rambling, old house. (And *who* they might be?) She tore her eyes away from the fascination, knowing by the fading daylight that it was nearing dinner time.

Giving her face and hands a quick rinse in the basin in her room, Anne went in search of the dining room. Kyla found her wandering and smiled. "In here," she said. Anne had to walk past the stuffed crow in its domed case and as she did, inadvertently held her breath. Pushing open the heavy wooden door she jumped as the Grandfather Clock in the hall chimed: *bong, bong, bong, bong, bong.* She entered and sat down, Kyla having set a plain but cheery table. "I've made risotto," Kyla said, "I hope you like that." Anne nodded and Kyla dished out the creamy risotto for them both. "Help yourself to salad and bread," she said. As they shared the delicious meal, Kyla and Anne shared what little they knew about the house and Agnes McNaughton. The next morning Anne thanked Kyla for her hospitality and leaving her telephone number, waved a warm goodbye.

It was several weeks later that Anne received a most unexpected call from the board of trustees overseeing the disposition of the rambling, old house. They'd decided that her father, Alexander, was the rightful heir to this property—but with one little *proviso.* That it could only be used as a spiritual teaching centre in perpetuity. Accordingly, the board had agreed that should Anne wish to assume control of Corbies Glen, they'd be willing to sign a one hundred-year lease in her favour. Anne was beside herself.

Chapter 25

ANNE SAT IN THE SOFT brown leather chair by the old, rather worn desk set before the big bay window. She gazed out over the mani-cured lawns and silently wondered what had transpired in this house over the decades. (What had her grandmother seen and heard?) In her hands she absently turned over and over the little red-coloured box with the gold string she'd found in the carton with the Karmapa's dental records while clearing out her Uncle Charles's house. She found it quite strange and intriguing that no one had ever bothered to open it.

Her hands trembling, Anne gently tugged at the gold string-- which slithered to the ground, the red-coloured paper following. Gingerly removing the lid of the box she gazed down into the open-ing and saw a worn leather pouch in the shape of a tear drop. Attached to one side were turquoise crystals and black feathers, which also had a turquoise and red drawstring at its neck. She carefully parted the drawstring and slipped her fingers inside the pouch, touching paper as she did. She pulled on it. As she withdrew the paper, a small photo of a young solider, along with a black feather, fluttered lightly to the ground. In her hand were two sheets of paper covered in Tibetan text and symbols.

"This looks like astrology charts".

Just then something struck the window with a dull *thud*—and Anne jumped. Her heart racing, she exhaled and smiled. It was only the resident crow flying into the window pane. She was glad for his presence and had gotten used to his unusual method of getting attention—*almost*. She'd come to understand that he was watching over her, protecting her against any malevolent force that might come her way. And he reminded her of the crow that had been accidentally killed on her first visit to Samye Ling--and the subsequent meeting with Akong Rinpoche that had completely changed her life--

She shook her head. She was still reeling from the tragic news that Akong Rinpoche had been murdered recently in Tibet. She, like so many others, was deeply shocked and saddened. And it had left her all on her own to complete the project he'd overseen. Until now, she hadn't fully realised how much she depended on his counsel. This void had left her feeling uncertain that she could accomplish on her own what was needed to make the Dharma centre a success.

As she gazed thoughtfully out the window, out across the manicured lawn and gravel driveway, she saw a black taxi approaching.......

Part IV: Palden's Story

Chapter 1

"Palden, get down from that wall, it is so high! Four-year-old boys should not be climbing like that! It is dangerous!" his mother called from the across the courtyard. Palden and his mother lived at a nunnery on the outskirts of Lhasa surrounded by the high stone walls—which Palden loved to climb.

"But, I love looking out at the countryside, Ama La! And I can see and hear so much from up here! Today I can even see the golden domes of Potala Palace! Do you think the Dalai Lama will be there today? I so want to go! Can we, Ama La?"

"No, not today," his mother replied.

Palden had been following a single kite released from the roof of Potala Palace to mark the first day of autumn. Within seconds, count-less other kites of various sizes and shapes then filled the sky above the palace, bobbing and twisting in the cool breeze. To Palden, every day was a good day to fly kites. His own kite was bright yellow in colour and had a long tail of multicoloured bows tied on the long string that held the kite secure. When his kite was aloft, he felt himself become *one* with it as it flew high into the sky; he felt free--free to soar above Tibet just like the birds that glided on the thermal currents, dipping and weaving as the air took them.

Palden took a quick glance at his mother; *She is so pretty*, he mused to himself. Today her brown hair was swept up and held at the back of her head with a turquoise clasp. She was wearing a long turquoise dress gathered at her narrow waist with a leather belt, the cuffs turned up to reveal a lighter, more pink colour than the deep maroon. And she wore her usual multicoloured apron tied round her waist--the large stones of the turquoise necklace that hung round her neck setting the whole ensemble off:

"Ama La, can we take Jalus for a walk, now?" asked Palden as he looked down at his mother's rather worn leather boots. Jalus, a Tibetan Mastiff the size of a small horse, was one of several dogs that had decided to make the nunnery their home and had attached themselves to the boy. Though light brown in colour, when the sun's rays shone on Jalus' long wiry hair, you could see streaks of gold mingled in with the varying colours. "Come on, Ama La, can we go?" Leaping down from the rough stone wall, Palden stood beside his mother, looking up into her kind face. Jalus sensed that they were about to go on a walk and was now chasing his tail; round and round he went in anticipation of the attention he was about to get.

As mother and son headed out the great wooden gates towards the valley so vibrant with green leaf-covered trees, rivers, and mountains, Palden was excited to explore its beauty; anxious to see the placid blue waters that meandered through the surrounding land. Accompanied by faithful Jalus, they followed the rough and stony, dusty path heading north along the river bank, the river flanked between the mountain ranges to the right and left of the nunnery.

"Look!" cried Palden as he caught a glimpse of the gleaming gold of the *chortens* in the distance. "Ama La, do you think we will ever be able to walk up to those monasteries, up there on those crags that look like they almost touch the sky? Look--the clouds are coming even lower!"

Pembuti took a moment to take in the breathtaking scenery; the picturesque buildings--some of which protruded outwards, suspended high above the rocky crags. She'd often wondered why these sacred structures, placed so precariously as they were, didn't pull away from the rock face-- knowing full well that if they did, no one would survive. It was a long ways down the steep and rocky slope beneath these overhanging buildings, and should any break free from their foundations, they would surely be smashed to bits on the unforgiving rocks below.

Mother and son loved the snow-capped mountains and the tufts of grey-white clouds that floated round them. Pembuti pointed to a lush green grassy spot near the river. "Let us sit there by the water," she said. A natural collection of boulders had gathered and she chose one and sat down to rest. Palden went to the water's edge and removed his socks and shoes, rolled up his trouser legs and began to paddle in the icy-cold water. Jalus raced to the edge but only paced nervously up and down along the water. "Tell me, Ama La," said Palden, "why do the monks live in such a distant place? And what do they do all day? Are they not lonely? And, how do they keep warm?"

"Palden, Palden . . . so many questions!" replied Pembuti, withholding a gleeful laugh. (She both loved and admired his seemingly boundless curiosity.) "It is all about choices, my son. The choices we all must make in our lives. One day you too will go to live in such a monastery and there you will learn the Buddhist way of life. From that, other choices will follow and you will make your own decisions about how and where you want to live your life."

"But, I want to stay with you *forever*, Ama La!"

"I know that is how you would like it to be, Palden, but a nunnery is no place for a boy to grow into a man. It is your destiny to go to a monastery, and so you shall. We will still see each other, but a time will come when you will be a monk and lead a monk's life. But for now, come, let us walk! The day is too beautiful to worry about the future!"

"But, I am happy *now!*" Palden pleaded. "I have everything I want! I have time to play, and I have lots to eat, and you and all the other nuns love me, and I have my best friend Jalus! Why would I have to leave?" Indeed, within the high walls of the nunnery, everyone had everything they could want: they lived a life of calm reflective meditation, shared communal meals and joyous gatherings, and took pride in completing all the duties that ensured the smooth running and peaceful atmosphere.

"My son, I know it is hard to understand, but you are the first-born male and it is your *duty* to go to a monastery to be educated in the ways of the Buddha. It is every first-born male's *destiny.*"

Palden's thoughts now drifted to the nuns and all that he'd be leaving behind when that fateful day arrived. The nunnery had long been his home--with its familiar scent of incense (as it wafted round the temple during their daily routine) and time spent in the temple (where he could dream and enter the world of his imagination where the paintings on the walls came alive in the flickering light of the butter lamps). He'd grown to love the sound of the conch shell being blown, sound of the symbols being clashed, and the loud deep resonance of the horns. These were the things that made up his peaceful, balanced life, and it was unthinkable that it would ever have to end.

Pembuti now sought to lighten her son's solemn mood. "I will be going into Lhasa tomorrow, would you like to come?" she asked.

"Oh, yes!" cried Palden, cheering up immediately. "I would very much like to come!"

The next morning, Pembuti decided they'd walk to Lhasa instead of taking the horses, she and Palden setting out on the five-mile journey after morning mantras and breakfast. As they walked they chatted about Lhasa and what they were going to buy. "Tell me, Ama La, what is the Potala?"

"Well, the Potala is a very busy place where all the important affairs of Tibet are conducted, and sits up on that small mountain you see when you climb up high on the nunnery walls," replied Pembuti.

"What kind of *important affairs*?" he asked quizzically.

"You see, within those palace walls are treasure-houses containing blocks of gold, sacks and sacks of gems, and curiosities from the earliest times. Those buildings are the living heart of the country, the focus of all thoughts and all hopes for the Tibetan people. And as you know, it is the home of His Holiness the Dalai Lama."

"Really?" said Palden, not really sure what his mother meant but already dreaming of going inside and investigating the treasures. "How long have those buildings been there?"

"Well, the buildings you see up there now are about three hundred and fifty years old—"

"Wow—that is really *old!*"

"Yes, they are! But they were built on the foundation of an even older palace, and before that, there was a very important fort on the top of that mountain! And people say that deep down inside that mountain, which used to be a volcano, there is a huge cave with passages radiating out from it, and at the end of one passage there is a beautiful lake." Palden's eyes were filled with wonder as his imagination took him inside the grand structure. "But that is enough about the palace—we better get a move on!"

As they approached Potala Palace, they saw Lhasa sprawled out in the sunlight below, the delicate pastel shades of the small houses dwarfed by the huge mountains; the meandering waters of the Kyi River that flowed through the level valley flanked by the greenest-of-green grass. In the distance the mountains were of a royal purple, surmounted by white caps of shining snow; the nearer mountainsides speckled with golden-roofed monasteries. As they walked toward Lhasa, they both fell into humble silence at the sight of Potala Palace, its immense bulk effectively constituting a small mountain.

"There, over there!" Pembuti said, pointing to the right. "See that small stand of tall evergreens--you can just see the temples and colleges peeking through--well, that's where the State Oracle of Tibet lives. A *very* important person to us Tibetans! Imagine, his sole purpose in life is to connect our world with other realms we ordinary people cannot see or understand!"

"I do not understand," said Palden; as yet unaware of any other realms of existence.

"You need not worry," Pembuti comforted her son, placing her hand gently on his shoulder. "As you grow older you will come to know these other worlds. But, there is time . . ."

Palden nodded and smiled.

Proceeding down the hill, at the bottom they turned towards Potala Palace and made their way through the throngs of sightseers and avid pilgrims. "Why are all these people here?" said Palden.

"These people have come from all parts of Tibet to see where the Dalai Lama lives. If they can catch even a *glimpse* of him they will leave feeling more than repaid for their long journey and whatever hardships they met along the way. Some of these pilgrims have travelled for months on foot just to reach this place, the Holy of Holies."

Nearly overwhelmed by the veritable sea of people round him, Palden said, "There are so many people here, Ama La!"

"Yes, said Pembuti, "all kinds of people come here to show their respect. Some farmers, some merchants--and look over there, nobles. I am sure they come from distant provinces. I can tell that by the beautiful fabrics of their clothes."

There mingling with the farmers, merchants, and nobles, Pembuti pointed out the herdsmen and traders, as well as the sick. Some of the infirm had come to Lhasa hoping to obtain a cure, while the beggars did not want to be healed as their illness or deformity provide them a daily living. Palden watched the pilgrims closely: some went on hands and knees, while others stretched the length of their body on the ground, rose, and stretched out again. Still others, the sick and crippled, hobbled along supported by friends or with the aid of walking sticks. Everywhere there were vendors, some selling hot buttered tea heated over a swinging brazier, others, various foods of other kinds. There were charms for sale and amulets said to be blessed by a Holy Incarnation. Old men were there hawking printed horoscopes and lucky charms, and farther down the road a group of cheerful men were offering hand prayer-wheels as souvenirs of the Palace. Scribes, too, were on hand: for a fee they would write a note certifying that the individual had completed circumnavigation of the circuit round the foot of the Palace. Now Pembuti and Palden reached the immense stone staircase which ran all the way up to the top of Potala Palace, running outside the buildings, Palden observing: "It's just like a street with stairs!"

"Yes, and did you know that at the very top of that building is the private residence of the Dalai Lama? --For no one may live more elevated than he!"

"So, he watches over everyone, then?" concluded Palden. Pembuti nodded agreement.

Pembuti so enjoyed the sound of the clacking prayer-wheels. In days gone by, before the Chinese arrived, the prayer-wheel was the only form of wheel used in Tibet because an old superstition had said that when wheels come into the country, peace will go out, and this was now proved true--since the Chinese had brought in their cars and tanks of destruction. Pembuti loved the bright colours (from the dresses and jewelry the people wore, to the colourful painted houses) and the noise of the traders (as they shouted their bargain prices), and the stealth and calmness of the monks and lamas. As Pembuti scanned the scene before her, taking in the shimmering gold reflected from the roof of the Palace (as well as the opulence of the monasteries) her soul felt uplifted. She delighted in all the happy, contented faces. These feelings warmed her entire being.

Pembuti (with Palden in tow) visited one trader then another, purchasing small quantities of flour, vegetables, and fruit; just enough to last a few days as this was more than enough for the two to carry home. Palden shivered; hugged himself. The temperature was dropping. He was tired and hungry and wanted to rest. Stopping at one of Pembuti's regular tea sellers they purchased two mugs of steaming hot butter tea and sat down on the wooden seats in the marketplace and sipped their drinks. Questions surfaced in Palden's curious mind.

"Ama La, why does Ani-Dolma always tell you to hurry up when you come to Lhasa?" he asked. "Why is it that she always looks so angry with you?"

"Well, she is not really *angry*," she explained, "but *worried*. She is concerned for our safety."

"What *worries* her so?"

"You see, Palden, even though Lhasa is a beautiful place, a wondrous place to visit, it is also a very strange place, with many different kinds of people. And our new occupiers, the Chinese, want to control us. They want us to think and believe as they do. Ani-Dolma worries because I support the Dalai Lama--but we are not even allowed to mention his name here. Lhasa can be a very dangerous place for us who follow the Dalai Lama, but we believe that it is *our* country, and that of our Dalai Lama, and we are entitled to follow him if we choose." (Palden raised his eyebrows warily.) "But, I think this is a conversation best saved for back home where there is nobody to overhear what we say. I promised Ani-Dolma we would not be too long. Finish your tea and we will head back before it gets too dark and cold."

As night fell and the temperature dropped below freezing, Pembuti and Palden trudged back to the nunnery. Too cold to converse, with each step the baskets they carried seemed to grow heavier. As they neared the nunnery gates they opened and Jalus came bounding out-- tail wagging, jumping up and down in relief that they'd finally returned. "Jalus! Jalus!" Palden cried over and over again.

Chapter 2

"Palden, Palden," called Pembuti.

"Yes, Ama La. I am outside with Jalus."

"Come here my son, I need to talk with you." Palden let Jalus run free as he joined his mother. "Soon it will be your fifth birthday, so I will be going to Lhasa to find a nice present for you."

"Then let me come with you--please, please!" begged Palden.

"No--your present must be a surprise, little one, so you will stay here," Pembuti explained. "You have plenty of chores to keep you busy until I return. I should not be gone long as I am taking a horse instead of walking." Palden stamped his foot and put his hands on his hips in frustration. "That is no way to behave, Palden! You will stay here and that it that!" Palden knew by her tone that it was useless to argue with her; that she most definitely would not change her mind no matter what tantrum he threw. At last Pembuti was ready to leave. Palden stood patiently in the courtyard as his mother saddled and reined a small grey and brown pony. Then just before she mounted the animal she bent down and gave Palden a kiss on his head. "I love you, my son. Promise to be good for Ani-Dolma while I am away." Palden nodded. "I will return soon with your present." Settled into the coarsely-woven saddle,

Pembuti took the reins in one hand and waved to her son with the other. As the horse walked slowly out the nunnery gates, Palden ran after her, waving wildly, stopping when he reached the gate posts. As his mother faded into the far horizon, dust rose high into the air and her horse cantered onward towards Lhasa.

That afternoon after seeing to all his chores, Palden sat propped up against the nunnery wall in the courtyard, playing with Jalus while throwing pebbles into a bucket. The sudden loud booming of drums coming from inside the temple jarred him awake--feelings of panic quickly washing over him. *I must have dozed off!* he said to himself. Getting up and dusting himself off, through sleepy eyes he saw Ani-Dolma approaching. "Follow me," she said in a light, crispy voice. "Time to go to the prayer hall, Palden."

There were many things about the prayer hall that Palden had come to truly love. The beautiful images, the intoxicating smells, the sound of pious voices joining as one. But nothing surpassed the peaceful feeling that came over him as he gazed at the countless butter lamps that struggled to shed their rays of light through the drifting clouds of incense smoke. These flickering lights that enlivened the shadows to shift across the giant sacred figures, seemed to bring them alive; as if they were bowing and swaying in response to the chanting . . .

Palden took his proper place at the end of one of the six long rows on the right-hand side of the temple and sat cross-legged on the gold-coloured cushion. He watched as the six rows opposite him quickly filled, the nuns taking their places on the brightly coloured cushions. (Each row had ten cushions placed neatly on the floor and ran the length of the temple.) Once they were all seated they began to chant sacred texts and songs based on special tonal scales, and the sound created had perceptible *power* (just as a single tone can shatter glass, so can a combination of tones build vibrational power. Palden had never witnessed this phenomenon himself but Ani-Dolma had told him this was so and he had no reason to doubt her).

The nuns' deep-red robes were a most impressive sight to see swaying in unison--with the tinkle of little silver bells and throbbing of primal drums. Blue clouds of incense coiled and twisted upwards towards the paintings of the many deities and every so often it seemed to Palden that in this uncertain light, one or another deity was gazing directly at him. Always the butter lamps were kept burning before the carved alter, and the seven bowls of holy water were cleaned and replaced several times each day. The flicker of the light, the beat of the drums, the drone of the trumpets all merged with the rhythmic chanting coming from the monks as they recited Buddhist scripture. As usual, Palden's eyelids became heavy and he began to drift . . .

Through slitted eyes, Palden watched as the colours from the *thang-ka* paintings came alive, the energy emanating from them reaching outward, swirling and weaving in and out of everything and everyone in the temple. Colours that merged into one and then another, linking together so quickly that momentarily they became a blast of white light--only to separate into their own constituent colour-rays. As Palden focused on these rays, a face began to form--that quickly drew towards him! A knot formed in his stomach, his heart skipped a beat, and sweat broke out on his brow as panic overtook him. He blinked to rid himself of this frightening image--but the black form only drew nearer! He opened his mouth to scream--but no sound would come; the face then separating into a chaotic mass of black swirling vortexes that then recombined to become a massive, horrifying face likes of which he'd only seen in nightmares. This dark and wrathful face then rushed directly at him—engulfing him in the blink of an eye. Instinctively he took a deep breath and felt his head becoming light--so light, in fact, that he lost all sensation of his body. And in the next moment he realised that he was no longer within his body--he'd *become* his breath. He was *free*.

Feeling himself quickly growing weak, Palden began to recite his mantras. And to his delight--in a flash of cold black light--he saw the wrathful face let out a scream and slowly fade to grey . . . then white . . . then became one with the atmosphere all round. Palden then felt a hand on his shoulder—and nearly jumped out of his skin. Turning, he found Ani-Dolma standing beside him: "Palden you must get up immediately. We must leave the nunnery, *now*!"

Still in a haze, Palden jumped to his feet and said, "*Leave*? Leave the *nunnery*?! But, *why*?" (What was Ani-Dolma talking about?)

"I will explain soon," Ani-Dolma said.

"But, we will wait for my Ama La to come back—will we not?"

"She is not coming back, Palden, and we need to leave. *Now*! I will tell you more when we are on our way." Grabbing him by the arm she and the other nuns began to hurriedly leave the prayer hall.

"But, why must we leave? --And leave without my Ama La?"

Ani-Dolma guided Palden to the room he shared with his mother, and swung opened the old wooden door. She knelt down and spoke to him eye-to-eye. "Soon--very soon--I will answer all your questions, Palden. But right now, you must trust me when I tell you that it is most important that we leave this place *immediately*," she said, a grave look filling her face. "And I need your help." It was something about the look in her eyes that made Palden realise that something was wrong; *terribly* wrong. Glancing over to the small table under the window he stared for a moment at a photograph of his mother. A photograph he'd always wondered about. She was standing there beside a foreign-looking man, a proud look on her face. He was a tall man with blond hair who wore a strange-looking brown-checked, fitted jacket and brown trousers.

Pembuti was smiling up at him; she wore a lovely long turquoise skirt, matched with a bright yellow blouse, and round her neck hung a large turquoise necklace. Palden smiled and in that moment felt an amazing love for his mother; her smile melting his heart. He then felt Ani-Dolma clutch his shoulder firmly, "*Please*, Palden, we must *go*! Bring the photograph if you like and put it in this bag!" He watched as Ani-Dolma quickly rushed round the room, throwing his clothes into a cloth sack.

"What about our picture of the Dalai Lama and the other special things on the table where we say our mantras? I must take them! Ama La will not forgive me if l leave them!" he whaled.

"Yes, bring those things as well. Put them in this bag—*quickly*!" she said, moving about the room frantically. "And when you've done that, take the bag and set it in the courtyard with the others. I've sent a few of the nuns to bring the horses in from the fields and they will return very soon. Then I want you to go to the kitchen and find Noma and ask her if our food supplies are ready." Noma, the kitchen-hand, could always be found somewhere near the kitchen, prepping food, emptying the rubbish, or generally tidying up--and was very grumpy by nature. Lifting the sack Ani-Dolma had helped him pack, Palden headed out of room—then stopped. He turned round. This room had been his home all his life; the room he'd shared with his Ama La. And he realised that he was about to lose this room, lose the only way of life he knew, and didn't even know where his mother was. And nothing would make sense until he understood why. Outside his room he bent down and rubbed Jalus behind the ears, who, as usual, was guarding the door. "Come, boy," he told his dog.

Out in the courtyard Palden felt the last rays of the afternoon sun shining down on him. They warmed him on the outside but on the inside he felt as though his whole world was crashing down. All the hustle and bustle of the nuns as they scurried about created feelings of fear; his once-perfect world was being invaded by chaos and all he wanted was his Ama La.

Now the nuns returned with a dozen horses and immediately went to work saddling them. Two yaks, already loaded with what Palden assumed were supplies, stood tethered to a rail. The nuns, normally calm, quiet, and slow-walking, were scurrying about in all directions with frantic intensity, carrying bags and provisions that were being lifting directly onto the backs of horses and yaks. Palden could not help but be drawn into the fear that seemed to be emanating from everyone within the nunnery walls. He walked to the centre of the courtyard and set his bag on the ground amongst the other sacks and baskets being loaded onto the animals. Suddenly a soft and gentle voice wafted up from behind.

"Hello, Palden," said Tenzin. (She'd been dreading seeing him after witnessing what had happened to his Ama La in Lhasa earlier that day.)

"Hi, Tenzin," he said politely. Then, "You went to Lhasa with Ama La today, so do you know why she has not returned?"

Tenzin ignored his plea. Looking down at the collection of bags and containers on the ground she said, "All packed for your journey?"

"Yes, I think so, but I do not even know why we are going!" Tenzin lowered her head and pretended not to have heard him. Palden then remembered that he was told to go to the kitchen and find Noma. "Are you coming with us, Tenzin?"

"Yes, Palden, I am." Palden nodded then turned and headed to the kitchen. There he found Noma shoving packages of foodstuffs into a basket.

"Well--out with it, Palden! What do you want?" Noma said in her usual crotchety tone, her overweight frame waddling its way towards Palden. "Come on—I do not have all day!"

"Uh . . . Ani-Dolma sent me to ask you about supplies."

"Well, *you* go back and tell Ani-Dolma that I cannot work any faster than I am! I am only one person! Everything will be ready when it is ready—and not before!" Glancing up at the boy, Noma could see that he'd been crying. She'd always told Ani-Dolma that Pembuti would bring trouble one day--and this was that day! She'd been right all along and was angry knowing that her life too would now change, as tonight she'd have to leave the nunnery for good and was too old (physically and emotionally) to make the long and hard journey the nuns were about to embark upon. She would now go and live with her sister, a day's ride away—and there was nothing more to it. The days serving the nuns was about to end. "Go back, now, Palden, and tell her what I said!"

As she looked into Palden's sad eyes, for the first time in many years she felt that her heart would burst. "Come here, boy," she said. As Palden came near, she reached out her fleshy arms and pulled him to her bosom, and holding him close—so close he could hardly breathe— smiled and said in a near whisper, "I will miss you, Palden, miss you very much!" She then spun him round and nudged him towards the door. "You go on now, Palden, *go!*" (Had he turned round in that instant he would have seen a tear stream down her cheeks.) Palden slowly shuffled out of the kitchen and walked back along the long corridor to the main entrance. Putting his weight against the heavy door he walked out into the cool late-afternoon air and made his way to where Ani-Dolma was busily loading bags onto their pack animals.

"Noma says you will get the provisions when they are ready," Palden reported. Ani-Dolma expected this response but felt it was important for Palden to say his goodbyes, and knew it would distract him from all of his questions—at least for the moment.

"There, Palden, your horse is ready and so are we--*almost*. If Noma would only hurry up with the provisions!" With that she saw Noma approaching, lumbering with two large hessian sacks, one in each meaty hand. "At last!" cried Ani-Dolma in a shrill voice. (Noma just kept silent.) As the sacks were securely tethered to one of the waiting yaks, Ani-Dolma took Palden by the arm and said, "Get on your horse, we have to leave now." Seeing Palden's growing look of fear she knelt down and said, "Palden, listen. The Chinese could well be on their way and you cannot be found here! *We* cannot be found here! And that is all I can say for now."

"But, where are we going?" Palden asked. "And how will Ama La find us?"

"We will talk more about this along the way--just get *moving*!" insisted Ani-Dolma.

Palden did as he was told. Mounting his horse and taking the reins, with a dig of his heels into the horse's flank and a tug at the right rein, he turned the horse towards the large wooden gates, now standing open. But then suddenly Jalus came bounding out to be included—causing Palden to jump off his horse and run to him.

"Palden, I know you are upset, but we must get going!" said Ani-Dolma from her mount.

"Jalus must come with us--he *must*!" cried Palden.

"Palden, we will have enough trouble feeding and caring for ourselves on this journey, without looking after Jalus."

"But, *I* will look after him! I will share my food with him!"

"Do you want what is best for Jalus?"

"Well, yes, I do!"

"Then you must understand that what is best for *you* is not what is best for *him*. And I know this is a hard lesson for a boy your age, but you have been learning the mantras. And you know that we must all look at our suffering and face our losses, understand our losses, and experience the feelings of our losses. Jalus belongs here at the nunnery. This is what is most important! You have become too attached to Jalus—and someday you will understand why this is not good. But now, we must *go!*"

Palden wanted so desperately for his Ama La to suddenly appear; just come riding up and say that it was all a terrible mistake. Climbing back on his horse Palden slumped forward, his eyes frightened, searching the faces round him, looking for someone to hold him and tell him that it was going to be alright. But he saw only resign on their sullen faces. Just then on the distant horizon he saw a woman on horseback. He called out to her--but there was no answer--so he called again and again with greater desperation. He could see her—and was *sure* it was his Ama La--but the figure was so far away and drawing no nearer. Just about to spur his animal and ride out to meet her he shouted, "Ama La! Ama La!" When a hand touched his arm it startled him—and he realised that he'd had his eyes closed. He'd seen his mother only in his mind. "It is time, Palden," Ani-Dolma said.

Chapter 3

⎯⎰

Ani-Dolma knew just where she was to deliver the boy, having been given a letter from Lama Kunchen on his last visit to the nunnery. He'd instructed her to take Palden to Tsurphu Monastery, telling her that she'd know exactly when the time was right. And Ani-Dolma knew beyond a shadow of a doubt that the time was *now*. With this letter tucked safely inside her warm yak-skin jacket, she sighed: such a long and arduous journey ahead, fraught with many perils. Added to that, they would only be able to travel perhaps ten miles per day--fifteen under the best conditions. Unable to exceed more than ten miles per day without suffering, the yaks had been lightly loaded, Ani-Dolma having instructed the nuns to pack only the minimum equipment as she wanted to reach Tsurphu Monastery as quickly as humanly possible.

"Please, Ani-Dolma, can you tell me where are we going?" pleaded Palden, now surmising that their destination was a guarded secret.

"All I can tell you for now is that I am taking you to His Holiness the Sixteenth Karmapa at Tsurphu Monastery, about sixty miles from here," she said. Having made this journey several times in the past, Ani-Dolma knew that the monastery was about seventeen miles up Dowo Lung Valley, on the north side of the river. They would first have to head for the town of Gurum, in Doilungdêqên County, in the Tibet Autonomous Region. Tsurphu Monastery is nestled in the centre of a valley facing south with high mountains. "We have a long journey ahead of us, Palden," Ani-Dolma said.

Ani-Dolma rode beside Palden while the other eight nuns and Tenzin rode behind. The two large yaks, carrying most of the provisions, brought up the rear of this little caravan. As the horses picked their way along the narrow stony paths, the flat fields seemed never-ending; the mountains never growing closer, their journey's end beyond sight. Immense peaks jutted out from continually-rising ground and flat tablelands like terraced gardens extending from the foot of these peaks like broad steps reaching higher and higher; some rich with rare herbs. As the caravan held a slow rhythmic pace, Ani-Dolma decided it was time to tell Palden the story Tenzin had told her earlier that day. Though Tenzin was known as an excitable young girl, who lived in Lhasa and knew Pembuti as well as most of the nuns at the nunnery, her honesty was unquestionable:

"Palden, I have something to tell you." Palden nodded, sensing that it had to do with his Ama La. "And, this is not going to be easy to hear." Again Palden nodded, as Ani-Dolma took a deep breath. "As you know, Tenzin was with your Ama La today, in Lhasa. And something terrible happened. As they went about their shopping, a Chinese soldier grabbed your Ama La and dragged her into a back passageway. Tenzin tried to help her by pulling the soldier away, but he was too strong. He struck her and knocked her to the ground."

"But--is Ama La okay?" begged Palden, fear rising in his eyes.

"Yes, she is, Palden, but there is more. It seems that just as the Chinese soldier turned his attention back to Ama La, a Khampa warrior was riding by and heard her screams, and went to take a closer look. When he saw the Chinese soldier attacking your Ama La he rushed to save her--the soldier then pushing Pembuti to the ground next to Tenzin. Tenzin saw the warrior draw his knife from his belt and plunge it into the Chinese soldier's chest--the soldier falling to the ground, dying from the wound. Then," continued Ani-Dolma, "the Khampa warrior pulled Ama La and Tenzin to their feet and told them that they would have to leave Lhasa quickly before the Chinese Army arrived. Tenzin knew that she and Ama La and the Khampa warrior were all in grave danger now from the Chinese. They would most certainly be severely punished for killing the Chinese soldier--imprisoned or even shot. And they knew that anyone who helped or hid them would also suffer punishment from the Chinese. So you see, Palden, they had no choice. They could not return to the nunnery. They had to run."

"*Run?* What do you mean, *run?* Run *where?*"

"Tenzin came back to the nunnery to tell us what had happened, and that Ama La had fled with the Khampa warrior." Palden had no idea how to feel about what he'd just been told. Tears welled up in his sad eyes. "By now they are far away, hiding with other freedom fighters somewhere safe," said Ani-Dolma.

"But, she can come back soon? I mean—she can find us and we can all live together again?"

Ani-Dolma shook her head. "No, Palden, I am afraid it will never be safe for her. You see, even Tibetan people can be Chinese informants. They sell or trade information to the Chinese about their own people. And sometimes the Chinese force people to give them information—even if they have to torture them to get it! And one thing we know for certain is that the Chinese will not give up until they find Ama La, Tenzin, and the Khampa warrior who helped them, and that we nuns are not safe for allowing you and your mother to live with us. This is why we had to leave so quickly--before the Chinese Army came looking."

Palden's heart sank as he realised all the pain he'd brought to the nuns he loved so dearly by his very presence. And knowing that his Ama La was miles and miles away by now, deep sadness set in and tormented his lonely, breaking heart. How could he ever know happiness and joy again?

As they neared the top of the long winding track that led to the snow-peaked mountain, their attention was drawn to the sound of gun shots. They reigned their horses, turned and looked back towards the nunnery. They watched in horror as billows of smoke rose up from within the old wooden walls, blotting out the night sky. "Jalus?!" wailed Palden. "What about Jalus and the other nuns?!"

"Run, run!" he heard Ani-Dolma say beneath her breath--the words caught in the wind and flung back--as rows and rows of colour-ful prayer flags on the roofs now disappeared into a massive cloud of smoke. Waves of fear shot up and down Palden's legs; he felt physically weak and thought he may fall off his horse! He shivered as he saw the tears rolling down the nuns' faces for the twenty nuns left behind who'd refused to leave; too old or too frail to travel. Ani-Dolma had tried her best to convince them all to leave, but most refused to believe that the Chinese would be so cruel as to drive them out of their home and place of worship. Ani-Dolma cried-- knowing that their bodies would forever remain where they'd fallen within the rubble of their sacred nunnery—now reducing to ashes. It crossed her mind that the Chinese may have taken some of the nuns captive, but quickly wiped that thought from her mind. What she'd heard of Chinese prison camps and how they treated female prisoners was more than she could not bear.

Ani-Dolma sighed and turned back to face the mountain towering above them, beckoning the others to follow. She gently kicked her horse into action. Slowly the party picked up the pace and resumed their long and arduous journey towards Tsurphu Monastery. Palden complained that his head hurt and his stomach heaved, and he was having difficulty breathing. Ani-Dolma was concerned that he was beginning to feel the effects of altitude sickness (as several of them were), but knew they had to press on without delay for their own safety. (They had no idea if the Chinese would follow or if there would be more Chinese soldiers along their path ahead—but had to anticipate the worst.) She retrieved a sprig of a certain herb from her saddle bag and handed it to him. "Here, chew this, Palden. It will help you to feel better." As he chewed he watched as Ani-Dolma fingered her prayer beads and murmured soft invocations: "*Om, mani padme hum . . . Om, mani padme hum . . .*" over and over. He remembered being told that this phrase meant, "Jewel in the Lotus."

After several hours, Ani-Dolma brought her horse to a halt and pointed to a nearby stream. The tinkling water flowed along the land then rushed over the edge of a cliff—falling thousands of feet below. (So far below that the sound of it crashing was lost.) "There is good pasture for our livestock and water for cooking, and plenty of yak dung with which to light our fire," she said. As the nuns dismounted and steadied their feet, Ani-Dolma dispensed the necessary instructions: "Firstly we must get the fires burning, so three of you go and gather rocks and place them in a large circle for a makeshift hearth. Three of you gather dung, and three of you, water. It is important that we work quickly and carefully, and accustom our eyes to the dark of the night sky."

Before long, with the aid of a goat-skin bellows, a roaring fire was started. Ani-Dolma and Tenzin then began to erect their small waterproof cotton tents, with Palden in charge of handing them the wooden pegs that secured the guy ropes to the hard, dusty earth. The tents were set close to one other and formed a half circle just close enough to the fire to be able to use the fire's light to see and glean a little warmth. Now as each of the nuns completed their tasks and night fell hard, they sat by the fire and drank freshly brewed butter tea and ate *tsampa*. The stars twinkled in the clear dark sky above and they knew the time by the appearance of the various constellations; they were their guides here— and in everyday life. Palden yawned. "Go to your tent now, Palden," Ani-Dolma told him. "We have another long day of travel tomorrow." Doing as instructed, Palden relaxed his aching, weary body on his hard felt mat and pulled a yak-wool blanket round him, and instantly fell asleep.

Chapter 4

In the morning the group awoke to a lovely, sunny day. They would be warm today, thought Palden. He breathed in the scent from the beautiful flowers as it wafted up to his nostrils. He watched the dragonflies with their shimmering wings as they flew quickly by--darting in and out of the flowers and bushes--heading towards the river. This was indeed a wonderful, calm and quiet place. Here they rested for two days before plodding on higher and higher--over crevices and vast ravines.

For the next four days they journeyed, riding most of the day and setting up camp at night. By the fourth day they were quite weary and worn; it had begun to snow, their supplies were running low, and they were in desperate need of rest. Then in the distance there appeared an encampment of nomad tents, with Palden relieved to see their prayer flags blowing in the breeze (although their colours were nearly obliterated by fiercely blowing snow). He'd not seen prayer flags since leaving the nunnery and his spirits were now lifted as he knew these flags were carrying their blessings out into the universe. He felt certain that now everything would go back to as it had been before . . .

"Stop!" called Ani-Dolma as she pulled back on her horse's reins. "Listen to those dogs barking!" Palden's ears pricked up--it sounded like a huge, ferocious pack of wild dogs. Ani-Dolma knew that if these animals were Mastiffs they could attack with little provocation as they were used as guard dogs by the nomads and were very good at their jobs—and potentially lethal to outsiders trying to enter their camp uninvited. Suddenly through the swirling, violent snow there appeared a massive man with a rifle slung over his shoulder, riding out towards them. He had long shining black hair and his cheeks glowed red with broken veins marking time spent herding animals in the gales and snowstorms in the high altitudes. He wore loose woollen garments tied round his waist with a belt braided from thick black yak hair. No words were spoken (it would have been too hard to hear in the winds that had whipped up and begun to howl round them) but he gestured for them to follow him into their encampment.

As the party entered the nomad camp, they saw that the loud, aggressive barking was coming from only three large Mastiffs, who were less-than-keen to welcome them. Palden was glad these huge dogs were chained up outside the first black yak-hair tent they came to, which by now was almost invisible--cloaked in snow. Two men appeared from the tent and beckoned them to dismount, the horses then led away to the stable, one man saying they would be fed and watered. Their host now held back the tent flap and gestured for them to enter. As they stepped inside the safety and warmth of the tent, they were greeted by a middle-aged woman who motioned for them to come and sit round the fire in the centre of the room. Shivering and throwing off their wet jackets, the group rubbed their hands together as they sat on the yak-skinned cushions by the welcoming heat.

The first thing Palden noticed was that there was an altar at the far end of the tent, where seven silver bowls filled with water set. Incense, flowers, and fruit had been set beside the silver bowls, placed in a precise row beside religious images, butter lamps, bells, and offerings to the Buddha. Palden knew well the routine, the ritual: he knew from his experience at the nunnery that each night they would empty and wipe clean the bowls then turn them upside down one atop the other, ready to be refilled in the morning. And as his mind flashed back to the nunnery, he could hear the dogs barking outside, bringing a tear to his stinging, wind-blown face. He wanted his Ama La and Jalus there with him now.

The middle-aged woman set freshly made *momos* (dumplings filled with yak meat), *tsampa*, and hot buttered tea down beside them. Digging in, Palden couldn't remember when he'd tasted food so delicious. They all sat round the fire and ate their fill, talking little. Finally the man who'd invited them in spoke: "My name is Samten and this is my wife, Jamyang. The weather is very bad tonight, you will stay here at least until morning. Where are you headed?"

"I am Ani-Dolma and we are headed to Tsurphu Monastery," she said, smiling at her host. "I am taking Palden" (she nodded towards the boy) "to meet with the Karmapa."

"The Karmapa?" replied Samten, glancing towards his wife.

"Yes, I have been charged by the late Lama Kunchen with seeing the boy safely there."

"But--*why* do I need to see him?" said Palden--instantly aware that he'd talked out of turn.

Ani-Dolma smiled at the boy's impertinence; understanding his need for answers. Even so, understanding the essence of His Holiness the Sixteenth Karmapa Rangjung Rigpe Dorje would be difficult to explain to a small boy—even one as bright as Palden. Seeking to pacify him she said, "Your great-uncle believed that you should go to Tsurphu to meet with him when the proper time arrived, and that time has arrived."

Recognising that Palden was far from satisfied with that answer, Samten said, "Oh, it is an honour to even be in the *presence* of the His Holiness the Sixteenth Karmapa! He is such an extraordinary man! And you will have the chance to *meet* with him! That is truly a great and wonderful thing, Palden! Most wonderful!" Palden looked to Samten for further reassurance. "You know, my grandmother lived at Den Khok, near Derge, where the Karmapa was born!" Samten said. "She actually knew his parents, who were from a noble family, and she served in their home, called 'Althup.' And I heard her tell the story of his birth many times! They say that while still in his mother's womb he could be heard reciting the 'Mantra of Loving Eyes.' Can you imagine! And when he did, many rainbows suddenly filled the sky! So indeed, the Karmapa is quite extraordinary!" Palden smiled; a look of relief coming to his face. "But, enough for now! My brothers and I will show you all to one of our spare tents. They are lighting a warm fire for you there as we speak."

Ani-Dolma thought for a moment she was going to cry. It had been such a strain for her to get everyone this far, to keep them safe and find their way through the now extreme weather conditions. She said to Samten, "We are so grateful to you. . . so *very* grateful."

"Please, finish your meal and I will personally take you to your tent," smiled Samten. Ani-Dolma could no longer hold back the tears. "Bless you!"

The next morning Palden woke after a fitful night of strange and frightening dreams to the clanging of bells and the echoes of voices. Tenzin was standing over him. "Up you lazy boy!" Ani-Dolma and the other nuns had already left the tent, so Palden quickly rose from his sleeping mat and threw on his warm clothes, pulled aside the tent flap and stepped outside--into deep snow up to his knees. Conditions were too treacherous to set out so it had been decided that they'd take advantage of Samten and Jamyang's hospitality a while longer. But after spending a few fun days with the nomads, Palden felt he now belonged with them. He'd made friends with the dogs and some of the children and begged Ani-Dolma to let him stay. But Ani-Dolma had a duty to complete; she had a five-year-old boy to deliver to His Holiness the 16th Karmapa (along with a special letter) and this she was going to do without fail.

As the nuns busied themselves cooking and cleaning and keeping the fire in their tent roaring, Palden went with Samten to the stables to help with the cleaning and feeding of the animals. "Samten," said Palden, "would it be alright if I lived here with you? I really love it here!"

Samten thought a moment how best to dissuade Palden from deviating from the path chosen for him. "Palden, you are young with a long life ahead of you. Although there is much to love here, there is much that cannot be learned here. Your future is not here in the wilderness but out there in the big world where there are many different lifestyles and many ways of living. One day you will come to understand why I say these words to you . . . Now, hand me that hay fork as we have much to do before we lose the light."

But, no, Palden didn't understand. He just wanted to belong somewhere. To feel that he was wanted. And at least for the moment, he did. So he worked hard all that day, stopping only for some roasted *tsampa* and hot butter tea. And in the late afternoon he helped gather all the dried dung which was kept in a large shed outside, then stacked up inside the tents within reach of the fires.

In the evening, Palden would lie curled up on a large cushion by the roaring fire inside their tent, listening to Ani-Dolma and the nuns chat amongst themselves and drink hot *cha*. Their talk focused round their journey and the Karmapa and the Black Crown Ceremony he often performed. Palden had now become quite intrigued by the Karmapa and felt that he was somehow *magical*. His mother had kept a picture of the Karmapa on her alter back at the nunnery, but he could not remember being told anything about him.

" Ani-Dolma, what is the *Black Crown Ceremony*? Is it . . . *magical?*" Palden wanted to know.

"Well, Palden, devotees believe that the *Black Crown* is the physical embodiment of the aura that surrounds the Karmapa. As you learned in your lessons, the Karmapa is the leader of the Karma Kagyu sect of Buddhism, which goes back more than nine hundred years." Palden's eyes widened. "And the Black Crown is the symbol of his enlightenment."

"But--" Palden attempted to say--

"It is late now, so off to bed with you."

As he lay on his mat, his eyes grew heavy; warm and snug under the yak-skin rug. As he drifted into deep sleep he imagined that he could see four black crows hovering above him, each holding one corner of a large black feather blanket in their beaks. Slowly they lowered the blanket until it came to rest upon his body . . .

Chapter 5

After a good night's sleep, Palden woke and got dressed, then hurried outside to find out where all the nuns had gone. He then saw that all their horses were saddled and ready to move on. Ani-Dolma emerged from Samten's tent: "Come, Palden, eat breakfast as quickly as you can. The snow has stopped and it is a lovely sunny day, and if we hurry we can make Tsurphu by early afternoon."

As the party rode out from the nomad encampment that morning, Ani-Dolma rode alongside Palden. She worried for the boy, so young and had already experienced so much loss. Now resigned to their destination, Palden asked, " Ani-Dolma, what *is* Tsurphu?" Ani-Dolma was pleased that he was now taking an interest in his destiny.

"Tsurphu Monastery is one of the most important Tibetan Buddhist sites in the whole world, Palden, with a very long history. It was founded by Düsum Khyenpa, the First Karmapa Lama, long, long ago in 1159, after first making offerings to the local protectors, the *dharmapalas*, and territorial divinities. Some thirty years later he revisited the site and established his main seat of power there. Now it is the seat of His Holiness the Sixteenth Karmapa, but there are many monks residing there, too."

Palden didn't understand what made the site so important, but he knew that if the Karmapa lived there, it must be a very special place.

Riding along a rocky shelf, Ani-Dolma warned the others of the dangerous down-drought which had now begun to push her horse sideways (one wrong move and any one of them could be blown over the crumbling ledge), instructing everyone to dismount and carefully lead the horses and yaks. As they shuffled slowly along the ledge their long robes were pressed tight against their backs, billowing out in front, pushing them--almost forcing them to run--while their bodies were pummeled with small stones and bits of debris as the wind shot up with gale-force speed from the crevices near the edge. Palden shuddered as he heard the shriek of the wind sweeping along the valley floor far below and Ani-Dolma was frightened for Palden; she worried that he would be lifted off his feet and carried straight up into the air and swept off—cast downward to the rocks at the base of the crevice. The mountains here seemed unending and eternal.

The group pushed onward through this seeming *lunar* landscape, finding it harder and harder to safely navigate and find sure-footing. For what seemed hours the nuns and Palden fought their way through the dangerous terrain until finally they saw Tsurphu Monastery situated in the shelter of a scrub-covered hill on the north side of a high, bare and narrow valley. In front of it flowed a small tributary of the Tolung River. Palden noticed behind the array of monastery buildings a wide ravine littered with very large boulders, stones, and clumps of green shrubs that added colour to the rather dull and grey scenery. As his eyes followed the course of this ravine up the mountainside, he saw a blanket of white fluffy clouds obscuring the top of the mountain range.

"We will head in this direction so that we can cross the river by that wooden bridge there," said Ani-Dolma, pointing to the right. A short distance from Tsurphu was a fast-flowing river that eventually led into panoramic alpine valleys and Palden watched the river as it crashed over rocks and boulders, its white foam racing onwards as it circumnavigated the monastery then proceeded onwards along windswept Yangpachen Valley. Invigorated now by the sight of the monastery, they pushed on with renewed resolve.

True to Ani-Dolma's prediction (and due in no small way to her guidance) by early afternoon they arrived safely at Tsurphu Monastery. At the entrance, Ani-Dolma and the rest of the party dismounted their horses, with Ani-Dolma approaching a monk busy sweeping the road with a large horsehair brush. She introduced herself and they talked for a few moments, then the monk scurried away in the direction of the main building. A short time later a group of monks could be seen approaching. As they neared, all the monks but one stopped and stepped to one side, who came forward, bowed before Ani-Dolma, and said, "Tashi Delek." Ani-Dolma recognised him as the Karmapa and returned the greeting. He said, "Ani-Dolma, please tell me what you are doing here and how we can help."

"Karmapa, I have here a letter from a mutual good friend, Lama Kunchen. He gave this to me before he died, instructing me to bring this to you when the time was right. Our nunnery was over-run and destroyed by the Chinese and we have fled. As you know, these are very hard times."

"Indeed, Ani-Dolma, times are changing. I have just returned from Palpung Sherab Ling where I gave lifetime secret transmissions of protector practices, and today counselled the monks on this subject." Ani-Dolma knew that he, the Karmapa, had been enthroned at Palpung Sherab Ling, and that it was indeed a wonderful place.

"In what state is the monastery, now?" asked Ani-Dolma.

"For the moment it remains a place of spiritual enlightenment and creativity. But I am greatly concerned about the thousands of sacred texts and the precious art collection there because I know that it is only a matter of time before Palpung will be destroyed by Maoist troops."

"So, you think Palpung is in danger, Karmapa?"

"There are thousands of *thangkas*, as well as Situ Rinpoche's Karma Gadri paintings, his glorious union of study and practice. We must do what we can to preserve our Dharma," he said. Calling to one of the monks standing nearby, the Karmapa instructed him to find the nuns refreshments and to tend to their horses. "Now," said the Karmapa, "the letter?" Ani-Dolma handed the Karmapa the letter, who scanned it quickly then pointed to Palden who, like the rest of the group, had dismounted. "Come here, boy," said the Karmapa. Palden did as he was bade and as the Karmapa gazed down at him Palden felt a sense of calm come over him--his fatigue, his worries, his pain and fear seeming to vanish. The Karmapa smiled at Ani-Dolma and said, "He is now where he is meant to be. I will take him under my direct guidance, Ani-Dolma. I thank you for bringing him to me."

As the Karmapa's hand rested on Palden's head, for a split second it was as if a window had opened in his mind and he could see things he'd never seen before. Scenes from other places and times flashed before him, none of which he could remember experiencing. It was as if in that moment time stood still and a stillness overtook him; as if he'd suddenly grown up and knew that he wanted to be near this monk, and wanted to learn from him. Now, he too knew that he was where he should be and for the first time since leaving the nunnery, felt complete peace and belonging. The Karmapa then instructed that shelter be found for Ani-Dolma and her group. He gazed directly into Ani-Dolma's eyes:

"You have done remarkably well, Ani-Dolma. But, it is time now to pass the responsibility on. To that young girl over there," the Karmapa said, pointing to Tenzin.

"Yes," agreed Ani-Dolma. "You are, of course, right. 'Tenzin' is the girl's name and she has matured considerably since we left the nunnery. Not long ago she had no cares and had a rather wild temperament. But over our journey she has come to learn our ways, our practices, and has begun to study our doctrines. I am much pleased with the changes in her and maybe one day she will become a nun. Time will tell."

"Tenzin," called the Karmapa. Tenzin sheepishly approached. "Tenzin, the time has come for you to take over for Ani-Dolma and lead your party to safety." (Tenzin looked a bit frightened at the prospect.) "Ani-Dolma will remain here for much needed rest. Remember all she has taught you."

Tenzin smiled at the Karmapa (it was hard not to be caught-up in his infectious smile)--but was stunned. *Surely one of the other nuns would be a better choice to lead them!* she thought. After all, they were spiritually trained, more experienced, and more intuitive than she. She was only a mere girl from Lhasa with little life experience—and less with Buddhism—and had never been charged with such a monumental task. But she said nothing—knowing not to question the Karmapa's insight and wisdom. With no further thought she found herself agreeing to lead the party to the best of her ability.

With that the Karmapa suggested that the nuns could rest outside the monastery in local accommodation and wished Tenzin and the nuns a safe and rewarding onward journey. Palden clung to Ani-Dolma's skirts, his heart ached that he was now going to be truly on his own. Ani-Dolma patted his head, saying, "You will enjoy being here, Palden. Do not fight the teachings you receive. Welcome them with open arms and your journey in life will be well-blessed."

Tenzin bent down face-to-face with Palden, tears welling-up in her eyes. She felt responsible for him somehow; she was overwhelmed with love and compassion for this young boy. Palden was embarrassed by this show of affection and could see that Tenzin was crying. As he stole a glance at Ani-Dolma, she hung her head, turned to walk away saying, "Good bye, Palden. I pray we will meet again one day. Until then, be a good boy."

Palden's eyes beamed. "I love you!" he said to Tenzin as a tear slipped from his eye and rolled down his face. He then felt a hand in his as the Karmapa led him away into the heart of Tsurphu Monastery.

Chapter 6

PASSING THROUGH A NARROW GATE between the high walls surrounding the monastery, Palden saw a wide paved courtyard with buildings on three sides, the west side open to the elements. This courtyard reminded him of the home he'd left back in the Lhasa nunnery. In the centre of the courtyard stood a stone pillar he later found out dated back to the reign of Ralpachan and described the founding of a temple at Changbu in Tolung. The Karmapa led Palden up a flight of steep stone steps that led to a doorway covered by a chain-mail curtain. As they reached the top, the curtain immediately swung open. "Please ask Rinpoche to come here as soon as he can," said the Karmapa to the monk who manned the curtain. Rinpoche had accompanied the Karmapa to Tsurphu and would later return to his own monastery, Lho Tsawagang Drolma Lhakang. The Karmapa led Palden into a quiet room. "Now, Palden, we must get started," he said. "From this time on you will live here at Tsurphu under my guidance. First, I will have Lama Tashi prepare a preliminary pre-life horoscope for you."

Palden was instantly fascinated by the room. It was full of relics, *thangkas*, paintings, written texts, and images of the Dalai Lama. The Karmapa grew intrigued as he watched the boy survey the array of objects, Palden's eyes eventually coming to rest on a bell and *dorge* set on the small wooden alter beside the main alter by the window. Palden picked it up in his right hand and smiled. "You like that," said the Karmapa.

"Yes," said Palden smiling, "I do." Then while holding the *dorge* in his right hand he picked up a heavy amulet suspended on a red ribbon with the other. He tried it on his neck. The Karmapa smiled. "Who does this belong to?" Palden asked.

"It once belonged to a lama I used to know quite well, Palden. His name was Lama Kunchen." (The sound of the name brought Palden to a complete stand-still.) "Lama Kunchen--your great-uncle! He wrote the letter which Ani-Dolma brought to me today. That amulet came into his possession, a present from a British soldier." Soft footfalls could now be heard approaching.

"Ah, Rinpoche," said the Karmapa as a small, heavy-set man entered the room, "please meet *Palden*. Palden, you will come under the direct instruction of Rinpoche, who has over the years received instruction from me. He is a certified teacher of Tibetan medicine. Rinpoche, this is Lama Kunchen's great-nephew, Palden," said the Karmapa. Rinpoche caught himself staring--his eyes drawn to the amulet that hung round the boy's neck. He'd seen the amulet many years before—worn by another. Memories of times gone by flashed before him and he remembered clearly the story of the circumstances of how the amulet had come to a new owner.

"Lama Kunchen, you say. Yes indeed, a most kind, wise, and worldly man! He taught me much as we travelled together round the country performing religious ceremonies and treating the ill," said Rinpoche. With that, Rinpoche bowed and took his leave. Metok, a young novice monk, now appeared in the doorway.

"Ah, Metok, good, please look after Palden. Show him round and make sure he has a bed and space for his possessions." Turning to Palden he said, "Go now and I will see you tomorrow." As Palden returned the *dorge* and amulet to the altar the Karmapa smiled and said,

"No, Palden, they are for you to keep, Palden." Palden smiled in disbelief. He was happy to have the sacred items as they somehow brought comfort and, for the first time in a long time, he had something that belonged to *him*.

Late that evening Palden was called to visit a very sick Ani-Dolma. Fearful to see her he wept as he sat at her bedside and held her hand, begging her not to die. He recited his mantras over and over but Ani-Dolma was exhausted; she'd fulfilled her final duty. She'd delivered the boy to the Karmapa and knew that Tenzin would now pick up the leadership mantle, leading the nuns to safety to begin a new life. Ani-Dolma was too tired and too old to travel and knew she'd only hinder their progress. At the first hint of day as the blackness of night cracked with pink, Ani-Dolma passed on. Palden held her hands and sobbed.

As the days rolled one into the next, Palden slowly fell into a routine at Tsurphu Monastery. Each morning at 5:00 he and the other monks were awakened by the sounding of horns by three or more monks on the roof garden of the monastery. The drone of the deep bass awoke his senses, preparing him and the other monks for the day ahead. These sounds balanced and calmed his mind, body, and soul as he learned to match his breath with the deep slow pulse of the horns.

When Rinpoche was away from Tsurphu, Palden's tutor was Yonten, a wise and knowledgeable lama who was kindly towards Palden. As Palden liked Yonten, he looked forward to these lessons with great anticipation. On this day they were together in mid-lesson in Lama Yonten's study: "Palden, you will learn over the months all about sound and how we can understand the sounds of our body, and reproduce them clearly. Once you hear these sounds, you will never forget them."

"So, what *is* sound, and what is important about it?" Palden wanted to know.

"*Sound*, for us, is a means of understanding how our bodies work and at what level of health our body is currently in. For example, have you ever laid your head upon your pillow then at the verge of sleep you hear the beating of your heart? . . . and the breathing of your lungs?" Palden contorted his face in thought. "Think, Palden, when we are in the temple and the sounds of the deep bass drum, close your eyes and imagine that the drum throbs out the rhythm of life itself. Then listen to the other instruments and link them to the sounds of your own body! Listen to the faint rushing of the blood through your veins and arteries, the muted whisper of your breath in your lungs, the gurgling of body fluids, all the other *creaking*, *squeaks*, and *rumbles* which make the music of life itself! These are the sounds of your body!"

Palden nodded his understanding. Smiled.

"In the Lamasery of the State Oracle, they put the medium into a trance using some of these sounds, and then he is entered by a spirit. Now, think of these sounds as *colour*. *Colour* surrounds us in our everyday lives. And think of nature's elements--earth, air, fire, and water--all of which support us each and every day. You will learn their importance, Palden, over the following months and years. But that's enough for one day! Off with you to find Rigsang! It is time to begin your chores!"

Palden headed for the kitchen. His first task most days was to clean the large stove of all the ash, then relight it. (This job held great responsibility.) Then he set about dusting the halls, after which he would find Lobsang and help with a more practiced job, the cleaning of the temple. There he would assist with changing all the water-offering bowls, then ensure that all the statues were spotless (with extreme care and attention to the precise placing of all the statues), as well as the musical instruments. And then the seating--even the cushions themselves--had to follow a specific method of cleaning and placement. Some days Palden would help out in the gardens, tend the goats and yaks, or help with the general maintenance of the monastery—all over and above his Buddhist practices and lessons. (Usually Palden would fall into bed exhausted by 9:00 in the evening and before he knew it--it was 4:30 in the morning and he was being called awake to start another day.)

"Palden, have you finished with the cushions?" said Rigsang. "It is nearly time for service." Within minutes, monks moved silently into the temple and sat down in the lotus style on the square cushions set two high, which raised them some ten-to-twelve inches off the floor. They sat in double rows, facing each other in pairs; the walls surrounding them brilliantly painted with deity images. The deep voice of the musical leader began to sing out the first passages. At the end of each passage, Palden listened as the leader's voice sank lower and lower until his lungs were emptied of air. Then all the monks droned their responses. Certain passages were accented by the beating of drums or the ringing of sweet-toned bells. The monks had to be extremely careful of their articulation as they believed that the discipline of a lamasery can be gauged by the clarity of its singing and accuracy of the music. Each day they recited their mantras over and over with the certainty that one day they would not need the help of the written texts.

As Palden sat with Lama Yonten he listened to one monk repeating, '*Om! mani pad-me Hum! Om! mani pad-me Hum!* Hail to the Jewel of the Lotus! Hail to the Higher Self, the Spiritual Self! There is no death.' Lama Yonten commented, "As one sheds one's clothes at the end of day, Palden, or discards them when they are worn out, so does the spirit, or the energetic energy colour of the body. Death is rebirth. Dying is merely the act of being born in another plane of existence. Man, or the *spirit* of man, is eternal. The body is but the temporary garment that clothes the spirit, chosen according to the task at hand upon the Earth. Outward appearance does not matter, only the spirit within."

Later that day in his study, Lama Yonten resumed Palden's lessons, beginning, "Today, Palden, let us discuss *auras*, the energetic coloured outlines which surround all living things; our life-force. It is by the intensity of those energetic colours that we can deduce a person's health, integrity, and general state of evolution. The *aura*, remember, is the radiation of the inner life- force. At death the light fades as the energetic colour—or what some call the 'spirit'--leaves the body on its journey to the next stage of existence. This energetic colour drifts a little--perhaps dazed by the sudden shock of being free of the body—and may not be fully aware of what is occurring. This is why we lamas attend the dying, so that they may be informed of the stages through which they will pass at death. If this is neglected, the life-force, the personality, may be earthbound by desires of the flesh. It is the duty of the lamas to break these ties." He paused then continued:

"During our waking hours on Earth our personality is confined to the physical body, and unless one is trained, it is not possible to separate them. When we sleep it is only the physical body which needs rest, the energetic colour disengages itself. The personality and physical body maintain contact by means of a link some refer to as a 'silver cord.' The body stays alive so long as this *silver cord* is intact. At death the cord is severed as the energetic colour is born into another life, just as a baby's umbilical cord is severed to part it from its mother. Birth, to a baby, is death to the sheltered life it led within the mother's body. While the silver cord is intact, the personality is free to roam during sleep--or consciously, in the case of those specially trained."

Palden closed his eyes and imagined what the silver cord might look like.

"The roaming of the energetic colour produces *dreams*," Lama Yonten said, "which are impressions transmitted along the silver cord.

As the physical mind receives them they are *rationalised* to fit in with one's Earthly beliefs--"

"*Rational*--?" Palden interrupted.

"Yes, Palden. *Rationalised*. The mind takes these impressions and finds ways to fit them into what we believe. Our view of how we see the world, or within the framework of what we know to be possible or probable." (Palden thought he understood—somewhat.) Lama Yonten resumed his train of thought:

"Sometimes in dreams we recall meeting with a distant friend or relative, and it comes as no surprise when they hear from that person soon after. With those who are *untrained*, the memory is often distorted and the result is an illogical dream or nightmare." (Palden now sat wide-eyed, taking in every word.) "In Tibet we learn about 'out-of-body' travel, and understand that the whole process is within our control. In this process, the *personality* is caused to leave the physical body--though still connected by the silver cord--and one can travel where one wills, and as quickly as one can think! Just imagine, Palden!" (Palden's eyes grew large.) "But if the individual is not properly trained they can experience an emotional or physical *shock*. This is usually a violent awakening by a sudden, inexplicable jerk to the consciousness. This is when the energetic colour is jerked back down the silver cord, and back into the physical body. When this takes place, the energetic colour is floating many feet above the body like a hot air balloon tethered to a long rope! Sometimes an external noise can cause the energetic colour to return to the physical body too quickly! When this occurs the physical body awakens suddenly--and there is the terrifying feeling that one has fallen off a cliff--and awakened just before they hit the bottom!" Although Palden didn't understand everything being explained, he liked the idea of leaving his body to travel whenever he wanted to—shivering at the idea of falling off a cliff!

Lama Yonten continued. "It is also part of our belief that the *prob-abilities* of the future can be foretold. To us, *divination*, by whatever method, is a science and can be trusted as *true*. And we believe in astrology—the movement of the stars, planets, and heavens. But always remember, Palden: *No* psychic power may be used for personal gain, for worldly ambition, or as proof of the reality of such powers! Only in this way can those not so gifted be protected."

Palden nodded in recognition. He knew he'd never use any *psychic power* he had to benefit only himself—though he wasn't really sure what *psychic power* was. But that was just one small detail because Palden loved his lessons. He loved the *magic* behind the teaching. He could indeed see colour round people and knew he could travel outside his body because he'd experienced it many times (though he'd hesitated to talk about it). But sadly, life for Palden was about to change again.

Palden had been living at the monastery not quite four months when a breathless lama came rushing in and told him to quickly pack his bags; that they were leaving. The Karmapa had made a decision to leave Tibet and felt that "the cause" (the protecting of the *Dharma*) was best served by moving to more peaceful settings. Palden became distraught at the thought of moving—*again*. (He'd just got used to Tsurphu and his new surroundings, and had become close with many of the monks there.) But he knew that the Karmapa must have good reasons for uprooting everyone, so he helped pack the most precious of the sacred statues, ritual items, relics, icons, paintings, books, and costumes that had been preserved at Tsurphu Monastery over the centuries. There was much to be done to prepare for the long journey.

Chapter 7

⤳

ON A BRIGHT SUNLIT DAY on the fourth day of the second month of the Earth Boar Year (1959) a huge entourage of one hundred and sixty lamas, monks, and laymen, as well as close relatives of the 16th Karmapa, left Tsurphu Monastery (the seat of the Karmapas since the 12th Century) and proceeded towards Bhutan to begin a most hazardous journey in freezing, icy winds, across snow-covered land. The exodus began quite early (about 2:00 a.m.), setting out by horse and foot and cart. It was a very typical journey in that in the daylight hours they travelled and in the evening they rested. And in each village they passed, people came running to receive blessings from His Holiness, who also gave ordinations.

Over the days that followed, the assemblage travelled in a land of fantastic contrasts. From a hot, humid atmosphere (such as they'd never before experienced) to a freezing fog-curtain--or ice, or snow, or blizzard (just a few yards away). But true to predictions made before leaving Tsurphu, the party arrived at Shabje Thang (in the Bumthang district of north Bhutan, near India) on the twenty-fifth day of the second month of the Earth Boar Year. Their sojourn had taken twenty-one days and all members of their group had survived. They were most cordially welcomed by Her Royal Highness Tsultrim Palmo, the Aunt of His Royal Highness the King, and many ministers and high-ranking officials of that government. At this time, discussions and negotiations began with the Government of India, considering future plans for the resettlement of the 16th Karmapa and his many followers, in their country.

The 16th Karmapa had given serious consideration as to where he could best create the conditions for the fulfillment of his mission to re-kindle and revitalize the Dharma, and decided on Sikkim (a landlocked Indian state located in the Himalayan mountains bordered by Nepal to the west, China's Tibet Autonomous Region to the north and east, and Bhutan to the east). The inhabitants of Sikkim were naturally inclined towards Buddhism, and the country was said to have been sanctified by a visit by Guru Padmasambhava in the distant past. Thus the Karmapa readily ac-cepted their kind invitation to establish himself in that country, and with the material and spiritual cooperation of Buddhists throughout the world, planned the creation of a Dharma Centre. And so it was that the 16th Karmapa led the party to Gangtok, the capital, where Sir Tashi Namgyal, the Maharaja, offered him the choice of several sites in his kingdom for the location of the new monastery; the Karmapa eventually selecting *Rumtek*. (There had already been a Karma Kagyu monastery there, built during the time of his ninth incarnation, Wangchuk Dorje.) The Maharaja graciously gifted seventy-four acres of land there to the Karmapa, in perpetuity.

Palden was now with heavy heart. He could go no further; he felt sick and the heat made him want to wither up and die. But that was not to be, just yet. Palden was standing with his tutor, Lama Yonten, when they and the other monks were directed into an official building where a lot of discussion and paperwork awaited everyone. Scratching his head, an official shuffled some papers and said, "Sikkim, you are heading to?" The monks all nodded in affirmation. "Well, there will be much work there for you . . . uh . . . food, shelter, a roof over your heads. You will like that," said the official.

With the final arrangements now in place, the group resumed their journey; some of the older monks and lamas rode on their horses, but most were on foot. Many carried heavy loads--as did the horses. Trekking along the dirt-track, stony road, the dust dried their throats, as did the humidity, but they still had the desire to chat:

"It must be amazing being the Karmapa," said Palden to Lama Yonten. "I would like to be him."

"Really, Palden? You would like to *be* him . . . or be *like* him?" (Palden could only shrug.) "Tell me, little one, how old are you now? About six, I should think."

"Yes, soon . . . I think." (The passage of time had had an unexpected effect on his memory.)

Lama Yonten smiled at the boy. "Tell me, Palden, do you believe in *magic?*"

"Well, not *really*. But, I think maybe the Karmapa is *magical*. And sometimes I *see* things--mists that turn into faces . . . black balls of air that swoop right at me . . ."

Again, Lama Yonten smiled at the boy. "Magic, spirituality, the supernatural—it is all interwoven, you know," he said. "The spiritual teachers of the Khans of Mongolia and the emperors of China were Karmapas known as 'miracle workers,' and reputed through their spiritual divination, prophecy, and ability to appear simultaneously in different places. They were even said to have the power to control weather!" (Palden's eyes widened at the thought of being in many places at once—or making a grey sky turn sunny.) "But it is interesting that you mentioned the colour *black*, as the Karmapa's spiritual potency is said to be preserved in the 'Vajra Crown,' the Black Hat Crown said to be invisible to all but the most pure in spirit."

"I remember hearing about the Black Hat," Palden said, nodding. "But, does he really *wear* this black hat?"

"Yes, he really does! At one of the most important of all Karma Kagyu rituals, the 'Vajra Crown Ceremony,' the Karmapa dons the famous crown! It is believed that he then *becomes* the living embodiment of Avalokiteshvara, the Bodhisattva of Compassion." (Palden knew that according to Buddhist beliefs, a *bodhisattva* is one of the four sublime states a human can achieve in life.)

"I love hearing your stories," Palden said excitedly, "please tell me more!"

"Well, you are tired, little one. We can talk more of this during your next lesson, if you like." Palden resigned that he was indeed tired. They'd been travelling for hours and Palden could barely keep his eyes open. But he was not free to sleep just yet.

As the party of now nearly two hundred came to a stop for the night, Palden had to help pitch tents, collect firewood, and fetch water from the river. With the dust of the road still burning his throat and the hot humid climate making it uncomfortable to breathe, a solitary tear rolled down his cheek as he thought of the nunnery--and Tibet. Making his way down to the rushing river he scooped up some cold water in his two hands and splashed his eyes. He then placed one of the wooden buckets into the water and allowed it to fill; repeating the process with the other. He lugged the containers back to camp--making several more trips until every water vessel in camp was filled to capacity. He then went to help gather firewood, running round the stony ground collecting twigs and branches until they had enough kindling and wood to last the night. Soon there were puffs of grey smoke and flames licking up from new fires all over camp, providing a comforting sight. Before long, water was boiling in several large pots and vegetables, rice, and butter tea were nearly ready.

Palden sat round the fire with some of the monks, who stoked the fire with long sticks. He looked at all the lovely colours rising up from the large fire pit; the array of reds, yellows, and oranges mesmerised Palden. He found the sight stirring to his soul. Lama Yonten interrupted his train of thought, using the moment as a lesson: "You know, Palden, colour is everywhere. As a young monk I was taught to sit still for hours on end. I had to sit in the lotus position while another monk placed a lighted butter-lamp on my head, and I had to balance the light and remain in that position until the butter was spent. And it would often take twelve or more hours for the light to extinguish! But, this type of silence and stillness brought forward a different kind of awareness in me. A new focus. And I can say that I truly benefited from that experience in ways I only now appreciate. Do you remember how butter lamps are made, Palden?"

"No, I cannot remember," Palden said, searching his tired mind.

"Well, traditionally, butter lamps were made from clarified yak butter. But now more often they use vegetable oil. Tibetans offer a lighted butter lamp to represent the illumination of wisdom, and they help us focus our mind and aid in meditation."

"But, how can a light do that, Lama Yonten?"

"The flames of the fire follow natural laws, as it is a fact that we all come to Earth when we are born. During our lifetime we climb upwards--or attempt to--by way of the 'Steps of Attainment.' And eventually our breath fails and our energetic colour leaves us. Then after an interval of time we are reborn to learn yet another lesson." (Palden nodded his understanding.) "Do you remember the sand mandalas the monks made back at Tsurphu depicting the 'Wheel of Life'?" (Again, Palden nodded.) "These mandalas symbolise the endless cycle of birth-life-death-spirit-birth-life--and so on. And when the intricately-designed sand mandala the monks have spent hours--sometimes months and months creating--is thrown to the wind, it represents the impermanence of everything—the transitory nature of the material world.

"There are many other religions, Palden, some Christians, for example, that believe that when they die Satan will get busy roasting them in the flames of hell! Or some believe that there is another place where they sit on a cloud surrounded by angels and take lessons in harp-playing!" (Palden's eyes widened at the funny image brought to mind.) "But we Buddhists believe that we learn what we need to know on Earth and that Earth is where we must go through suffering to learn the lessons needed for our energetic colour to reincarnate--or not, as the case maybe. Some call the energetic colour the 'soul' or the 'spirit,' and some by other names. But the name does not matter. It is the *understanding* that matters."

Exhausted, Palden's eyelids began to droop, so Lama Yonten nudged him, saying it was time that he went to his tent and slept. They had to be up bright and early as tomorrow they would reach Sikkim and there would be much to do.

Chapter 8

⎯⌒⎯

THERE WAS NO PAVED VEHICLE road at that time from town to the monastery, so it took over a day to make the trip between Gangtok and Rumtek on foot. At last the party arrived safely in Sikkim, on the twenty-fifth day of the fourth month of the Earth Boar Year, a remote and peaceful area beside a mountainous wedge between China and India in the tiny Himalayan Kingdom ten miles south of Sikkim's capital, Gangtok. Perched on a foothill of the great Himalayas, the site possessed many natural attributes considered auspicious for the placement of a monastery: seven streams flowing toward it, seven hills facing it, a mountain behind it, snow-capped mountains in front of it, and a river spiraling in the shape of a conch shell below. At the time of the Karmapa's momentous arrival, Rumtek consisted of a monastery (mostly in ruins) and about half a dozen huts at the verge of being overtaken by jungle. There was neither adequate accommodation nor facilities for preparing food, so the building process took first priority. And forthwith the Karmapa began to design the Rumtek Dharma Chakra Centre, the design drawn solely from inspiration and memory—with some of the features modelled after Tsurphu Monastery, the seat of the Karmapas in Tibet.

As promised, the Indian Government provided significant financial assistance for the construction of the new centre. The Karmapa was given assurances that there would be a free supply of food and clothing for the people there, as well. The Sikkim Government also generously donated funds towards the preliminary construction costs and even provided free timber. A road was constructed, electric cables brought in, and portable water provided. The Indian Government also provided a large grant for the immediate construction of an assembly hall and residential quarters for the monks. But even with such generosity, these funds were insufficient to complete the project so the 16th Karmapa contributed a significant sum from his own resources.

Work on clearing the site began in 1962. For the first month, all those able-bodied began to clear the land by hand, then construction on the complex began in earnest. It was indeed a formidable task of clearing the jungle-like mountain terrain; there were many hardships and the remote area had no trained builders, craftsmen, or masons. More daunting, until the road was completed, supplies were carried up steep paths on the backs of pack animals and the workers themselves, making delivery of equipment arduous, the ordering of building supplies complicated. During the rainy season, working conditions became increasingly dangerous. While the manual work was being undertaken (and before the foundation stone was officially laid), the Karmapa held special *pujas*, expressions of honor, worship, and devotional attention. At the end of the ceremonies, the Karmapa explained that he'd consecrated the surrounding area as the "Mandala of Chakrasamvara," one of the highest-ranking deities of Tantric Buddhism.

It was hard-going for all, and slowly Palden fell into routine and began to put his past behind him. Everyone worked tirelessly clearing land and constructing, and in-between, prayers, lessons, and teaching resumed. Each day they rose before sunrise—working virtually non-stop-and finally getting to bed by 10:00 at night. And by 1966 Rumtek Monastery was finally completed and the relics brought from Tsurphu were installed. Once the building was finished, special attention was given to its decoration and painting.

At a grand ceremony on Losar, the Tibetan New Year, the Gyalwa Karmapa (*Gyalwa*, his honorific title) officially opened his new seat. For Palden, each day was new and exhilarating and he began to take great pleasure in monastery life. No matter how much building or general work there was to do each day, everyone took time to reconstitute the life they had in Tsurphu—much to Palden's liking. Many people of the region built small houses all round and settled there, the centre becoming one of the best examples of the Karma Kagyu tradition in India-- and in all Asia. At the Karmapa's invitation, many new, young, and old lamas arrived at Rumtek, joining those who'd escaped from Tibet, gathering to receive teachings from the Karmapa.

His new routine much to his liking, Palden skipped across the court- yard, entered the new building constructed for the monks, and made his way to Lama Yonten's room. Reaching the new door that smelled of freshly-cut pine, he knocked. "Come in." Palden smiled when he saw his favourite teacher sitting cross-legged on a large red cushion in the centre of the room. The learned lama smiled back, and beckoned Palden to sit on the cushion opposite him.

"Today, Palden," said Lama Yonten, "we are going to talk a bit more about meditation. But before we can *meditate*, we must understand the meanings of the words used to describe the various meditation sys- tems. First, the *Vajrayana* system. This is a complex system of Buddhist thought and practice which has evolved over several centuries and has three separate routes to enlightenment—and includes learning about *Yidam* deities. *Yidams*, you see, are the unblemished reflection existing from the beginning of time and the inborn true nature of our minds that manifest in specific forms and colours. These deities, Palden, you should not confuse as being *outside* one's own mind, but rather, they are images that work *with* our minds. The purpose and goal of this practice is to attain perfect *Buddhahood*—and lamas and guru yoga are important to this system."

"Well, what is *guru yoga*?" asked Palden.

"*Guru yoga* is the practice of merging one's mind with the 'wisdom mind' of a master. The practice involves visualizing the guru, either in his own form or in the form of a deity, requesting his blessings, receiving his blessings, and then merging minds."

Palden had no idea how to imagine merging his mind with someone but had a more urgent question to ask: "And a *lama*? Is a lama a *guru*? . . . a *master*?"

"*Lama* is the title given to any teacher of the *Dharma* in Tibetan Buddhism. In history the term was used for venerated spiritual masters or heads of monasteries, but now it is used as an honorific title conferred on a monk or nun or practitioner who has reached the designate level of spiritual attainment and authority to teach—like myself. Or it may be part of a title such as Dalai *Lama* or Panchen *Lama*, applied to a lineage of reincarnate lamas. The Karmapa, a manifestation of Avalokitesvara, is a *bodhisattva* and is an *enlightened* being who embodies the compassion of all the Buddhas."

"Bod-i-*sattva*?"

"In the Tibetan Buddhist tradition, a *bodhisattva* is anyone who is motivated by great compassion, who has generated a spontaneous wish to attain *Buddhahood* for the benefit of all sentient beings. *Buddhahood*, of course, is the state of perfect enlightenment--*enlightenment* meaning '*awakened*.' And according to Tibetan tradition, great enlightened teachers are said to be able to consciously control their rebirth in order to continue their activity for the benefit of all sentient beings. One such teacher is the *Karmapa*."

"So this is why the Karmapa is so important to us?" said Palden.

"*Us*—as well as all other living things! And as you grow, Palden, you will come to understand just how remarkable a man he truly is!" (Palden took a deep breath and exhaled; reminded now of what Ani-Dolma had once said about the Karmapa, what seemed a lifetime ago.) "Now, let us review what we have learned of the *pujas*. The *pujas*, you remember Palden, are expressions of *honor, worship*, and *devotional attention . . .*"

After his lesson, Palden rushed out into the courtyard as there was much work to do. In the courtyard was much excitement; a different *energy*, Palden thought, as he tuned into an unusual *buzz* that encompassed the monastery. As he strode across the open space he met with Lama Kipu. "You know, Palden, there is a large gathering of monks coming in today for the empowerment and teaching tomorrow. And there is much to do. I believe Akong Rinpoche is planning to attend. The Karmapa has insisted that you are to go with the car to meet him when he arrives in Gangtok, and you are to look after him during his stay. Seeing to his needs will be your responsibility. In the meantime, we must prepare everything for tomorrow, so follow me."

As expected, there was much hustle and bustle the following day as everyone got ready for the empowerment ceremony and influx of new arrivals at Rumtek. As Lama Yonten rushed here and there he shouted to one of the attendants, "Arrange a car to go to Gangtok now. I am certain Akong Rinpoche has arrived and is waiting to be picked up. *Hurry*--the empowerments are about to begin! And make sure you give Palden a *kata* to take along!" The attendant wandered off to find the white silk scarf the Tibetans call a *kata*, which symbolises purity and compassion, and often given Tibetan dignitaries and other people of honour.

Palden met Rinpoche as planned, and when the esteemed monk caught sight of Palden his face broke into an enormous smile--a smile that penetrated to the very core of Palden's being. "Rinpoche," said Palden as he presented him with the *kata* and bowed reverentially.

"Well, well, Palden! How you have grown!" said Rinpoche, placing his hand on Palden's shoulder. Palden smiled as he ushered Rinpoche to the waiting car, both taking seats in the back.

Recent rains had left the dirt-track road leading back to Rumtek quite slippery--even for the *Jeep* with its large, specially-designed tires, which proved no match for such road conditions. As the car careened round the sharp bends of this narrow road, the rear end would sometimes slide—the driver frantically jerking the steering wheel left then right—trying to right the vehicle. Rinpoche fingered his prayer beads, a string of small round brown wooden beads attached to his wrist, to keep himself calm as he casually chatted with Palden. The sheer drop to the valley below became quite apparent as the car neared the edge of the road on numerous occasions, Palden clutching his seat as he looked down into the deep ravine below. On this treacherous journey to the monastery, Palden asked Rinpoche something he'd always wondered about: how Rinpoche had survived when he escaped from Tibet.

"Palden, back in Tibet, my simple lifestyle, my spiritual training from the Karmapa, my learning to look into the mind and understanding suffering, and even our simple habit of eating small portions of food—all this prepared us for what we would endure. And let that be a lesson to you, Palden. Use all the teachings you receive at Rumtek and realise how lucky you are to be living under the direct care of the Karmapa. You are still quite young—about ten years I think? But you are *wise* Palden, wiser than your years," smiled Rinpoche as their car rumbled through the potholes at the gates of Rumtek.

At the precise moment, the Karmapa entered the temple. He gazed out at the rows of monks sitting in the lotus position on coloured cushions; two cushions in the front row remained unoccupied. As he surveyed the room and looked at all the people, he smiled and thought, *Now life indeed has the same quality as Tsurphu Monastery.* Today as he looked at the monks sitting in precise rows he noticed lay people amongst them; some Western visitors, some from the surrounding villages. As he lowered himself into his chair (raised on a platform in front of his audience) he took a deep, cleansing breath. He felt his body become light. He closed his eyes as the time had not yet arrived for him to commence. He waited for another to arrive. When he finally opened his eyes he instructed all those who'd gathered there to recite the Vajrasattva Mantra. The Karmapa knew Rinpoche was near. He smiled. Moments later, Rinpoche, accompanied by Palden, made their way to the front of the assembly and took their seats. Thus the teachings and transmissions, the first phases of the gathering, began . . .

Later that day, after the opening observances, Rinpoche found Palden in the temple cleaning the water bowls. After the customary exchange of bows, Rinpoche smiled and motioned for Palden to take a seat beside him. He wanted to make certain Palden understood the gravity of tomorrow's ceremony. "As you know, Palden, the Karmapa is going to perform the Black Hat Ceremony tomorrow."

"Yes, and I am really looking forward to attending."

"Your teachings have explained the significance of this ceremony?"

"Yes, Rinpoche. I have been well-taught in its history and spiritual significance."

Rinpoche smiled and nodded. "Very good." As the pair headed out of the temple and into the bright streaming rays of the afternoon sun, Palden knew that he'd better hurry as he still had a lot to prepare before the Black Hat Ceremony the following night.

Palden spent all the next day helping make arrangements for the grand ceremony. A great deal of attention had been applied to detail regarding the area the Karmapa would occupy. Finally the area was ready and soon people began to arrive and take their places on the neatly laid-out rows of brightly-coloured cushions. Palden too arrived, taking a seat near the back. He looked up at the dark sky, the stars twinkled their lights, and the moon shed its long bright rays that effectively illuminated the space below. Palden could see clearly in every direction. (Sometimes in meditation he felt that he were flying--weightless--in another world.) He jumped when he felt a hand on his arm--and looking up saw Lama Yonten. "Let us move to the front, Palden. I have a mind to sit with Akong."

As they made their way to the front, where a square brocade seat had been set up for the Karmapa, they nodded at Akong Rinpoche and then sat down beside him. Rinpoche smiled at the two and together in silence they awaited the Karmapa's grand entrance. Within minutes, all the cushions were taken, the benches filled, and there were people standing on the perimeter as the Karmapa came forward. His golden robes billowed out in the soft breeze as he climbed the two steps to his seat, then sat down cross-legged and became very still.

Once all eyes were set upon him, the Karmapa carefully lifted the Black Hat out of its special box and placed it on his head. Raised higher than everyone else, it was as if he were looking straight ahead to some far away, inner place; his right hand raised to balance his hat, his left hand in his lap, rolling a crystal rosary between his practiced fingers. The lamas stood round him, their instruments raised. Horn tones rose, the rhythmic sound of the drums resonated with the beat of Palden's heart, and he began to become one with the sounds. He began to resonate with the high frequency energy--feeling weightless yet anchored to the ground. As he rose higher into super-consciousness, the Karmapa seemed to fade from his vision, and all he could see was the Black Hat. He blinked and recognised that the Karmapa was now in a trance--holding the hat firmly in place. Majestic yet detached from the physical world, he lifted the Black Hat aloft, poised it above his head as if suspended in mid-air, then re-placed it--crowning his head, and holding it there.

The horns maintained a clear, high, piercing crescendo—the drums banged, the symbols clashed, while feelings of love and compassion enveloped Palden. Now it seemed the stars were more radiant than moments before. As Palden looked round he could see that the gathering masses were transfixed; a huge orange sunset appearing in the background. As if time had come to a standstill, Palden was completely awake in this moment and believed that he'd just received a most powerful blessing. (The Buddha of Compassion became manifest.) The ritual, a special blessing, seeing the Karmapa in deep meditation, provoked many to weep and as the tears flowed a spiritual awareness, an *awakening*, came over Palden.

When the ceremony had concluded, the Karmapa returned the Black Hat to its special box. He then bent forward and extended a red silk thread to each person who passed before him, palms joined in greeting. Palden wrapped his thread round his neck, lost in the moment as like no other. Akong Rinpoche then pulled Palden aside:

"Palden, I am leaving tomorrow. My future is not here. I have been given an opportunity to travel to *England*, a land far away. I am most fortunate that a sponsor has provided for me to go there to learn English. I believe this is my path and that there are many auspicious signs for my journey. However, I do believe we will meet again, Palden. But for now, my young friend, study well. I know that you are interested in astrology, but I feel that you should look into medicine as well. You would do well with medicinal herbs, I think. Think on this, Palden, and in the meantime, study well."

Becoming known as a quiet, serene place where people from all over the world came to visit, pilgrims from India and Westerner countries alike came to Rumtek to listen to the teachings of the Karmapa. By now, in addition to the rigorous educational curriculum which included mathematics, Buddhist philosophy and psychology, Tibetan grammar and literature, Tibetan medicine, astrology, and meditation practices, for Palden there was the continuing work of running errands and helping carry building materials. Palden found the study of mathematics difficult but knew it was essential for astrological work—the field he intended to pursue. Unlike many zodiacal systems used round the world, Tibetan Buddhist astrology is no mere hit-or-miss affair, but works out according to proven scientific principles. Over the following months Palden became interested in medicine, coming to see that it was better to treat an individual according to their astrological "type" than to prescribe something haphazardly in the hopes that because it had cured one individual, it would automatically do so for another.

There was no time to dream of his beloved Tibet now, but sometimes in class Palden's eyes would blur and he could see pictures from his past, replacing the wall charts dealing with astrology and various herbs. The latter were changed each week and Palden and the other students were expected to be entirely familiar with the visual aspects of all plants. But it was the outdoor excursions that took Palden and the other students away from Tsurphu that he most enjoyed. There they would gather various herbs and other vegetation which on their return to Tsurphu they would prepare and use as remedies.

One day while Palden sat in the courtyard contemplating his future, Lama Yonten approached. "Ah, there you are, Palden, I have been looking for you," he said. "Come--follow me. I have instruction for you. No time for daydreaming today!" Together they strolled across the courtyard towards the meditation rooms and once inside and seated comfortably, Lama Yonten spoke. "Today, Palden, your lesson regards relaxation and meditation. Today you will experience the sensation of relaxing every part of your body. And you will use what you learn today to derive pleasure from meditating on the realities of life and on the

Higher Self." (Palden gave him his undivided attention—as he always did.)

"In Buddhist discipline, Palden, everything is done to train the mind. For example, by touching a particular spot on the neck just *so* (the lama indicated the spot on Palden's neck) a person can be rendered unconscious in a fraction of a second—as just a little pressure can paralyze the brain. Harmlessly, of course. In Tibet where there are no anesthetics, pressure is often used when extracting a tooth or even performing surgery. It is incredible what we can do when we understand how the mind and body works."

Chapter 9

THE YEAR IS 1974 AND Palden has exciting news: "Lama Yonten!" said Palden. "I am travelling with the Karmapa and the others to India!"

"Well, Palden, you are now nineteen year of age, you have studied well, and you have proved yourself worthy to accompany the Karmapa—which, of course, will develop further your knowledge and experience. You will visit sacred sites most will only dream of--Bodh Gaya, Sarnath, Sanchi, Ajanta, Ellora and Nagarjuna Sagar! And I am sure you will travel abroad in years to come, so this will help prepare you for that stage of your life." Still, Palden felt an uncertainty about leaving Rumtek for the first time. Recognising this, the Karmapa had asked one of his personal attendants to involve Palden in their daily travel arrangements; including management of their tour. Soon, for the first time in his life, Palden looked forward to travelling: he couldn't wait to see the auspicious Buddhist sites and meet with new and interesting people. And not long after their return, Palden found himself charged with making arrangements for the Karmapa to visit Scotland:

"Rinpoche, it's Palden calling from Sikkim."

"Palden, so nice to hear from you."

"Tell me, how are the plans coming along for the Karmapa's visit to Scotland? As you know, the Karmapa is intending to visit several places but had thought perhaps a four-week stay at Samye Ling would be good."

As Rinpoche sat in his favorite chair in his room at Samye Ling, in Scotland, telephone pressed to his ear, discussing the Karmapa's forthcoming visit, he studied a crow sitting in the tree just outside, looking directly at him through the window. He smiled. Palden liked talking with Rinpoche; liked his sober, authoritative manner. Even though Rinpoche was thousands of miles away, Palden could feel the sincerity, the compassion, the resolution that was Rinpoche. Holding the phone in his left hand, Akong idly brushed an errant piece of lint from his maroon *chuba* as he assured Palden, "Everything that can be in order for the Karmapa's visit, has been."

"I am rather sad," said Palden, "the Karmapa has asked me to remain here at Rumtek, so I will not be travelling to Scotland with him."

"Perhaps not *this* time, Palden, but I have no doubt that one day you will visit Samye Ling--as well as other places here. And I look forward to that day. In the meantime, if you have anything you need me to do on this end, just let me know. I am only too happy to help."

The Karmapa's visit to Scotland was an unqualified success and shortly after, under his supervision, construction of a temple began at Samye Ling, all the work being performed by members of the community--and Akong himself. The 16th Karmapa was now able to establish direct contact with all those seeking the 'Way of Dharma,' functioning as in his previous incarnations as guide, teacher, and true living example.

Over the next few years the Karmapa remained busy; travelling, teaching and opening new Dharma Centres. But his health was quickly failing. On the evening of November 5, 1981 (the day of Liberatrice;

Tara) he was admitted to Mount Zion hospital near Chicago, Illinois. Under constant observation, doctors entered the Karmapa's room to discover that his life-support machines had *apparently* turned themselves off, all present thinking, 'He's playing a joke on us!' A moment later, the machines started up again . . . worked for five minutes . . . then stopped again; never resuming. The Karmapa was officially pronounced dead at 8:30 pm, his death a final lesson on the impermanence of the material world for all present. But his passing would bring unexpected uncertainty to the future of Rumtek.

Over the next four years, Palden's concerns regarding the running of Rumtek affairs steadily grew, primarily due to the varied opinions (and mounting factions) surrounding the Karmapa's reincarnation prediction letter. More specifically, the existence of *two* prediction letters, an inner and an outer letter: the outer one requesting that certain mantras be said over a period of time, then once completed, the inner one was to be opened. Palden believed that those in primary positions of control were stalling, and was unsure what could be done about this matter.

Akong Rinpoche had recently returned from visiting Tsurphu, his first visit since fleeing Tibet, having been given permission from local authorities to open new schools and centres there. These new developments beginning at Tsurphu were good news, as well as the news about the fund-raising and rebuilding of the monastery. The Chinese had forced the villagers to tear down the monastery brick by brick then used dynamite to blow up the fifty-five-foot-high brass statue of the Shakyamuni Buddha! And sadly, relics of the Buddha stored inside had all disappeared.

Despite growing tension regarding the Karmapa's reincarnation prediction letter, for the next few years Palden remained loyal to the monastery, eventually receiving word that a search party had left Tsurphu Monastery (in Tibet) with a prediction letter, looking for the reincarnation of His Holiness. Directed to a family in the village of Bakor (*ba* meaning "cow" in Tibetan), near Lhatokgar, in the province of Lhatok (*Lha* meaning "god" or "divine" and *tok* meaning "thunder"), the search party discovered that the couple had an eight-year-old son born on June 26, 1985 and that his birth had been accompanied by many miraculous signs.

As a matter of course, Akong Rinpoche travelled to Tibet to meet the boy believed to be the reincarnation of His Holiness the 16th Karmapa. Rinpoche knew that as one of the few individuals authorised to identify the new reincarnation, it was important for him to see the boy for himself to ensure that he was the true and rightful reincarnation. By tradition, the family of the boy has to be *formally* asked to give up their son, so Akong himself presented them with money, food, bolts of cloth, and a precious Buddha statue he'd carried from Sikkim. Shortly after, special prayer flags were flown and juniper incense sticks were burned at Tsurphu.

It was June when a convoy of vehicles comprised of a dozen *Jeeps* and tow trucks made its way up the dirt-track road to the gates of Tsurphu Summer Palace, behind them a large party of Khampas on horseback dressed in their finest garments. The third *Jeep*, a Chinese governmental vehicle, was swathed in white *khatas*. Seated next to the Chinese driver was the young Karmapa, dressed in a tunic of striking yellow brocade. The Karmapa had formally returned to Tsurphu.

It was some weeks later that Palden jumped at the sound of the ringing telephone. He'd been sitting at his desk at Rumtek dreaming of Tibet, and pondering the fate of their monastery. He recognised the voice immediately as that of his dear friend Akong Rinpoche:

"Palden," said Rinpoche, "if you have a moment, I have a story I think you will find most interesting."

"Always, for you, my friend," said Palden.

"Before His Holiness the Sixteenth Karmapa died, I asked him for something special to remember him by; his tooth, which would be an auspicious relic for me. The Karmapa conceded, but I was never provided that tooth. Well, weeks back as I sat before the young reincarnate Karmapa, the boy reached out and handed me one of his milk teeth. Seems he had kept the tooth ready to present to me, under the yellow silk cushion he was sitting on. 'Rinpoche,' he said, 'I promised you this in my last life and now I have fulfilled that promise!'"

"That is truly *extraordinary*, Rinpoche! So you are now convinced that this boy, Apo Gaga, is indeed the reincarnation of the Sixteenth Karmapa?"

"Yes, Palden, I am."

But even with Rinpoche's full endorsement, some of the lamas at Rumtek remained doubtful of the authenticity of the late Karmapa's prediction letter and the acceptance of this young boy as the 17th Karmapa. Added to the uncertainty, the Chinese government's approval of the new Karmapa was being portrayed as an historic event by the Chinese. Palden and others questioned if the Chinese weren't, in fact, moving in on the Buddhist lineage to gain political control. By this point, the Dalai Lama had officially "recognised" Apo Gaga as the Seventeenth Karmapa, but the Chinese were well aware that while still in exile in India, he would have no control over the boy. Thus, Palden's fears were only waiting to be realised.

Due to increased tension at Rumtek (which had escalated to violent confrontations by this time) Palden and Lama Yonten decided that it was time to leave and together said their fond farewells to the remaining monks. Palden would spend the next phase of his life in India. Rumtek would be left exclusively in the custody of its monks and the Karmapa Charitable Trust. But this was hardly the end of the problems surrounding the Karmapa or Rumtek. Apo Ga was enthroned at Tsurphu, given the name "Ogyen Trinley Dorje," the 17th Karmapa.

Upon arrival in India, Palden accepted a secretarial position at the main offices at Gyuto Tantric University, in Dharamsala, India. It was a beautiful setting full of harmony and peace, nestled in the foothills of the Himalayan Mountains. One of the first things he did in his new capacity as secretary was place a phone call to Akong Rinpoche in Scotland:

"Rinpoche, my friend, I have arrived in Dharamsala and have moved to Gyuto," said Palden.

"Sounds wonderful!" Rinpoche said.

"My new position is as secretary and I am responsible for organising various events. I feel it was the right move for me—especially now that I am near the Dalai Lama!"

"That is truly *wonderful*, Palden! I am pleased that you have found where you need to be!"

"Yes, Akong! I feel this is exactly where I *should* be!"

By this point the Chinese had paraded the new Karmapa before the public in Tibet, and Akong had been travelling to Beijing for talks with members of the United Front (the department responsible for decision-making concerning Tibetan affairs) to plead on the Karmapa's behalf that he be permitted to travel. Though the Chinese had agreed to allow him to visit India, they had so far not delivered on their promise. And since the Indian government was trying not to get involved in Chinese politics, they were not pushing for his visit. But now, yet *another* issue took centre stage: The Chinese government had made insulting comments to the Karmapa about the Dalai Lama and dissent had flared up at Tsurphu. Monks had been arrested for openly stating that the Chinese were trying to manipulate the Karmapa, and as a result, the Karmapa refused to have his picture taken with the Chinese--even though he'd been given gifts.

As tension at Tsurphu mounted, a plan was hatched for His Holiness the 17th Karmapa to secretly leave Tibet and join the Dalai Lama in India. And not long after, His Holiness arrived in Dharamsala--his daring escape making world headlines. With the Karmapa's momentous arrival in Dharamsala, Palden now busied himself with his new official duties. He was over-joyed that he would now live and work beside His Holiness, remembering well the 16th Karmapa--his tutor, friend, and one who'd led them out of Tibet to safety. As Palden organized his papers he thought back with fondness to the time he'd spent at Rumtek. Brief case in hand he was soon outside in the bright morning sun; he smiled at the novice monks as he headed for the taxi that would take him into Dharamsala. Today he had a meeting with the Dalai Lama.

When he arrived in Dharamsala, Palden discovered that he had more than hour before his appointment, so he decided to take a slow walk round the various stalls selling wares from India, Tibet, and other places. And as he sauntered over to a stall hawking a variety of Tibetan items, his attention was drawn to a tall, slim lady standing at the stall. He could only see her in profile but there was something quite familiar about her. But no matter how hard he taxed his brain he couldn't recall how he knew her. Disturbed by this, he decided to tap her on the shoulder and ask. As his hand rested upon her, she turned round. And in that moment he realised that it was Tenzin; Tenzin who'd been with him all those years before at the nunnery; Tenzin who'd been there the last time his mother had been seen. Older but still just as beautiful! She looked at him, obviously confused.

"Tenzin!" Palden said excitedly.

"*Yes?*" she said, now looking directly into his face.

"Palden? Palden from the nunnery? *Ani-Dolma!?*"

Tenzin froze. "Oh--" was all she could utter as she began to cry and flung her arms round him. Suddenly images of his boyhood came flooding into his mind. In mere seconds they both revisited the pain of years before--Tibet and all the suffering they'd both endured.

Palden held her out at arms-length and said, "I have an hour to spare, Tenzin. Shall we have coffee?" Tenzin nodded and looped her arm in his.

Arm-in-arm they made their way to a near-by rooftop café. Although the restaurant was not that high up, the mist had begun to roll in low over the mountains and forests--so low that it descended round the restaurant like a cloud. From this vantage point Palden and Tenzin could see all that was happening below: people strolling round, monkeys swinging tree-to-tree, and the odd cow sauntering carelessly on the road, bringing confusion to all who tried to pass. The loud hooting of the buses, the din of car and motor-bike horns had become mere background sounds to Palden.

As they sipped tea and reminisced, Tenzin told Palden of her escape; told him of the horrors--the unending freezing snow and blinding sun, and of one young girl's desperation to become a nun and live near His Holiness the Dalai Lama. Sadly, Tenzin explained, this poor child was shot dead by a Chinese sniper; one of several Chinese soldiers who'd been tracking their party for miles. She told of how the rest of the Tibetans had scrambled off in different directions--struggling through the deep snow to distance themselves—even as more bullets rang out. In the end, over twenty of their party were left dead or bleeding in the snow.

"I was beyond exhausted, Palden; like all the others. Older monks and others of the village did not survive. They dropped like dead weight to the frozen ground and there was nothing we could do but watch them die--just leave them where they fell! The sun blinded us, our shoes wore out--as did our food rations--and finally our energy ran out. We were frozen to the bone. But by some miracle, several of us managed to survive! It took us nearly ten months and when we arrived in India we were not the same people who set out from Tibet. Some of us ended up here in Dharamsala, some went into retreat. Some just disappeared."

Tears fell from Palden's eyes for what his friend had suffered. Then he asked, "Did you ever see my mother again, Tenzin?"

Tenzin sat for a moment staring at him. "What do you mean, *see your mother again?*" she said, her face suddenly taking on a dire look.

"Well, I just wondered if on your travels you may have come across her . . ."

"Palden, tell me you know where your mother is!" cried Tenzin—sorrow filling her eyes.

Palden's heart began to pound in his chest. "*Seen* her? Seen her *where?*" he said anxiously.

She took Palden's hands in hers. "Palden, she lives *here*, at the local nunnery . . . has for several years! She escaped Tibet on foot--over the Himalayas--and arrived here in a very poor health—but she made it, Palden!" cried Tenzin. "She survived!"

Palden made no attempt to hold back the tears that now came flooding out. "I--I must see her *now*," he said, jumping to his feet. "I--I cannot believe I did not know this! How is this possible? After all these years believing she . . . *please*, take me to her! Please—after I meet with the Dalai Lama--can we me meet in two hours?" said Palden, his head swimming.

Filled with joy and anticipation, Tenzin said, "Of course, Palden. Of course." They chose a meeting place, Tenzin agreeing to take Palden to see his mother.

Chapter 10

MEETING AS PLANNED AT THE market where they'd found each other earlier that day, Tenzin took Palden's hand and together they headed for the nunnery. Although Palden knew well where the nunnery stood, they both took comfort in Tenzin leading the way. As they approached the nunnery gates, Tenzin explained what had transpired:

"About ten years ago during a visit to Kathmandu, I visited a refugee camp where they make traditional Tibetan carpets. As I watched the women work, my eyes were drawn to one woman who was helping with the wools. When I got closer I recognised her, it was your mother. And when I called out her name, she looked directly at me. We embraced and cried until we couldn't cry any more. I spent over a month trying to get her a visa and papers to travel to India, and managed with what little savings I had to bring her here to Dharamsala."

Tenzin stopped and held Palden's hand tighter. "Palden, your mother has been through a *very* difficult time. On and off for twenty-five years she was in a Tibetan prison where she was tortured and suffered horrible punishment for her support of the Dalai Lama and her Buddhist beliefs. But she refused to abandon her beliefs and refused the Chinese brainwashing that their way of life is the only way. Your mother would rather have died in Tibet than leave, but there was *you* to consider."

"Me?" asked Palden.

Resuming her lead, Tenzin said, "Yes, Palden, *you*! *You* were her incentive to leave so she joined a group escaping Tibet bound for Dharamsala, as they desperately wanted to be near His Holiness, but she only made it as far as Kathmandu. The journey almost killed her. She had a stroke, was frost bitten—and nearly lost her toes--and was severely malnourished. By the time she arrived here, she had pneumonia and was not expected to live. I am sure there is much more to tell, which she will want to tell you herself."

At the gates they were invited inside then led by an elderly nun to a small room in a building just outside the nunnery proper. Tenzin entered the room first, reminding Palden to bear in mind that his mother was much older now and the hard life she'd endured had taken its toll.

"Thank you, Tenzin. I appreciate your words. I will see her now." As they entered, Palden's eyes struggled to adjust to the dim light.

"Palden, we must keep the curtains drawn in the morning to protect her eyes," Tenzin said. "Her eyes were badly damaged by the blinding snow on her long journey from Tibet to Kathmandu."

As Palden walked slowly towards a large blue armchair set beside a small, wood-frame bed, he heard a feeble voice whisper his name. Through the dim light of the room he could just make out his mother's wrinkled and weathered face, her eyes barely visible between half-closed lids; the left side of her face slightly drooping. This, he knew, was due to the stroke she'd suffered. This was his mother! —And he suddenly felt angry!

He *should* have done more! He *should* have gone back to Tibet and found her! He *should* have looked after her and if he had, perhaps she would be well, healthy, and happy!

He bent over his Ama La and gently kissed her forehead. Taking her frail, cold hands in his he sat down in the chair beside her. They sat in silence for what seemed an eternity. Slowly he felt her hands begin to warm. As he looked deeply into her widening eyes, he saw pain; eyes tired and heavy with a haunted look. Then suddenly it was as if the suffering of the past was insignificant:

"Oh, Ama La--I have no idea what to say to you other than I have missed you so. Suffering, understanding, learning how to accept and live with a clear frame of mind free from suffering has been part of my learning. Now seeing you my joy is overwhelming but my compassion for your suffering is more than I have ever thought I could feel," Palden said, his heart and mind a churning sea of emotion.

Reaching out her hand, Pembuti's lips parted as if to speak—but then her eyes grew heavy. As she drifted off to sleep Palden sat thinking: If *only* life had been different; if *only* the Chinese hadn't invaded; if *only* he'd been allowed the chance to be with his Ama La throughout his life. And though her eyes were closed, Pembuti was in the moment; fully aware of where she was and that now--here in this very room--sat her son. And through her suffering she was overwhelmed by his presence, the touch of his now mature hands, and was reminded of the deep love she'd felt for the two lives that had grown inside her all those years ago . . .

But, Pembuti was tired. She had too many scars to heal and no longer the will to live—or even fight back. Yet, now, here was her son. The son she thought she'd never see again—yet hoped beyond hope to reconnect with before her final day. And as she lie there, head rested on the soft pillow, she pondered on her inner-strength. The depth of her resolve. Is love enough reason to go on living? A smile parted her dry lips as she felt warmth and love flow into her from the hand that now firmly clasped hers. Drowsy, her eyelids grew heavy and her vision blurred. As her hand gave in to the tender touch, her thoughts travelled back to a time when she'd felt such wondrous love before. It was the last time she'd seen her son--decades ago. If only she'd known when she clasped his tiny hand that day that it would be the last time she'd see or touch him--she'd never have gone to Lhasa. And if only she could get those lost years back. As she drifted off to sleep, she recalled her final words to Palden that fateful day:

'Come here my son, I need to talk with you. Soon it will be your fifth birthday, so I will be going to Lhasa to find a nice present for you,' she'd said. 'Then let me come with you--please, please!' Palden had begged. 'No--your present must be a surprise, little one, so you will stay here,' Pembuti explained. 'You have plenty of chores to keep you busy until I return. I should not be gone long as I am taking a horse instead of walking.' The little Palden had stamped his foot and put his hands on his hips in frustration, causing her to say, 'That is no way to behave, Palden! You will stay here and that it that!' And then as she mounted her horse, she bent down and gave Palden a kiss on his head saying, 'I love you, my son. Promise to be good for Ani-Dolma while I am away. I will return soon with your present.' She never imagined that anything could change her plan—yet it happened . . .

After the dreadful incident in the marketplace—the killing of a Chinese soldier—Pembuti spent the next twenty years fighting for the freedom of Tibet alongside her Khampa comrades. All the while her heart ached when she thought she may never see her son again; wishing she could kill *all* the Chinese—such was her anger! Her own mother, Dawa, had been killed by them (which had led to her father leaving her in the nunnery to join the fight), and now she was forced to leave behind her own son, knowing that going back to the nunnery could endanger all their lives! She had no option, that dark day, but ride onwards to a life that would take her back to her ancestral roots. She would live as her parents and their parents before had—as a nomad.

As she thundered off that day she took a sly glance at the Khampa Goba—the warrior who'd intervened on her behalf--and saw similarities between him and her father. She remembered her father; he'd been renowned for his horsemanship and fearless character, and with that memory a pang of longing gripped her heart. This Khampa had rugged features and was quite handsome, his long black hair pleated and pulled forward to the front of his chest. She noticed his heavy boots and flowing khaki robes that flapped like whips as they rode on the wind—Pembuti finding it hard to keep up even though she was an accomplished horsewoman. Across the rugged terrain they galloped--at last reaching an encampment hidden in a lush green valley north of Lhasa. They'd travelled over three hours and as they dismounted and walked their horses the last few miles through the thick of the forest, Pembuti began to sob uncontrollably:

"There is no time for tears," Goba had told her. "They will not help you to understand that this is the *only* way now. There is no going back! You will now join us and help with the organisation of our camp, and you will be made welcome." When they reached the camp Pembuti found many men but few woman; as well as some children. "This is Pembuti," said Gobi to the rest of the group, who'd now gathered outside to see the newcomer. Made welcome, Diki, daughter of one of the group's leaders, was instructed to look after her. The young girl took Pembuti into her tent and pointed to a spot by the fire. There she was given hot steaming butter-tea and roasted *tsampa*, gratefully accepted as Pembuti was famished. Diki then led her to a corner of the tent where she laid out some warm yak-skin blankets on a mat. Feeling all the intense emotion of the day, moments later, Pembuti was fast sleep.

The next morning Pembuti was awakened before sunrise; the camp was already buzzing with activity and Diki had a list of chores for the new addition. After breakfast, Pembuti gathered and stacked wood for their fires, then collected yak dung from the grazing fields. Then she milked the goats, churned butter, and helped grind and roast *tsampa* from barley. The day was long and the work hard, but all the women in camp did their part. There were eight tents in the camp and each had six-to-eight occupants, so there was much to do.

The men had gone out on patrol that morning scouring the country-side for Chinese, but travelled far from camp so as not to draw attention to their base. Travelling in the light of day was, of course, dangerous, but enabled the Khampas to locate Chinese camps—which they could attack or set traps for at night. All quite risky considering that the Chinese were far better equipped with guns and had many more men. The Khampas routinely organized Chinese ambushes--and killed Chinese soldiers when possible--but their general aim was to create as many obstacles for the Chinese Army as possible through sabotage of the roads, bridges, and transport the Chinese needed to advance their army.

About a month after Pembuti had arrived at this camp, a commotion outside her tent alerted her: she worried that the Chinese had found them. She opened the flap of her tent slowly, prepared to fight or run, and there in the yard were eight men on horseback. As she watched, one of the men slipped off his horse--his foot catching in the stirrup, causing him to hit the ground with a *thud*. As the horse began to walk forward, the man was dragged on his back a short ways until one of the camp women stopped the horse. Pembuti ran forward to release the man's foot from the stirrup but as she approached--stopped short: she recognised the man. It seemed impossible--but as she looked closer she knew without a doubt that it was him. It was her father! And blood was seeping through his heavy dark jacket; a sticky red mass spreading. She ran to him, screaming for help, then fell to the ground beside him and cradled his head in her arms, crying, *Help me!*

Goba ran to her and knelt down, lifting her father up in his big arms and carrying him to the nearest tent. Suddenly everything seemed to slow down; Pembuti felt as though she were out of her body looking down on her father and was unable to help. Goba yelled to her, "Boiling water! *Now*, Pembuti!" Soon Amrita, an elder of the camp who knew herbs and potions, rushed into the tent and announced, "He has been shot! We need to remove the bullet then ensure there is no infection!" Turning to Diki she said, "Child, bring me the lotion labelled *Hibiscus rosa-sinensis* from my medicament shelf. We will use this to cool the body of fever. We will also need the *bya rkan*g, the antiseptic. *Hurry!*"

Over the following days, Pembuti's father slowly recovered; Pembuti at first spending day and night at his side. But even as his strength re-turned, her father acted withdrawn and distant and said little. Pembuti had come to accept that she'd never see him again and now that they had reunited, her loving father was not how she remembered him. As soon as he regained full strength he made it clear that he intended to return to fight the Chinese--no matter how much Pembuti pleaded with him not to—Pembuti finally resigning, "If you insist on going back to fight then let me come with you! You know I am a skilled rider and I too can shoot a gun!" But her father was having none of it and for the first time explained himself:

"Pembuti, I have done things I do not want you to be part of. Terrible things I know I must do again. After your Mother, the love of my life, was so cruelly taken from me--and you, my family, my home, my land, and my way of life—I vowed revenge." He explained that back then he had not appreciated what he had—that simple way of life. He'd been in his natural element, surrounded by loved ones, and although their lives were fraught with harsh weather and abject poverty, they'd been happy--like generations before. And now there was nothing left—not even the freedom to follow the Dalai Lama if he chose. And he knew with a burning passion that he had to continue--no matter what the cost--to eliminate the Chinese from his land. Most of his friends were dead, the monasteries lay in ashes, and now the land was being mined by those who'd taken his country by force—and only force would reclaim it. He wanted everything to just go back to how it had been—but knew in his heart could never be.

"*No*! I am coming with you!" Pembuti told him. "I can at least hunt for food and cook and help maintain the camp! I will be a *great* help to you! I am *coming*!" Pembuti had thus made up her mind. She would look after her father, help him, care for him—and that was that! And so one day not long after she, her father, and the other Khampa men rode out of camp heading for new pastures in search of Chinese . . .

Chapter 11

THERE WAS LITTLE CONVERSATION BETWEEN father and daughter as they set out that day. And no matter how many times Pembuti asked about her childhood, Anil simply turned away--as if he hadn't heard. Over the ensuing months they encountered many Chinese soldiers; some the Khampas ambushed and killed, others too numerous for the Khampas to take on. Pembuti watched in horror as the Chinese—one after another--fell dying to the ground, reminding her of when her mother, Dawa, had been shot dead. And now her very survival depended on her marksmanship. Although she'd never before considered killing a man, she quickly learned that survival was a matter of the quickest gun; the face of the first soldier she killed always haunting her. (In the moment she'd aimed and pulled the trigger she felt nothing but rage. Still, she was elated; in her heart and mind she'd avenged her mother's cruel and pointless death.)

As they made their way across the sometimes barren countryside, she often remembered the beautiful turquoise necklace her mother had been killed for—*had sacrificed her life for*--and the other jewels she had so joyously played with as a child. For fleeting moments she thought about her baby girl and wondered if she were still alive; what fate had befallen her. Would she be playing with the necklace and jewels? Was she happy? Had Alexander managed to get himself and the baby safely back to Scotland? And as for her son--she had no idea what became of him. The nunnery had been reduced to rubble, as had Tsurphu. Had he managed to escape? All these questions she knew may forever go unanswered.

But as she thought of her own children, she also considered the Chinese men who she and other Khampas had killed. Did they have children? She wondered about their parents and the suffering they'd face knowing their child was dead. And slowly, confusion and guilt at these killings began to consume Pembuti; to eat away at her soul.

One day while riding along with her father, skirting a chain of foothills known for Chinese occupation, Pembuti began to worry about being killed or captured and put into prison. Although her father had used this very argument to dissuade her from following in his footsteps, there were so many stories circulating round the campfire of the atrocities that happened to innocent monks and lay people who'd been thrown into Chinese prisons that the images were sometimes too hard to shake from her thoughts. Just moments later as they picked their way along a narrow path littered with boulders and scree, a shot rang out . . . and in that split second her father lunged forward and fell to the ground. As Pembuti quickly wheeled round, she saw the Chinese soldier some distance away raise his gun again and take aim at her. The other Khampas who rode ahead reigned their horses and shouted back, '*Move*, Pembuti! *Move!*' pointing up the steep hillside to the boulders that were now thundering down. In that same moment Pembuti saw blood running from her father's head; the bullet having penetrated the back of his skull.

Realising that her father was dead and that she could do nothing to help him, she kicked her horse in the flanks and rode as fast as she dared along the narrow path towards the others. The boulders boomed and crashed onto the path behind them, blocking the way for the Chinese to follow. Pembuti reached the others and together, without a word, they headed for the safety of the ravine ahead--tears streaming uncontrollably down Pembuti's angry face. The Khampas stopped and, obscured now by vegetation, dismounted and began to talk:

"We have lost one of our finest!" Gado said.

"They were so *quiet*--I never heard them coming!" remarked Jetsen. "We are fortunate that no more of us were killed! And so lucky the shot started the avalanche!"

"Pembuti, this is indeed sad for you, but we each knew the dangers your father knew in recent years," said Jetsen, "and there was no other life he would have wanted. He died a hero! He was a true and proud Khampa!" He paused then said, "And, he was so very unhappy since your mother was killed, Pembuti. He will be at peace now. But I think it is time for you to return to Lhasa as that is what he would have wanted."

"My mother lives in Lhasa and I know you would be welcome to stay with her," Gado spoke up. "You will not be recognised now--you have changed, a few years older, eh?"

Pembuti thought for a moment. To return to Lhasa with all its memories--of Palden, Tenzin, Ani-Dolma and the others--tore at her heart. Yet she knew that here was an offer that would at least guarantee a roof over her head. Some place safe—away from the killing. "Okay," she resigned, still in shock that her father now lay dead, unable to find any other words of gratitude.

"Good. We will head for Lhasa," said Gado, "stop and rest once the sun has set." Looking at his comrades he said, "Everyone must be on the lookout for Chinese. The area will be swarming with them now that they know we are here." The group then made their way quietly under cover of the surrounding vegetation. Nearly five hours later, as night fell, they stopped and set up camp. The weather had taken a turn for the worse and now it was snowing wildly. They tethered and fed their horses under a canvas tarpaulin, then set up their tents. After a small repast of hot butter-tea and roasted *tsampa*, they bedded down for the night and slept until first light.

The next day as they neared Lhasa they spotted Chinese patrols: some on foot, some on horseback, others in *Jeeps*. "This is where we must leave you, Pembuti," said Gado. "Wait here until dark and then lead your horse on foot into the city as quietly as you can. Be on the lookout for Chinese soldiers and remember: trust nobody! Not even a kindly monk! And tell *no one* of your past, Pembuti! You would be wise to invent a story of where you have come from and why you are here—a believable story! Perhaps you have come from a village near Tsethang City in the Yarlung Valley--this you must remember is to the southeast of Lhasa in Nedong County of Lhoka! And you must sound *convincing*!" He paused then suggested, "You have come to bring news of your mother's death to your aunt who lives in Lhasa, and you plan to stay for some weeks. But say nothing more to *anyone*!" Pembuti nodded. With that the Khampas rode off, leaving a cloud of dust behind. Pembuti sent her love outward towards them knowing she'd never see them again. And it saddened her as she'd grown accustomed to life with them, as well as having become hardened to stalking and planning, ambushing--and even killing--Chinese soldiers.

That night as she entered Lhasa, Pembuti saw that much had changed. Many new buildings had appeared--yet the streets were almost deserted. Heading for Gado's mother's house as inconspicuously as she could, she led her horse past a group of women adorned in turquoise jewellery; Pembuti slid her left hand inside her closed wrap-around and felt her neck, remembering the turquoise necklace she'd once so proudly worn. (She wondered why her fellow Tibetans had come to believe that turquoise guards against the evil eye and brings good luck and health as she'd had little of that.) Further along she came to a group of women sitting behind tables at the side of the road selling fruit, vegetables, sweet meats, and candles with wooden wicks. A few ruddy-cheeked, stalwart men with beardless faces and coarse features with contented, cheery expressions, wandered round the narrow streets as if careless. Glancing up, Pembuti saw a mass of new buildings covering the hillside, its terraces of many windowed houses, as well as the hundreds of windows of the enormous imposing building--on one, the most striking of mountainous land—set Potala Palace. Her eyes travelled to the great stairway on either side leading down to the main entrance and the gardens below, zig-zagging outwards to enclose a diamond-shaped inner space. Dark curtains of purple-coloured yak-skin cloth draped the verandas to protect the aging frescoes from rain and sun.

Pembuti smiled as she caught sight of the tall prayer flags erected at the main corners of the streets. Stealthily slipping by the white-washed, flat-roof brick houses with the beams of the eaves highlighted in various colours--reds, yellows, greens, blues, and browns--she went over the directions given her by Gado in her head. The chatter of caged birds hanging outside some of the houses lifted her spirits: she spotted larks, rose finches, as well as doves. Many of the windowsills had pots of brightly-coloured plants, while numerous small incense kilns were beside the doors of most houses. Just as she reached what she believed to be the house of Gado's mother, she felt a hand touch her shoulder— jerked and stifled a scream. Turning round she came face-to-face with a young Tibetan boy who put his finger to his lips and gestured for her to give him her horse's reins. As he led the horse away, he pointed to the old wooden door of a small stone building. Inside, Pembuti found Akar; a little old grey-haired woman sitting by a fire. When she smiled, Pembuti noticed that she had few remaining teeth.

"Word has reached me of my son Gado's travels," she said, "and I have been told of you. It seems you have suffered much in your life. But now it is time to rest. You can be of help to me as I am old and frail and need someone like you round the house. I have prepared a bed for you over there," she said, pointing to a spot in the corner. "Come now, child, let us eat and drink."

As Pembuti looked round her new home she realised that there were but two rooms: one where they ate, the other where they slept. Hanging from pegs on the walls were clay and iron cooking utensils, bladders of butter, as well as strings of cheese, bits of meat, yak-hair rope, cooking ladles, and pots and pans. Setting on the floor were tubs of water alongside vats of grain and other foodstuffs. This all reminded her of her childhood, when she lived in a tent with her parents who had similar ways of doing things. Akar pointed to an upended log set beside the fire. "Sit," she said. Pembuti was comforted by the roaring fire in the hearth in the middle of the room, although it was rather smoky due to there being no chimney. "Dote, my son, here, will tend to your horse," said Akar, pointing to the young boy who'd just entered, breathless.

As Pembuti lifted a mug of steaming herb tea to her lips she felt exhausted, but for the first time in a long time glad to be within four walls. She'd forgotten the sense of security walls provide. She looked round the room and saw on the floor against the back wall a box on which a shrine with the image of the household deity set beside a religious image and a few charms. There was a second box beside the altar and was suddenly reminded of the box she once had where she kept her special trinkets, knowing that this one would also likely contain the family's treasures--probably charms, fine cloths, and their astrological charts. Akar placed a plate of *tsampa* in front of Pembuti on the wooden box used as a table. By and large, Pembuti quickly felt at home.

Chapter 12

It wasn't long before Pembuti came to realise that Lhasa was a much more dangerous place than she'd imagined. The walls had ears and the Chinese had spies *everywhere*. Most every day she witnessed a monk or ordinary Tibetan carried off in one of the *Jeeps* driven by the Chinese. Some were beaten mercilessly with bamboo rods for simply saying "Long live the Dalai Lama" outside Potala Palace. And Pembuti began to feel anger well-up inside her once again. She couldn't fathom why the Tibetan people were not allowed to show support for His Holiness; why they weren't permitted to recite their mantras. And she decided it was time to rebel against such cruel authority--as her father had.

One day soon after as Pembuti traversed the Lingkhor (the sacred path walked in a clockwise direction as a sign of religiosity), she turned right and crossed the road to continue along the Lingkhor Circuit. As she passed Potala Palace (on the side of Marpo Ri: "Red Mountain") she stopped and took a moment to marvel at the palace itself. She looked in awe at the immense inward-sloping walls broken only in the upper parts by straight rows of many windows; the flat, multi-leveled roofs of this thirteen-story palace. An errant flash of sunlight glinting off the gilt canopies of the roof tops blinded her. Rubbing her eyes she was then drawn to the central part of the palace; painted crimson and called "the Red Palace," this colour distinguished it from the remainder of the building. She'd hoped that one day her son Palden would study and practice here--learn his mantras and prayers in the great libraries brimming with precious scrolls and books. Pembuti had learned as a child at the nunnery that within the Red Palace were chapels, shrines, and halls adorned with rich decorative paintings, carvings, and other bejewelled craftsmanship. She sighed. She had no idea where her son was or if he were even still alive.

As Pembuti continued on her path, a group of Chinese soldiers approached waving knives--pretending to stab at her as they circled menacingly. Breathing slowly to control her fear she looked down and kept walking, daring not look them in the eyes. They glared at her, made mocking sounds and gestures, and she could almost feel their eyes burning into her back. Only when she'd walked a safe distance away did she dare turn round. To her relief they were still standing exactly where she'd left them, only now they were laughing as they talked and smoked their hand-rolled cigarettes. She continued on.

Pembuti make her way to Norbulingka (meaning "treasured park"), the site of the Dalai Lama's summer palace, located a little less than a mile from Potala Palace. Surrounded by a stone wall some twelve feet high, the palace within had golden turrets and consisted of three buildings used for official and state business. An inner enclosure, also protected by a high wall, was used by the Dalai Lama as a pleasure garden and contained a beautiful artificial lake with two islands upon which two summer-houses were built. At the north-west corner a wide stone causeway enabled one to reach the islands and the summer-house on each, where the Dalai Lama spent many hours each day in meditation. Inside the park were barracks housing some five hundred men who served as the Dalai Lama's personal bodyguards (and army, if necessary).

Pembuti strolled across the beautiful countryside and through an ornamental gateway leading to the inner enclosure. All manner of birds were pecking food from the ground as she entered--but took no notice of her—and she had to get out of their way! The lake was placid, like a highly-polished metal mirror. Here Pembuti lingered a while, this somewhat magical place offering her the sanctuary she needed. The fire of revenge still burned hot within her but here in this tranquil, idyllic setting she found peace and compassion--if only for the moment. Still, even now she felt the urgent need for a plan:

She wanted the Dalai Lama back in his rightful place. She wanted her children back in her life. But, *how?* the question remained. She certainly could not *kill* all the Chinese! So, what could she actually do to help the Tibetan people and benefit her own life? She knew only too well what happened to those who opposed the regime; she'd witnessed people dragged away in Chinese government vehicles simply for handing out leaflets saying *Long Live the Dalai Lama!* Yet she knew she had to do *something.* She thought perhaps she could bring Tibetans together and they could spread the word of solidarity for Lhasa and the return of His Holiness.

As Pembuti made her way back to Lhasa, a plan began to form in her mind. And by the time she reached town, she'd worked out many of the details. Although she wanted to act quickly, she knew that any plan would require careful organization. Meticulous preparation. (This was very dangerous business!) And so with Gado's words still ringing in her ears, for the safety of his mother Pembuti moved out to share a room with Rinzen, one of her new friends who was herself a freedom fighter. Pembuti knew she had to choose her comrades carefully (there were spies and Chinese-sympathisers round every corner) and be absolutely certain they would fight for the freedom of Tibet and safe return of the Dalai Lama. So she watched and listened in cafés and other meeting places round Lhasa and began to note who was *pro* Dalai Lama and showed enough passion to fight for his return. Eventually she'd compiled a list of some twenty people she felt she could approach with her plan, ultimately inviting them to attend a secret meeting.

At the meeting, each person was asked to declare their allegiance to the Dalai Lama and their preparedness to help gather support for his return to his rightful home, Potala Palace. Soon a group of twenty loyal men and woman was formed and together began to formulate their long-term strategy. Leaflets were printed with the words *Freedom for Tibet, Long Live the Dalai Lama* and they drew reinforcement from friends and family. Steadily the group grew in number. Although they wanted to stay local and spread the word covertly, they knew they had to take their message outside to those Tibetans who'd been brainwashed with promises of good fortune from the Chinese, as well as those who'd been bullied and blackmailed to join the Chinese reformers. Pembuti insisted that she be the one to leaflet Lhasa; she knew there was every chance of being caught but also knew that the thousands of leaflets they'd printed would help the morale of Tibetans and rouse them to demand the return of their precious Dalai Lama.

The day finally arrived when Pembuti, joined by a number of other Tibetans, headed to the centre of Lhasa. Weighed down with arm-loads of leaflets she began to quickly hand them out, saying 'Join us! Join us!' Some dropped the leaflets immediately and walked away in fear--not wanting to get involved. Others took them and smiled--nodding their support. Pembuti was nearing the end of her supply when a *Jeep* screeched to a halt beside her: four armed Chinese guards jumped out, manhandled her into their vehicle, and drove off. The next thing she knew she was waking up on the hard and dirty concrete floor of a prison cell. The year was 1987.

The uprising viciously crushed (sending some group members into hiding) Pembuti and nearly one hundred other Tibetans were subjected to severe flogging in wide-spread mass-accusation trials. (There was talk that many had been executed in other cities throughout Tibet for rebelling against the Chinese regime.) Life in prison was hard. Often brutal. Pembuti and the others were made to listen--day-in, day-out--and repeat in parrot-fashion, Chinese propaganda. Pembuti now began to understand how the Chinese government had succeeded in controlling the Tibetan people. Monks and nuns were especially persecuted; lay people oppressed and intimidated. Most days, Pembuti, a nun or monk was tortured. There was no formal sentencing and no right of appeal; all inmates were forced to work--cleaning, building, carrying, and serving their Chinese overlords. *Tsampa* was rationed and they were given only a small bowl of cabbage soup each day.

Pembuti was amongst the most restless and vocal, beginning each day by loudly reciting her support of His Holiness the Dalai Lama; spitting at the guards who demanded she remain quiet. "Release me! Leafleting Lhasa is not a *crime*! You are in *our* country uninvited—you dogs!" Such outbursts were met with the tying of her arms with coarse rope behind her back, gaging her with filthy rags, and hard hits across her back or legs with a bamboo rod—causing excruciating pain that left her limp, weak, and bloody. But still she persisted, and the beatings continued.

"We are here to liberate you from your uncivilized life!" she was repeatedly told. "We are here to *help* you—do you not understand this, stupid woman?!"

Blinded by pain and misery, Pembuti coveted the pistols her captors kept in their holsters and knew that if she had the strength she'd grab one and shoot them dead--one after another.

Each day she was interrogated for refusing to memorize and recite the Chinese propaganda relentlessly spewed upon her: "You are a political prisoner and like the rest here, you will read and repeat our *truths*! Whether you like it or not, you will be re-educated! You will be tested and if you fail to answer our questions correctly, you will be punished! Do you understand?!" Each interrogation was concluded by slaps to the face or kicks to the stomach (from the more sadistic guards). Eventually, this led her to a new strategy: Pembuti would feign adherence. She realised that while inside prison she was helpless, useless, and unable to spread the word of the Dalai Lama or freedom for Tibet. So she outwardly changed. She learned all the *truths* and could recite them *verbatim.* She kept her political and religious ideas to herself and never spoke back. Finally, after eight years of imprisonment, she was released and allowed to return to Lhasa.

Once back in Lhasa, Pembuti could not contain herself. Along with a group of activist nuns, Pembuti (and the others) shouted slogans and distributed pro-Tibet leaflets in public squares and were, as no surprise, immediately arrested by Chinese police and taken back to prison, charged with "endangering state security." Now a repeat offender (and political subversive), Pembuti was placed in a section of the prison for female political prisoners. As before, each time Pembuti (and the other prisoners) refused to participate in the official state propaganda recital, they were beaten. Over the ensuing years, Pembuti staged numerous hunger strikes and other demonstrations--and each time the beatings were more severe than before. (Several times she was beaten so severely that she had to be force-fed so the lessons and beatings could continue.)

Labelled a "dissonant ring-leader," Pembuti had five years added to her original eight-year sentence, most of it spent in constraints.

After serving more than twenty years behind bars, Pembuti was finally set free and allowed to return to Lhasa. But there her freedom was so curtailed that it was nearly impossible to exist; nothing to do all day and no faith to follow. (A pariah in her own town, most fellow freedom-fighters avoided her.) Eventually she was asked to join a new underground movement of Tibetan rebels. But having already attempted every strategy they were planning, she did her best to persuade them to think beyond Lhasa. To target a much more significant site:

Nepal. Thus an escape committee was organised with this plan of action in mind.

On a cold and windy day soon after, Pembuti and a party of twenty-five men, woman, and children quietly slipped out of Lhasa—one-by-one. Slowly, so as not to arouse suspicion, they left Lhasa at varying times; all on foot, utilising a single yak to carry their provisions. Eventually every member of the group arrived at the arranged meeting place along the Lhasa River, where they began their long trek to Nepal (located in the Himalayan Mountains and bordered by China in the north, India in the south, east, and west). Glancing back, Pembuti could just see Iron Hill with its medical college sitting proudly in the morning sun, and Potala Palace was like a glimmering speck in the distance on the conical-shaped hill. Through rich fields of oats, wheat, peas, barley, and potatoes, past water mills where flour was being ground under large stone wheels, they traversed. She knew this would be the last time she'd see all this incredible beauty and felt deep sadness and pain in her heart. She took one last look at the rock sculptures carved out of the cliffs along the roadside.

A long and arduous journey ahead of them, they had few provisions: a few tents, some prepared *tsampa*, a ration of cured meat, some butter and herb tea. Wearily they trudged on using as much daylight as available and at night they set up camp near the river so they had a supply of fresh water for cooking. But it was the bitter cold that was most daunting. Day and night the cold (combined with the treacherous terrain) hindered their progress and sapped their energy. As they trudged onwards along dangerous rocky paths they repeated their mantras, said prayers for His Holiness the Dalai Lama, and twirled their prayer wheels against the unrelenting wind. The rock faces rose in almost sheer cliffs above them; some rocks had split into shimmering steel columns. Pembuti noticed perched on the top of one of these imposing pinnacles the ruins of an old castle, and on a knife-ledge lower, ruins of a second fortress. From the lofty position of this fortress, Pembuti realised, a panoramic view of the trade routes from India, Nepal, Bhutan, and Shigaste--straight to Lhasa--was available. But the track was so narrow that they had to walk single-file-- over masses of rocks that had fallen from above. They were forced to weave in and out of giant boulders, climb muddy slippery slopes, upwards and across cliffs of granite hanging precariously over the rushing swirling tide of the muddy river below.

At last they came to another rich valley where they saw rich crops of oats, peas, rape, mustard, and coriander. As Pembuti looked at the unfolding scenery she could just make out, bobbing up and down on the surface of a large pond, some beautiful pink-coloured blooms of lotus flowers. She walked quickly towards them, drawn in by their natural beauty, wanting desperately to hold one in her hands. She knelt down and reached out towards the bobbing blooms, gently cupping her hands round the one nearest her, bending down to breathe in the rich intoxicating aroma. She knew that the lotus flower reflected the purity of heart and mind, and represented long life, health and luck. As her fingers fondled the soft delicate petals she took this moment to pray for their safety on this difficult and dangerous journey. Dusk was now falling and she knew that soon this beautiful flower would close and withdraw beneath the water, only to reappear at dawn in all its brazen glory. She closed her eyes and inhaled deeply; she wanted to remember this smell and the euphoric sensation of love, happiness and joy it brought to her being, always. She let go the lotus flower as she felt herself fall forward towards the deep dark, muddy waters where the lotus roots were deeply embedded, hearing . . .

"Pembuti! Pembuti!" Then as the warmth of the lotus faded, someone grabbed her hand and a warmhearted sensation overtook her.

Chapter 13

PEMBUTI OPENED HER EYES—CONFUSED, FOR there was a man holding her hand. It took a few moments to remember where she was and that this was her son, Palden. "How do you feel, Ama La?" said Palden.

"Well enough, I suppose, for an old woman," she whispered with a hint of acceptance; hint of good humour.

He stood above her and smiled down into her drowsy eyes. "You know, Ama La, I am a trained doctor in Tibetan medicine. And I know I can help you to get better. Will you let me try?" A look of hesitation flashed across his Ama La's face. "I can prepare herbs and curatives that will not only heal your body, they will heal your soul. Enliven your spirit. Will you accept my help?"

Pembuti thought for a moment. She felt certain that her son could help her, but the question was, did she *want* help? Or did she want to die? Was it time to leave this life or should she prolong her existence? As she looked up into Palden's face, his eyes pleaded with her, and in that moment she knew she would have to accept his help. She'd given him nothing throughout his difficult life and this was one small thing she could give him now: "Yes, Palden. I will be happy to accept your help."

"Good, Ama La!" Palden smiled broadly for the first time since entering his mother's room.

"I remember back on the Tibetan Plateau, using herbs and plants we found in the countryside. Is it like that?" Pembuti asked.

"Yes, Ama La, it is *just* like that! I shall go now and return shortly with the first remedy," he said, bowing and kissing her damp forehead.

Outside the room Palden found Tenzin waiting. "I am certain I can help her become well, but I worry about her will to live. Her mind is feeble. And she seems to have little desire to go on. I am going now to prepare a medicament which will strengthen her mind, body, and spirit." Tenzin smiled her hope and support.

Over the next few days, Palden spent many hours with his Ama La, who was slowly responding to his herbal treatment and Tenzin's round-the-clock care, and to the special, fortifying diet Palden had prescribed for her. Pembuti began showing interest in everyday affairs again, coming more into the present; but still clung to her guilt and painful memories of her past, which Palden tried to address. But after checking his mother's progress on his next visit, Palden sighed and sat down beside her bed. She was not recovering as quickly as he'd hoped; her speech was still slurred and she was easily winded. And when she spoke it seemed to sap all her energy. Even so, she was more alert and *wanting* to get well.

During one of his recent visits with the Karmapa, Palden had related the story of his recent meeting with his mother and how happy he was to at last have her in his life—though she was rather ill. It took him by surprise when the Karmapa made what seemed to be an odd request: "Palden, I would like you to take your mother to Samye

Ling in Scotland as I feel that the medicine--the *true* medicine--she needs will be found there. The clear Scottish mountain air will do her *unimaginable* good," the Karmapa said, a look of certainty on his wise face.

Palden wondered how his Ama La would react to this idea, and wondered if she was even well enough to undergo such a long, strenuous journey. Meanwhile, Pembuti was reflecting on her life—having no idea where all the years had gone. It was to her as if only yesterday she was a young girl playing outside her tent on the Plateau. She now asked herself where all her anger had come from. When it all started. How was it that she could kill so easily another human being? (She'd lost count of how many lives she'd taken.) Where had all her Buddhist beliefs gone; had she abandoned them or had they deserted her? Why had she not chosen (as she'd been taught) to meditate and send prayers out to those who killed, tortured, and abused her homeland and its people? Killed her mother and father? Was that not the best way to change the minds of the new and even old generations? And now, her son wanted to treat her . . . to keep her alive! Was this the universe's way of affording her time to rectify all the wrong she'd done? To make up for abandoning her son?

"*Scotland*!?" Pembuti rasped at the top of her frail voice—disbelieving what she'd heard him say. "Why--*how* would I go to *Scotland*, my son? I am old, Palden. My best days are behind me. I can barely walk on my own!"

Taken aback by the thought of such foolishness, Pembuti's thoughts flew back in time; back to a young Scottish doctor who'd taken her baby daughter away from her. Away to this place, "Scotland," on the other side of the world. And now her son was suggesting that she should accompany him to this distant, foreign place! And suddenly, something deep inside her resonated with this idea; something so powerful that she found herself agreeing to make the arduous journey she had little confidence she could complete. And for a moment she found herself awash in pure joy—her mind more alert than it had been in recent memory: Could she find her Scottish doctor there in Scotland? Find her lost daughter?

"If the Karmapa believes it is what I should do, I will not go against his wishes," she resigned.

A week later after a hot and jarring, frightening taxi ride from Dharamsala to Gaggal Airport (swerving in and out of traffic), Pembuti began to have second thoughts about Scotland. The thought of flying—and more stomach-churning taxi rides--now terrified her. As they waited in the hot and steamy airport for their flight to be announced, mother and son did not share the same emotions. Palden's heart soared at the thought of taking such a wondrous journey with his Ama La while Pembuti feared she'd have to disappoint her son. Just then the *Tannoy* loudspeakers boomed out that *Buddha Airways* flight to Delhi was now boarding. When Pembuti saw the old and battered, small twelve-seater plane, her fears mounted. Palden held on tightly to his mother's arm as he guided her on-board and into their seats. Pembuti had thought she knew the risks they were taking—but now had great doubts. But if she were ever to find her lost daughter, it had to be now. Summoning the courage which had gotten her through the most horrendous times of her life, she looked at her son and said, "Tell me what you know about this *Scotland.*"

Delhi Airport was jammed with throngs of people rushing about—as if aimlessly. The chatter, the almost constant blare of the loudspeakers, and the din of hustle and bustle was deafening. Pembuti clung tightly to Palden's arm as he pushed his way through the shifting masses. Her first visit to this bustling metropolis, Pembuti was overcome with the mayhem of all the vehicles; the loud clamour of horns as the drivers vied for their place in the pecking order of the almost non-existent taxi stand. The air outside was hot and stifling and Pembuti found herself feeling light-headed and drawn. As they forced their way through the sea of people, Palden was suddenly met by an older man with a deeply-lined face, small beady black eyes and bristly white hair. After initial pleasantries, Palden introduced his mother:

"Ama La, this is Raju, my very dear friend. This, Raju, is my mother."

Raju bowed and smiled. "Let's get out of here. The car is over there," he said, pointing to a nest of vehicles.

Seated in the back of Raju's old and battered black *Toyota*, Pembuti took in all the exotic scenery as Raju wove in and out of traffic at unnerving speeds, skillfully avoiding numerous cows and people wandering the streets, seemingly aimlessly. Pembuti noticed that the vehicles seemed to adhere to no traffic signs nor road rules but nonetheless managed to somehow navigate without colliding. At last they came to a stop outside a dress shop on a narrow street on the outskirts of Delhi, Palden announcing, "We're here."

Alighting from the car, Raju ushered Pembuti through a door at the side of the shop. The three entered a dimly-lit hall and came to a stone staircase, which Palden helped his mother scale at her own pace. At the top was a large open balcony and Raju led the way, carrying their bags. They entered a door at the far end of the balcony. Inside was a kitchen, lounge, and another stone stairway leading up to another floor. Setting down their suitcases, Raju went to the cooker and lighted the gas, then placed the chrome kettle on the ring. "Tea," he announced, but Pembuti wanted only to rest. The stifling heat and the trip there had sapped her of her strength.

"Not for me, thank you, Raju. Is there somewhere I can lie down for a few minutes. I am afraid I am a bit light-headed."

Raju waved towards the sofa and said, "*Please . . .*"

As Palden and Raju talked, Pembuti sat on the old and tattered brown sofa and was soon fast asleep—and light-years away--finding herself decades younger and at the nunnery. It seemed that only moments had passed before she heard, "Time to wake up, Ama La, we must eat. We must be up early in the morning for our flight so it is food and then bed," said Palden. Pembuti rubbed her eyes.

"What time is it, Palden?"

Glancing at his watch, Palden said, "It is 5:00. You have been asleep for about one hour."

After a delicious meal of okra and vegetable curries (Pembuti unable to remember when she'd tasted anything so good), Raju showed her to her room. It was small and the stone walls bare--in keeping with the bare, stone floor. The single bed had surely seen better days but Pembuti was thankful for it and after washing up, changed into her sleeping gown. She was soon fast asleep on the multicoloured spread that brightened up the rusty wrought-iron frame. The next morning the three rose bright and early and after a quick breakfast of potato curry headed off in Raju's old car for the airport. There, after an exchange of handshakes, bows, and expressions of "thanks," mother and son set off on the final leg of their journey.

After a long and exhausting twenty-four-hour trek across the continents, Palden and Pembuti arrived at Samye Ling Monastery. Ushered to their accommodations, twin rooms within the original Johnstone House building, mother and son were brought a light supper, after which they bathed and retired for the night; both wanting to be well-rested for tomorrow. A meeting had been set for Rinpoche, Palden, and Pembuti for the next afternoon.

The next day as mother and son sat waiting for Rinpoche to arrive, they sat in silence, each to their own thoughts. So deep were they in contemplation that they didn't hear Rinpoche enter the room. Though catching Palden and Pembuti momentarily off guard, they were instantly warmed by Rinpoche's smile as they all formally greeted one other. Palden introduced his mother to his old friend, with discernible pride, who in turn smiled and welcomed her to Samye Ling.

Now in the habit of presenting Palden with a riddle at each meeting, Rinpoche said, "Ah, you see the three lamas, Palden."

Palden thought for a moment; curious and confused. *Three lamas?* He was reluctant to admit that he did not, but could not lie. "I feel as if I am being watched," Palden offered by way of reply.

Rinpoche pointed to the near-by window, smiled and nodded. "See, Palden--out there on the branch of that tree? The three crows?" Palden looked and indeed--staring directly into the room intently--were three black crows. It was only natural for Rinpoche to think of the three as *lamas*.

After catching up on recent events in their respective lives, Palden turning much of the attention towards his Ama La, Rinpoche made a suggestion: "Palden, I believe that you and your mother should visit a Dharma centre in the Highlands, which I believe may have much to offer you both."

"Dharma Centre?"

"Yes, Palden. It is a project which I have overseen for a number of years now involving a young Scottish woman who has visited me here on several occasions—and on one visit, presented me with a Peace Tartan Scarf." Palden looked to his mother for a reaction. "You see, this young woman, who is not a Buddhist, is developing the centre alone and could very much benefit from your help. And as tomorrow I am on my way back to Tibet, I believe the time has come for me to hand over the role of overseer, and I would like to hand that role to you, Palden. I am certain that both you and your mother will benefit greatly from meeting this young woman and living at her centre. I wish you both well, I know that your journey will be rewarding."

Palden smiled and clutched his mother's hand firmly. Things were moving quite quickly now—and in ways he'd never conceived. Momentarily his thoughts flitted to Tibet and then India. It seemed that he was destined to move his life to a new land. To start anew. And now that he had his beloved Ama La with him, life was wonderful. Pembuti smiled proudly at her son.

"Thank you, Akong! Of course, I graciously accept!"

Chapter 14

ANNE GAZED THOUGHTFULLY OUT OF the window, out across the mani-cured lawn and gravel driveway, watching the black taxi approach. She followed it as it slowly wound its way up the driveway to the front steps. She watched as a middle-aged Tibetan looking man and an elderly wom-an stepped out and came to the door. She smiled. (*A man and woman from Tibet might be just what I need to make the Dharma centre work!* she mused.)

Curious, she headed out of the study and hurried down the stairs, coming face-to-face with her two visitors--whom Kyla had invited in. (Kyla had asked to stay on and help Anne as she too had quickly fallen in love with this rambling old house.) As Anne reached the bottom, a flash of turquoise caught the old Tibetan woman's eye--the blue-green stones of Anne's necklace reflected sharply in the sun. An old gold-framed photograph on the wall then drew the woman's attention--instantly recognising the facial similarities of the man to those of a handsome Scottish doctor who'd once befriended her in Tibet. The Tibetan man offered Anne his hand and spoke in a soft and pleasant tone:

"My name is Palden, and this is my mother, I call her Ama La which means mother in Tibetan" he said graciously.

"Very nice to meet you," Anne said, studying both their faces. "I'm Anne, and this is my assistant, Kyla".

"Anne, just before Akong Rinpoche made his final trip to Tibet, he suggested that my mother and I visit you here and offer our help in running your Dharma Centre. I know this may seem like a strange idea, but in his wisdom he thought this may benefit us all. No doubt you know that Akong was since murdered, but we are here to fulfill his wishes and offer our help, should you require it."

As Anne stood speechless before these two strangers, smiling, it suddenly occurred to her that each time she became confused, sidetracked, or lost for answers, something would occur to allow her to stay on her path. Just when she'd been grieving for Akong and lamenting her sense of hopelessness, an offer of help had *literally* landed on her doorstep! And suddenly her whole world lit up. There was hope! She was no longer struggling on her own! The plan to establish the Dharma Centre in Scotland would forge ahead as planned!

Chapter 15

"THERE'S ONE LAST ROOM YOU should see," said Anne. "It's a private room, not really part of the centre at all. I use it as my study, office, and *sometimes* meditation area. Come—it's just down the hall."

It didn't take long, even allowing for Pembuti's slow pace, for them to tour the house and arrive at a dark wood-paneled door at the end of the upstairs hall. Anne grasped the well-worn and tarnished brass handle and turned it. As the door swung open, a smallish room with an open fireplace on one wall was revealed. Free-standing shelving units occupied two of the remaining walls, the last wall taken up by a large bay window. A leather armchair set close to the fire, allowing whomever sat in it to have a view of the ancient Alders outside. The room was finished off with a bureau-type table with files and papers stacked on it, and a couple of high-backed chairs. The warmth in the room came from the dying embers of the smouldering fire.

"I don't use this room often," explained Anne, "but I always try to remember to feed the fire and keep the fire going. Some of my own paperwork is in here, but it's mostly old photos and odd papers from long ago." As Anne pointed to some old photographs that hung round the walls and occupying some of the shelves, Pembuti had already sat herself comfortably in the leather armchair.

"It has been such a long journey already—and I am not so young as I once was," Pembuti said in her best English. "I think I had better rest a bit."

"Yes, that is a very good idea, Ama La," nodded Palden. "Good to save your strength. Anne and I can look through these old photos and papers and she can educate me on more things *Scottish*, although maybe I can teach her about things *Tibetan*." Palden surveyed the room. "I see that there are ornaments and pictures of Tibet here," Palden said, picking up the astrology charts that Anne had looked at earlier. "These are very old Tibetan astrology predictions," he said knowingly as he began to translate. "Year of the Wood Cock, 1885. Baby girl: Karlha. Birthmark: On the back of thigh a round black circle. There will be two main obstacles to overcome in your life. The first has to do with love and loss. Although you will not marry you will take a husband as such, but this relationship will not last for a long period. There are forces out to destroy you in the Year of the Iron Ox (1901), your body will be weak but your mind strong. The wheels of life, birth and death are turning.

Anne's heart began to flutter. Laying the first chart aside he picked up the second. He translated:

"'Year of the Iron Horse, 1870. Baby boy: Yutso. You will love to quarrel and to fight. A feud will break out and if you take part in this you will invoke the dark forces of the wrathful deities. Be warned not to provoke an altercation during this feud as this will bring forth endless suffering for yourself and family, and generations to come. Should you partake in this feud then your young life will suddenly come to an abrupt end. Be forewarned--'"

Pembuti raised her head and looked to Palden when she heard the name "Karlha." Karlha had been her grandmother's name. She'd died giving birth to her Mother the day after the sky burial for her grandfather, Yutso. She smiled. Everything in this room now felt so familiar to her.

While Anne and Palden sifted through more documents, Pembuti stared into the dimming flames of the log fire. Without forethought she reached out with her left hand and removed the wrought-iron poker from its metal stand next to the fireplace and prodded the dying embers. The fire sputtered and crackled back to life and filled the room with a sudden burst of light. Hearing the fire flame-up, Palden and Anne turned round to see Pembuti straining to lift herself out of her chair, headed for the big bay window.

"Careful, Ama La," scolded Palden. "You should rest more. Just stay where you are."

"You do not need to fuss over me," replied Pembuti. "I heard a noise outside the window and just wanted to see what it was."

Just then the light from the blazing fire caught the stones of Anne's necklace and sent prismatic bolts of turquoise round the room—reflected directly into Pembuti's aging eyes. She raised her old and weathered hand to shield her face. Anne instinctively covered the necklace with her open hand as if to subdue the dramatic light it cast.

"My father gave me this necklace," replied Anne, feeling the need to explain.

Just then the noise outside the window that had drawn Pembuti's attention repeated. The old woman turned and faced the window expectantly: "See, there!" she said, pointing out the window. "There-- on that branch! A *crow*! And a *big* fellow! I *thought* I recognised that sound!"

Outside the window a great oak tree stood swaying back and forth in the breeze as a solitary black bird clung to a bare branch, staring in. And as Palden and Anne approached the window, they saw the crow fluttering its wings and seeming to caw out a cryptic message. Pembuti smiled and turned her attention to what interested her more:

"Anne, that photograph, over there on the shelf . . . " Pembuti said, squinting her eyes and pointing a bony finger. "The one with all the soldiers standing round. Could I see it?"

Anne walked to the shelf and picked up the faded, black-framed photo. It stood amongst a dozen or more others and Anne wondered how Pembuti had singled it out. She crossed the room and handed it to the old woman. "It's a picture of my father, from his time in Tibet," explained Anne. "That's what's written on the back."

Pembuti's face lit up. A smile spread across her thin lips that made her eyes dance like those of a child. "No, it is a picture of *us*! *All* of us!" said Pembuti, looking up into Anne and Palden's confused faces. "The doctor was a fine man! A very good man!"

Anne looked at Palden and saw recognition in his face as he nodded and smiled. A moment later the photograph came to life as never before:

"Are you saying . . . ?"

"Yes! This is *us*—you Anne and you Palden, as babies!" she said, tears welling up in her ancient eyes. "And me standing there with Alexander, the kind doctor I entrusted with taking you out of Tibet and to a better life here in Scotland! I could never forget that day!"

Pembuti, Palden, and Anne reached out their hands to each other as mother, son, and daughter.

And as their hands joined, the room filled with the sweet aroma of pine and juniper; with the sound of children giggling beneath pale yellow city street lights, and beneath the sun basking the lush green of open, high meadows. With the view of snow-capped, wind-swept mountain peaks, and the piercing turquoise and blue colours of mirror-still lakes and fast flowing rivers; to the crimson red of flowing robes. All this and more filled the little room. So much so that it spilled out like waves sent rippling by a pebble, through the big old house and into its very fabric—across time. And on across the lawns and trees, across the duck pond touching the water lilies, it passed like a great enveloping wave to touch everyone and everything that reached out for it.

Epilogue

THE EARLY MORNING TRANQUILITY WAS shattered by the piercing *beep-beep-beep* of the alarm clock. The young man moaned as he reluctantly turned his head across the soft cotton pillow to look at the flickering red numbers on the clock's display; just to confirm that it was in fact that time of day again. A raised and dismembered voice added to his shattered peace:

"Are you up, yet?" In point of fact, it didn't sound like a questioning voice but a statement of impending fact. "I need you to move some of that new feed-stuff out of the back shed and into the trailer." (Another statement of fact booming out of thin air.) The lad knew the voice. It was his father; his voice having carried up from the kitchen downstairs. There was no need to reply; one wasn't expected nor welcome.

Reluctantly the duvet was thrown off the bed and a still-tired pair of legs swung over and onto the floor. As the soles of his feet winced at the coldness of the timber floor, the young man felt round with his toes for the fabric touch of his jeans, which had been thoughtlessly discarded the night before. Once located, the garment was collected by outstretched hands as the boy raised himself, reluctantly, to his feet.

"And I hope you're remembering," came another fact from the voice, "that you're to go up to the big house round mid-morning. They've got problems with some of the doors up there. Not opening and closing properly or some such."

The young man had, in fact, forgotten that particular chore, the reminder spurring him to quicken his pace and pull on his jeans and T-shirt, and rummage under his bed for his trainers and cleanest dirty socks. Moments later he pushed sleep-eyed through the kitchen door.

"Thought that would get you moving!" smiled his dad, the voice no longer separated from its body.

"Don't know what you mean," replied the son as he reached into the fridge to take out a small container of orange juice.

"Of course you do," continued the father. "I'm not stupid you know. A've been there and done that."

The lad just shook his head as if to disregard his father's comments, but knew what his father was on about.

"She's a pretty enough young thing, so she is--and no mistake," his father said, giving his son a sidelong glance.

The young man quickly gulped down the last drops of orange juice and set the empty carton on the kitchen table, gave his dad an embarrassed frown and headed out the back door. A couple of hours later he sought out his dad and confirmed that the new feed-stuff was now loaded onto the trailer, as instructed.

"Remember to take some tools with you this time!" scolded his dad. "Not much of a *handy* man if you arrive at the big house with nothing to be *handy* with!" he said, a wry smile spreading across his face.

The lad gave his father another frustrated look and went off to look for the small tool kit. Once found, the kit was dropped into his backpack and he set off for the big house.

The big house was about a mile-and-a-half's walk from the little farm the boy's father owned and worked. It was quite a stately pile, the big house, and his father had helped out when the new owner had moved in. The house had got a bit run down and as one of the nearest neighbours, his father had put the owner in touch with local tradesmen and suppliers and such. But for smaller jobs, he'd volunteered himself to help when he could. That job had now passed down to his son.

As the young man hiked the short distance to the big house, along the narrow tarmac road, he occasionally had to move over onto the grass verge to allow cars to pass. There wasn't much traffic on that road, usually locals coming and going on their daily business, but sometimes a lost tourist's car with Dutch or German plates would happen by. But when not jumping aside to avoid curious motorists, the lad would take in the soothing views over the hedge-lined fields of neighbouring farms and the gardens of the farm cottages that were spread out along his route to the big house. He'd played with his pals in some of these gardens as a young boy--one daring the others to see how deep they could get into the gardens without being spotted by the owners. Sometimes it wasn't much of a challenge as many of the cottages had been made holiday homes, and were unoccupied for much of the year.

Eventually the narrow road opened up onto a junction with the main road and as the boy turned left he could see in the distance the imposing outline of the big house, set back on its own grounds, a piece off the main road. He soon reached the entrance to the estate—something he could hardly miss: Two tall ancient-looking stone columns stood on either side of a wide, gravel driveway, and perched on the top of each was a majestic stone eagle with outstretched wings. As he turned into the driveway, he looked up and saw a large crow perched beneath the wing of the eagle on the right—closely watching him.

The driveway wasn't particularly long--but long enough when you were trying to tread through deep gravel, and the lad always wondered why it had never been upgraded to tarmac. As he crunched his way along, between the rows of spruce trees set on either side of the drive-way, his gaze took in the once formal lawns and the duck pond in the near distance whose edge was now blurred with water lilies. Eventually the driveway gave out onto a semi-circle of gravel, and there at its base stood the old house.

As he approached the rise of curved stone steps leading to the old worn oak door, the young man stopped and wondered if she'd be there. He recognized two of the cars parked on the semi-circle: the dark green *Range Rover*, which belonged to the new owner, and the silver *Mercedes* Saloon, driven by one of the owner's friends. But today there was a third car. He thought it was familiar--but wasn't sure. If she was coming up to the house she usually sent him a text, but she hadn't been in touch. Anyway, he'd know soon enough. He rang the doorbell and waited.

A few moments later the door swung in, opened by a young woman, delicate and petite. Her long auburn hair played over her shoulders in waves and framed in a smooth porcelain-fine face, pronounced by high cheeks bones and a sharp-but-sensual jaw line. The lightness and spar-kle of her blue-green eyes were offset by the intensity of her full, pink lips. They smiled at one other.

"Hello!" said the lad brightly. "Long time no see!"

"Yes, I had to go back down south for a while," explained the girl, "but I'm here now helping for the rest of the summer."

"Did anyone tell you I was coming to fix the doors?" the young man said.

"Oh yes, yes--they did tell me," confirmed the girl, glancing behind. "I think it's the library door and the main door into the big dining room that's the problem." (They exchanged a longing glance.) "I--I won't hold you back . . . and you know your way round . . . " she said with a smile; her words trailing off.

The young man blushed slightly. "Okay, I'll get to it then," he said, slipping by her.

"Oh--when you're finished, come looking for me. We can catch up on things. I'll most likely be in the kitchen."

The boy smiled. "Okay. Will do . . . "

The lad did in fact know the house quite well. For the first few years he'd come to the house to help his dad when it was more than handyman's work that was needed; just after the new owner had moved in. That was when he'd discovered her. Bumped into her, *literally*, during one of her visits. While the older folk were busy going on about removing walls and building new ones, they'd been left alone to explore the house and the grounds. And at first it had been just playful fun; teasing each other about eerie noises, things that went bump in the middle of the night, and ghosts that *surely* inhabited the old house. But slowly, as growing teenagers, their friendship grew and progressed.

Shaking himself from his memories, the lad arrived outside the library and set himself to figuring out the problem with the door. (His father had taught him long ago what to look for.) As he pushed it back and forth it began to squeak, and when he tried to close it, the handle wouldn't turn. *Maybe it just needs some oil*, he thought. But the squeaking of the door brought back a memory of the girl. It was during her last visit, just a few months before . . .

They'd been sitting in the house all day looking through some old papers and photographs, but it was such a nice afternoon that they decided to go outside for walk on the grounds. They'd set off across the lawn--teasing and goading each other with nudges and casual touches--and soon found themselves outside the old barn. Slightly ajar, the old barn door squeaked as it moved in the breeze. They wandered inside.

The atmosphere was still--but not calming. Away from prying eyes their playful prodding and goading quickly turned into longer, more intimate touches. To this boy, the girl was something that had to be touched to make certain she were real; caressed to experience the fineness of her soft and supple skin. He found that his touches made her smile. He kissed her lips and let his hands roam across her body. Soon they were lost in the touching, the kissing, and the fire of each other's body, and no words were spoken nor necessary . . .

As they lie half-dressed beside each other on the straw of the barn floor, they gazed warmly at each other and smiled. The young man cupped the girl's face in his two hands and kissed her gently. He then rose to his feet, adjusted his clothes, and put out his hand to help her up. Fully dressed, together they left the still and now calm atmosphere of the barn . . .

The sound of the door squeaking receded from his ears and the handle began to turn in the lad's able hand. He pushed the library door firmly closed with a *click*. Oiling the door had done the trick! Now on to the dining room door. Like the first, that too would only re-quired some oil to get it opening and closing properly. Jobs completed, he then made his way to the kitchen to look for the girl. And right enough she was there, unpacking groceries and stacking them in wall cupboards.

"That's a lot of supplies you've got there!" said the young man cheekily—by way of announcing his arrival.

The girl looked round from her work and smiled. "Yes, there's a residential course next week so they'll need to be well-fed."

The young man sensed that something wasn't quite right. "Say, are you okay?" he asked, taking a step towards the girl.

"Yes, yes I'm fine. Nothing to worry about," she replied, turning her back.

But the lad knew something was worrying the girl. "Uh . . . is it something I've done or said?"

"No it's not you . . . " said the girl, trying to reassure him, and herself.

"But, there must be *something* up," he said. "I mean, you didn't text me to say you were coming up—like you always do."

The girl stopped what she was doing and sat down on a chair at the kitchen table. (This was the cue for the young man to sit on the seat next to her.) "Well if you must know, I'm *late*," mumbled the girl.

"Late?" queried the lad. "*Late* for . . . ?

The girl gave him an exasperated look. "You know, *late*! *Remember*? The *barn*?!" she said, giving a look only he could translate.

"Oh--*that* late!" he said, rising from his chair and beginning to pace the floor.

"Lord only knows what's going to happen *now*?!" sighed the girl. "What will they all *say*? And *think*! I'll have to go away--and what about you? Your father will go mad!"

The young man sat back down, moved his chair closer, and took the young woman's hand in his. He smiled at her. It was a reassuring smile; a knowing smile. She smiled back. Hers too, a reassuring, know-ing smile. In silence they sat until the sound of adult voices intruded on their moment:

"See, young people today, where are they when you need them?" said one voice, jestingly. The lad smiled at the girl, recognizing the voice as his father's.

Her grandmother now stood directly before her and looked into her eyes, the girl felt as if her grandmother was looking right into her very soul. She knew she could never keep a secret from her.

"Something to tell me?" said her grandmother as she cast her eyes over her granddaughter and the boy.

The room remained silent.

"Blue, I think, yes, powder blue for the small bedroom upstairs, it will need re-decorated very soon I believe" muttered her grandmother out loud.

The two young people looked into each other's eyes and smiled. There was no need to go away! No need to go *anywhere*! They had everything and everyone they needed, right here! The young girl's hand moved absently to the small metal box that hung round her neck on a coral string. She felt loved, cherished, and protected. All was fine in their world.

When His Holiness the 17th Karmapa, Ogyen Trinley Dorje,
saw the handwriting and signature belonging to His Holiness
the 16th Karmapa on the 1974 Scottish tour programme,
I believe that he recognised and acknowledged it as his
own--a belief further supported by his suggestion that
I put this signed tour programme in a book for the world to see.
I ask you now, why would His holiness the 17th Karmapa ask me
To reveal this document with His Holiness the 16th
Karmapa's handwriting and signature if he is not the
true and rightful 17th Karmapa?
Can the 17th Karmapa's decision to show the world
this document prove
once and for all that he is indeed the rightful 17th Karmapa
and end the on-going Karmapa Controversy?

Author Biography

VISIONARY AUTHOR, CLAIRVOYANT, AND SELF-DEVELOPMENT Expert, Alison Demarco has touched the hearts and souls of countless individuals worldwide for over three decades. An expert on human nature, Alison identifies individual personalities and temperaments through her tried-and-tested system and believes that the only pathway to self-development is to understand who we truly are: how we think, how we communicate, and how we behave. Trained in a Facial-and Body-Temperament Recognition, the Language of Colour, NLP (Neuro Linguistic Programming), and Energy Medicine, Alison knows how important these tools are to securing a peaceful, happy, healthy, and prosperous future.

Author of *Dark Storm Golden Journey* and *Lomond's Awakening*, Alison has appeared on numerous national and international TV and radio programs, as well as being featured extensively in newspaper and magazine articles. She is an experienced and entertaining speaker and lecturer, runs workshops worldwide, offers numerous self-development webinars, as well as facilitating her award-winning Elite Communicator Courses.

Demarco makes her home in Edinburgh, in the United Kingdom.

www.AlisonDemarco.com
Email:-admin@alisondemarco.com

Credits/Acknowledgments

Rumtek Dharma Chakra Centre website: http://rumtek.org/

Vajrayana, Wikipedia contributors, The Free Encyclopedia: https://en.wikipedia.org/w/index.php?title=Vajrayana&oldid=684578043

Lama, Wikipedia contributors, Wikipedia, The Free Encyclopedia: https://en.wikipedia.org/w/index.php?title=Lama&oldid=686998982

Kagyu Samye Ling Monastery and Tibetan Centre: http://www.samyeling.org/about/

Kagyu Samye Ling Monastery and Tibetan Centre, Wikipedia, The Free Encyclopedia: https://en.wikipedia.org/w/index.php?title=Kagyu_Samye_Ling_Monastery_and_Tibetan_Centre&oldid=683927163

Rangjung Rigpe Dorje, 16th Karmapa, Wikipedia contributors, Wikipedia, The Free Encyclopedia: https://en.wikipedia.org/w/index.php?title=Rangjung_Rigpe_Dorje,_16th_Karmapa&oldid=687251948

Karmapa, Official Website of the 17th Gyalwang Karmapa: http://kagyuoffice.org/in-tibet/the-sacred-letter-of-prediction-of-his-holiness-the-16th-gyalwang-karmapa-1981-1992/

Potala Palace, Wikipedia contributors, Wikipedia, The Free Encyclopedia: https://en.wikipedia.org/w/index.php?title=Potala_Palace&oldid=687243461

Tsurpu Monastery website: http://www.tsurphu.org/

Black Hat (Black Crown), Black Crown, Wikipedia contributors, Wikipedia, The Free Encyclopedia: https://en.wikipedia.org/w/index.php?title=Black_Crown&oldid=681436612

Sikkim, Wikipedia contributors, Wikipedia, The Free Encyclopedia: https://en.wikipedia.org/w/index.php?title=Sikkim&oldid=687270020

23501520R00302

Printed in Great Britain
by Amazon